ONE AND DONE

JAMES CHANDLER

Severn River
PUBLISHING

ONE AND DONE

Severn River Publishing
www.SevernRiverPublishing.com

This is a work of fiction. Names, characters, businesses, places, events and incidents are either the products of the author's imagination or used in a fictitious manner. Any resemblance to actual persons, living or dead, or actual events is purely coincidental.

ISBN: 978-1-64875-101-1 (Paperback)
ISBN: 978-1-64875-102-8 (Hardback)

For Hannah and Abigail,
I loved you first.
No father ever had finer daughters.

1

Greg Goodrich of the Custer, Wyoming, Police Department was three-quarters of the way through a twelve-hour shift and patrolling Teton Avenue when he saw a man sitting on the sidewalk in front of a convenience store. He'd had about his fill of drunks and tweakers, but given the time and the early October weather, and sensing a problem, he pulled in front of the store without turning on his lights. Exiting the vehicle, he drew a flashlight and shined it on the man. "What's going on, sir?"

"I guess I got a flat," the man slurred, covering his eyes with one hand to block the light.

"Where's your car?" Goodrich looked around, shivering slightly in the cold.

"Oh, my car's home. I walked tonight, 'cause I knew I'd be drinkin'."

"Good decision," Goodrich said. It was three a.m., and the store clerk was laughing at him through the frosted front window. She'd clearly dealt with the man already. "You got any ID on ya, buddy?"

"I think so." The man attempted to reach for his wallet.

Goodrich watched him closely, always on alert. Something about him was familiar.

"So, tell me about the flat," Goodrich said, taking the driver's license handed to him and calling it into dispatch to check for warrants. He continued to look around the parking lot for a car, fully expecting to make an arrest for drunk driving.

"Well, how 'bout I show you?" The man reached down, fumbled with the leg of his jeans, and then tried to hand Goodrich an artificial limb. "See that? I lost the adapter between my socket and my knee, there," he said, pointing and grinning. "I got a flat."

Goodrich looked at the leg, then the man, then the empty pant leg while listening to the dispatcher talking on the device in his ear. "You're Sam Johnstone, the lawyer—right?"

"I am," the man answered. "I am indeed."

"I've never seen you without a tie," Goodrich observed. "You're the guy that walked Tommy Olsen a while back?"

"Well, that's not exactly what happened, but close enough, I guess. Guilty as charged, Officer." Although still seated, Sam was teetering unsteadily.

Goodrich reached down and put a hand on Sam's shoulder to stabilize him. "Mr. Johnstone, why don't you put that leg back on and I'll give you a ride home tonight, and you can work on fixing that flat tomorrow?"

"Sounds good to me, Officer."

After he helped Sam to his feet and into the patrol car, Goodrich locked the door and walked into the store. "Good morning," he said to the clerk. "This guy drive here?"

"Oh, I don't think so," she said. "Not unless he parked somewhere else. I was outside smoking a cigarette when he came staggering up, talking about how he lost his men in Afghanistan and had a flat. I didn't see no car and he was freaking me out, and I was just about to call 911 when I seen you."

"Okay, good enough. I'll get him home."

"Aren't you gonna bust him for public intoxication?"

"No. This guy's a hero. I think I'll cut him some slack."

"He don't look like a hero."

"Well, he is."

Minutes later, as they neared the address Sam had given him, Goodrich looked at Sam and said, "Counselor, probably not a good idea for you to be shit-faced drunk and out on the streets on a night like this. Just sayin'."

"I hear you. Didn't intend to get drunk." Sam shook his head slowly and looked at his legs. "Sometimes I don't stop when I should."

"If you need some help, I know a guy."

"I already got a guy."

"You gonna tell him about tonight?"

"Maybe."

"You should," Goodrich said. "Look, normally I'da run you into the jail for public intox, but after all you done for this country, well . . . We're here."

"Thanks for the ride," Sam said. "You need something, you let me know."

"Got it, Mr. Johnstone. You need some help?"

"Naw, I can get that far," Sam said. He exited the car, and with an exaggerated wave turned and staggered toward his front door, adding, "I'll be fine."

Goodrich made up his mind. "Better safe than sorry," he said. He exited the vehicle and caught up with Sam, extending an arm and putting Sam's over his own shoulder. "Let's get you inside."

Sam was snoring on the couch when Goodrich locked the townhouse door behind himself.

Three weeks later, an uneasy Sam was at Custer College addressing twenty-five freshmen. He'd never considered himself particularly bright, and his grades gave no indication he was wrong. He'd spent four years in college chasing women, playing baseball, and otherwise goofing off before graduating with a liberal arts degree. That wasn't a particularly valued credential, and Sam recognized that if not for his status as a disabled veteran, he would probably not have been admitted to law school years later. Nonetheless, at the request of Marilyn Smith, a casual friend and the criminal justice instructor at the local community college, he was back in a classroom on a late October afternoon—this time to talk with the students regarding the criminal justice system. Marilyn had completed a short introduction about him and asked if anybody knew him.

"He's the guy that got Tommy Olsen off," one student offered.

"Actually, he was convicted by a jury of his peers," Sam said. "But the right thing was done eventually."

"I don't know how you can do it," a student ventured. "I couldn't represent someone I knew was guilty."

Sam smiled. He'd had this discussion on more than one occasion during his career. "A lawyer's job is not to determine guilt or innocence. A lawyer's job is to protect the rights of the accused, to see to it that the State is put to its burden of proving each element of each charge beyond a reasonable doubt."

"That's a bunch of crap, man."

Sam looked at the speaker, a large young man wearing a light jacket with the college's name emblazoned across the front. "I'm listening," Sam said through slightly clenched teeth.

"You all are in business to make money, and the way you make money is to do as little as possible. Do a deal, throw your client under the bus, whatever."

"I like money," Sam offered. "But there are a lot of ways to make money. I do this because I believe in the system, and I think that most defendants are good people who've made bad decisions. There are exceptions, of course, but for the most part I view my job as one where I'm trying to get my client out of a bad situation in the best shape possible. Sometimes it's not possible."

"Like if he's black?"

Sam could hear the intake of air around the room. "Who cares?" he asked, looking steadily at the young man.

"You care. Because you're white. That's the way you were raised."

"You've got no idea how I was raised or what I think. But here's a clue: white or black or brown or whatever, if you're an American citizen I think you've got rights and I'll bust my ass to protect them. I did it for the Army while your mom was wiping your ass, and I'll do it again tomorrow."

While the rest of the class laughed nervously, the young man looked steadily at Sam, clearly unpersuaded.

"And there's one more thing. You're Davonte Blair, the basketball player, right?" Sam could feel the other students shifting nervously in their chairs.

"Yeah."

"I read the sports page," Sam said. According to the local newspaper, Davonte Blair was an NBA-quality basketball player who had failed to qualify academically to play at the NCAA Division I level. How he'd landed here Sam had no idea. "Mr. Blair, you didn't get to be who you are because you enjoy losing. Well, I don't like to lose, either. I didn't like to lose when I was a college baseball player. I didn't like to lose when I was leading men in Afghanistan before I got blown up. And I don't like to lose in a courtroom. When I take on a case, I do it with the intention of winning—however I define it."

Davonte smiled. "I get that."

"Well," Marilyn interjected, happy to see the tension had been lifted, "does anyone else have a question?"

"So, what happens if you have a client who you are absolutely, positively certain committed the crime?" another student asked.

"Again," Sam answered, "it's not my job to determine guilt, so if I have a client against whom I believe the State can prove the elements of the crime or crimes beyond a reasonable doubt, I look at my ability as an attorney to raise reasonable doubt in the minds of the members of the jury. Then I work to raise that doubt."

"But if you 'win,' the defendant would be getting away with it!"

"No, if the defendant is acquitted by a jury of his or her peers, that means the State failed to meet its burden of proof."

"That's not right, though."

"I'm not in the 'right' or 'wrong' business. I'm in the 'lawful' and 'unlawful' business. Remember, in our system, we seek justice, not truth. If we sought only truth, we would not be afforded the rights we have. That's why a woman can be caught red-handed doing something illegal—possessing marijuana, for instance—and be exonerated if her rights were not respected during the search and arrest."

"That's people getting off on technicalities," a student complained. He was a tall, skinny young man with thick glasses.

"What I have found," Sam began, "is that if someone else

beats the rap on a point of law, it's a 'technicality.' If you get off, then it's a righteous suppression. I've yet to have a client demand I overlook an officer's failure to observe his rights and insist on pleading guilty." Most of the students were smiling now, and Sam was getting more comfortable.

"That sounds good, but if you are a brother in the 'hood, none of that matters. You get busted, you're goin' down," Davonte said.

"That's not the failure of the system, though, is it?" Sam asked. "That's the failure of the actors in it, isn't it? The Constitution affords the same protections for the rich white kid from Loudon County as 'the brother in the 'hood,' as I think you phrased it."

"That sounds good, but that ain't the way it is," Davonte said.

"It may not be the way it is in practice. But if it isn't, the place to look is at the actors in the system. Why do the voters in those places continue to enable failure? Why are they re-electing and reappointing people who can't get the job done to positions of public trust? The system isn't perfect, but it's the best one we have, and for my money the best one any people on earth have ever had," Sam said.

For another half hour, Sam answered questions about being a lawyer, the legal system, and defendants. After the class had been dismissed, he and Marilyn sat and talked. "I appreciate you taking the time," she said. "You're something of a celebrity."

"Well, I'm glad to help. Looks like you've got some bright students here. A couple of them asked tough questions."

"You gave some straight answers. It's unusual to find someone who believes in the system as strongly as you do. Mr. Blair spoke out, but I can tell you that he's not the only one who believes the system is rigged against some groups."

"The system is genius. It's the people in the system who fail us," Sam said. "And I've practiced in a couple of places now, and in my experience the system functions ninety-nine percent of the time. But that doesn't make for books and television and movies. How boring would a book be if the system worked?"

"Again, thank you for being here," she said. "My students come from limited means and they set limited goals. It is wonderful to have someone like you come to meet with them."

"You're very kind."

"Will you come again?"

"Of course," Sam said. "You call and I'll be here."

The rhythmic sound of the basketball hitting the empty field house's hardwood floor was interrupted only by the soft swish of the ball passing through the net. Over and over Davonte took a shot, then ran to another spot on the floor and received a pass from one of the two much smaller young men serving as rebounders. The only words came from Davonte: "Got to be at my chest, man." "Hurry up!" "Now. Now!" Eventually, he said, "One hundred," signifying the end of the drill.

The three young men walked over to the folding chairs that would be occupied by the home team during a game and sat down. While Davonte drank water and looked at his phone, Kaiden Miles and Ronnie Norquist talked among themselves.

After a few minutes Davonte stood, looked down at the two managers, and said, "Let's go." Kaiden and Ronnie grabbed a basketball apiece and ran to their positions. This time, Kaiden looked at a stopwatch while Ronnie rebounded shots by Davonte, who shot, moved to another spot just beyond the three-point line, received a pass from Ronnie, tossed the ball to the floor with a spin so it came back to him, and then shot again. Kaiden called off the times as the drill went on: "thirty seconds," "one minute," "ninety seconds," and then—as the three-minute mark approached—counted down the last ten seconds as Davonte and Ronnie sped up the drill accordingly. After the time expired, Davonte took a final pass from Ronnie near the free throw line, dribbled the ball once, and effortlessly dunked the ball with two hands while Ronnie looked on in admiration. "Thanks, man," he said to the two managers. "See you in the morning."

"We'll be here," Kaiden said as Davonte walked away.

"Man, I'd give anything to be able to dunk like that," Ronnie said. "Just once."

"Yeah, me too," Kaiden said. "But what I'd really like is for him to pay me my damned money."

"Kaiden, be cool. You'll get your money," Ronnie said. "Davonte is gonna be a pro in a year. He'll pay you. You just need to be patient, man."

"That go for you, too?"

"I'm working on it," Ronnie said. "I told you, as soon as my financial aid comes through, I'll square up with you, man."

"You better."

"Just you wait." Ronnie smiled. "Davonte goes pro, and he's gonna take us to the top with him. We're all gonna be golden!"

2

Sam was having dinner at a tavern on Yellowstone Avenue with Veronica Simmons, the assistant to one of the judges in town. They had dated off and on since shortly after his arrival in Custer. The restaurant was across the street from the courthouse and near his new office, making it a convenient place to meet for a casual dinner. She was drinking a glass of Chardonnay and he was having tonic water, having eschewed alcohol since the debacle at the convenience store a couple of weeks prior. "What is this crap we are listening to?" he asked, grabbing a fried pickle.

"It's country music," Veronica said. She was looking somewhat dubiously at a chicken wing.

"Have one," he urged.

"A little too fattening for me," she said.

"Really? That's not George Jones—or even George Strait," he said, waving a wing in the air to indicate the music.

"It's the new stuff."

"I'm not into it. Sounds too much like what you'd hear on adult contemporary."

"Hick-hop," she said. She dipped a piece of fried cheese into a cup of marinara sauce and popped it into her mouth.

"Now that's funny!" He laughed. She covered her mouth, grinning as well. Looking around the tavern, he noted several patrons he had represented, two of whom were not supposed to be in a bar or liquor store due to their probationary status. Both avoided eye contact with him.

"So, how are you doing?" she asked. "I mean really."

"I'm doing fine."

She looked at him for a moment. "I never know whether that is true, or if you are just saying that."

"I don't generally say things that aren't true," Sam said. "Or at least that I don't think are true."

"I can't tell. I don't really know you, I guess."

"You know me," he said, shaking an ice cube from the plastic glass into his mouth. "Well enough to have dinner with me. Well enough to sleep with me." He winked and crunched an ice cube, making her wince.

"Doesn't that hurt?" she asked. He shrugged in response. She drank some wine. "I really don't know anything about you."

"What do you want to know?"

"Your life in two minutes or less. Go."

Sam looked steadily at her, trying to decide whether to comply. When he'd made his decision, he looked at his watch and began. "Raised outside Bozeman. My dad was a drunk. Sold used cars and chased barflies. Mom died when I was a kid, leaving my dad and an endless string of alcoholic women to raise my big brother and me."

"I didn't even know you had a brother," she said.

"You're cutting into my time," he said. "May I continue?"

"Yes. Sorry."

"He was three years older. Killed a guy some years back.

Went to prison. Haven't seen him since." He ignored her look of shock. "I hated school. Didn't like my teachers and they didn't care much for me. I got into a lot of trouble drinking, doing drugs, and fighting. Stayed in school so I'd know where the parties were and because I liked to play sports. Went to college. Drank a lot, played baseball. No future in that. Got bored after graduating. Was working with a national company for a couple of years in marketing. Had a big account selling cat food. Woke up one day and realized I'd never be satisfied if the measure of my life boiled down to the volume of cat food I sold."

"You probably weren't a great fit."

"I faked it. One day I got moderately drunk and walked into an Army recruiting office. Told them I wanted to wear that green beret. Had no idea what it involved or what it meant, just thought it looked cool. Did basic training, Officer Candidate School, and Infantry Officer Basic Course at Fort Benning. Then Ranger School while I was in the 101st Airborne at Fort Campbell. Got picked up for Special Forces Qualification School, but before I could get into my class, my unit got activated and I went overseas. Did a tour in Iraq, came back, and got assigned to Fort Drum and the 10th Mountain Division. That's light infantry. Was again ready to ship to the qualification course when I got picked to command an infantry company getting deployed to Afghanistan. Couldn't turn that down. Took command, got deployed, and got blown up after just a few weeks in the country." He crunched more ice. "Never did get that green beret—still pisses me off."

She was shaking her head sadly.

"Spent almost a year getting fixed up. Could have stayed in, but honestly, I'd lost my enthusiasm. Went to law school using the GI Bill and VA disability. Didn't fit in, didn't do great, but got through. Through some connections I had—and I think a little bit of pity—I got a job in a firm in Washington, D.C. until I screwed up and got fired. Paul offered me a job. Here I am. How's my time?"

Veronica smiled briefly, but it disappeared. "That's terrible about your mom." She shook her head again.

"It was. I was six."

"And your dad? Is he alive?"

"Not sure," he said.

"You hold a grudge."

"I do."

They were quiet for a moment. "I have a favor to ask," she said, brightening.

"Did I pass your test or something?" he asked, eyeing her near-empty wine glass and signaling the waitress. "How can I help?"

"I want you to accompany me to a charity gala. It benefits battered women and children. I need a date." She smiled at him.

"Sorry." He shook his head. "No can do."

"Sam, it's important to me. I'm on the board of directors and—"

"Veronica." Sam held up a hand to stop her. "It's not that I don't want to go. It's that I *can't* go. Not right now."

"It's important to me!"

"I know that. And I'm sorry," he said. Seeing the look in her eyes, he repeated, "I'm sorry."

"We wear the scars of where we've been," she said, and sighed heavily before swallowing the last of her wine. He was thinking of how it would taste on her lips. "Will you think about it?" she asked.

The waitress brought their steaks. "I'll think about it," he said. "But for right now, the answer is no, and if you want someone to go with you, you'd better find someone else." He picked up his knife and fork. "I'm okay with that."

She sat back in her chair and stared at Sam. They finished their meals in silence.

"Veronica . . . Mr. Johnstone, how are you tonight?" Ron Baker of the Custer Police Department had approached their table unnoticed.

"Fine," they answered simultaneously. Baker smiled.

"Making your rounds?" Sam asked.

"Yup. Keeping the peace. Well, that and seeing how many of your clients aren't doing what they are supposed to be doing, counselor." Baker waved his hand at the near-empty bar area and smiled at Veronica. "Veronica, you look great, as always. Sam here ought to have you on the dance floor. I would."

"Not gonna happen," Sam said, shaking the ice in his tonic water.

Baker said nothing. He had a faraway look in his eye.

"Ron, if you'd like to ask me—" Veronica began, but Baker waved her off and pointed to his ear.

"He's getting a call," Sam said.

Baker nodded and said, "Roger," to whoever was on the line. Looking at Veronica and Sam, he said, "Gotta go. Saturday night in Custer. Somebody's beating on the wife."

"Be safe, Ron," Veronica said, and got a wave in response. She turned her attention to Sam. "Are you ready to go?"

"I am." He chugged the last of the tonic water and put the cup down. "Let's do it."

Moments later, on the way to her house, they passed Baker's patrol car, parked in front of a convenience store. Through the glass, they could see Baker talking with the clerk.

Baker had been a patrol officer for five years, but as he was pulling his cruiser into the parking lot, it somehow seemed longer than that. Dispatch had indicated a possible kidnapping and/or domestic at a convenience store on Yellowstone Avenue. The clerk, he was told, had the information he needed. Entering the store, he wasted no time. "What's going on?"

"A man and a woman were in here a while ago," the clerk began. "They bought beer, chips, and stuff, you know?"

"Okay," Baker said. "And?"

"And when the guy turned around to grab a package of jerky, she mouthed, 'Help me,' to me, so I called 911 as soon as they left."

"Did they drive away?"

"Yes. White Chevy truck."

"Good. Only a couple thousand of them around here. Did you get a plate?"

"I did. It was County 25, 4-2-2-1-0."

"You're sure?" he asked. She nodded. "Okay, let me call that in." Having done so, he returned to questioning her. "Real quick, how about a description of the couple?"

"Well, I didn't look real close at him. He is a big one—I'd say six-three or four. My ex was six-two and he's at least that tall." She was smacking her gum and looking off in the distance, trying to recall what she had seen. "And he was big. Not a skinny type at all. Kind of chunky. Had sleeve tattoos on both arms. Jeans. Sweatshirt that said 'Custer High School Wrestling.' She was real pretty, once—cheerleader type, you know?"

"Okay, thank you—Lisa, is it?" Baker said, looking at her name tag.

"Yeah. Lisa Crandall," she said. "And the woman has a black eye and a busted lip. She'll be easy to recognize."

"Thank you, Ms. Crandall. I'm sure there'll be someone along to talk with you soon," Baker said as he headed out the door. Back in his car, he relayed the vehicle information to dispatch and just moments later was given the address of a residence on Long Street matching the registration. He knocked on the door and a large man fitting the description of the suspect answered.

"Mr. Smith?" Baker asked.

"Yeah," the man said. "What do you want?"

"I want you to step outside and talk with my partner here," Baker said, indicating Corporal Mike Jensen, who had arrived soon after he did. "I'm going to talk with *her*." He indicated a woman sitting on a couch in the living room of the small, shabby home. Surprisingly, the man complied.

While Jensen spoke with the male suspect, Baker interviewed the alleged victim—Raylene Smith—who in fact had a black eye and a busted lip. Ms. Smith was extremely upset and in significant pain, and explained that she and her husband, Albert, had been having some issues due to his excessive drinking. Notwithstanding, the two of them had been drinking together most of the day when, for reasons she could not recall, an argument broke out. She had told him to leave, which he did—after he had thrown her cell phone through the large-screen television. He returned an hour later even more intoxicated, she said, and kicked in the front door when she would not let him in. He punched her in the face and then dragged her into the bedroom before trying to strangle her. She was able to get loose when their dog bit him. She then convinced him she needed to go to the store to get some dog food. When they arrived, she alerted the clerk while the suspect was getting something and bringing it to the counter.

Baker then spoke with the suspect, Albert Smith, who was sitting on the front steps. "What's going on tonight?"

"Nothing," the big man said. Baker was eyeing him closely. He had the feeling this one wasn't going to end well. "Nothing you need to know about."

"Well, something's going on. We got called because someone was afraid your wife was getting hurt."

"Whatever happened to her has nothing to do with me."

"Are you telling me she did this to herself?" Baker asked.

"I'm telling you she is drunk," Albert said. "She's always drunk. Probably fell and hurt herself. She does that a lot."

"Really. You expect me to believe that?"

"I don't care what you believe. I'm just telling you I don't know what happened. We had a verbal disagreement. I left and she was fine; when I got back, she looked like that."

"Did you kick that door in?"

"Hell yes," Albert said. "That bitch can't lock me out of my own house away from my dog and stuff!"

Baker looked at Albert for a long moment, then walked up the steps and looked at Raylene and around the living room of the filthy little house. She was sitting on the couch rocking back and forth with her arms wrapped around herself. He felt the anger well up in him and took a deep breath. "Albert, turn around. I'm going to place you under arrest for suspicion of domestic battery. I want you to listen closely while I advise you of your rights."

"Are you kidding me? I didn't do anything!" Albert said, struggling with the officer trying to put the cuffs on his wrists. "Raylene, you tell these bastards I didn't do anything!" Another officer had joined the fray.

"Get him out of here!" Baker ordered, drawing his taser, just in case. "I don't want to listen to this."

"You'll be listening soon enough, asshole! I'm going to sue you—" Albert's voice trailed off as the officers took him outside, placed him in a patrol car, and shut the door.

"Raylene," Baker said, putting his taser back in its holster. "I'm going to have an officer accompany you to the hospital so we can get you looked over. You'll be safe for tonight."

"I wish you hadn't done that," she said, continuing to hold herself and rock. "Every time y'all arrest him it just makes it worse."

"Raylene, when are you going to get out of here? I'm afraid that one of these times he is going to hurt you bad." Then, quickly realizing what he had said, he added, "I mean *real* bad. I'm sorry."

"I know what you mean. But you don't understand. Albert loves me. It's just that sometimes I say stuff that makes him mad. And there is so much pressure on him to make a living and pay the bills and . . . well, it just all wells up in him and then—"

"And then he beats you."

"Well, I wouldn't call it that," she said.

"Well, I would. I am. Now, get what you need. I'm taking you to the hospital and then to the women's shelter."

3

Twelfth Judicial District Court Judge Preston C. Daniels had been on the bench for two decades. In that time, he had seen a lot of defendants come to court drunk. While to a normal person it might seem bizarre, to a judge it indicated either a lack of coping skills or a level of alcoholism that had them consuming a little more than necessary to stiffen the backbone.

"Mr. Park, court security is telling me you smell like a brewery," Daniels said to the defendant. "So I'm going to have you submit to a portable breath test here this morning to ensure you are fit to proceed. Do you understand?"

"Oh, yes, Judge," the defendant said. "I maybe had a little too much to drink last night, but I'm okay this morning, sir."

"Well, why don't you kind of hold your tongue there, okay?" Daniels suggested. "You'll remember that you're on bond and are not supposed to be drinking at all. So before you say anything else, why don't you just go into the back with the officers there, and we'll see where you're at?"

"Okay, Judge," Park said. "But I want you to know that I'm okay. I wouldn't do nothing to disrespect you."

"I'm sure," Daniels said as Park was led away. "Ladies and gentlemen, let's take a brief recess."

In his chambers several minutes later, Daniels heard court security approach. "Judge," the officer said, "looks like he's about a .06. How do you want to proceed?"

"Well, he's legal to drive, right?"

"Presumptively," the officer said.

"Okay, well, let's go back out on the record." Daniels stood and donned his robe. "Give me a minute."

After the security officer had left, Daniels closed his door and spent a brief time in meditation. He was irritable. It was never a good idea to go into court in a bad mood, especially now, while he was serving a period of judicial probation following his being sanctioned for decisions he'd made during the trial of Tommy Olsen. He'd come to grips with the sanction over time, and while he would never agree, it didn't really matter. He took a deep breath and reminded himself to be careful. Back on the bench, he began to proceed with sentencing when the young public defender stood. "Your Honor, I'm made to understand my client showed positive for alcohol."

"That's my understanding as well."

"Well, then, I object to continuing this proceeding. He might well not be capable of understanding today's proceedings."

"Mr. Anderson, your client has a blood alcohol content of approximately .06. That's a three-beer buzz. I'm going to go out on a limb here and postulate that your client—who has nine lifetime DUIs—is fully capable of following today's proceedings with a three-beer buzz. Appeal me." The young public defender looked at his client and then at Daniels, clearly uncertain of what to do. Daniels decided to cover the young man. "Your objection is noted, Mr. Anderson," Daniels said. "And is overruled. I'm going to find that Mr. Park is fit and competent to proceed."

"Thanks, Judge." Park shook his head. "Be embarrassing to be found too drunk to proceed with a .06."

After the hearing was over, Daniels called for his long-time judicial assistant, Mary Perry. "Mary," Daniels said. "Can you get me Rebecca Nice on the phone, please? I need to talk to her about next week's trial."

"Do you want me to get Mike Sharp on the line, too?"

"No, just get Rebecca. I'm not worried about an *ex parte* communication."

"Judge, don't forget that you have an initial appearance on that sexual assault this afternoon."

"I know that, Mary. Just get Rebecca on the line if you would, please." Daniels stood and walked over to the cabinet but didn't find what he was looking for. "Mary—"

"Judge, you need to be on your best behavior. You know that you are still on probation with the Commission on Judicial Conduct and probably being watched by the Wyoming Supreme Court because of the Olsen case. And I'll remind you that you have always said a trial court judge's job is to follow the rules and to apply the law. But during the Olsen case you made the decision to . . . well, let's just say you *adjusted* the rules. Now they are watching you, and you need to be careful."

"Those were judgment calls! Judicial discretion! Half of those people don't have the slightest idea what they're talking about, and the other half haven't been in my chair for a long time. More importantly, you know what? I'd make the same damned decision again!"

"Judge, please watch your language!"

"Mary, let me remind you: being my handmaid is not your job."

"Well, Judge, whether it's my job or not, I'm gonna do it."

Mary put her hands on her wide hips. "For your information, my future might very well be tied to yours. There is no guarantee that I will have a job if you get fired and another judge gets appointed. Your probation runs in six months. After that you can do whatever you want, but between now and then, I've got bills to pay, so it's in my best interest to keep you out of trouble. And that's exactly what I intend to do!" She turned and left his chambers, slamming the door behind her.

Directly downstairs from Daniels, Circuit Court Judge Melissa Downs was getting ready for court. She had taken the bench less than a year prior, following the suicide of her predecessor, Judge Jonathon Howard. The ensuing scandal had been the talk of the town for a long time and was only now beginning to dissipate. She'd never given much thought to becoming a judge; in fact, she'd been quite content as a civil practitioner specializing in business litigation in Cheyenne. But when her husband decided that marriage "wasn't for him," she'd applied for the judgeship in a fit of pique and—much to her surprise—was appointed by the governor. The move to Custer had been uneventful, and her nine-year-old daughter was settling into school.

The circuit court was informally known as the "People's Court." In contrast to the district court over which Daniels presided, where the stakes were high and the pace somewhat ponderous, circuit court was fast-paced and wildly unpredictable. For Downs, the biggest surprise had been the paperwork—she discovered she could measure it daily in feet.

She was reviewing a petition for a stalking order of protection when her clerk came to retrieve her. "Ma'am, everyone is here. It's a change of plea on a charge of sexual battery for one of our regulars."

The defendant, represented by Sam Johnstone, had appeared in court on a felony count of sexual assault a couple of weeks earlier and waived his preliminary hearing, and Downs had bound him over to district court for further proceedings. The parties had subsequently reached a plea bargain wherein the matter would be reduced to a misdemeanor, so the parties were back before her. After calling the case and hearing the terms of the plea agreement from Deputy County Attorney Catherine Schmidt and Sam, Downs obtained the defendant's plea and imposed a sentence—time served and a nominal fine. Eschewing the delivery of a lecture, Downs left the courtroom.

"Thanks a lot, Sam," the defendant said. "I mean, I appreciate it. That little bitch—"

"Shut your mouth," Sam said, quickly glancing at Cathy. "You got your deal. Now get your ass out of here. I don't want to see you again."

"Hey, counselor, I paid you good money."

"And I earned it. Now leave."

The defendant looked at Sam for a long moment and extended his hand. Sam looked at it and said simply, "I don't want to get any on me."

"Well, you sorry bastard! Who the hell do you think you are?"

"I'm the guy who is gonna beat your ass for feeling up that little girl if you don't get out of my face right now," Sam said quietly.

Looking at Sam in shock, the defendant slowly backed away. "I'm gonna report you to the bar association."

"Do it," Sam said. "Just make sure you spell my name right." After the man departed, he looked at Cathy, who had

been watching silently. Smiling wryly, he said, "Another satisfied customer."

"I appreciate it," Cathy said. "I didn't want to put that little
girl through a trial."

"And I didn't want to have to cross-examine her," Sam said.
"I just hope—"

"Me, too," she said. "I'm praying he'll keep his hands—and
everything else—to himself for both our sakes."

4

The campus field house was rocking with excitement. At six foot nine and 240 pounds, Davonte didn't look like the other players on the court, and by halftime he'd outscored the opposing team by himself. With an array of three-point shots, drives, and dunks, he had scored forty-one points, gathered twelve rebounds, and had even dished out a couple of assists while dazzling observers and opponents alike.

"Why are we here?" Lucy Beretta asked her husband. "You care nothing for basketball."

"We are here to show support for the team," Vincent Beretta replied. He'd been president of Custer College for just under two years, and in that short amount of time he had presided over an expansion of the junior college's offerings, to include the athletic program.

"Well, I'm not sure why I'm here," Lucy said, examining her nails.

"You're here because you are my wife," he replied, smiling tightly and waving at one of the college's boosters. "We need to put on a good front here until I can get hired somewhere else."

"I can't believe you brought us from Vermont all the way

out here," Lucy said. "It's the first week in November and it's already snowing."

"If you'll recall, you agreed to this," he said.

"Well, I didn't think it would be this . . . remote. My God, we're 150 miles from a mall!"

"That's why God created overnight delivery, sweetheart," he said, and, looking at the crowd, mused, "Good turnout tonight. I know the people are here to see Davonte, but the video will show a full field house. That is going to reflect well on the college. Just look at this crowd!"

"It will reflect well on you, as well," Lucy noted. She was watching an overweight woman in yoga pants several sizes too small take on the stairs. "My God—where are we?" she muttered.

"Coach Fitzsimmons is building a solid program, and Devonte will draw more student athletes of high quality," Beretta said, ignoring her question. "At some point the program begins to sustain itself."

"Who would have thought you—of all people—would oversee the building of an athletic department?" Lucy laughed softly.

"Athletics are one of the quickest ways to increase attendance at a small college. For one thing, you get the student athletes and their significant others. Moreover, winning brings the strap-hangers who want to be a part of something successful."

"I suppose," she said. "Who are those tall guys against the wall there?"

"Don't point, dear," he said, taking her hand and putting it in her lap. "Those are a couple of coaches from prominent NCAA men's college programs. Coach told me they would be here tonight to watch Davonte. He is bringing national exposure to our program."

"Good," she said. "If he gets out of here, perhaps we can follow him and get back to civilization."

Beretta looked at his wife of seven years for a long moment, then turned his attention to the game as Davonte drained a twenty-five-foot jump shot to open the second half, then stole the inbounds pass and dunked the ball effortlessly. "I certainly hope so," he said. "I know one thing: I don't know a thing about basketball, and even I can tell that Davonte is unusually good at what he does."

———

Several seats away, Sam and his law partner, Paul Norquist, were enjoying the first home game of the year from the season ticket holders' seats they received for their generous donation to the college's athletics program. Paul was pointing out members of the audience when Daniels sat down beside them. "Evening, men," Daniels said. "Mind if I join you?"

Paul and Sam nodded at Daniels. "Evening, Judge," Paul said. "How are you?"

"Doing well, doing well," Daniels said. "My goodness, that young man can play, can't he?"

"He is amazing." Paul shook his head. "Coach Fitzsimmons has recruited some ballplayers, but no one like this. Ronnie says he was a McDonald's High School All-American and had offers from most of the Big Ten and Atlantic Coast Conference schools."

"Why is he here?" Daniels asked.

"Non-qualifier, supposedly," Sam said.

"What's that mean?"

"NCAA schools require incoming student athletes to meet certain academic requirements. Those who don't are loosely termed 'non-qualifiers' and cannot compete at the highest level."

"So, what then?" Daniels asked, stuffing a handful of popcorn in his mouth.

"They have some options, one of which is to attend junior college."

"So, come here—"

"Spend a couple of years, then go on to school," Paul said.

"Or," Sam said, watching Davonte steal a pass, easily outmaneuver a hapless defender, and dunk the ball, "get drafted and go play for money."

"Seriously?" Daniels asked.

"That's what Ronnie is saying," Paul observed. "Says the kid and the coaches here expect him to go in the lower half of the first round."

"So, how is Ronnie doing?" Daniels asked, observing Paul's older son on the sideline in his role as manager. "He's sure grown."

"He has, Judge," Paul said. "He's doing very well. He likes school, and managing is giving him some experience traveling. He's good buddies with Davonte, there. And by hanging with the team he's meeting some guys with backgrounds way different than his own."

"I'll bet that's true." Daniels chuckled, then turned his attention to Sam. "How are you tonight, Mr. Johnstone?"

"Doing well, Judge. Just out for a couple of hours to watch some basketball."

"Not like you saw in D.C. in your previous life, though, is it?"

"Not exactly," Sam said, recalling evenings spent watching the Washington Wizards as well as teams from Georgetown, George Washington, and George Mason play NCAA Division I opponents. "But I'm not sure I've seen anyone better than that guy." He indicated Davonte. "That guy can play with anyone."

The post-game party in Davonte's dorm room had wound down, and those remaining—Davonte, Kaiden, Ronnie, and a young man named Trent Gustafson—were drinking whiskey and vaping THC oil.

"Davonte, you were something else tonight," Kaiden said, handing Davonte the vape pen. "Sixty-one points! Holy shit!"

"Dude, these people never seen no one like me. Back in Detroit, now, there's some ballers." Davonte inhaled deeply from the vape pen.

"Whatever, man. You were awesome. Those D-1 coaches got a show tonight!" Ronnie added.

"Just gotta keep getting the rock and doing my thing, man." Davonte handed the pen back to Kaiden.

"Someday I'll be watchin' you on TV, man!" Ronnie said.

"You will, you will," Davonte agreed. He leaned back on the bed and looked to the ceiling. "Next year, if everything goes right."

"You'll comp us some tickets, right?" Kaiden asked.

"You got that midterm paper done?"

"Ronnie's doing it." Kaiden looked at Ronnie. "He says it'll be done in plenty of time—right, Ronnie?"

Ronnie was sharing a couch with Gustafson. "Yeah, I'll have it done."

"Better be good." Davonte looked at Ronnie and then Kaiden. "Or you ain't gonna get shit, man."

"Ronnie knows the deal," Kaiden assured him. "He'll get it done, email it to you by Friday. Then you copy and paste, and you email it in."

"Who are you, man?" Davonte said, indicating Gustafson.

"This is my . . . uh . . . friend, Trent," Kaiden said. "He's from Fort Collins."

"Where's that?" Davonte shifted so he was on his elbows and could look at Gustafson directly.

"Colorado," Gustafson said, returning Davonte's stare.

"Weed legal there, right?"

Gustafson merely nodded.

"Looks like he's Ronnie's friend, too," Davonte observed. "He solid?"

"Oh, yeah. As a rock, man," Kaiden said, trying to sound street-wise. "He knows what's at stake."

"Can't have no mistakes, man," Davonte said, and again laid his head back on the bed. "Man, that is some good shit."

"It's that same stuff I had last time. You said you liked it." Kaiden eyed Gustafson.

"Whatever. Some of my boys will be in town next week. You need to have some of that around for them, too."

"This shit is expensive—they gonna be able to pay?"

"Pay what, man? These are my boys," Davonte said. "They ain't payin' shit. Put it on account for me."

"I can't do that, Davonte," Kaiden said. "I'm in about twenty-five hundred dollars. Been borrowing my ass off to keep us in this stuff."

"You been sellin' some, right?"

"Yeah, but we've been burning a lot," Kaiden said with a sideways glance toward Gustafson. "I can't cover."

"Then you better figure it out, 'cause I expect you to cover me and my homies when they get to town." Davonte took another hit from the pen and noted Gustafson's raised eyebrow. "I mean, if you wanna keep hanging out. 'Cause, you know, if you can't—"

"Davonte, I can't do that, man! I need you to pay something, now!" Kaiden had stood and was looking down at Davonte, who was looking back up at him in surprise. "I need to cover my costs."

"That's your problem."

"No, asshole, it's your problem, too!"

Davonte sat up. "What're you sayin', little man?"

"I'm saying that if I don't get shown some good faith here—some respect—that I might go have a talk with Coach Fitzgerald, or maybe write an anonymous note to the newspaper, or maybe whisper in one of those visiting coach's ears."

Davonte was fully alert now. He stared at Kaiden and then looked at Ronnie and Gustafson. Ronnie averted his eyes, but Gustafson again held Davonte's stare. "Little man, are you threatening me?" Davonte asked.

"Yeah, I am. I'm tired of you taking advantage of me and disrespecting me," Kaiden said. "I'm tired of you making promises and not keeping them. I'm tired of you—"

"Get your shit and get out," Davonte said quietly.

"I'll leave, but that ain't changing nothing." Kaiden looked at Ronnie and then Gustafson, as if seeking support. Ronnie was staring fixedly at the floor. Gustafson was watching the events unfold without emotion.

"Leave or I'm gonna throw your ass out, boy," Davonte said.

"Fine, but I want my money!" Kaiden said, and to Ronnie's surprise, walked over and got in Davonte's face. "Or else!" he yelled. With that, he grabbed his backpack, pulled it on, and left, slamming the door behind him.

"That sorry sonuvabitch," Davonte said. "Little mother—"

"Let it go, Davonte," Ronnie said. "He'll calm down. He'll square you."

"Nobody talks to me like that," Davonte said. "Back home, you get killed for talkin' shit like that, man." While Ronnie and Gustafson watched, Davonte picked a basketball off the floor with one hand and again lay back on the bed. He began shooting imaginary shots toward the ceiling, catching the ball, and repeating the drill. After a couple of moments, he stood and walked over to the table in the small kitchen. He sat and began putting on his shoes, muttering to himself.

"Where are you going?" Ronnie asked.

"I'm gonna go find Kaiden and beat his ass."

"He's got people to answer to." Gustafson spoke for the first time.

"Not my problem," Davonte said, finishing with his shoes and standing.

"Could become a problem," Gustafson said. "His source will want his money. If Kaiden doesn't come across, the source might start looking for the end users."

Davonte looked at Gustafson for a long moment. "Don't threaten me, bitch," he said. "You two little queens need to lock the door on your way out. And don't touch my shit."

5

Downs had advised the defendants of their constitutional rights as a group, and as a courtesy, would proceed with those defendants having an attorney first. "The first matter before the court is State v. Albert Smith. Defendant is present and represented by Mike Sharp. The State is present and represented by Catherine Schmidt. Mr. Sharp, will your client waive a verbatim reading of the charges?"

"He will, Your Honor."

"Thank you. Because these are both felonies, the court will not take a plea here today. Mr. Sharp, are you in this matter for the long haul?"

"Yes, Judge."

"All right. Defendant has retained counsel. I'll hear from the parties regarding the terms and conditions of pre-trial release. Ms. Schmidt, what is the State's position?"

"Your Honor, this is the seventh time law enforcement has had contact with this couple. Mr. Smith has twice been convicted of domestic battery, and in each instance the victim was his wife. While we don't see the defendant as a flight risk, we do believe he poses a danger to the community. We'd ask the defendant be held in lieu of fifty thousand dollars—"

"Fifty thousand dollars? Are you kidding me?" Albert said as Sharp attempted to quiet him.

"Mr. Smith, I'll tolerate no outbursts," Downs said. "You and Mr. Sharp will have an opportunity to speak about bond here in a minute."

"Fifty thousand dollars is ridiculous," Albert said as Sharp went pale.

"Mr. Smith," Downs said slowly, recalling that in her recent judicial training she was advised to 'kill 'em with kindness.' "I'll not have that kind of language. Again, if you'll act appropriately, you'll have an opportunity to address me momentarily. Ms. Schmidt, anything else from the State?"

"No, Judge."

"Mr. Sharp, what is your client's position?"

"Judge, my client believes this is all a mistake. His wife, he tells me, had been drinking and she tripped and fell into a doorknob. He's asking that he be released on his personal recognizance so that he can get back to his job and support Mrs. Smith and the couple's dog."

Downs sat quietly for a moment and was about to speak when she heard a voice in the back of the room say, "Your Honor?" She looked at the gallery, and a hand went up.

"Yes?" Downs said. "Do you have something to say?"

"Yes, ma'am. I'm the . . . uh . . . I'm Raylene Smith. It's all a mistake, Judge. I want Albert home. He's a good provider. I need him."

Downs looked at the small, frail woman. She had obviously tried, but the pancake make-up wasn't covering the bruises, and her lip was swollen like an aging Hollywood starlet's. Smith was staring at Downs smugly.

"I've heard the arguments of counsel. I don't find a release on personal recognizance appropriate," Downs began, seeing Albert's face turn beet red, "and as I believe the defendant presents a real danger to members of the community, he will be held in lieu of fifty thousand cash. No contact with the alleged victim or the dog. Don't be at the victim's address—"

"That's my house! That's my dog! You can't do that!"

"I can and I have," Downs said. "Mr. Sharp, please get your client under control."

"Yes, Judge." Sharp put an arm around Albert's large shoulders, and the man easily shrugged him off. Downs continued her recitation of the terms. When she had concluded, she ordered court security to have Albert taken back to his holding cell. After he had been removed, she looked over the remaining defendants. "Anyone else feeling froggy today?"

―――

The high school's small stadium was filled for the home-coming game with one of Custer's bitter rivals, and the community was out in force. Sam hadn't been to a high school football game since he last played in one twenty years prior. Sitting with Paul and Jeannie, he took it all in, taking occasional deep breaths to alleviate the anxiety caused by being in close quarters with hundreds of strangers. It was his favorite time of the year, but despite the apparently friendly confines, he mentally rehearsed the actions he would take on contact. He had an escape route selected and was studying the bulge in the waistband of a large man seated a couple of rows in front of them when Jeannie, who was sitting between him and Paul, put her hand on his arm. "I get so nervous watching the boys play," she said.

Sam smiled. "I can't believe that. When you used to come

to my—uh, Paul's and my—games, you spent most of your time soaking up rays and drinking beer from the cooler."

She laughed, and he remembered how he loved to hear her laugh. "For the record, those were wine coolers. And this is my son."

"And he is a good one," Sam observed. As he watched Paul, Jr.—"P.J."—play tailback, he couldn't help but see Paul's natural athleticism. He leaned around Jeannie and said, "The apple didn't fall far from the tree, Paul."

"A little time in the weight room and he might have a shot," Paul observed. "Ronnie worked harder, but he didn't have the ability P.J. does."

They watched as P.J. took a pitch-out from the quarter-back on the right end. Sam stood with everyone else and heard Jeannie screaming for P.J. as he turned the corner on the helpless defensive end. The outside linebacker had been blocked, the cornerback was tied up with a receiver, and the safety took a bad angle. It was no contest, and fifty yards later P.J. flipped the ball to the referee in the end zone. Sam was exchanging high-fives with Paul and Jeannie when the Junior ROTC cadets fired the small cannon that Sam hadn't seen. Instantly, Sam was down in the snow-covered bleachers between the seats, scouting for enemy fighters. "Get down! Incoming!"

"Sam! It's okay! Sam!" someone was saying.

"Jeannie, get your head down!" Sam yelled, and grabbed her sleeve and tugged her down next to him. "We've got enemy in-bound!" he yelled, and peered over a bleacher. Oddly, the enemy fighters were on the run. They must have been conducting a raid, trying to disrupt operations but nothing more. The bleachers were emptying fast and he was deciding whether to conduct a pursuit when he felt something on his sleeve.

"Sam!" Jeannie was shaking his arm. "Sam!" She was now crouched in front of him in the bleachers. "Sam!"

Sam looked at Jeannie and saw the tears in her eyes. "What's going on?"

"They fired the cannon and you. . . you thought you were back in combat," she said.

Sam looked around and saw parents and children looking at them from afar. The referees were holding the ball, unsure of what had caused the disturbance. Off-duty police officers had put down their hot dogs and were scurrying toward him. "Oh, man," he said. "Jeannie, I am so sorry."

"No, Sam," she said, taking his hands in hers. "You don't have to be sorry."

Paul had been talking to the crowd, attempting to calm them. "Sam, come on," he said, putting his arm around Sam's shoulders and leading him toward the parking lot. "Let me give you a ride."

On the way to his house, Sam again tried to apologize, but Paul wouldn't hear of it. "Sam, after what you've been through. . . I just wish I would have thought to warn you. And just so you know, I called Veronica. Thought maybe some company would be good. She's out with some friends, but she said she'd be here soon."

When they pulled into Sam's driveway, Sam turned to Paul. "I'm sorry, man."

"Need me to come in?"

"No. Just tell P.J. 'great game' for me, would you?" Sam said.

"You got it. Take it easy, buddy. I'll see you Monday."

When Veronica got to Sam's house, he was slow to answer the door. She was just about to call him when the door opened a crack and she could see him peering out. "Sam, what is it?" she asked. She could smell the booze on his breath. He opened the door and she followed him into the small living room, noting a half-empty bottle of scotch and a glass on the floor next to the couch. "Paul called me. He said you had a . . . problem at the game."

"I didn't expect that cannon fire after that first touchdown. It, uh, it freaked me out. Having a little trouble catching my breath now." He was holding his chest and pacing the room, covered in sweat. "I—I can't breathe," he managed to say.

"We need to get you to a hospital," she said. "You might be having a heart attack."

"No!" he managed in a near-shout, and then, seeing the fear in her eyes, added, "I'm fine. I just need a minute. This happens sometimes."

"It might be a heart attack," she repeated. "Sam, you can't continue on like this."

"I'm okay. I just go to a . . . dark place, sometimes."

"Sam, I don't know what you've been through. I can't even imagine it. I've never had to kill others to survive," she said. "What can I possibly say? But it is hard being with you when you are like this."

He was sitting heavily on his couch. "Something happens and it comes back: the smell of death and all the things that cause it, noises so loud you feel like an ant under a lawn mower."

"Can you take some time off?" she asked. "Maybe talk with Paul and tell him you need time—"

"I don't need time off! I just need to stay busy!" he said. Her reaction told him he'd been too loud. He couldn't tell whether she was afraid *of* him or *for* him. "Look, I'm working on it, I promise. Just give me a minute." He lay down on the couch and closed his eyes.

She watched him until at last she heard his rhythmic breathing. She took his hand and brought it to her lips, kissed it, and covered him with a blanket. Then she left quietly, locking the door behind her.

Sam started the next day with a couple of aspirin and had stopped for a greasy fast-food breakfast burrito, but he was still feeling sick by the time of his first court hearing. His client was scheduled to plead to a charge of possession of a controlled substance in pill form. Addicted to opioids, she had been going from veterinarian to veterinarian, getting prescriptions for gabapentin and taking them herself. When she'd passed out at a family gathering on Labor Day, the EMTs had discovered her purse was full of pills and notified law enforcement.

Downs had reminded the woman of her rights and the possible repercussions of a guilty plea, and had taken her plea and sentenced the woman —who had no criminal history—to a suspended jail sentence, treatment, and a nominal fine. After Downs left, Sam accepted congratulations from the family for the light sentence, encouraged his client to follow up with treatment, and thanked Cathy Schmidt for the prosecution's cooperation and consideration in reaching a deal. After Cathy left, Sam chugged an entire bottle of water, then put his file in his briefcase and was getting ready to walk back to the office when he heard a small voice behind him.

"Mr. Johnstone?"

"Yes?" he said, turning to face a small, frail woman. "Call me Sam."

"I—I need a lawyer," she said. "I read your name in the newspaper."

"What's going on?"

"I don't have any money," she said, removing a wisp of hair

from her eye. He could see the green and orange under the makeup.

"Well, some things are more important than money." He nodded at the chair next to him. "Why don't you have a seat?"

"Thank you." She sat down, then folded her hands in her lap and looked up at him. At some point, she was probably pretty. But years of bad decisions, and apparently beatings, had left her with deep lines from the pain and worry. "I need an order of protection," she said at last. "My husband. He . . . beats me."

"I haven't done a lot of that kind of work," Sam said. "There are experts in that area over at the women's shelter. I think they keep an attorney on retainer."

"I need someone who won't be afraid of Albert," she said. "He is very big, very angry, and everyone in town is afraid of him. They tell me you are a hero."

"That's an exaggeration," Sam said with a smile.

"I just know what I'm told. I need someone who will scare *him*," she said.

"I don't know," Sam mused. "Guys like that, they don't scare easy. And I'd be working as your lawyer, not your big brother."

She smiled. "My big brother beat Albert up once, a long time ago."

Sam nodded and watched her closely as she thought back to that time. "But then he got cancer and died," she said. "Since then, well . . ." She looked at the desktop.

Sam thought about it for a moment. "Okay," he said at last. "Here's my card. Call Cassie, my secretary, and tell her I said to get you in as soon as possible. Is your husband in jail?"

"For right now."

"Okay, I'll get the petition filed as soon as I can. In the meantime, do you have somewhere to go?"

"I'm home. Someone's gotta feed the dog."

"Got any family you can stay with?"

"No. All gone."

"Friends?"

She shook her head. "We don't have any."

"Okay." He gathered his briefcase and stood. "I'll get on this right away."

"I can't pay you much," she said.

"We'll figure something out, Ms., uh—I'm sorry, I didn't catch your name?"

"Raylene. Raylene Smith. My husband is Albert Smith."

"Okay, Raylene. I'll get on this right away, okay?"

"Okay."

"In the meantime, you stay safe," he said, and extended his hand. She hesitated, then placed her bony hand in his. Her eyes were filled with tears.

"Thank you, Mr. Johnstone."

"Call me Sam."

"Thank you, Sam," she said, and turned and walked out of the courtroom, dabbing at her eyes with a tissue.

6

Custer Police Department Chief of Detectives Kenneth "Punch" Polson was in his cubicle typing a report when Corporal Mike Jensen called him.

"Polson."

"Boss, I'm out at the college," Jensen began. "I'm taking a report on a missing person."

"Kid miss class, or what?" Punch asked. The "e" on his keyboard kept sticking and it was making him irritable.

"This is a little more than that, boss."

"Yeah? What's going on?"

"Young man by the name of Kaiden Miles has been missing for a day or so."

"So how did we get notified?"

"His roommate," Jensen said. "Apparently, these guys are roomies and managers for the college men's basketball team. The kid says they were at a party a couple of nights ago—Thursday, after the game—and he got tired and went back to the room. He said that the Miles kid never came home, but he didn't worry about it. Figured he might've met someone. But when Miles didn't attend any classes Friday, and when he didn't see Miles at the dining facility, and when he missed practice and didn't come home for a second night, he reported him missing to the campus police."

"And he got ahold of us?"

"Yep."

"So, the kid—Kaiden, was it?" Punch asked.

"Yeah. Kaiden Miles."

"He can't have been missing too long," Punch said. "Shit!" He'd typed "receeeeeipt" three times in a row.

"No, a little more than thirty-six, maybe forty-eight hours now."

"Local kid?" Punch was looking at the word he had re-typed. It still didn't look right.

"Born right here in Custer. Raised on his family's cattle ranch outside of town," Jensen explained. "I did a quick check —no criminal history except for a single minor in possession from when he was a senior in high school."

"Have you spoken with anyone who knows him yet?"

"I've got a couple of officers going through the dorm now asking questions."

"What's his family say?" Punch asked. He re-typed the word. "It's 'I before E'—right?"

"What? Well, yeah, I think," Jensen said. "Except after 'C,' maybe. They are worried. Say it ain't like him. Great kid, yadda, yadda. Mom says something bad must've happened."

"He ever disappear before?"

"Not that they are telling me," Jensen said.

"Who's the reporting party?"

"Ronnie Norquist."

"Any relation to Paul?"

"Not sure. I got his number," Jensen said. "You want to talk with him?"

"I will, yeah," Punch said. "You on scene?"

"I'm at the campus security office. Kid was assigned to West Hall, if you want to meet me there."

"I'll be right there."

Ten minutes later, Punch called Jensen from the dorm entryway. "Hey, how the hell do I get in?" The door was snowed in.

"Which door are you at?" Jensen asked.

"I don't know. South, I think?"

"Just a minute," Jensen said. Punch could hear him talking with someone. "They're telling me someone stole the snow shovel at that end of the dorm. Can you walk around to the east side?"

"Who the hell would steal a snow shovel?"

"I dunno, boss," Jensen said. "People steal anything. Come around."

Punch did so, and minutes later he and Jensen were in the missing student's dorm room on the Custer College campus. "How old is he?" Punch asked, looking through papers on the young man's desk.

"Nineteen, according to the family," Jensen replied. He was on his knees looking under the bed. Jeb Richter, Custer College's head of campus security, was standing in the doorway of the small room, officiously watching the two of them.

"Jeb, how are you?" Punch asked.

"Fine, Punch."

"Who saw him last?"

"Well, after he left the party, I think maybe a freshman girl coming back to the dorm, as far as we know right now," Jensen said. "She's a little quiet. I think she was doing the walk of shame." Punch saw Richter smirk.

"Get her name?"

"Yeah."

"I'll talk with her later if necessary," Punch said. "Anything on the security cameras?"

"I wanted to talk with you about that, boss." Jensen looked at Richter out of the corner of his eye.

"What is it?" Punch said.

"Jeb says the school president says we're gonna need a warrant."

"To look at common area video? Why?" Punch was looking around the room. It was a mess; property was strewn about the place. The two sides of the room were almost identically slovenly; the biggest differences were the missing kid's bed covers were blue while his roommate's were red, and there was a watch cap on the missing teenager's bed. He turned his attention to Richter. "Jeb, what's going on?" Richter had been a Custer County sheriff's deputy some years back. "Why do I need to get a warrant to look at common area footage?"

"President Beretta is a little uptight." Richter shrugged. "What can I say? I got my orders."

"Sonuvabitch." Punch shook his head. "Okay, you stay here," he said to Jensen. "Leave everything as is—I'll want to see things as they were." Turning to Richter, he continued, "Jeb, I'd like to have this room secured. No one in or out—can you do that?"

"What about the roommate? He's got a right—"

"Hold him off, can you?" Punch asked. "And let's get the crime scene photographers on standby; I'm gonna want pictures of this place."

"Crime scene?" Richter asked.

"Just to be sure," Punch said. "Look: just do this much, okay? When Jensen leaves, just lock the door and don't let anyone else in, please. I'll get you whatever you need to cover your ass."

Two nights later, Punch and his wife Rhonda were just sitting down to dinner when his phone rang. Punch looked at the number, then at Rhonda, then at the beef roast. He quickly reached with his fork, and as Rhonda shook her head disapprovingly, stabbed a roasted potato and shoved it into his mouth, then picked up his phone.

"Kenneth, do you have to answer that?" Rhonda asked.

"I do, honey." Punch swallowed the potato and wiped his mouth, then looked at her and smiled. She was mouthing the word "rude" at him. "Polson," he answered, then covered the speaker and explained to her, "I'm on call. It's a Cheyenne number. Might be important."

"This Detective Polson?"

"Yes," Punch said, putting a large helping of roast beef on his plate and spooning gravy over it. He gestured to her to ask if she wanted any. Rhonda shook her head.

"This is Investigator Jerry Johnson with the Wyoming Division of Criminal Investigation."

"How can I help you?"

"You working a missing persons up there on a kid named Miles?"

"I am," Punch said, staring at the roast and wanting to eat. He looked at Rhonda questioningly. She shook her head.

"I've got some information you're gonna need," Johnson said. "Can you be in your office by nine a.m.?"

"I usually manage to drag my ass in by then, yeah," Punch said.

"No offense. Just wanted to make sure you'll be there."

"I'll be there. What's going on?"

"I'll let you know when I'm up there tomorrow morning."

"Roger," Punch said, and hung up.

"What's going on, honey?"

"Kid missing from campus," he said, taking a forkful of beef and savoring the smell before putting it in his mouth. "DCI has some information on him. They're coming up to see me tomorrow."

"Well, then, eat your dinner," she said, helping herself to an exceptionally small portion of everything. "We've got that band concert here in an hour."

"Ugh!"

"Kenneth! He's your child."

"I know. I can't believe my son is playing a tuba."

"It's not a tuba," she corrected him. "It's an oboe. Now, eat. You can help me with the dishes when we get back."

The next morning was a Tuesday, and Punch was in well before nine a.m., as usual. He thought DCI Agent Johnson seemed a little stiff, but okay otherwise. "Coffee?"

"No thanks. Been pumping coffee since I left Cheyenne a little after four."

"That's a couple hundred miles of dodging deer and antelope," Punch said, closing his office door. "How were the roads?"

"They sucked. All the way. Blowing snow."

"Fall in Wyoming," Punch said. The two men sat quietly for a moment. "So, what do you have for me?"

"That kid Miles. He's been missing four or five days now, right?"

"As far as I can tell."

"He was working for us."

"How so?" Punch asked. He had a pretty good idea, but it never hurt to make someone feel like they were telling you something you didn't know.

"He came into the fold here about six months ago. He got busted for dealing weed on campus," Johnson said. "Your folks got ahold of me, and once I explained the maximum possible penalty to him for dealing weed on a state property, he was all about agreeing to work as a confidential informant, and away we went."

"So you've been supervising him?"

"As closely as we can," Johnson said. "I'm watching a lot of 'em, and I don't worry so much about weed dealers. It's that damned meth that worries me. But a dealer is a dealer. Preying on other people."

"How did you get onto him?" Punch asked. He'd bought a half-dozen donuts earlier that morning and was offering Johnson one.

"No thanks," the agent said, patting his stomach. "It wasn't difficult. He was apparently supplying half the campus. His name came up in a discussion with a couple of our other confidential informants. Someone else we're watching is a guy named Trent Gustafson. Major dealer. He sold a pound to this Miles kid, who we followed here to your campus. We sent one of our small-timers out and Miles sold a quarter to that kid. Then we had a couple more buyers do the same thing. We got enough to hold him by the short-and-curlies."

"Did you charge him?"

"No. I met with him and convinced him to start working with us in return for him not being charged."

"So how's he done?"

"I guess he's been selling the hell out of the stuff. But he hasn't had to testify against anyone yet," Johnson said. "Word is, he was about to leave the reservation."

"Really," Punch said. He was thinking about having another donut.

"He didn't want to play anymore, so my guys say. I told them to get ahold of your county attorney and have her staff draw up a warrant to have him arrested," Johnson said. "So, have you spoken with his family yet?"

"Just some initial communication—where he might've gone, things like that," Punch said. "Does the family know?"

"I don't think so. Confidentiality was a part of the deal," Johnson said.

"Yeah, well, nineteen-year-olds are not known for keeping secrets," Punch said. "From what I'm told, his mom seems to think he walks on water."

"Haven't seen anything that would tell us he's been running his mouth. FYI, we think his source—Gustafson— really is a badass. Not someone you'd want to cross."

"So, what do you want me to do?"

"My working theory is that one of his buyers realized what was going on and that young Miles got scared, took his supply, and headed for the hills," Johnson said. "Of course, if he was stiffing Gustafson, well . . . just wanted you to know."

"I appreciate it."

"We all have to work together," Johnson said. "I would appreciate it if this just stayed between us."

"You got it," Punch said.

Johnson was eyeing the box. "That donut offer still good?"

Punch handed him the box, hoping Johnson wouldn't take the chocolate one. "Knock yourself out."

After Johnson left, Punch returned to his paperwork. He was just about finished with an affidavit he was preparing in connection with a ring of car-hoppers when Jensen knocked on his door with a gloved hand.

"Come in, Jensen."

"Hey, boss," Jensen began, shaking the snow off his gloves and removing them. "We've got a kind of development in the Miles case."

Punch pushed himself away from the desk and turned to face Jensen directly. "I'm listening."

"The kid was gay."

Punch stared at Jensen, waiting for him to continue. When he didn't say anything, Punch got impatient. "So?"

"Don't you remember that case down in Laramie a few years back?" Jensen asked. When Punch's expression didn't change, he continued, "Matthew Shepard?"

Punch realized where Jensen was going. "That was twenty years ago!" he said. "For Christ's sake, the kids on campus here weren't even alive when that went down. Besides, no one gives a rat's ass anymore, do they?"

"I dunno, Punch. I think you're wrong," Jensen said, shaking his head. "My guys tell me that right now, planning is underway on campus to hold some sort of a rally or protest in support of this kid and against homophobia."

"What? Why? We've got no evidence to indicate that the kid is dead, let alone missing or was killed because he was gay. In fact, all the evidence is to the contrary."

"What evidence is that?"

"Jensen, close the door and sit down," Punch said, and when Jensen had complied, he explained, "Miles was a CI. You've got to keep that under your hat."

"That does change things, boss," Jensen said, and stomped a snow-covered boot on Punch's carpet.

"Really?" Punch looked pointedly at the snow on his carpet.

"Sorry."

"Don't worry about it." Punch shook his head and smiled despite himself. "But look, the most likely explanation is that he took off rather than continue to be a CI. Happens all the time."

"Well, I just wanted you to know what is going on at that campus," Jensen said.

"I hear you," Punch said. "And I appreciate it. Now, as far as your looking around—any update?"

"Not yet. What are you gonna do?"

"Watch some video," Punch said. "Richter has it cued up. Then I'm going to have a talk with his roomie, that Norquist kid."

———

Richter had been a cop for a few years, but when the night shifts and frequent absences had begun to take their toll on the family, he had applied for and landed the job as head of campus security for Custer College. He still maintained contact with local law enforcement, and he had the coffee on well before Punch showed up to review video with him.

"Still take it black?" he asked after the men shook hands.

"Black is good," Punch replied, sitting at the table in the conference room. While Richter poured coffee, Punch looked around the room. "Jeb, you got a pretty good gig going here."

"Oh, yeah. No denying that. Biggest issue I have is all the paperwork."

"For what?"

"These guys have meetings to get ready for meetings, and reports in preparation for reports. You think *you* gotta push a pen, you got another think coming." Richter shook his head. "These academics . . . I don't know. I do know I measure my email in the dozens of messages every day."

"No shit?"

"Oh, yeah." They swapped stories of their shared past for a few minutes, before Jeb turned serious. "What day are we looking at?"

"Well, let's start with the 6th of November. That's the morning we think he disappeared, right?"

"Right," Richter said. "Just so you know, we started installing cameras this summer. We got a couple in the union, and one or two outside, but that's it. Budgets, you know."

"Okay, well, let's cue it up."

Richter started the video and passed the controller to Punch, who sped through it until he saw a figure wearing a pullover sweatshirt, jeans, and tennis shoes and carrying a small black backpack leave the dorm around 1:20 a.m. "Is that him?" Punch asked.

"It's a dude," Richter said. "But I never knew the kid."

"Looks like him," Punch mused. He was looking at a photograph in his hand. "See if anyone follows him."

Less than five minutes later, Richter spoke up. "That's Davonte Blair," he observed. "The basketball player."

"Can't be too many guys on campus who look like that," Punch agreed, nodding. "We've got two guys leaving the dorm, heading south. You have another camera to the south we can take a look at?"

"There's one in the parking lot, and it looks north, but it is a helluva long way from the sidewalks."

"Let's take a look."

Richter showed Punch how to switch the video to another camera, then set the camera to the approximate time they estimated they would see the two men. They watched the video for a few moments and saw nothing.

"There!" Punch said, seeing a figure that resembled the smaller man. "Looks like him."

"I agree," Richter said, watching closely. "And there you go," he added as Davonte walked from left to right across the camera's field of vision. "He's about ten seconds behind him—gaining on him if he is, in fact, following him."

"Any other camera we can see them on?"

"I don't think so. There's the one in the parking lot. There's a couple in the field house, and the rest are in the hallways of the classroom buildings. Really, they are there for active shooter situations."

"Makes sense," Punch said. "Let's speed this up and see if they come back." Together they watched the video in fast motion until Punch said, "There!" He stopped the video, backed it up, and watched it again.

Davonte could be seen walking from right to left across the camera's field of vision, his pace much quicker than it had been earlier. He was looking to his left and right and holding what appeared to be the small black backpack. "What time is that?" Punch asked.

"About 1:45 a.m."

"Okay, you got video of Miles's dorm?"

"No. That's West Hall. Those cameras are gonna be installed next spring."

"Of course," Punch lamented. "You might as well make me copies of the footage from every camera on campus. I'll get a subpoena to you."

"Agreed. Times?"

"Let's go with 1:20 a.m. to six a.m."

"What cameras?"

"Anything outside," Punch said. "And anything in the field house. They both had business there; maybe one or both went over there for some reason."

"Got it. I'll have it on a thumb drive when they tell me to fork it over," Richter said.

"I appreciate it," Punch said. "I owe you one."

Custer College had spent a lot of money on the new facility, Punch was thinking as he looked around the place. The high ceilings revealed clear plexiglass panels affording natural light as well as a view of today's partly cloudy skies. The building apparently housed not only the coffee bar but also the bookstore, admissions office, advising, testing, financial aid, and the tutoring center. Accordingly, there were a lot of students walking about in addition to the ones lounging on the overstuffed furniture. He had gotten ahold of Ronald Norquist and asked the young man to meet with him. Punch was drinking coffee and ogling the young women when he approached.

"Detective Polson?" Ronnie asked.

"Yeah. How'd you know it was me?"

"Well, you're the only old guy in here. My name's Ronnie."

"Have a seat, Ronnie," Punch said sourly, and handed the young man a business card. He indicated the seat across the small table from himself. "So how's it going?" Punch asked. He stared at Ronnie, who alternated between looking at his feet and at those who walked by. The one place he didn't look was in Punch's direction.

"It's okay, I guess," Ronnie said, focusing on the latte between his hands. "I'm worried, you know?" He looked around the student union and nodded at a couple of young women passing by. "Does my dad know you are here?"

"No," Punch said. "You're eighteen. No reason to tell him."

"What do you want to know?"

"Are you surprised he left?" Punch asked.

Ronnie sipped his latte. Some of the foam remained on his upper lip. Punch didn't think he'd started shaving yet, so between the baby face and the foam Ronnie looked something like a giant tween. "Is that what you think happened?" Ronnie asked.

"That's my working theory," Punch said. "What do you think happened?"

"I don't know."

"Do you know any reason why he would leave? Know anyone wishing him ill?"

"No," Ronnie said, still looking around the union. Anywhere but at Punch.

"When did you see him last?"

"We had a party after Thursday's game in Davonte's dorm room," Ronnie said.

"Were you drinking?"

"Well, yeah, a little. But it was quiet, you know?"

"Anything else going on?" Punch asked.

"What do you mean?"

"I mean was anybody smoking weed?" He watched Ronnie closely.

Ronnie looked around the room and then back toward Punch. "Detective Polson, I can't afford to get in trouble. My dad will kill me."

"I already told you," Punch began, "there's no reason for your dad to know anything that we're talking about. I'm just trying to find out what happened with your roommate."

"So, yeah, Kaiden had some weed," Ronnie admitted.

"Kaiden always had weed—right?"

"Well, yeah, he did," Ronnie said, and almost smiled.

"Look, we vaped some weed and played some video games. Then I left and went home because I was tired, and I had a final on Tuesday. Yesterday."

"How'd you do?"

"Okay, I think."

"What's your major?" Punch asked.

"Well, I'm just getting my basic stuff out of the way here," Ronnie said. "But I plan to major in theater when I get to the U. I do the school plays."

"Gonna be an actor, huh?" Punch asked. When Ronnie nodded, he continued. "You go straight home?"

"I did," Ronnie said, looking at the floor.

"Who all was at this get-together?" Punch asked.

"Do I have to answer?" Ronnie was tapping his foot on the floor.

Punch let him fret for a minute. "Is there a reason why you wouldn't want to?" he asked.

"Well, I don't wanna be a narc."

"I'm trying to figure out what might have happened to Kaiden," Punch said. "Seems like if you cared about Kaiden, then you'd want me to know everything." He watched as Ronnie struggled to decide what to do. "It might be important. And for your information, my investigations are confidential."

Having made his decision, Ronnie took a deep breath. "Well, there was Kaiden, and me, and this other guy. His name was Trent—"

"Gustafson?"

"Yeah. How'd you know?"

Punch ignored the question. "Who else?"

"And, uh, Davonte. I mean, some other guys had been there earlier, but they had all left. Except the four of us."

"No girls? No women?"

"Uh, no," Ronnie said.

"Why not?" Punch asked. He had a pretty good idea.

"Uhh, I'm not sure?"

"So I'm assuming everyone there was vaping dope?"

"Well," Ronnie began, "I kind of wasn't really paying attention. I mean, we were gaming. I didn't exactly see them vaping, but that's what they always did."

"But you saw Davonte there that night?"

"Of course. It was his room."

"So, everybody is gaming and vaping dope and then what?" Punch asked. "Why did the party break up?"

"Because Davonte and Kaiden were arguing."

Punch's interest was piqued. "Yeah? What about?"

"Do I have to say?" Ronnie asked. Punch didn't answer, but merely stared at Ronnie. It worked. "About money," Ronnie said at last.

"Yeah?"

"Yeah. And then Kaiden left. Then Davonte left. Then, well, then me and Trent left."

So far, Ronnie's story was matching what Punch already knew to be true. "Together?" he asked. "Where'd you go?"

"Well . . . yeah," Ronnie said. Beads of sweat were forming on his forehead and he was looking around the union again. "To my room."

Punch sat back, looked at Ronnie, and then around the union. Students were bustling back and forth, trying to get a moment's respite before heading through the driving snow to their classes. He finished his coffee. "Ronnie, fair to say you and Trent could corroborate each other's whereabouts for the rest of the night?"

"Well, for a while. I mean . . . yeah."

"Was Kaiden ever there?"

"No."

"Had he been there, could you tell?" Punch asked. "Like maybe before you and Trent got there?"

"Not sure," Ronnie said. "And honestly, I just hit the sack. I didn't look to see him there."

"You don't know where Kaiden spent the night?"

"No."

"Do you think he might have stayed with Davonte?" Punch asked.

"He, uh, might've, except they were mad at each other."

"Were they an item?"

"What? No! I mean, Davonte is gonna be in the NBA some day! He's big-time!"

Punch looked at Ronnie for a long moment. Ronnie looked away. "Ronnie, is there something I need to know? You're kind of protective here."

"No. I mean, it wasn't like that with those two," Ronnie said, and then looked at his phone. "I gotta get to class."

"Ronnie, were you surprised when Kaiden didn't make it home?"

"No."

"Did you think he was with Davonte?"

"Well, yeah—but not in the way you mean," Ronnie said, standing and gathering his gear. He was buttoning his coat when he stopped suddenly and looked down at Punch. "I mean, Davonte followed him outside. He said . . ."

"Said what?" Punch asked. He waited while Ronnie debated answering, then softly repeated, "Said what?"

"He said he was going to beat Kaiden's ass," Ronnie said, looking around him. "Detective Polson, does my dad need to know?"

"Know what?" Punch asked, turning both palms upward and shrugging.

"Thanks, Detective Polson." Ronnie cracked the briefest of smiles. "I gotta go."

"Go," Punch said, and waved him off, admiring a couple of very attractive young women walking by, talking and laughing. He was in no hurry to drive in the snow.

7

The next day, Punch and Jensen were back at the college under Richter's escort. This time they were in the dorms to visit Davonte Blair. Punch knocked at the door, then repeated the knock and listened closely. Eventually, the door opened.

"Mr. Blair? I'm Detective Polson and this is Corporal Jensen," Punch said through the crack of the door, flashing his badge. "We'd like to talk with you if you have a minute."

"What about?" Devonte answered.

"How about you let us in, and we'll explain?" Punch asked, and then turned to Richter. "You might want to leave this to us. Else you might have to make an arrest."

"Huh?" Richter said.

"What if I don't?" Davonte asked.

"Well, Mr. Blair, if you don't let us in, then I guess I'm gonna have to go and get a warrant so I can investigate what I think is the smell of raw marijuana," Punch said. He made a show of sniffing, then turned and looked at Jensen. "Can you smell what I smell?"

"Oh, yessir," Jensen said. "I smell the strong odor of raw marijuana emanating from Room Number A12."

vaped a little weed and played some video games. Says you and Kaiden got in a little disagreement. Says Kaiden got pissed and left."

"Yeah?"

"Yeah," Punch said. "And here's where it gets interesting: he says that a few minutes after Kaiden left, you got dressed, said you were gonna go kick Kaiden's ass, and you left, too."

"He said that?"

Punch ignored him. "Now, you're a college man, and I'm just a cop. But I'm sure you understand why I would find that of interest, right? I mean, Ronnie saw Kaiden leave, then you leave . . . and then Kaiden disappears."

"Sounds like Ronnie's been talking a lot." The big man's hands were still now.

"Enough." Punch nodded. "And if all that's true, I'm thinking that you were the last person to see Kaiden." Punch used the toe of his boot to move a discarded towel that was lying on the floor. Underneath, he could see marijuana shake on the carpet. "So, since I'm looking for Kaiden, I thought, 'What better place to start than with Mr. Blair, who appears to have been the last guy to be seen with him?'"

"I don't know nothin'," Davonte said, shaking his head and then running a hand over his face, top to bottom.

"Were you with those guys that night?"

"I can't remember," Davonte said.

"Did you have a disagreement with Kaiden?"

"No."

"Threaten to kick his ass?"

"No."

"Did you follow Kaiden?" Punch pressed.

"No," Davonte repeated.

Punch and Davonte looked at each other, expressionless. "I've already looked at the video on campus, and I know he

Richter was walking down the hallway as fast as he co
Punch smiled and turned back to the door, which was r
open. Davonte stood just inside, looking down at the six-f
Punch and the slightly shorter Jensen. "Come in," he said i:
deep baritone.

"Why, thank you, Mr. Blair," Punch said. He quick
scanned the room. It looked like dorm rooms he'd been :
before, except for a six-inch-high stack of letters piled at th
foot of the bed. Many of them were unopened, and most wer
outwardly adorned with the logo of an athletically prestigiou,
university. "Can we sit down?"

"Make yourself at home, cop."

"Why, thank you, Mr. Blair," Punch said, and with the back
of his hand vigorously swept the letters off the bed. Settling in,
he looked at Davonte and smiled. "You know Kaiden Miles?"

Davonte stared at Punch until he realized Punch wasn't
going to look elsewhere. "Sure. He's our manager."

"You know him off the court?"

"We hung out a little bit, yeah," Davonte said. "What's it to
you?"

"You know he's missing?"

"I know he ain't been around."

"His roommate—Ronnie Norquist, you know him, right?"
Punch asked.

"He's a manager, too."

"Ronnie reported Kaiden missing a couple of days ago."

"Yeah?"

"Yeah. Ronnie says you and him and Kaiden and Trent
Gustafson were partying the other night."

"That's what he said?" Davonte was looking at an expensive athletic shoe, rolling it back and forth in his enormous
hands.

"That's what he said," Punch said. "Says the four of you

left and then you left, and I'm thinking you were following him." Punch watched the big man closely. "What's got me curious is why you are lying to me now."

"I don't know what happened to that dude, man."

"So, what happened?" Punch said. "When's the last time you saw him?"

"I ain't answering no more questions without a lawyer, man."

"Jensen, you still smell what I smell?"

"I do, Punch," Jensen said. "In fact, the smell is getting stronger. I think it's coming from that Crown Royal bag right next to you. In fact, I'll bet if you stood up, you could see in there without touching anything."

"And if I did that, then—"

"Then you'd probably have probable cause for a warrant to search, boss."

"How do you think those big colleges would feel about a recruit getting busted for weed?"

"Well," Jensen said, tipping his hat back, "what I hear is they are getting real sensitive to the use of illegal drugs or other lawbreaking by prospective players. I think that might dissuade some of them. Did I use 'dissuade' right, boss? Because I never went to college either, you know."

"You did fine," Punch said, looking to Davonte, who was studying the floor. "Hey, Jensen. Someone told me Davonte here might be a real NBA prospect. What do you hear about the draft prospects of guys busted for drugs?"

"I hear it results in a guy losing several positions in the draft, or even dropping out of the draft entirely," Jensen said. "Could cost a guy millions, is what I hear."

"Wow. That'd be a shame." Punch shook his head sadly and watched Davonte do the math.

"All right, cop. I seen 'em all that night," Davonte said,

standing and beginning to pace the room. "We vaped a little weed, played some war game on the box, then he left. I left after that to go see one of my teammates."

"Alone?"

"Alone."

"Where was he going?" Punch interrupted.

"I don't know. We had a little argument and he left."

"What time was that?"

"I don't know. I was wasted, man." Davonte shook his head slightly and looked to the ceiling. "That shit he had. . ."

"So, he left and—"

"That's it."

"Did you two have an argument?"

"Not really. Why would I argue with him?"

"Ronnie says it was over money."

"Ronnie needs to watch his ass."

"Or what?" Punch asked. "He'll disappear, too?"

"Yo, man, you listening? I just told you, I don't know nothing about that!" Davonte stopped pacing and looked down at Punch.

"But you saw him leave?"

"I did."

"Never saw him again?" Punch asked, looking up at the young man.

"Nope. Like I said. Kinda rode the buzz for a while. Talked with Ronnie and that Trent dude. Went to my buddy's house. Fell asleep. Woke up a few hours later and came back here."

"Can anyone corroborate that?" Punch asked, and then, seeing Davonte's blank stare, rephrased the question. "Can anyone say they saw you that night—I mean after Kaiden left and you left? See anyone else?"

"Just the dude whose place I crashed," Davonte said after a long pause.

"Never seen or heard from Kaiden since that night?"

"Never. God's truth," he said, and sat back down just as Punch's neck began to cramp.

"Okay." Punch stood. "I'm gonna go with that for right now. What's your travel schedule?"

"Uh, we play somewhere in Idaho this weekend. Idaho one night, Utah the next, I think."

"So, for the time being I'm going to be okay with you traveling for basketball, but other than that, I'm gonna need you to stay around here."

"Can you do that?"

"If I have to get a court order, I will, Davonte," Punch began. "Of course, that would involve me completing an affidavit, meaning I'd have to spell out everything I know, including you hanging with a bunch of dudes getting high. Know what I mean?"

"I'll be around, cop," Davonte said. "Just be cool."

"Oh, I will be," Punch said. "One last question."

"Yeah?"

"Where'd you get those cuts on your hands?"

"Games, man," Davonte said, turning his hands and looking at them. "These guys can't stop me, so they hack me."

"Mind if Jensen here takes a couple of pictures?"

"Why?"

"Why not?"

"Go ahead, man," Davonte said, putting his hands in front of him. "Then get on out of here."

Punch hadn't slept well and was up early. He had a bad feeling about Kaiden Miles. It had been a week since the young man's disappearance, and people were getting antsy. According to

Jensen, no activity had been observed on Miles's phone, which was a bad sign for a guy his age. This morning, though, Punch had to testify in a drug case he'd made months ago. The plan was to get in and review the file and then get to the courthouse a little early to talk with the prosecutor. He was brushing his teeth when his phone rang. He answered lest it wake Rhonda.

"Did you hear what was on the radio just now?" It was Jensen.

"No. Rhonda's still sleeping. What are you talking about?"

"Miles's mom gave a radio interview to the Custer station. She is all over us for looking at this as a missing person case. She is convinced he is the victim of foul play, and she said we were flat on our asses."

"Good God almighty!" Punch said, then took a minute to spit and rinse. "Everything we've got right now indicates that he took off. We don't have squat saying it was anything other than him disappearing because he wanted to."

"I know that, boss. You know that. But she is convinced that it's foul play. She's pointing out that he had no suicidal tendencies, that there was no note, that he had good grades last semester, and that he had told her he was going to go on down to the University of Wyoming next fall."

"What's becoming clear to me is that she didn't know her little angel was a CI, did she?"

"I don't think she had a clue."

"Well, you spoke with her, didn't you?"

"I did. She either doesn't know anything or she's a helluva actress."

"Well, I'm gonna let DCI know," Punch mused. "Maybe they can whisper in her ear, and if mom knows that the apple of her eye was a drug-dealing CI, maybe we can get a little breathing room, huh?"

"Sounds good to me, boss."

"All right, I'll be there in a couple minutes, but I gotta get to the courthouse. I'm testifying this morning."

"Lucky you."

———

Sarah Penrose, reporter for the *Custer Bugle*, had been on hold, waiting for Custer Police Department Chief of Police William "Buck" Lucas for more than five minutes now. She was getting irritable and was about to hang up when she heard his deep voice. "Hello?"

"Chief Lucas, this is Sarah Penrose," she said. "What can you tell us about the investigation?"

"Which one?"

"The one into the disappearance of Kaiden Miles."

"I'm not prepared to comment at this time," Lucas said.

"Can you confirm that Kaiden Miles, a student at Custer College, is missing?"

"I cannot."

"His mother says he is missing," Sarah said. "She said your department is failing to investigate, at least in part, because he is gay."

"What does that have to do with anything?"

"So, are you saying that you are investigating his disappearance?"

"I'm not saying anything right now," Lucas said. "We'll have a comment later."

Sarah sat at her desk and looked at her phone, hearing a dial tone. "This might be it," she said.

"What was that?" asked Jimmy Brown, the paper's photographer. He was cleaning his camera.

"If this is what I think it is, JB, you and I might be on our way to the *Denver Post* here soon."

"You think this is that big?"

"I think it is huge," Sarah said. "And even if it isn't, I think with a little creative journalism we can make it that big. Remember Matthew Shepard?"

"I've heard of the case."

"The gay University of Wyoming student killed by a couple of rednecks? This is going to be bigger. Way bigger."

"How do you know?"

"Simple," she said, turning to her keyboard. "I'm going to make it bigger."

———

Sam was sitting in the local Veterans Administration outpatient clinic. Twice each week, he was shown to a small room with a desktop computer, a chair, and not much else. Moments later his counselor, Bob Martinez, would appear from parts unknown via video-teleconference. Sam was wandering around the tiny room when he heard Martinez's voice. "Mr. Johnstone, how are you?"

"If I was okay would I be here seeing your sorry ass?"

"Thanks, Sam. Love you too, brother," Martinez said, smiling. He'd been Sam's counselor for a little more than a year now. "Seriously. How are you doing—really?"

"I'm okay," Sam said. He took a chair.

"Okay is good," Martinez said, making a note. "Any thoughts of harming yourself or others?"

"Was behind a guy on his phone this morning who sat through a green light. Gave some thought to cutting his throat."

"Nice. Anything else?"

"Some clown in front of me at lunch ordered a quad shot, vanilla soy something-or-other with foam and sprinkles," Sam said. "That's summary execution material there, right?"

Martinez laughed. "Anything else?"

"Yeah, any producer in Nashville who is cranking out this hick-hop crap I'm hearing on the country music station. I think a couple of bunker-busters would do the trick."

"Hick-hop?" Martinez laughed aloud. "I love it! And I'm with you, for what it's worth." Then he turned serious. "Okay, Sam. How is it going?"

"I'm all right. Hanging in there."

"Good. Work your program to deal with the booze and you can get better. How's the drinking?"

"One day at a time."

"You're talking to me," Martinez said. "No bullshit. Where ya at?"

"I do pretty good some days, and not so good other days."

"How many times did you drink in the past week?"

"Three, maybe four?"

"You can't remember?" Martinez asked.

"I'm not counting—you are," Sam replied.

"Any blackouts?"

"No."

"Any incidents?"

"Yeah."

"Tell me," Martinez said, and for the next few minutes he listened closely while Sam recounted the events at the football game. "Yeesh. What did your sponsor say?"

"We haven't been talking."

"Why not?"

"He relapsed," Sam said. "I need to find a new guy, I guess."

"Find one who won't buy your bull. Sponsors are impor-tant," Martinez said. "Have you been doing the meditation I suggested? Those mental exercises? The reflections and prayers?"

"No, not really," Sam admitted. "I'm busy. I have trouble meditating—my mind goes a hundred miles an hour."

"Sam, you can't be too busy to get and stay sober and to deal with your PTSD," Martinez explained. "I know it is diffi- cult and time-consuming, but you have got to find the time. Now, let's talk about next steps. This football game thing concerns me." They spoke for another thirty minutes or so. As always, Sam felt immeasurably better and departed the session resolved to put into action all of Martinez's suggestions.

Beretta was in his corner office on the second floor alternately watching the mid-November snow fly and looking at a spread- sheet. He was losing interest and thinking about calling it an afternoon when his secretary, Mona Ogletree, called him. "President Beretta, Sarah Penrose from the *Bugle* is on line two —do you want to speak with her?"

"Of course, Ms. Ogletree," Beretta said, unconsciously straightening his tie as he reached for the phone. "Ms. Penrose, President Vincent Beretta here. How might I help you?"

"Mr. Beretta—"

"*President* Beretta, if you would," he said sharply. "After all, we are speaking in my official capacity, are we not?"

"We are," Penrose said. "*President* Beretta, what can you tell the Custer community and the people of Wyoming to assure them in the face of this apparent hate crime?"

"Hate crime?" Beretta said, jumping to his feet. "What are you talking about?"

"I'm talking about the disappearance of one of your sopho-mores—a young man named Kaiden Miles."

"What makes that a hate crime?"

"I'm told he was gay, and given the history of gay males in higher education in this state, I feel certain that my readers —your constituents—will be interested to hear what steps are being taken to protect the LGBTQ+ population from attack."

"What? I don't know anything about that!"

"You don't know anything about the disappearance of one of your students from his dorm last week?"

"Well of course I do, Ms. Penrose," Beretta said. "I just didn't know anything about him being gay."

"Oh, come now, Mr. President," Penrose said, making notes. "Surely you've seen the signs on campus. My sources tell me there were protesters in the student union yesterday."

"I—I've been out of town briefly," Beretta said. "No one has told me anything—"

"Surely you've seen the messages posted on your own social media sites?"

"I—I've not looked."

"President Beretta, now that you've been informed of what's going on at Custer College, what can you tell our readers?"

"Uh, Ms. Penrose, what I can say, uh, is this. . . As an educator and the leader of Custer College, I am deeply committed to, uh, a campus environment where every indi-vidual can live, work, and learn in a caring, safe, and supportive environment. I—I am deeply concerned when issues of homophobia or, uh, anything else target individuals or groups," he said, pausing for a drink of water. "Such behavior is against our core principles and will not be tolerated."

"What steps are being taken to protect other members of the Custer College community?" Penrose asked.

"I can say we, uh, we are cooperating fully with local law enforcement authorities in their investigation. At the same time, we, uh, are . . . we are protecting the rights of our students. We want to ensure that all students, especially students from historically oppressed groups, are treated, uh, fairly and, uh, are supported throughout the process."

"What kinds of support are you providing?" Penrose asked.

"We are making our counseling staff available to students from these groups," he said, buzzing for Ms. Ogletree and scribbling, "Get me the counseling office!!!" on a piece of paper as he spoke. "And we are augmenting our college police force with off-duty officers from the local community," he added.

"Are you working with the sexually and gender diverse communities of Custer at all?"

"Yes, uh, I have reached out to the local chapter of gay and lesbian students, and while we have no reason to believe that additional students, faculty, or staff are at risk, I have nonetheless assured that group we are working to ensure their safety."

"What else can you tell us?"

"I will have no additional comment at this time."

"Thank you, *Mister* Beretta," Penrose said, hanging up.

"That's President—" he said to the dial tone, before getting up and walking quickly to his door. "Ms. Ogletree! Stop whatever you are doing. I need to speak with the head of our counseling office, then with Chief Lucas and our head of security. Then get me someone from one of the gay and lesbian groups —in that order, and now!"

"What's going on?"

"The shit is hitting the fan, that's what's going on! Why

didn't you or someone else tell me about the student protests?"

"Protests?"

"Sarah Penrose says there were protesters in the student union yesterday!"

"I got lunch there yesterday, sir," Mona said. "There were two protesters, if you could call them that. One had a sign calling for divestment of anything involving oil and gas and the other one had a sign reading, 'Where's Kaiden?'—whatever that means."

Buck Lucas had the door to his office closed with a sign on it reading, "Knock and enter quietly." The rather bleak sun was shining through his office window and he was on his stomach on the floor, trying to stretch and hoping the feeble rays would warm his back. Probably due in part to the change in weather, he'd slept poorly and had gotten in before five a.m. Now, the situation involving a missing campus sophomore was causing him discomfort just a little bit south of there. When the phone rang, he fumbled around, trying to reach it before grasping it and growling, "Chief Lucas."

"Chief Lucas, this is President Beretta."

"Vince, how's it hanging?" Lucas asked, knowing that Beretta hated to be addressed using his given name and figuring he'd be appalled by that greeting. "How can I help you?"

"You can find that missing kid and do it fast!" Beretta said in his falsetto. "We are dying over here. Have you seen the protests going on?"

"Well, my officers tell me that there are some people who

are holding signs and walking around on your campus, yes. But you have a security force. What do you want from me?"

"I want you to solve the disappearance of Kaiden Miles, is what I want!"

"We are doing the best we can," Lucas said. "I've got Punch Polson on it—world of confidence in him."

"And I heard he was dragging his feet because this young man was gay," Beretta said. "In fact, that story in the newspaper seems to say just that."

"Well, all I can tell you is that story is bullshit."

"Do you think maybe you should bring somebody in? Like maybe the FBI? I'm not sure a small-town police force like yours is capable of solving this crime."

"Vince, right now, I've got a missing person," Lucas said. "That's all I've got. When and if I feel like we can't do the job, I'll get someone in here who can. Until then, we'll handle it. And when I need your advice, I'll ask for it."

"All I'm saying . . . All I'm saying is that maybe your guys could use a little help," Beretta said.

"And I assure you, when in my judgment we need some help, I'll ask for it," Lucas said. "I've done it before."

"I just don't want to have another situation like you had in Laramie years ago," Beretta said. "Your community cannot withstand that kind of a situation."

"You mean *our* community, don't you, Mr. President?"

"Well, yes . . . Of course, that is exactly what I mean."

"That's what I thought, Vince," Lucas said. "And I'm glad to hear it. I'd hate to have to talk with the board of directors if I thought differently. I mean, I went to high school with most of 'em. Dated the board chair, in fact. You see Greta, you give her my best, will you?"

"Don't you threaten me, Chief! I'm telling you I want this solved, now! I am not going to have this kind of shit-show on my campus! Diversity and inclusion are important and make us who we are. You need to get this thing solved right now, or—"

"Or what?" Lucas growled. "Vince, I don't care whether that kid is straight, gay, trans, or doesn't know what he is. He is someone's little boy. I believe that every human life has value, and I don't prioritize one over another for any reason. Ask around, and you'll find I am an equal opportunity asshole. I'm on my people to get this thing solved, and solved as quickly as possible—and you want to know why? Because that family deserves it, if for no other reason. Now, why don't you go and count pencils or administrators or whatever it is you do all day? I've got things to do!" he concluded, slamming the phone down so hard it nearly broke.

"Chief, what's going on?" his secretary asked. She'd heard the commotion and had knocked and come in.

"Nothing! Just get Polson's ass in here now!"

———

Several days later, on a snowy November Saturday morning, Punch was at his kitchen table, buttering a piece of multigrain toast, when a call came in. "Boss, we've got a body," Jensen said.

"Where?"

"On the edge of the creek that runs along the south end of the college."

"Who found it?" Punch asked, taking a huge bite of the toast.

"Couple of joggers," Jensen said. "Older couple. Had their lab with them. Dog got off the trail and wouldn't come back, so they went down to the edge of the water and saw the body."

"This our guy?" Punch asked, chugging coffee and getting to his feet.

"Can't tell. No one's touched anything. Head and shoulders are in the water."

"Hoodie and jeans?"

"Yeah. We can see that much," Jensen said.

"Okay," Punch said, putting on his shoulder holster, "I'll be there shortly."

By the time Punch arrived, Goodrich had cordoned off a sizable area up and down Cavalry Creek and running perpendicular to the walking path, so if one envisioned the scene as a rough square, the body was at the center of the south side, with the walking path being the north side. Two strips of yellow crime scene tape formed the east and west sides of the square. Punch sighed and looked about him. A few bystanders were huddled behind one of the plastic tapes, but beyond that it looked like word had yet to get out. Jensen walked up to meet him. "Morning, boss."

"Good morning. Anything good?"

"Not really. I've kept everyone away so you could get the first look. Crime scene guys are on the way."

"Okay, where's the photographer?"

"Over by the truck. Want him?"

"Yeah, let's get him in to take pictures of the scene first," Punch said. "I want pictures of all the footprints in the snow before we start mucking things up."

"Got it," Jensen said, and then turned and waved at the photographer. "Yo, Thorp! You're on!"

"Go with him, Jensen. Make sure he doesn't dork anything up."

"Roger," Jensen said. "Folks who found the body are in the back of Goodrich's car, keeping warm." Punch turned to go see the couple. "Hey, boss?"

"Yeah?"

"You got some crumbs on the front of your shirt."

"Thanks," Punch said, wiping himself down. He walked over to Goodrich's vehicle, opened the front passenger-side door, and after moving several notebooks, paper bags, and an empty holster, squeezed his way into the seat. The couple was huddled in the back seat, clearly upset by what they'd found.

"Not good," the man said.

"It was horrible!" said the woman.

In short order, Punch got their story. There wasn't much to it. They'd let their dog off his leash and he'd gone down to the creek and wouldn't obey their commands to "Come," so the man had gotten irritated and had gone to get the dog. "I was gonna drag Barney—that's my dog's name—back up to the trail," he admitted. "But then I saw the feet and the legs and I yelled at Barney and I think I scared him. He came that time."

"Did you touch anything?"

"No."

"Did you see anyone around?"

"No, but it was still kind of dark. Even though we're partly retired, me and the wife still get up early," the man said proudly. "Barney wouldn't let us sleep in, anyway," he added.

"Any footprints other than yours around the body?"

"Well, Barney's," the man said. "But I didn't see any others. Tell you one thing, though."

"What's that?"

"I think he'd been there for a while."

"Why do you say that?"

"Well, because you can tell his body was frozen, and it didn't look there was much snow under him, so he musta been there before we had that last big snow. What was that? Ten days, maybe two weeks ago?"

"That's good detective work." Punch smiled. "I'll look into that. Ma'am, do you have anything to add?"

"No, I don't think so."

"Okay, well, let's do this: I'll have you leave your contact information with the officers, and we'll have to get you in at a later time to make a more complete statement."

"Thanks, Detective," the man said. "Is—is that the young man that's been missing?"

"We're not sure. We'll go about the business of identifying the remains here soon enough. I'll be in touch. Here's my card; give me a call if you think of anything between now and then," Punch said as he left the vehicle.

"Detective Polson." Penrose matched Punch's stride as he walked to his car. "Sarah Penrose from the—"

"I know who you are," Punch said. He was walking quickly, thinking about everything he needed to get done. "I don't have anything for you at this time."

"Can you confirm you have discovered a body?" she asked, walking beside him.

"I can."

"This is a crime against a gay man, right?"

"I don't even know if it is a crime yet," Punch said.

"Is it Kaiden Miles, the young gay man who has been missing for ten days?" she asked.

"We don't know yet," he said, opening the car door. "We've yet to recover the remains."

"Is the body that of a male?" Penrose asked.

"We're unsure at this point."

"Detective, how can you be unsure of something as simple as that?" she asked, holding the recorder toward him.

Punch looked at her for a time, considering his options. "Can we go off the record for just a minute?"

"Why?"

"Because I want to tell you something, but I don't want the mother of this person to know the details of what I'm going to tell you," he said. "No one should ever know something like this."

Penrose thought for a moment, then nodded and made a point of switching off the recorder.

"We haven't recovered the body yet," Punch began, "because it looks like after the person passed away, they either fell or were dragged halfway into the creek, which then froze over and thawed. Looks like animals may have been feeding on the body. So all we've been able to see at this point are feet, legs, and an ass—and I can't tell if they belong to a man or woman. Jeans, socks, and tennis shoes. Nothing to indicate gender yet. Now, eventually, we'll be able to get the body out of the creek—I hope without it falling apart. Then the medical examiner will look at it and make his findings. At that point I'll get information to our press liaison, who'll put something out, okay?"

He looked at her steadily. She was rather pale now, and nodded her understanding. "Thank you, Detective. I'll just say the remains are unidentified."

"Thank you," he said, then closed the door and started the car. Before he was out of the parking lot, Penrose was on the phone with her editor, dictating.

8

Sam habitually got to the office before six a.m., so as usual he made a pot of coffee, turned on some country music, and checked the sports websites for the box score from the previous evening's college football games. After perusing the sports, he checked the weather, as he was hoping to get some fishing in over the weekend. He then read the local news. According to reporter Sarah Penrose, a yet-to-be-identified body had been found near Custer College, but she was hinting strongly it was that of the young man who'd been reported missing. According to the reporter, the missing young man was a manager for the college's basketball team and—why this was included was a mystery to Sam—he was gay. After finishing the story, Sam began drafting an estate plan for an elderly couple he'd met with the day prior. He was still doing that when Cassie arrived with the morning's distribution.

"Good morning, Sam," she said.

"Good morning. How are things?"

"Fine. Did you hear they found a body?" she asked. Sam knew she also had a child attending the local college.

"I read about it. Very sad."

"If it's Kaiden Miles, my daughter knew him," Cassie said, putting the stack of paperwork in his in-box. "It's a small school, of course."

"It is," he said.

"I just hope they find whoever did this, and fast. The kids are very upset. I'm just hoping it doesn't have anything to do with his being gay."

"What is that all about?" Sam asked.

"What do you mean?"

"Why is it important that he is gay?" Sam asked. "That got played up in the online account."

"Don't you remember the Matthew Shepard case?"

"No. I'm not from around here, remember?"

"Oh, right," she said, sitting in a chair on the other side of his desk. "About twenty years ago, two men in Laramie killed a University of Wyoming student. They wrote and said horrible things about him being gay. It was on the national news."

"So, two idiots killed a guy because he was gay," Sam said. "What does that have to do with this?"

"Well, a lot of people from out of state seized on that story and decided that Wyomingites are homophobic."

"Because of one incident?"

"Well, that and the fact that Wyoming law doesn't deal with discrimination based on gender or sexual orientation. It's a real sore point for some people. My sister lives in Seattle and she told me some of her gay friends won't even visit Wyoming for fear they could be killed."

"Seriously?"

"That's what she said." Cassie shook her head. "If this is a hate crime, it's going to be bad."

"They're all bad," Sam said.

"Oh, I agree, Sam. I'm just saying if this is because he was gay—well, that's just going to reaffirm every stereotype of Wyoming out there."

"Interesting," Sam said. "What was that kid's name again?"

———

Beretta was having breakfast and reading the paper. "Holy crap!" he said, putting down his bowl of oatmeal.

"What is it, dear?" Lucy asked. She was wearing her workout clothes, drinking coffee, and eating a bran muffin. After he left for work, she would go to the gym and meet with her personal trainer for an hour. It was expensive on a small college president's salary, but she insisted upon it.

"Look at this! It sounds like they found a body—and on campus, no less. Damn it! Why didn't I get a call from Jeb Richter? Why am I having to find out from the damned newspaper? What the hell are we paying him for?"

"His poor family; they must be so distraught," Lucy said.

"I'm sure they are—but what about me? I can't afford this kind of publicity, Lucy! We're this close to getting out of this hellhole." He held his thumb and index finger inches apart. "I just sent off my expression of interest for that job in Massachusetts!"

"I just feel so bad for his family," she said. "They lost their child."

"And now we're going to have the press descending on us like locusts. It's going to be terrible." He stood, handed her the paper, and put on his suitcoat. "My press officer is inexperienced, we've really got no place to hold press conferences, and we've got some students on this campus who are . . . well, they're damned insensitive to what's going on in the world, let's just say that!"

"It says here that her 'sources' told her it was Kaiden," she said. "Maybe it's not."

"That's a little more than I'm willing to hope for right now," he said, bending over and putting a spoonful of oatmeal in his mouth. "Sonuvabitch! I cannot believe my bad luck."

Punch had been called to the principal's office.

"What is this?" Lucas asked, turning his monitor so Punch could see the online article's headline: SOURCES: BODY LIKELY TO BE THAT OF MISSING GAY STUDENT. "How the hell did she come up with that?" Lucas demanded.

"No idea," Punch said. "I specifically told her we had no idea what gender the body was. I told her we'd put something out as soon as we know."

"She says 'sources' told her."

"She's making that up," Punch said. "I told her we'd get something out when we knew. According to Jensen, she had that story up half an hour later. The only sources she has are between her ears."

"You're probably right," Lucas said. He stood and looked at his watch. "I've got a meeting with the mayor here in ten minutes. So, is it that kid?"

"I think so," Punch said, drinking from a red coffee cup shaped like a shotgun shell. "The guys who recovered the body told me it was a male, approximately the right height and weight. But Dr. Laws hasn't looked at it yet. Supposed to start the examination here in an hour or so."

"Okay, keep me posted," Lucas said. He moved his mouse to look at the comments below the story, then straightened and gestured at the screen. "What the hell is wrong with people?"

"You mean in general, or is your question more specific than that?"

"I mean whoever wrote this story—this Sarah Penrose. What the hell difference does it make if the kid was gay?"

"Well, I suppose it's a reaction to that kid getting killed down in Laramie."

"That was twenty years ago!"

"I know."

"My department pursues all crimes, regardless of the nature of the victim! I've got a dozen people who're gay in jail right now, and a couple more who identify as something other than what you'd think they are given the plumbing God gave 'em! We accommodate—no one can say we don't!"

"I understand, Chief. But you have to understand that a lot of people from elsewhere—"

"Don't know what the hell they are talking about!" Lucas was pacing his office now. "You read that crap people are saying in the comments?" he asked, gesturing toward the monitor. "You'd think we were some sort of cavemen here."

Punch sat quietly, nodding.

"All this is going to do is complicate everything, Punch. We've got a dead kid who—whatever his sexual orientation, color, political persuasion, or favorite football team—deserved better. Let's get this thing figured out, now!"

"Got it," Punch said. "I'm going to get everyone started before I go see the medical examiner."

"And I'm gonna tell the mayor you are on this and feeling positive about a quick arrest."

"Chief, we don't even know a crime was committed yet," Punch cautioned.

"Don't confuse me with facts," Lucas said. "Now go!"

Two hours later Punch was in the morgue. "So, Doc, what do you know?" he asked Dr. Ronald B. Laws, M.D., Custer County's contracted medical examiner. Laws had done a residency in pathology some years ago before turning to internal medicine. He was in private practice locally and contracted with the elected coroner "Doc" Fish to do the actual work of the medical examiner.

"Well," Laws began, "not a lot. I can tell you that it is a young adult male. Slender build. Maybe 5'10", 150 pounds."

"How long before you'll have an identification?"

"I should have something for you later today."

"Can't you tell by looking at him?"

"No," Laws said, pulling back the sheet covering the body. A distorted, purplish mass presented itself where the face should have been. "He's unrecognizable."

Punch looked at the purple mass and quickly averted his eyes. "He's that. Any idea how long this guy's been dead?"

"How long has the Miles kid been missing?"

"Ten days, maybe two weeks?"

"That's consistent with what I'm seeing here, I think. This body has been partially preserved due to the low temps and the fact that it was in the snow. Well, except for the upper torso and head, which were in the water when it wasn't frozen. But post-mortem decomposition is obviously well underway."

"Obviously," Punch mimicked. "What happened there?" He pointed to an obvious injury to one of the body's hands.

"Not sure. Could have been done before he died, or it could be animals."

"Any idea on cause of death?"

"I'll get to the X-rays here shortly, but there are obvious injuries to the head," Laws said. "Preliminarily, I'd say he had a broken jaw and suffered a severe head injury." He pointed to the misshapen jaw and area of interest on the back of the skull. "Might have taken one to the eye, as well."

"Got beat up before he died?" Punch asked. He was thinking about an irritated Davonte following Miles out the door.

"I would think so, but again, I'll know more later."

"Can you keep me updated?" Punch asked. "There's a lot of interest in this one."

"I've heard," Laws said, removing a large scalpel from a plastic sleeve and raising it to examine it under better light. "I'll let you know when my report is ready, of course. Sure you don't want to hang around? I can always use an extra pair of hands."

"Positive," Punch said as he left the morgue. "Thanks, Doc."

The canyon walls seemed to reach the azure sky. Aside from the sound of water against rock and the wind in the stand of Engelmann spruce lining the creek, Sam heard only the occasional screech of a hawk. The big birds were circling above, hunting for mice and varmints moving around on the snow. He was fishing for Yellowstone cutthroat, a native species nearly depleted following the introduction of brook trout into this remote watershed. The brook trout had been eradicated a few years back, and when a client of Sam's had let it be known that this water now had sizable cutthroat, he'd vowed to make it before winter fully set in. It was a glorious late fall day, unseasonably warm, and he'd spent several hours catching and releasing decent fish. The walking was easy, which he appreciated. As bizarre as it sounded, his missing left leg had been troubling him of late, and he'd had second thoughts before heading out, but knew in his heart that if he didn't go, he would likely regret it. Except for a major storm a few days prior, it had been a dry fall, so the ground was firm under the couple inches of snow remaining. Working his way upstream, Sam saw only undisturbed white stuff—no signs that anyone else had walked the banks. He was appreciating his good fortune when he saw a large trout finning in the shallows behind a boulder the size of a footlocker. He flipped his fly into the current on the side of the rock, watched it drift into the slack water downstream, and set the hook on the fish when it struck. He was kneeling in the creek, removing the cutthroat from the hook, when the hair on his neck stood on end.

He was being watched.

He dropped his rod with the fish still on the line and drew his pistol from the shoulder holster. Slowly, he crawled to the bank, keeping the weapon dry and scanning the hillside for enemy. Despite the buzzing in his ears he was acutely aware of his own breathing. Seeing nothing, he prepared to make a three-second rush to a boulder in a nearby stand of bare aspen, which would afford him both a better view of the draw he was in and a more defensible position. With a quick look behind him, he rushed uphill to the trees. "I am up, I am moving, he is aiming, I am down," he thought to himself, just as he'd been trained at Fort Benning. At the end of his rush he slid into a slight depression in the earth behind the boulder, rolled, and began scanning for signs of enemy.

He held his breath to slow his breathing and steady his aim if necessary, then focused on a brush pile approximately twenty yards uphill. The Taliban would be in there. He saw movement and prepared for the assault. He flattened himself and with one hand unsnapped the case holding his hunting knife, extracted it, and placed it in the dirt next to him. The buzzing had disappeared, and his hearing was now acute. He took a deep breath and awaited the assault, reminding himself to aim center of mass and wait until the enemy was within ten yards to fire. Seeing movement in the brush, he extended the pistol in front of him with both hands, held his breath, and readied himself for the attack. But instead of Taliban fighters rushing his position he saw only the back end of a mountain lion sprinting up the side of the snow-and-brush-covered hill to his west. Relief flooded through him, and—still shaking—he rolled over on his back in the melting snow, closed his eyes, and laughed until he cried.

Jon Middleton was the Custer Police Department's computer forensic examiner. With the help of the local internet service provider and Miles's mom—who had given him some basic information about the young man—he had been able to figure out Miles's passwords and personal identification numbers, and had reviewed and copied everything on Miles's smartphone and laptop. He was at his desk looking at a computer when Punch entered his office. "Jon, what do we have?" Punch asked.

"Plenty," Middleton said. "The kid was indeed gay, if the porn he'd been accessing is any indication. Here, let me show you—"

"I'll take your word for it," Punch said. "No different than if he was straight and looking at girls, right?"

"Well, yeah."

"What else?"

"I think he was selling weed."

"Really?" Punch asked, feigning ignorance. "Why is that?"

"Look at this," Middleton said, bringing up a text passage

he had copied and saved on his desktop. "He's talking about pizza here, but I don't think that's what he is selling."

Punch read the passage. "Yeah, that'd be some expensive pizza." They shared a laugh before Punch, turning serious, asked, "You get me a list?"

"I did. I even printed it out for your dinosaur self." Middleton indicated a file folder full of papers. "There's a lot of names in his contacts."

"Okay, thanks. I'll look through this stuff. But to cut to the chase here, who was the last person he spoke with?"

"Guy named Davonte Blair. Before that, guy named Ronnie Norquist. About the same time. Middle of the night on the 5th, early morning on the 6th. Not unusual, though."

"Really?"

"Yeah. I'd say the three of them were in contact daily, if not hourly."

Punch nodded at Jensen, who had just walked into Middleton's office. "Well, they knew each other from the basketball team," he observed.

"At least," Middleton said.

"What's that mean?"

"It's all in there," Middleton said, indicating his report. "Unless you want to look at the pictures."

"Do I?" Punch opened the report.

"Probably not."

"Okay," Punch said. He read for a moment. "That it?"

"No. Check this out." Jensen dropped a spreadsheet on Punch's desk. Punch took a look at it, squinted, and looked up at Jensen. "Give me the short version."

"Jon's given us a record of everywhere Miles was on the night he disappeared, as well as all of his texts and everyone he spoke with on his phone," Jensen said. "We've even got a record of the websites he was looking at that night."

"Anything interesting?"

"Everything stopped at around 2:30 a.m. on the 6th," Middleton said.

"That's consistent with what we knew," Punch observed.

"Right, and his phone tracks with Norquist saying Kaiden left Davonte's apartment at between 1:00 and 1:15 a.m. Looks like he went to his dorm, then out to where his body was found."

"What else?" Punch asked.

"This is good. Last text to Miles was from Davonte. Lemme see." Jensen looked through his notes. "Here it is: 'Need to talk. Meet me at your place. Now.'"

Middleton was nodding. "Good stuff, Jon," Punch said.

"Thanks," Middleton said.

"Okay, Jensen, get a warrant for Davonte's phone—now." Punch pointed at the clock. "I want to find out what else is on there, and I don't want to have to wake Downs or Daniels."

Punch and Ronnie were in an examination room at the police station. It was mid-morning and Punch had asked Ronnie to come down to the station to talk. "Ronnie, I asked you to come in and talk to me because we've had some new developments," Punch began, gesturing for Ronnie to sit. "And some of them involve you."

Ronnie remained standing and looked at Punch uncertainly. "Do I need a lawyer? My—my dad is a lawyer."

"I know who he is," Punch assured him. "Why would you need a lawyer?"

"Well, my dad says that you should never talk to the cops if you . . . well, you know."

"Ronnie, I'm just trying to get some information. I'm trying to find out who killed your friend. Sit down." Punch again gestured toward the chair across the desk.

Ronnie sat, shifted uncomfortably, and looked at Punch. "What do you want to know?"

"Well, I'd like to ask you about a couple of things," Punch began. "Things you didn't tell me when we spoke last time."

Ronnie feigned innocence. "Like what?"

He was a terrible liar, Punch thought. "Like the fact that Kaiden was dealing weed."

"I don't know anything about—"

"Ronnie, don't try to bullshit me, okay? I've imaged his phone. I've got it all in writing. No one is paying a hundred and fifty dollars for pizza, okay?"

"I know he sold a little weed on the side, but—"

"You should. You were a pretty regular buyer, right?"

"Maybe I do need a lawyer." Ronnie started to stand.

"Sit down, Ronnie. I couldn't give a crap about you buying weed from Kaiden," Punch said. "I'm interested in who would want to kill him."

"I—I don't have any idea."

"Think, Ronnie. He owe anyone any money?"

"Well, not that I know of. His mom sent him money every month. He always seemed to have enough to get by," Ronnie said. "I mean, we're in college. No one has any money, know what I'm saying?"

"I do," Punch said. "Where did he get his weed?"

"I don't know. He was kind of secretive about that."

"Denver?"

"No, someone brought it up here to him."

"Was it Gustafson?"

"What? Why would you think that?"

Punch looked at Ronnie for a long moment. "Ronnie,

remember when I said that I wasn't really interested in the weed thing right now?"

"Yeah?"

"Yeah, well, that's true. But if I find out that Kaiden dealing weed had anything to do with his death, and if I find out you had information that could've helped me find out who killed him and you withheld it, well, then I could get real interested real fast. Get me?" Punch asked. "So, let me ask again: Did anyone owe Kaiden money?"

"Yeah, lots of people—according to him," Ronnie said.

"You?"

"Well, yeah."

"How much?"

"Maybe one fifty or two hundred. Am I a suspect?"

"Everyone is a suspect." Punch unwrapped a piece of gum and stuck it in his mouth. He offered one to Ronnie, who declined. "Who else?"

"Well, to hear him talk, lots of people."

"Davonte?"

"Well, yeah."

"How much?"

"I don't know, Mr. Polson. I swear. I just know that Kaiden said he was gonna have a talk with Davonte about his bill."

"Did they talk?"

"Well, yeah. They had a little argument the last night. That's . . .that's what kind of broke up the party. Them arguing —I told you all this."

"What was said?"

"Well, Kaiden told Davonte if he didn't get some money, he was gonna tell someone—I don't know who—and Davonte was saying he'd pay Kaiden when he signed with the pros."

"Did they fight?"

Ronnie laughed despite himself. "Kaiden fight Davonte? No way. Kaiden's my size. We can wear each other's clothes."

"So they didn't mix it up?"

"Not that I saw. Why?"

Punch ignored the question. "Who left first?"

"Like I told you last week—Kaiden. That I remember. Then Davonte. Then me and Trent."

"And you never saw Kaiden again?"

"Never. I swear," Ronnie said. He was staring at the desk.

"What was Kaiden wearing that night?" Punch asked.

"I don't know."

"Think."

"Jeans. Tennis shoes. A hooded sweatshirt with Custer College on it, I think. He always wore that."

"Anything else?"

"Like what?"

Punch looked steadily at Ronnie without answering. "Thanks, Ronnie. You can go. I'll be in touch."

After Ronnie had left, Jensen—who had been watching through the one-way glass from an adjoining room—entered. "What do you think, boss?"

"I'm thinking he's not telling me the truth—or at least, all the truth. He's holding something back."

"So, how is the investigation going?" Rebecca asked. She and Punch were in her office. "Was it the gay kid?" She had been re-elected last November despite a subordinate's malfeasance during the Tommy Olsen case. Rebecca had quickly dismissed the woman, who had withheld evidence from Sam before and during the trial. The attorney had gotten her conviction, but Daniels had granted Sam's motion to set aside the verdict and for a new trial when Sam had found out—courtesy of Punch, Rebecca suspected—that the attorney had withheld exculpatory information from him. Nice's office had eventually convicted Olsen's wife of the murder, but the entire situation had given them a black eye.

"It was Kaiden Miles, if that's what you are asking. Doc Laws just confirmed it."

"Suspects?"

"Some people we are looking at," Punch allowed.

"The black guy?"

"Word travels fast."

"I'm the county attorney." She shrugged and looked steadily at Punch. When he didn't speak, she asked the question. "I know you've been talking with Paul Norquist's son, too. Progress?"

"I'm not sure we are getting anywhere," Punch admitted. "I'm not finding anyone willing to admit the guy is violent. I mean, he looks violent—"

"Because he's black?"

"No, because he's six foot nine and acts menacingly. He pulls it off. But he's got no record of violence. I've had my guys calling back to the Detroit area where he is from. They've spoken with teachers, coaches, former girlfriends, people who lived nearby—all with the intent of finding someone who will tell us he is a bad guy. So far, nothing. Similarly, I've had my officers questioning people on campus and in the community. Insofar as I can tell, this guy lives in the dorm, walks over to the student union to eat, hits the gym, and goes back to the dorm, where he gets high with his teammates and the managers and plays video games."

"Oh, come on now," Rebecca said. "No disenchanted girlfriends?"

"Nope."

"No unhappy one-night stands who think he got a little rough?"

"None."

"Punch, I don't have to tell you that with as little evidence as we have, you are gonna need some negative sentiment," Nice said. "We need someone who's had a bad experience with him or will otherwise cast a shadow on his character."

"I know that would be good, but right now I can't find anyone who will say anything other than he is singularly focused on basketball," he said.

"You talking with his support system here?"

"Of course."

"They hanging tight?"

"Oh, yeah. The people that surround him are hand-selected," Punch said. "I'm told this guy is a professional athlete in waiting. The people in his inner circle want to be there when he hits the big-time, so nobody's going to say anything that might derail their car on the gravy train."

"Nice analogy, there."

"I thought so," Punch said. "Takes time to come up with stuff that's figurative yet colorful."

"What else?"

"Lab's looking at everything we could find at the scene—his clothing and stuff. There was a watch cap left behind. Hoping they can scope some DNA off it."

"This is thin."

"It's gonna be thin." Punch nodded. "Crime scene is crap. Unless someone rolls over or we get a witness or some sort of solid forensic hit, it's gonna be purely circumstantial evidence. Gonna be tough to convict—who's going to prosecute?"

"Probably Cathy."

"Good. She's tough, but fair. And honest."

Rebecca looked at Punch for a moment. "I know. I thought Ann . . . well, I just didn't see that coming."

"She was an officer of the court. Who would expect a prosecutor to hide evidence?"

"Keep looking, Punch," Rebecca said. "But we gotta move fast. This town is coming apart at the seams. The county commissioners are in a panic; one or the other of them seems to call every hour."

"I hear you," Punch said. "But I work on evidence, not emotion."

"Then get it—soon. We need an arrest. Now. Before this town blows up."

Downs looked in the mirror in the private restroom in her chambers. She leaned forward to fix her hair, then grabbed a bottle of antacids and swallowed two. She walked back into her chambers, took a drink of water and a deep breath. "Remember," she said aloud as she released the breath. "You are in control."

Moments later she entered the courtroom and the preliminary hearing began. Sam was sitting in the audience with Raylene Smith. He had explained to her that preliminary hearings were generally rather perfunctory. The State, he had told her, was required to put on only enough evidence to convince an ordinary person that a crime was likely committed, and that the defendant probably committed it. Cathy Schmidt was certainly capable of that, and it was a near-certainty that Albert Smith would be bound over at the hearing's conclusion.

"What about bond?" Raylene had asked.

"Raylene, I can't see a new judge modifying bond. She made her decision last week. She's unlikely to change it."

"But I need him home," she had said. He had sighed. Days

earlier she wanted an order of protection; now she wanted him home.

As Sam had expected, Cathy made quick work of meeting the State's burden. Mike Sharp, Albert's attorney, asked few questions. Having heard the evidence, Downs announced her decision. "Mr. Smith," she began, looking first at Albert Smith and then at his wife, who was sitting immediately behind him in the audience. "The purpose of today's preliminary hearing was to determine if there is probable cause to believe that the offense charged was committed, and that you committed it. As you've observed, the State was not required to prove beyond a reasonable doubt that you did this. The court will find that there is probable cause to believe that on or about November 4 in Custer County, Wyoming, the crime of felony domestic battery was committed, and that you did so. Your case will be transferred to district court for all further proceedings. Is there anything else we need to discuss here this morning, counsel?"

"Your Honor," Sharp said, rising. "My client would like to revisit the issue of bond."

"I'm not inclined to modify bond, Mr. Sharp," Downs said. "Just ten days or so ago, I made a decision and provided a rationale for the bond I set. Has something changed?"

"I understand, Judge. But he's been unable to make bond and it is causing a real hardship on his family. Mrs. Smith is here and can add details if you wish."

"I don't need to hear from her," Downs said. She turned her attention to Cathy. "Ms. Schmidt, what is the State's position on modification of bond conditions?"

"No change, Judge. Ask that bond be continued."

"Thank you, counsel. Bond will be continued in the amount of fifty thousand dollars cash," Downs said, and rose to leave the courtroom.

"Sell the trailer, Raylene!" Albert Smith yelled.

"But we won't have anywhere to live!" Raylene said, beginning to sob.

"Get him out of here!" Downs said. "I ordered no contact," she added as the big man was taken away by court security. Downs gave Raylene and Sam a disapproving glance as she left the courtroom. Afterward, Sam sat with Raylene, trying to get her to move out and leave Albert.

"I can't do it, Sam. I just can't," she said. "Now, I brought some money for your fee. Here's fifty dollars. It's all I have—"

"Keep it."

"Sam," Raylene said. "I know. . . I know you don't understand. No one does."

"I'm trying, Raylene. Let's not worry about the money, though. Plenty of time for that later, okay?"

"Okay, Sam." She stood and pulled on her coat. Ten years ago, it was clean and probably fit her. "I'll—I'll see you later, okay?"

Sam was back in the office when Cassie came in. "Good morning, Sam," she said. "Paul wants to see you if you have a minute."

"Okay, I'll be right there," Sam said. He got a coffee from the small kitchen, and a couple of minutes later he wandered into Paul's office.

"Close the door if you would," Paul said, and after Sam had done so, added, "Sit down, Sam. I wanted to talk a little bit."

"What's going on?"

"Would you like the good news or the bad news?"

"Always better to start with the bad news and end on a high note."

"Well, Sam, the bad news is you haven't covered for three months or so." Paul slid a spreadsheet toward Sam. "I know you've had appointments with your counselor and stuff, but we've had to draw on our line of credit twice now, and I'm getting concerned."

Sam looked at the spreadsheet intently, shaking his head. "Damn, Paul, I thought I was doing a little better than that. I've got some stuff coming in here this month. I did a trust a week or so ago. That'll help."

"Okay, Sam. But keep an eye on it. We can't go on like this forever. As much as I wish we were in this for altruistic reasons, we've still got to make a living."

"I promise, Paul. I know I need to hold up my end of things. I appreciate the opportunity. You know that."

"I know you do," Paul said. "Want the good news?"

"Sure," Sam said.

"I know that you don't get the paper, but I thought you'd be interested." Paul handed the local paper to Sam, who took a quick look at the headline on the back page. The story had to do with a survey run by the newspaper asking readers to name their favorite restaurant, store, dentist, and the like. Under "Best Attorney" was Sam's name and picture. He looked at it for a second, and then at Paul.

"Paul, I'm sorry," Sam said.

"What are you sorry about?" Paul asked. He looked tired, Sam thought.

"Paul, you've been named 'Best Attorney' about ten years in a row." Sam looked at the plaques lining Paul's wall. "I come in, and because of the Olsen case—"

"Sam, there's more to it than that. You've represented a lot of veterans and other folks who needed it—and at a discount, I might add," he added with a slight smile.

"And that gets us back to that, huh?" Sam nodded toward the spreadsheet.

"We'll figure it out," Paul said, standing. "And hey, we can always use good press. Let's use it to our advantage. Now, go bill someone's ass off, will you?"

"Got it," Sam said, and started to leave. Then, thinking better of it, he turned to face Paul. "I just want you to know how much I appreciate you giving me this opportunity. I mean . . . It has changed my life."

"We're friends." Paul waved Sam off. "You don't have to thank me."

Moments later, Paul's secretary Monica came into his office with a stack of documents. "Paul, you said you wanted to see the discovery in the Bank of the Bighorns case. Here you go!" she said brightly.

"Just leave 'em, Monica," he said. "I'm going to take the rest of the day off."

Punch found Richter in his on-campus office eating a donut. "Man, have I got a job for you," Punch said.

"That's not gonna happen, Punch. This is a good job." Richter licked some sugar from his fingers. "Aside from the occasional fistfight or someone smoking weed in the dorms, I've got a nice, quiet gig. Check some locks, watch the video."

"So the Miles case has upset your rhythm, huh?"

"You know it. What can I do for you?"

"I'm looking for Davonte Blair."

"He's probably in the gym," Richter said. "He's always in the gym."

"You okay with me heading over to the field house?"

"Oh, yeah," Richter said.

"All right, Jeb, I'll keep you updated."

"Thanks, Punch."

Moments later, Punch entered the field house and could immediately hear the rhythm of a basketball being dribbled, followed by the sound of the ball passing through the net and then landing on the floor: dribble-swish-bounce, dribble-swish-bounce. Punch came from the north side and stood unseen, watching Davonte. Time after time Davonte shot the ball from far beyond the collegiate three-point line, watched it go through the net, picked it up after one bounce, then dribbled back beyond the three-point line and shot it again. After making ten shots in a row, he picked the ball up on one bounce, and instead of dribbling back out to the three-point line, viciously dunked the ball with one hand.

"Mr. Blair," Punch said, walking onto the court. "Detective Polson, Custer PD."

"I remember, cop," Davonte said, dribbling the ball away from Punch.

"I wanted to follow up with a few questions," Punch said.

"Told you all I know," Davonte said, making a shot from the top of the key.

Punch rebounded the ball and bounce-passed it to Davonte. "We've had a development."

"Yeah?" Davonte asked as he shot the ball and jogged toward the baseline.

"Yeah," Punch said. The shot was good, and he rebounded the ball and chest-passed it to Davonte. "We identified the body."

Davonte shot the ball from the baseline—it was long—and jogged slowly to the other side of the court to retrieve it. "What's that got to do with me, man?"

"It's your buddy, Kaiden Miles."

"And I'm thinking you misunderstood me," Davonte said, dribbling the ball. "We didn't have a relationship. He was a manager."

"That's odd," Punch began. "According to what I found on his cell phone, you and Mr. Miles were in contact on an almost daily basis."

Davonte dribbled over to the first row of seats and sat down. "Look, cop, the dude was the team manager. He took care of stuff for me, you know?"

"Like supplying you with weed?"

Davonte drank red liquid from a plastic bottle. "He maybe had a little once in a while," he said.

"Oh, come on, Davonte, I've read the damned texts. Want to look at the ones on your phone to refresh your memory?"

Davonte drank again from the bottle. "Look, I called him lots of times. He got my stuff for me. And we were . . . friends, I guess."

Punch looked at Davonte for a long moment. "You didn't ask me about the body."

"And?"

"Most people would ask questions like, 'Where did you find him?' 'Who found him?' 'What happened?' You didn't ask."

"Man, I seen bodies before. I ain't from some hokey shit town like this." Davonte was on his feet now, dribbling the ball steadily.

"Davonte, I checked," Punch began. "You're not from inner-city Detroit. You're from Berkley, Michigan. If there's anyone in this town born with a silver spoon in his pie hole, it's you. So don't play the street bro with me, okay? You can play that game with the kids in the dorm, but I'm not buying it."

"You don't know what it's like to be black, man!"

"I don't. I don't know what it's like to be black, and I don't know what it's like to be from some rich suburb of Detroit, either," Punch said. "There's a lot of things I don't know, including and especially why the last guy to see Miles has absolutely no interest in what happened to him—unless he already knows, of course."

Davonte stopped dribbling the ball. "Can I be straight with you?"

"It would be in your best interest," Punch assured him.

"I owed him some money, 'cause he fronted me some shit. He was callin' me on it and I didn't have the money. So, him disappearin', well, let's just say that didn't bust my balls, okay?"

Punch looked at Davonte for a long moment, assessing him. "In some of those texts, you called him a fag."

"That's just talk, man."

Punch thought he saw movement at the south entrance. He moved slightly so he could appear to be looking at Davonte while he scanned the facility. He saw what he was looking for. "Mr. Norquist, will you join us?"

While Ronnie made his way slowly across the gym floor, Punch turned his attention back to Davonte. "Yeah, well, look at it from my perspective, okay? I got a dead guy in the creek here on campus. His acquaintance—you, who just happens to owe him a couple thousand bucks for weed—is calling him a fag and telling him to 'get screwed' over the money. You were telling him you will pay him when you sign a contract with the NBA. That's what you told him, right?"

Davonte didn't answer, but nodded, still bouncing the ball on occasion. Ronnie walked up and the two young men exchanged a look. Punch saw it and continued. "Miles was telling you he had guys to answer to, and that if he didn't pay, they were going to come down on him, right?"

"Well, yeah."

"Yeah. And you were the last one to see him before he disappeared, right?"

"Wrong," Davonte said. "Whoever killed him was, cop."

Punch watched both Davonte and Ronnie. "I didn't say anything about him being killed."

"What?" Davonte asked.

"What makes you think he was killed?"

"I don't know, man!" Davonte shook his head.

Punch turned from Davonte to Ronnie. "Ronnie, I'm glad to see you here. I need to ask you and Davonte here for a little favor."

"What's that?" Ronnie asked. Davonte merely looked at him.

"Well, it sounds like we might be able to collect some DNA off of a watch cap that was found near Kaiden's body. You know anything about that?"

"No," Davonte said.

"So, we shouldn't find your DNA on that hat, should we?"

"No reason to."

"You never touched it?"

"Nope."

"That'll make it easy, then. We took dozens of other swabs, as well. Now, police work can be quite complicated, but I like to keep things simple. Rather than an investigative genius like you see on television, I work backwards. I rule everyone out, and whoever is left is my suspect."

"So he *was* killed," Davonte said. "Why are you screwing with my head, man?"

Punch ignored the question. "The quickest way to rule you guys out will be to see that your DNA was not at the scene. I just happened to have brought a little kit that will enable me to take your DNA so I can get it to the lab and rule you out," Punch said. "Davonte? What do you say?"

"Sure, man." Davonte shrugged. "Ain't got nothing to hide."

"Great. Ronnie, what say you? Want to give me a little sample so I can rule you out?"

"I don't know . . . Maybe I should call my dad." Ronnie hesitated.

"Maybe you should." Punch nodded. "Tell him to meet us down at the station, would you?"

"What? Why?"

"Well, if I've got to go to the trouble of talking with a lawyer, I might as well have you in the station so I can get everything recorded. If we're gonna get the lawyers involved, I gotta do things right, you know?"

While Davonte opened his mouth and Punch obtained a swab, Ronnie watched closely, obviously thinking. "Okay. Thanks, Davonte," Punch said. "Ronnie, you ready to head downtown?"

"Just do it," Ronnie said.

"Why, thank you. I'm sure your father would be proud. By the way, any reason for your DNA to be on that hat?" Punch extracted the swab from the kit. "Say, 'ah.'"

"I don't think so," Ronnie said. "I mean, I don't know why it would be."

"Good," Punch said. After he had taken Ronnie's sample and put it into its protective pouch, he put both pouches in a little bag and wrote his name across a piece of tape that covered the opening. "By the way, Davonte, where are you playing this weekend?"

"Colorado, I think. Thanksgiving tourney down there."

"Well, same rules. You can go to Colorado for hoops, but

other than that, stay around here, okay?" Punch instructed. "And same for you, Ronnie," he added.

The Custer County Civic Center had proven to be a wise investment. The buildings were multi-purpose and hosted everything from state basketball tournaments to concerts. Tonight's event was a charity Thanksgiving gala, and as Sam opened the door for Veronica, he heard the buzz of the crowd and felt his stomach tighten.

"Should we have a plan in case something goes wrong?" Veronica asked.

"No. Everything will be fine," Sam said.

"Well, I'm so happy you agreed to come," she said. "Let's just relax and have fun. We won't stay long, I promise."

"I hear you."

"Come on, I want you to meet some people. Maybe you can find someone to go fishing with."

"I like to fish alone," he said, helping her take off her coat.

"You like to do everything alone," she countered, and then waved at some people across the big room. "Will you get me a drink? I see someone I need to talk to."

"Of course," he said. He headed to the bar and was waiting for the bartender to pour Veronica's Moscato when a couple of drunks lined up behind him, talking loudly and profanely. One had on a leather vest adorned with what looked to be motorcycle club colors; the other wore a button-down shirt, jeans, and boots. They were already loaded, and already loud. Sam felt himself getting irritated and took a deep breath. He was self-conscious in his suit and sensed a trickle of sweat under his arms. When he finally got his drinks and turned away from the portable bar, the biker said to Sam, "Only guys in this town wearing suits are undertakers, lawyers, or dead!"

Sam simply looked at the man, who was looking at his buddy and laughing. "Excuse me," Sam said, and attempted to move past the two men. The cowboy stepped in front of Sam, blocking his path to Veronica. Sam felt his heart rate begin to quicken. He looked the cowboy in the eye and said levelly, "Excuse me."

"Yeah, we heard you the first time, buddy."

"And I'm not going to say it again," Sam replied, looking from one to the other. He stepped forward, expecting trouble, but to his relief, both men stepped aside.

"We'll talk with you later, buddy," the biker said.

"Look forward to it," Sam replied.

After dinner had been served and the silent auction had been declared over, the tables were cleared and the band began playing. Veronica looked at Sam. "Are you going to ask me to dance?"

"I don't dance. I didn't dance when I had two legs. I'm not going to try it now."

"Oh, God," she said, and put her hand over her mouth. "The wine. I'm sorry."

"No problem."

"Would you mind if I dance with someone else?"

"Go for it," Sam said. "I need to use the little boys' room." Moments later, he re-entered the ballroom and saw Veronica two-stepping with the cowboy. He'd always wanted to learn but had never taken the time, and then he'd gotten blown up. Seeing her with the cowboy made Sam unaccountably irritable, and he got in the bar line for another cola. When his turn came, he ordered a double whiskey. Downing it without leaving the line, he ordered another.

The bartender raised her eyebrows. "You driving?"

"Nope," Sam said. "I've got a ride."

"Too bad," she replied, pushing the plastic glass across the small bar to him. "Something changes, let me know."

Sam smiled at her and drank the contents of the glass. "One more time."

Returning to his table with his drink, he sat down and felt the warmth from the whiskey emanating from his throat and stomach down through his leg to his foot. For the first time in weeks he felt like he could breathe. The band was covering an old Keith Whitley ballad and it sounded good. He was comfortably numb and sipping the amber liquid from the third double when Veronica returned to the table, accompanied by the cowboy and the biker.

"Sam, I'd like you to meet Rocky and Levi. I went to school with them," she said. "Rocky and Levi, this is Sam, my . . . friend."

Sam stood and shook hands with each. "We've met, sort of." He sat back down and took a long pull from his drink.

"Sam, are you drinking?" Veronica asked. "You told me you wouldn't."

"Things changed," Sam said.

"Oh, Sam, I wish you wouldn't!"

"And I wish you'd leave me alone," he said.

"Hey, now, that ain't no way to talk to her," the cowboy said, stepping forward and looming over Sam.

"I need you to step back," Sam said. "You're making me uncomfortable."

"Am I? Well, what are you going to do about it? I mean, Veronica here tells me you're a real live American hero. That true, boy?"

"Seriously, I just need you to get out of my space. Please," Sam said quietly. The blood was rushing in his ears and he could hear his heart pounding. His vision had narrowed like he was looking through a rangefinder. He felt his skin tightening and the hair on the back of his neck standing on end.

"Veronica, I need to leave now," Sam said, attempting to stand.

"Sam—" she began.

"Where you goin'?" the cowboy asked. He pushed Sam back down in his chair and moved toward him. The limited vision Sam had earlier was gone. When he opened his eyes, the cowboy was on his back with his eyes wide open. He wasn't moving. Veronica and the biker were staring at Sam, eyes wide with fear. People throughout the hall had gone quiet. Some were slowly coming to surround Sam, Veronica, the biker, and the cowboy to see what had happened. Sam was seeing stars, and he felt faint.

"I'm a cop. What happened?" It was Goodrich. Sam recognized him but couldn't think of his name.

"Levi pushed Sam," Veronica said. "And Sam, well, he—he beat him up."

Goodrich looked at Rocky. "That what happened?"

"Yeah, I guess," the biker said. "It happened kinda fast. Look, Officer, Levi was just funnin' around. This guy's freakin' crazy! He's dangerous!"

"Is that what happened, Mr. Johnstone?" Goodrich turned to Sam.

"I think so," Sam answered. "I, uh, I didn't mean it," he added, rubbing his right hand with his left. "He was pushing me and I got . . . scared, I guess."

"Anyone call 911?" Goodrich asked, looking around. Seeing several heads nod, he put a hand on Sam's shoulder and said, "Let's you and me go for a walk, okay?"

Sam and Goodrich spent a few minutes in the civic center office, the officer getting Sam's version of events. Satisfied, Goodrich stood. "Well, it sounds like you had a right to defend yourself given you were afraid and all. But I gotta tell you, knocking Levi out like that, well, that's not gonna make any fans."

"I understand," Sam said. "Look, I need to get out there and grab Veronica and get her home."

"You okay to drive?"

"Oh yeah. That was a buzzkill."

A smile creased Goodrich's face. "I've been there," he said. "But seriously, Sam—can I call you Sam?"

"Yeah."

"You've got to get some help."

Back in the ballroom, Sam looked for Veronica. Her purse and coat were no longer at the table. "You looking for Veronica?" It was the bartender who'd served him earlier. She was bussing tables now.

"Yes."

"She left with Rocky while you were with the deputy." Picking up the dish-covered plastic tray, she asked him, "You sure you don't need a ride?"

"Sam, I've been thinking," Paul said. It had been two days since they last discussed the firm's finances. They were in his office with the door closed. "About the bottom line, I mean."

"Yeah?" Sam rubbed the sore knuckles of his right hand with his left.

"Yeah. Look, you know John Francis?"

"I think we've met. He's an older guy, right?"

"Yeah, I think he might be seventy or so. Anyway, he is getting ready to retire and he called me and was asking if we'd take over some of his clients. I assured him we would. He does a lot of real estate, estate planning, things like that. And the school district keeps him on retainer," Paul said. "Around here, most school districts aren't busy enough to employ counsel, so they keep an attorney on retainer. In Custer County, John's the guy. He's been the guy for twenty-five years. Knows that stuff inside out."

"And?"

"Well, Sam, I told him you might be interested in taking on that contract."

"Paul, I don't know anything about school law," Sam said. "That's getting pretty complicated, isn't it?"

"Oh, hell yeah. Between Americans with Disabilities Act, mainstreaming kids with no business being in a regular class, food allergies, bullying, and guns in school, not to mention contracts and normal human resources challenges and all that stuff, it's a bitch."

"Stuff I know nothing about," Sam said, sipping from a cup of coffee. He winced, thinking Levi might have gotten a shot in.

"Sam, you could learn. They'll send you to school. Three weeks, on their dime."

"Damn, Paul, I don't know." Sam spread his hands. It hurt to do that.

"Sam, this account would almost cover expenses by itself every month."

"Yeah, but what about medical expenses?"

"Whattaya mean?"

"I might stick a pencil in my eye. I'd hate it." Sam put the cup down on Paul's desk.

"Damn it, Sam, you're not paying your fair share of expenses! I come to you with a solution and you're dismissing it out of hand. That's bullshit!" Paul pounded the desk with his hand.

"Whoa! Wait a minute, Paul," Sam said. "I really don't want to do this. You can understand that, right?"

"I can, yeah. But you need to understand that you've got to cover. I appreciate you helping vets and doing some criminal stuff. I've allowed it, but that's not paying the rent."

"I'm your partner now, Paul."

"I understand that, but we still get a little say in the other guy's practice, right?"

"Right," Sam said, standing.

"Look, Sam. This is an opportunity to represent a great client, make some money, and do good things for kids in the community. Just tell me you'll look at it, okay?"

"I'll call John this afternoon," Sam said, grabbing his cup and walking toward the door. "Open or closed?"

"Thanks, Sam," Paul said. "Leave it open, if you would."

10

"Thanks for coming down," Punch said to Davonte. They were in an interview room at the detention center. Punch had gotten ahold of Davonte and asked him to come in, but he hadn't really expected him to do so. "Can I get you something? Bottle of water? Coffee?"

"Water be good." Davonte settled his huge frame in the little plastic chair as best he could. Punch was reminded of himself at a parent-teacher conference. He handed the bottle to Davonte and watched his huge hand engulf the thing. "So, I've got another request," he said.

"Yeah?"

"Yeah." Punch sipped from a coffee cup, then set it down and leaned forward to look directly at Davonte. "I'd like to collect your fingerprints. Still just collecting information. Working to rule you out as a suspect."

"Am I under arrest?"

"No. And you're free to leave anytime. Just get up and walk out." Davonte moved as if he was going to stand. "Of course, if you did that, I'd wonder why you didn't want to cooperate."

"Because I got rights, man," Davonte said. He was thinking

about his criminal justice class. "Shouldn't I have an attorney?"

"Well, you're not under arrest, so technically you don't have the right to one," Punch said, adding for effect, "yet."

"I don't know." Davonte looked at Punch steadily. "So, if I'm not under arrest, I can leave?"

"Right. But if you're innocent, your prints will help clear you."

"Wonder how many brothers behind bars been told that?"

"None I put there—how about that?" Punch said, sipping his coffee. "So, aren't you interested?"

"In what?"

"Who did this," Punch said. "You're not one of those jerks who treats the manager like crap, are you?"

"Naw, it's not like that. It's just . . . I'm not wanting to get involved, man."

Punch stared at Davonte until the younger man looked away. "What do you say, Davonte? Want to clear this up?"

Davonte rolled the water bottle around in his huge hand, clearly conflicted. At last, he nodded. "Let's do it, cop."

Punch looked at the one-way mirror on the wall and nodded. "You got your boys behind the wall in case the brother goes wild?" Davonte asked.

"Naw," Punch said. "They're behind the glass in case *I* do. Now, let's go down to booking and get these prints and get you out of here. I do appreciate your cooperation in this."

After Davonte had left, Jensen wandered into Punch's office. "What do you think, boss?"

"I don't know. He's obviously got the size and strength. I guess I don't know why he would bother. Hopefully, the DNA and prints will clear him."

"How? We don't have DNA or prints on anything yet."

"Yet."

Penrose was near giddy with excitement as she hung up the phone. Her source had told her that Detective Polson was interviewing Davonte Blair in connection with the murder of Kaiden Miles. She now had a gay college student killed—perhaps by an African-American college athlete! This was pure gold.

She dialed Punch's direct line.

"Polson."

"Detective Polson, this is Sarah Penrose with the *Bugle*."

"How'd you get my direct line?"

She ignored the question. "I'm calling because my sources tell me you just interrogated Davonte Blair in connection with the death of Kaiden Miles."

"Your sources are wrong."

"How so?"

"Well, for one thing, I was merely gathering information from a student I have reason to believe was acquainted with the deceased," he said.

"So, you're denying you interrogated Davonte Blair?"

"I am. He was free to leave the entire time. Showed up voluntarily and left when he had nothing more to offer. Ms. Penrose, he's a private citizen and a college student—why not leave him alone?"

Again, she ignored the question. "Did he have an attorney with him?"

"He did not."

"Is he a suspect?"

"In what?"

"In the murder of Kaiden Miles."

"Murder?"

"Stop it."

"Everyone is a suspect until I rule them out. I can say that at this time we are pursuing multiple lines of inquiry."

"Will you keep me apprised of the situation?"

"We'll cut a press release as soon as—and if—something changes."

"Thank you, Detective," she said.

"Thank you," Punch said, and hung up. He was about to walk to the break room for a donut when Corporal Jensen stuck his head in the door. "Boss?"

"Yeah?"

"We got an ID on some of that DNA."

"A match?"

"Yeah."

Punch's direct line rang. Caller ID indicated it was Sarah Penrose. He picked up. "That was fast," he said. "Amazing, really."

———

Sam was looking at a warranty deed when he heard what sounded like a ruckus outside his office door. Stepping to his window, he moved the shade so he could see clearly. Perhaps fifty mostly young people walked by, many of them carrying homemade signs and placards with messages depicting support for Kaiden Miles ("Kaiden We Won't Forget!"), denouncing the investigation into his death ("Custer Cops Don't Care About Gays!"), or attempting to drum up support for the cause ("Justice 4 Kaiden!"). He was thinking about demonstrations he'd observed in various far-flung foreign locales when Paul put his hand on his shoulder. "I'm sorry, Sam," Paul said when Sam jumped at his touch. "What do you think?"

"Everybody has a right to assemble," Sam said. "Some

places don't have that. I think I'd pick a warmer day, though," he added, observing the heavy coats and scarves covering the marchers.

"Yeah. This is where I don't want to be Buck Lucas," Paul said. "It's not enough you've got a dead college kid. Now you've got rabble-rousers bringing an angle to it. We don't need that."

"What do you mean?"

"Well, in this town everyone gets along. I don't think anyone really cares who or what you sleep with. Haven't had any issues with gay marriage. Our judges do 'em and no one bats an eye."

"Well, there's a history in Wyoming—you'll grant that."

"Okay, we're not San Francisco or Minneapolis—but how long we gonna have to live with that?"

"Well, just a few years ago you had a judge refusing to perform gay weddings. And that kid got killed down in Laramie—what? Twenty years ago? So it really hasn't been that long."

"But no one here had anything to do with any of that!" Paul said.

"I know that. But, Paul, there are papers to sell and websites to get clicks on."

"And you can say whatever you want about rural white people if you live on either coast."

"I won't argue with that," Sam allowed. "I had folks in D.C. ask me if I rode a horse to school as a kid."

"They think we're all just a bunch of redneck mouth-breathers."

"That either."

"It ain't fair, Sam," Paul exclaimed. "It's tearing this country apart!"

"Well, it isn't doing us any favors."

"Chief Lucas, this is President Beretta."

"Hey, Vince, what's going on?" Lucas asked. He was tired and cranky and worried about having a murdered college kid in a creek. "How can we help you?"

"My sources are telling me your investigator has been interviewing a number of my students."

"He better be."

"What do you mean?"

"I mean I've got a dead college student. Looks like he was killed on campus. At least, that's where his body was found. So, the procedure would be to start by looking at people close to the victim, and then expanding from there—*close to the victim* in this case meaning dorm rats and others on campus."

"What evidence does he have against Davonte?"

"You know I'm not going to answer that."

"Well, can you assure me that your detective is not on some sort of wild goose chase?" Beretta asked.

"I can tell you that Detective Polson is the best we've got. What's the issue? Seems like a couple of weeks ago you were urging me to hurry up and close this deal," Lucas said. "Seems like you'd want me to solve this as soon as possible."

"Well, I do, of course. But I just don't know why you aren't looking at some of the homeless downtown, checking the bars and places where methamphetamine is sold. You know, those kinds of people."

"Well, unfortunately, the kind of people who murder college men are usually, normally, generally, and almost always other college men."

"I understand, Chief," Beretta said. "I don't like it, but I understand it. Can you keep this quiet?"

"Can you give my men a place on campus to do interviews?"

"Maybe. I'd have to clear it with my board of directors, of course."

"Of course," Lucas said, smiling to himself.

"Sam, Paul, good to see you both," Daniels said, extending his hand. They were at the county bar association's fall gala. Most of the town's attorneys had shown up with dates, and the booze and talk were flowing freely. Sam was reminded of formal army officer functions from days gone by. "The people's choice for 'Best Attorney' ten years running now," Daniels continued, looking at Paul and then Sam. "And the new title holder. That's what we call a power firm."

"Thank you, Judge." Paul took the judge's hand. "Very proud of my partner here. And I won't lie. I kind of liked having that trophy in my office, but if it's got to go, then at least we kept it in house. But I won where it really counts," he said, looking at Jeannie and then at Sam.

Daniels had no idea what he meant, and turned to Sam, who was smiling tightly. "Sam, well done," Daniels said, extending a hand. "No surprise from this end."

"You were kind of hard on me during the Olsen trial. I was wondering what was going on." Sam was extremely anxious and didn't want to be there, but had agreed to make a twenty-minute appearance at Paul's insistence.

"You did fine. Probably woulda got an acquittal if Ann had disclosed evidence like she was required to, or if you hadn't had your man testify," Daniels said. "Oh well, who's up for a drink?"

"I'm in," Paul said.

"Sam?" Daniels asked.

"Don't think so, Judge. Not at the top of my game."

"Okay, your loss. I'm buying."

Daniels headed for the bar with Paul and Jeannie in tow. Sam wandered the room, mingling as best he could. He desperately wanted a drink, and he was thinking about following the judge when he heard his name.

"Sam Johnstone, is it?" The question came from a small man with dark, curly hair. He was accompanied by a slim, dark-haired woman of about thirty-five. She was at least three inches taller than the man, and stunning.

"It is." Sam extended a hand. "I'm sorry, have we met?"

"I'm President Vincent Beretta from Custer College. This is my wife, Lucy. We're guests of our in-house counsel, Marilyn Easterling-Grabarkowitz. Do you know her?"

"No. I'm sure I would have remembered. Pleased to meet you." Sam released Vincent's hand and took Lucy's. Hers was warm and soft. She had beautiful eyes, almost black.

"You're an attorney," she said, holding his hand tightly.

"Guilty as charged."

"And a hero, I hear," she added. She kept ahold of his hand.

"Not in my eyes."

"How do you do it?" She let her fingers caress his palm as he extracted his hand.

"Do what, exactly?" He looked to Beretta, who was flushed.

"Defend guilty people."

"Well, I try not to do that," Sam said. "I try and defend only the good guys." He smiled.

She smiled back at him over the rim of her wine glass. "How do you know who is good and who is not?"

"I give a pretty fair third degree."

"Do you now?"

"Lucy, I think we'd best move along," Beretta said, trying to break up the exchange. "I see Marilyn has cornered the mayor and her husband across the room. I want to introduce you."

"Would you defend the boy's killer?" Lucy asked Sam, freeing herself from her husband's grasp. "My husband wants to see that gay boy's killer brought to justice as soon as possible."

"Well, that's the job, right?"

"It's the job, but it's not going to happen again, is it Sam?" It was Paul, who was back from the bar with Jeannie. "Sam's interested in expanding his practice, Mrs. Beretta. He's looking to cash in on his newfound fame, right, Sam?"

Sam nodded slowly. "Well, yeah. But I'm always looking for an interesting situation."

"But only if it covers the overhead, right?" Paul laughed tightly, then turned to Lucy. "Perhaps the college might find Sam of use?"

"Oh, I'm certain we could find a position for him." Lucy let her eyes wander over Sam from head to toe. "I'd hate to see you defend that boy's killer, though. That would be . . . against my interests. I must go. Vincent is beckoning," she said, and was gone.

"I think that woman has a position in mind for you, all right, but I don't think it has anything to do with the practice of law." Jeannie had moved beside him and was whispering in his ear while Paul watched from several feet away.

"Really?" Sam said. "I thought she was . . . nice."

"Sam Johnstone, I'm telling you right now," she said. "Stay away from her, or she'll peel you like a banana and eat you."

"Who's eating what?" Daniels asked. He had a fresh drink —a double, if Sam was right—and an unlit cigar in his mouth. Seeing no response, he asked, "Who's up for some fresh air?"

"Me," Sam said. "Getting a little warm in here, anyway." He followed Daniels out the back door to the large deck.

Punch was again in conference with Rebecca Nice. She had skipped the preliminaries and was down to the business at hand. "What do you have?" she asked.

"Not enough," Punch admitted. "Davonte was the last guy to see the victim alive, I think. He had some cuts and bruising on his fists—he'd definitely been in a scrap recently. He was into Miles for almost two grand in drugs."

"Two grand! Where the hell does a college kid get that kind of money?" Nice asked.

"From what I can tell, his mom's got money. And I think Miles figured he'd get paid by Davonte or his agent. If he didn't, he could always threaten to go public."

"Maybe he already did?"

"I'm looking into that."

"Good. What else?"

"Not a lot. The cause of death was blunt force trauma on the back of his head. We haven't found the weapon yet. Davonte's a lot of things, but I don't see the guy popping someone from behind. He's more an in-your-face kind of guy."

"We need to solve this one, Punch," she said, standing and walking to her window. "I don't need to tell you that with these idiots marching around calling us all homophobes, the city council and county commissioners are getting nervous. And now that you interviewed that black kid . . . well, supposedly national media is inbound as we speak. I've got a request for an interview in my inbox already."

"Great," Punch groused. "Look, I'm going to tell you up front I don't expect we're ever going to get a lot on anyone on this one. The scene is screwed. We think he died near there, but that snowstorm, then him lying in the water, the animals . . . well, altogether, it served to screw up the crime scene and to pretty much eliminate any sort of forensic stuff."

"Really?"

"Yeah. I've got my guys looking at everything, of course, but I don't have a good feeling," Punch said. "I keep going back to having no weapon. And we've looked at what little video there is from every security camera and closed-circuit feed not only on campus but elsewhere, and we haven't gotten squat from an evidentiary standpoint, other than Blair following Miles. That's it."

"Damn," she said. "I don't like the sound of that at all."

"Well, it's worse, really. I mean, Davonte had a reason to kill him, but don't forget the victim was a CI. If word had gotten out about that, we'd be up to our asses in suspects."

She opened her desk drawer, then a small bottle of antacids, and swallowed two. "Did it?"

"Not as far as I can tell. No indication that anyone knew."

"So, assuming that's the case, Blair remains our best suspect?"

"Well, him and whoever was supplying Miles, because we know Miles had been shorted two thousand dollars by Davonte, and I don't think Miles was independently wealthy, so he definitely owed someone."

"Any ideas?" she asked.

"A guy named Trent Gustafson. But I think he's got a pretty solid alibi."

"What is that?"

"Spent the night with Paul Norquist's kid."

She raised her eyebrows. "Really?" she asked. "Well, whatever." She nodded in the direction of the protesters marching outside the justice center. "Punch, can you hear those idiots outside?" When Punch nodded, she continued. "Find me a suspect, or the shit is going to hit the fan."

"I know. I'm waiting for a final opinion from the tech guys who are looking at the phones I had subpoenaed. I'm hoping that will shed some light on the situation and maybe tell us a little more about what Miles was doing, and where, and maybe with whom, around the time he bought it."

"Good."

"And I've got a call in to the lab. There was a watch cap on the scene we think belonged to Miles. I had it checked for DNA. I've had Davonte and some others swabbed. If that comes back a match, we might have something."

"What's he say?"

"Says no reason for his DNA to be on the cap."

"So if his DNA is on that cap—"

"Well," Punch said. "He'll have some explaining to do."

"If that happens, arrest his ass," she said. "Right, wrong, or indifferent, we gotta get this done."

Sam was in the courthouse to pick up distribution and to meet with Cathy on a case involving one of his clients. He'd been retained by the woman's sister after his client had been busted for breaking into people's homes and stealing their cats, taking them home and adding to her growing menagerie. According to the affidavit of probable cause, when the cops had raided her apartment, they'd discovered more than sixty felines in the filthy home. Due in large part to the obvious mental illness involved, Cathy had made him a reasonable offer, and he was in a pretty good mood as he walked by Downs's office—so much so that when he saw Veronica at her desk, he decided to stop in.

"Hi," he said, standing just inside the door. His heart was pounding.

"Hi," she said. She was working on a file of some sort.

"I wanted to apologize," he said. "I got scared and—"

"You got drunk and beat up Levi," she snapped. "You almost killed him!"

"Veronica, he was pushing me!" he said. "I asked him to stop. Before you saw us, he'd been bullying me in the line. I was defending myself."

She didn't look up from the file. "You were drinking, which you promised you wouldn't do. And then you beat up one of my friends. Sam, I am so embarrassed I can't even go anywhere."

"Why? You didn't do anything."

"I brought you. That's what I did."

Sam stared hard at her for a long moment. "Well, you won't make that mistake twice, now will you?" He turned and left the office.

Seconds later Downs exited her office. She looked at Veronica and asked, "Are you okay?"

"I'm fine, Judge."

"Was that Sam Johnstone I heard out here?"

"Yes," Veronica said, and sniffed.

"What did he want?"

"He was just stopping in to see a file."

"Okay, well, if he had any sense, he'd be stopping in to see you," Downs said. "You two seem pretty compatible to me."

Punch was at his desk eating a sandwich when Jensen knocked on the door. "Boss, I got the state crime lab on line two."

"Yeah?"

"Yeah. They got something."

"I'm listening," Punch said, taking another bite of his BLT.

"They matched Blair's DNA to some of that on the hat."

Punch finished swallowing and took a gulp of coffee. "Send 'em through," he said. When the phone rang, he answered it eagerly. "Polson."

"This is Amanda Desmond. I'm a forensic scientist with the Wyoming state crime lab."

"Outstanding," Punch replied, wiping crumbs from the top of his desk and setting a yellow legal pad in front of himself. "What can you tell me?"

"I'm the technician assigned to look for DNA on that hat your guys sent down."

"So, what can you tell me?" he asked. He was hoping for something definitive.

"I can tell you that the hat has DNA consistent with at least two of the samples you sent me."

"Whose?"

"The victim," she began. "No doubts there. The other one I can be fairly certain about is from a . . . Davonte Blair."

Punch felt his heart skip a beat. "You sure?"

"Of course. I did the tests myself."

"I didn't mean to offend you," Punch said. "This is important."

"All my tests are important," she snapped.

He took a deep breath. "Uh, yeah. So, anything else I should know?"

"The DNA on the cap came from a mixture. So, there is a little more statistical uncertainty than might otherwise be the case. I have to remind you that, given the few cells I had to analyze, I cannot say that the DNA was not a secondary transfer."

"Meaning?"

"Meaning that Blair, for example, might never have touched the hat. He might have touched something that someone else touched, and then that person touched the hat."

"Christ," Punch said sourly. "What else?"

"Well," she said. "There might be a third person's DNA in the mixture."

"Well, isn't that special," Punch groused. "Can you narrow it down a little?"

"Not yet."

"Why not?"

"Because again, the samples were so small, and they were mixed together like a, well, kind of like a soup," she explained.

"Soup?"

"Yes. That's a good analogy. Please understand that we've got the DNA of at least two males, and I feel pretty certain about the samples I've identified, but I'm unsure whether there is additional DNA I'm looking at."

"Are you still working on it?"

"Of course. I'm going to attempt to use a probabilistic genotyping software program to try and sort the multiple DNA samples present," she said.

"Probabilistic—"

"PSG for short," she said. "It's a software program that can look at the different profiles mixed in the sample. It employs sophisticated biological and statistical models to determine the probability that the sample contains information from a known donor."

"Yeesh," Punch said, then brightened. "So, you could find more of Blair's DNA in this mixture?"

"Oh yes. Or someone else's."

"Okay," Punch said, doodling on the legal pad. "But you can tell me without a doubt that Miles's DNA is on that cap?"

"I can. It is statistically near certain."

"And Davonte Blair's DNA is on that hat—right?" Punch asked.

"To a degree of scientific certainty, yes."

"But the DNA for the third person—you can't be sure?"

"Correct," she said.

"Do you have any ideas?" Punch asked.

"I do," she said.

"Who?"

"Well, I think it might—might—be the case that the remaining DNA in the mixture matches that of one Ronald Norquist. You took his sample, didn't you?"

"I did," Punch said. "You'll keep me updated?"

"Of course," she said. "You'll get a copy of my report. But any level of proof less than scientific certainty will receive only an oblique mention. I have to include all my findings for completeness, but if there is no scientific certainty it is only an educated guess, so his name will not appear. So, read the report and you'll know."

Jensen was on the phone with Middleton. He'd been calling him every morning for three days. "We're dying here," he had said. This morning Middleton had called.

"I finally got the data downloaded."

"Can you get it to me?" Jensen asked.

"Of course."

"Do this. Put it on a thumb drive and bag it like anything else. Then get over here and run it by me, and then we'll sit down with Punch later and tell him what it all means?"

"I gotta clear it with my boss," Middleton said.

"Okay," Jensen said. "If you run into a problem, let me know, and I'll have Punch call."

"Call who?" Punch asked. He'd walked up behind Jensen unseen. When Jensen hung up, Punch continued. "You gonna get me something on Davonte's phone, or what? We probably cracked the Enigma code faster than we can get into a college guy's cell phone, for Christ's sake."

"What?" Jensen looked blankly at Punch.

"Never mind," Punch said. "Where are we?"

"Middleton should be over this afternoon to show us what he's got."

"Good. Tell him I need it in English," Punch said. "I talk with those computer geeks and I'm sure the expression on my face is like a cow looking at a new gate."

"Right, boss."

Several hours later, Punch, Jensen, and Middleton were sitting at the meeting table in Punch's office. Middleton had brought along a laptop and was sitting between Punch and Jensen, pointing at the screen. "This"—he indicated a small, blue, teardrop-shaped icon on the screen —"is the approximate location of Davonte's phone the early morning hours of the 6th of November." The teardrop was superimposed over a map of Custer. "See, he is—"

"His phone is," Punch said.

"Yeah, right. Correction, his phone is moving from here to here," Middleton indicated. "Then, at approximately 2:45 a.m., the phone stops near here."

"How near?"

"Hard to say."

"How hard?" Punch pressed. "What's the accuracy?"

"Depends." He shrugged. "Depending on the location of towers, Wi-Fi arrangement and availability, time of day—it can range from three meters or so to maybe a hundred meters."

"Crap." Punch popped an antacid. "So, take me to the location closest to here," he said, pointing to the spot on the map where Miles's body was found. He watched as Middleton complied. "So, at 2:45 a.m., Davonte was there?"

"Well—"

"Let me rephrase: at 2:45 a.m., Davonte's phone was within one hundred meters of that dot?"

"Yes," he said. "And probably closer."

"Okay. Let's talk phone calls and texts. Whatcha got?"

"Well, I can tell you that the last text sent to Miles came from Blair's phone and was sent at approximately 1:25 a.m.," Middleton said.

"Jensen, does that square with what Miles's phone showed?" Punch asked.

"Yes, sir."

"Okay, Jon, what else?"

"It's really sort of a volume thing," Middleton said. "Literally hundreds—maybe thousands—of texts between the deceased and Mr. Blair."

"Subject?"

"Well, drugs primarily. Talking about other people. Teammates of Blair's, I think. Toward the end, the messages got kind of contentious," Middleton said. "Apparently, Mr. Blair owed Mr. Miles quite a bit of money. Miles wanted his money; Blair didn't have it but promised it when he went pro—he was an athlete, I take it?"

"Basketball." Jensen shook his head. "This is all the same stuff we had on Miles's phone, boss."

"I know." Punch was tapping his fingers on the desk and thinking about calling Rebecca when Middleton continued.

"There's another thing."

"Yeah?"

"I think the guy was gay."

"He was," Punch said to Middleton, who looked surprised. "We've spoken with his mother and most of his friends. Everyone knew Miles was gay."

"Oh, not him," Middleton said. "Blair."

"What?" Jensen said.

"Oh, yeah, a look at his phone . . . well, there's a considerable amount of gay porn on it. Lots of sexting messages between Davonte and another guy," Middleton said.

"Everyone look to be over eighteen?"

"Oh, yes."

"Well, whatever turns you on, I guess," Punch said. "No big deal."

"And here, if you want to see. . . Miles was threatening to go public with Davonte being gay," Middleton said. "Or at least bisexual or whatever."

"Don't you think it's a possible motive, boss?" Jensen asked.

"No. It's the twenty-first century," Punch said. "Who cares?"

"A lot of people do," Jensen said. "Just look at all those people marching around town. And boss, it only takes one. What if Davonte didn't want that coming out?"

"You think he killed someone because he didn't want it known he was gay or bisexual or whatever?" Punch shook his head. "Doesn't make sense; people are celebrating being gay, bi, trans, whatever. I know more about people's sex lives than I ever wanted to know."

"I'm just saying I think we need to take a look at it," Jensen urged.

Sam was waiting for his teleconference with Martinez to start. Martinez was always on time; the fact that he was running late was aggravating an already irritable Sam. At check-in, one of the nurses had given Sam a form Martinez used. It was loosely based on the Alcoholics Anonymous tenth and eleventh steps and would require Sam to identify his feelings since the last meeting, any thinking errors, resentments, and how he dealt with those. "Well, this is going to suck," he said aloud.

"Why is that?" Martinez asked. Sam hadn't seen or heard him enter the room at the far end. "What's going on? How are you?"

"I'm screwed," Sam said. "I went to a function with Veronica last month."

"And?" Martinez made a note in the omnipresent spiral notebook. "How did it go?"

"Well, I got drunk and one of Veronica's friends threatened me and I knocked him out," Sam said.

Martinez put down the notebook and looked directly into the screen. "Give me the long version."

For the next few minutes, Sam spoke while Martinez listened, only occasionally asking clarifying questions. Finally, Sam sat quietly, his eyes wet with tears. "I'm screwed."

"No, you are not," Martinez said. "Sam, you've been through a terrible, terrible thing. You—"

"That was more than ten years ago! I can't go on like this. I—"

"Sam, give me a second, okay?" Martinez said. "I want to talk for just a minute about you. Just sit and listen, would you?"

"Sure," Sam said.

"You had a terrible childhood. Your mother died, your dad was a drunk, your brother wreaked havoc. Then, you entered the army and were grievously wounded. Those kinds of injuries do not simply go away. On top of that, you lost some of your men and—"

"Five."

"You lost five of your men—"

"Right."

"Then," Martinez said, holding up a hand to silence Sam, "you blamed yourself for their deaths."

"It was my fault!"

"For the purpose of this discussion, it does not matter."

"It matters to me!"

"Are you going to let me finish?"

"If you'll hurry the hell up," Sam said. He was pacing the small examining room.

"Then, and most importantly, you did not seek treatment for your condition until recently."

"I didn't know I had a condition until recently!"

"I'm aware," Martinez said. "So my point is that while the salient events may have happened ten or more years ago, you've only recently begun to deal with the issues caused by those events. Instead, you did what has always worked for you: you set whatever was bothering you aside and you moved forward. But this time, what had always worked for you was working against you, and that condition built up in you until it was more than you could deal with. That's what's been going on these past few years, Sam. Your past is catching up with you. Now, you've got to give yourself some time to heal."

"I don't have time, Bob! I've lost my girl and my partner is pissed off at me. My business sucks right now. I'm edgy as hell. Look, can you just prescribe—"

"I could, but I'm not going to."

"Why not? Maybe just a little something to take the edge off?"

"Because there's virtually no way you'd take the medication as prescribed. You'd be abusing those meds in a week. I can't have that. You don't do anything in moderation."

"Screw you, Bob."

"Feel better?" Martinez asked.

"I'm trying!"

"I know. Let's work on that," Martinez said. "Now, I'm going to email you some workbook pages. I want you to sit down somewhere quiet and complete the sheets I assign . . ."

Moments later, Sam climbed into his truck and took a deep breath. He thought about what he and Martinez had discussed. It was all such a load of crap—workbooks, breathing exercises, prayers, meditation . . . He looked at his watch. He was meeting with the firm's accountant in fifteen minutes, and not looking forward to it.

———

Punch and Jensen had been sitting in an unmarked car outside Davonte's dorm for almost four hours and were getting squirrely. "I need to take a leak," Jensen said.

"Well, go, but hurry up. Need you here if he shows up, damn it!" Punch barked.

"Where am I gonna go?"

"It's a college campus. Must be six hundred acres. Think you can find a tree?"

"Isn't that against the law?"

Punch looked sourly at Jensen. "It is, but who's going to cite you? Seriously, go find a bush or just go here. But hurry and get back!"

Punch sat alone in the car, watching the dorm. He absolutely did not want to do this. The case was not ready, and he'd told that to Lucas and Nice in no uncertain terms.

"I don't have enough," he'd told them repeatedly.

"You don't understand," Lucas had countered. "We've got assholes from all over the country tearing this town apart. We've got to arrest someone—right, wrong, or indifferent."

"That's not how it is supposed to work!" Punch had protested.

"I don't care how it is supposed to work," Rebecca Nice had said. "I just know that if we don't do something, we're going to watch this town get torn in half."

Now, as he quaffed antacids and waited for Jensen to return, Punch knew that things were about to take a turn. Whether for better or worse, he didn't know. A few minutes later, Jensen came back, breathing heavily. "He's coming!"

"From where?"

"From that other dorm over there." Jensen pointed.

"The back door is locked, right?"

"Yeah, Jeb told me he locked it with a chain, so we'd be able to see. We've got to let him know when we've got Davonte, though, so he can unlock it. He says it's a fire hazard."

"Don't let me forget. I don't want to—"

"There!" Jensen pointed, and the two men scrambled out of the car and jogged the short distance from the parking lot to the front door, where they intercepted a startled Davonte.

"What the hell?" he said.

"Mr. Blair, you're under arrest," Punch said, hoping the young man would cooperate. "Suspicion of murder."

"You gotta be bullshitting me, man."

"No bullshit. Please turn around and put your hands behind you."

"What if I don't?"

"Mr. Blair, momentarily, you are going to be in custody," Punch explained. "In fact, a lawyer would say you have been seized at this point. This can be done easily, or we can do it the hard way." He looked up at the big man, hoping Davonte would go easily.

"What do you have now that you didn't have before?" Davonte asked Punch.

"Well, among other things, eyewitness statements placing you near the scene, more stuff from your phone, cell phone tower locations, and—best of all—your DNA on Miles's hat. Altogether, enough."

"This is bullshit," Davonte said, turning around.

Punch quickly affixed the handcuffs, taking a deep breath when they were emplaced. "Come on over to the car. I'm going to read you your rights, then I'm going to give you a ride to the detention center." Davonte, escorted by Punch and Jensen, made his way to the car before being seated and advised of his rights. "Any questions?" Punch asked.

"Yeah, one."

"What's that?"

"You dumb cops ever get tired of arresting the wrong dude? I heard you arrested some soldier a while back for something he didn't do."

Neither Jensen nor Punch answered, but Jensen mouthed, "Ouch!" as they got into the car and headed for the jail.

11

The *Custer Bugle* had been in Bill Gordon's family for generations. As readership dwindled he had taken on more and more responsibilities, and today, he was on deadline for an editorial he was writing regarding school funding. He was focused and typing when Penrose burst into his office. "Oh my God, Bill!" she said. "Do you have a minute?"

"Absolutely, Sarah." He sat back in his chair and removed his readers. "What's up?"

"Sounds like they've made an arrest in the Miles kid's murder."

"Good. Have a seat." He gestured to the chair on the other side of his desk. "I'm glad. It's creepy, having someone like that running around."

"Yes, of course. But you know what's better?" She looked at him expectantly.

"What's that?"

"The guy they've arrested? He's black! And an athlete!"

Gordon looked at Sarah closely. "So . . ."

"So, there are just so many angles we can take with this story," she said. "We've got black versus white, black versus gay, straight versus gay, athlete versus gay, and probably some I haven't even thought of!"

"Sarah, a young man is dead," Gordon said. "That's tragedy enough. I'm not certain that we need—or want—any angles."

"Yes, he's dead. And there is nothing we can do about that. What we can do, and what we should do, is to highlight the *why* of his death."

Gordon looked at Penrose for another long moment. Her lips were pursed, and she was rocking in her chair. "Don't you think, Sarah, that before we get to the why, we first report the who, the what, the when, the where, and the how as we get the facts?"

"Oh, I'll get all that, of course," she said. "But the story in this case is the *why*."

"Just out of curiosity, why do you think that?"

"This is Wyoming! The kid was gay!"

"Where's the suspect from?"

"Detroit," she said. "I think a suburb, actually. But that doesn't matter. What matters is that Miles—a young gay man —was killed by an African-American man."

"Allegedly. And what do you have supporting the homo-phobic angle?"

"A lot."

"Really?"

"Well, I don't exactly have it yet, but my sources are telling me that Davonte did not like gay people."

"And how do they know?"

"Things he said. Things he posted. Things he wrote."

"Sarah, he's what? Eighteen years old, nineteen maybe?" Gordon asked. "You want to be held responsible for things you said when you were eighteen?"

"He's an adult, Bill. Legally, he's responsible for everything he says or does, to include murder."

"I understand that," Gordon said. "Look, Sarah, suppose I agree with that. What does it mean? He's not from Wyoming."

"He's going to college here. He's got an attitude shared by many here."

"And one opposed by many here, Sarah," he said. "And there's a third faction, one that I think is way bigger than the others."

"What's that?"

"There are a lot of people who don't give a damn one way or the other who someone sleeps with. They just want to be left alone, free from learning about anyone's sex life."

"Then they are part of the problem, Bill. Don't you see? Acceptance and apathy are not enough."

"How can leaving someone alone to live life as he chooses not be enough?"

"Because for eons gay people have been discriminated against. It's not enough to merely accept them; we need to ensure these people are made whole."

Gordon turned to his keyboard. "I'm on deadline for this editorial," he said. "Write your story, Sarah, and I'll look at it. But again, focus on the elements aside from the *why*, please. You might find one young man killed another young man simply because they got in an argument or for no reason at all. Get the facts. We will deal with the social ramifications—if any—after that."

A couple days later Sam was in court with Raylene Smith. Albert Smith, having been bound over to the district court for further proceedings, was appearing for his felony arraignment. Sam had agreed to accompany Raylene to observe.

Although he had no direct role in the proceeding, because he represented her in her civil domestic violence proceeding, he wanted to accompany her. They sat in the last row of seats and watched as her shackled and bound husband was brought in to face the judge.

"He looks so small," Raylene said.

"Raylene, he's 6'3" and weighs 250 pounds and has been beating on you for thirty years," Sam whispered.

"I know, Sam," she said. "But I can't help it. I love him."

Sam bit his tongue. It wasn't rational, but he knew enough to know he wasn't going to change it.

Daniels entered promptly at eleven a.m. and began immediately. "Good morning, ladies and gentlemen, court is in session. We are on the record in the matter of State of Wyoming vs. Albert Smith. The State is represented by Ms. Schmidt. The defendant is represented by Mr. Sharp. Is everyone ready to proceed?"

"We are, Judge," Schmidt said.

"Defense is ready as well, Your Honor," said Sharp. Sam hadn't worked with the man much—just enough to dislike him.

Daniels then proceeded to advise Smith of his rights, as well as the charges against him and the maximum possible penalty. After ensuring that Smith understood, Daniels had him stand. "To the allegation that, on or about the 4th of November, you committed felony domestic battery, how do you plead?"

"Not guilty, Judge," Smith said.

"Be seated, Mr. Smith," Daniels said, writing on a pad in front of him. "The parties will be heard regarding bond. Ms. Schmidt, what says the State?"

"Your Honor, we think Judge Downs set a fair and well-considered bond. Mr. Smith has been convicted of domestic battery multiple times. We think it is clear he represents a significant danger to the community, and especially to Mrs. Smith. We'd ask that bond be continued as set by Judge Downs."

Daniels nodded noncommittally. "Mr. Sharp?"

"Your Honor, the defendant would request a personal recognizance bond. He—"

"That's not going to happen, Mr. Sharp. These are serious charges. Your client has a history, as you know."

"Judge, I'm not trying to minimize the charges at all. But I'd remind the court that my client is to be deemed not guilty of all charges until and unless proven otherwise. He is otherwise a productive citizen with a job and a mortgage and a wife to support."

"Yeah, right," Sam said under his breath. "He's a danger." Raylene looked at Sam but said nothing.

"Moreover, Judge," Sharp continued, "I've been in contact with Mrs. Smith and she wants him home. I have a copy of the letter she prepared for me just yesterday. May I approach?"

Sam sat still, except to shrug when Daniels looked at him. Raylene leaned over to whisper in his ear. "Sam, I'm sorry, but—"

"Please don't say another word," Sam said through clenched teeth while looking straight ahead. "We'll talk outside here in a minute."

Daniels read the letter and then looked at Raylene. Apparently satisfied, he said, "I'm not convinced this is the best decision I'll make today, but at the request of the defendant and the alleged victim, I'm going to modify bond. Defendant will be held in lieu of fifty thousand dollars cash or commercial surety. Mr. Smith, if you get out, follow these terms and conditions . . ."

While he was outlining the terms and conditions of the

new bond, Sam grabbed Raylene's arm and escorted her from the courtroom. In the hallway, he saw Fricke and Frac. Nodding to them, he escorted Raylene a little farther down.

"Raylene, what the hell?"

"I need him, Sam," she said, her eyes welling up with tears.

"For what? My God, Raylene, he treats you like trash! He's going to get out and eventually hurt or kill you!"

"Sam, I know he's sorry. I—I made him mad. He just lost it for a minute. I know he loves me!"

"Raylene, no man who actually loved you would treat you like that! It's part of a cycle. There's a tension-building phase, then an abusive incident, then a honeymoon phase. You're in that honeymoon phase now, but as soon as you're back together the tension will start building again, until . . . well, you know."

"Sam, I'm old and fat and I don't bring any money into the house. I couldn't have kids and so it's just us. I owe him—"

"Nothing! You don't owe him anything! Can't you see that?" Sam's voice was raised, and he could see people looking in their direction. Worse, he could see Raylene cowering. He softened his voice as best he could and put his hand on her arm. "Let me take you to the women's shelter, at least. That way, you don't have to stay in the home with him."

"But I'll be alone."

"I know, but—"

"Sam," she said, taking his hand, "I'll—I'll be fine. This has happened before. He'll be sorry. We can get some counseling."

"Raylene, I just . . . I can't . . ."

"Sam, you've done so much for me already," she said. "I'm fine. I feel safe. Just tell me how to get him out of jail. I sold one of our old cars and I have the money."

Sam explained the procedure and watched as she walked

quickly to the side door. He might have sworn there was a bounce in her step.

———————

Sam was still angry when he got back to the office. He slammed his briefcase down and was taking off his coat when Cassie appeared in the door. "Sam, there is a Mr. Blair on the phone. He wants to talk with you."

"The practice of law would be so much fun without clients," he said, taking his chair. He took a deep breath. "Put him through."

"Sam Johnstone," he said when the phone rang. His head and his nonexistent leg hurt, and he searched in his desk for a hydrocodone.

"This is Davonte Blair. We met a while back. You came and spoke at my class. I'm in jail for a bullshit charge."

"What charge is that?" Sam asked, having a pretty good idea.

"Murder. These assholes think I killed Kaiden Miles."

"How can I help you?"

"Get me outta here."

"Well, it's a little more complicated than that," Sam said. He took two pills with tepid coffee left over from earlier that morning. "If you want to retain me, there's the little matter of my fee."

"All about money, huh?" Davonte observed. "I thought you were all about justice when you spoke at my class."

"Welcome to the real world. I have expenses. Rent. Paper and pens. Secretaries. Bartenders."

"You'll get paid."

"By whom?" Sam asked.

"What do you care?"

"I prefer to be paid by my client," Sam said. "If I'm going to be paid by someone else, then I want to know who it is."

"Money's all the same."

"Not to me, it isn't," Sam said. "I know who the source is, or you find yourself another boy."

"How much?"

"I don't know yet," Sam said. "And I haven't even started with my conditions. I don't need this," he lied. "I have plenty to do, and I don't know if I want to take this on. It will depend."

"On what?"

"Well, where the money's coming from, for one. And more importantly, what you have to say when we talk."

"I didn't do it," Davonte said. "That's all you need to know."

"Davonte, I don't care whether you did it or not," Sam explained. "I'm only interested in whether you're going to listen to me."

"What?"

"Something you didn't understand?" Sam asked. Davonte was quiet at the other end of the line, clearly thinking. "Let me help you, Davonte," Sam said. "There are people who will take the case, no questions asked."

"I need someone who believes me," Davonte said. "Someone who can get me off."

"You pay enough money, you'll get both."

"But you're different, huh?"

"I am," Sam said. "Tell you what: I'll come see you here shortly. We'll talk."

"See ya," Davonte said, and hung up.

Sam walked down the hall to Paul's office. He was reading a contract. Sam noticed the reading glasses. "Got a minute?"

"Sure," Paul said. "Close the door." After Sam sat down, Paul ran a hand through his thinning gray hair. Sam remembered when Paul's hair was long, dark, and thick under his ever-present baseball hat. "What's up, Sam?"

"I like the readers," Sam teased.

"Bite me. This getting-old thing sucks."

Sam smiled. "Got a call from Davonte Blair. He's been arrested for killing that Miles kid."

"He wants to retain us?"

"Apparently."

"You agree?" Paul asked.

"Of course not," Sam said. "I told him I wanted to talk to you."

"You quote him?"

"No. Basically told him it would depend," Sam explained.

"On what?"

"I left that open, but told him there would be conditions, the primary one being that he would listen."

"Will he?" Paul asked.

"Don't know." Sam shrugged. "Maybe if it is part of the deal. I think we ought to at least talk to him. Might be that we're not a good fit."

"I don't like it." Paul shook his head. "I think this one has media circus written all over it. Ronnie says there are groups on campus making this a gay thing already. Get a black guy accused and you've got that to fight in addition to the prosecution."

"What do you mean, 'that?'"

"I mean that whoever defends him is going to have to battle the race angle as well as everything else."

"Do you really see that as an issue?"

"Not for a jury, no. They'll do the right thing. But I'm worried more about the press and the publicity, Sam. I mean, I've done some criminal work, but . . . well, murder defense is a whole different ballgame." The old friends sat and looked at each other. "What's he say?" Paul said at last.

"Says he didn't do it."

"You believe him?"

"Haven't even thought about it," Sam admitted. "Does it matter?"

"I suppose not," Paul said. "I don't know, but . . . I mean, I know it's your practice, but I'll say it again, just like I did with that Olsen guy: this is all I've got." Paul gestured around the room. "This one is going to be controversial. I want to go along."

"I'll set it up," Sam said. He stood and was leaving when Paul's voice stopped him.

"Sam, I know you want this one, but we've got to get the money. And a lot of it."

"Agreed."

The Custer County jail had been on site for almost a century. As Sam and Paul walked down the long, windowless hallways, Sam was reminded of some of the buildings at Fort Benning: staid and colorless, but functional. They were escorted to the counsel room by a long-time jailer. "Boys, I'm gonna have to look through your bags and do a quick pat-down."

"No problem, Tom," Paul said. "How are the kids?"

"Doing fine, doing fine. Got me a grandkid that's going to be a ballplayer, too," Tom said while patting down Sam. He stopped at Sam's leg. "I'm sorry, I forgot."

"No problem," Sam said.

"Paul," Tom continued, "if he's half as good as that P.J. of yours, he'll be something!"

"Well, thanks, Tom," Paul said. "Gotta keep him healthy. He's still a little small."

"He'll fill out. He's got speed—and you can't coach that," Tom observed with a smile. "Ya'll go on in. I'll be here in the hallway, if you need something."

Sam entered first, followed by Paul. Davonte had been issued the orange jumpsuit. His hands were cuffed together, and he was chained to the table on the far side of the room, the links running from the cuffs through a C-shaped weld on the top of the table. A pane of plexiglass separated the two ends of the table. "Forgive me if I don't get up," Davonte said.

After the door was closed, Sam began. "Davonte, this is my partner, Paul Norquist. As I mentioned, we work together on these things. We wanted to meet with you tonight to see if it is possible for us to represent you."

"Okay." Davonte shifted his weight in the tiny plastic chair. "Ronnie is—"

"My son," Paul said.

Davonte nodded. "What do you want to know?"

"I want to start with what happened after you got arrested," Sam said. Both Paul and Davonte looked at him blankly. "That was last night—the 22nd, right? Now, where were you?"

"Outside my dorm."

"And what happened?"

"I was gonna go get some food—"

"Just what happened from the arrest on, please."

"So, I'm walking out, and that Polson dude and that hanger-on who is always with him came up to me and Polson told me I was under arrest," Davonte said. He sat back and waited.

"And then what?" Sam asked.

"He told me to put my hands behind my back. He threatened to use his taser on me. That ain't right, is it? They can't do that, can they?"

"And then what?" Sam asked, ignoring the questions.

"They cuffed me and then put me in the back of that police car, then they took me to the police station," Davonte said. "They searched me. That was humiliating, man!"

"And then?"

"They, uh, took my prints—for a second time. Put me in a cell," Davonte said. "Gave me some paperwork to ask for a phone call and a bond."

"Did you say anything to them while all this was going on?" Paul asked.

"Told 'em they had the wrong guy and they could kiss my ass," Davonte said. "Told 'em I was gonna sue their asses off when this was over."

"Did you talk about what had happened at all?" Sam asked, looking at Paul. This was the key question.

"Not other than to tell him I didn't do it. Told 'em I wanted a lawyer. The Polson guy, he read me my rights and said he had probable cause to believe that I was the guy who killed Kaiden—which is bullshit."

"What evidence did he say he had?" Sam asked.

"He said . . . like, video and phone records and texts and cell phone tower stuff."

"That it?"

"And DNA. On a hat. And cuts on my hands," Davonte said.

"Other than the inventory, did you make any statements or sign anything?" Sam was watching Davonte closely.

"No. Well, I mean I told him that it wasn't me."

"Okay, but you didn't tell them why, or discuss an alibi or anything like that? Nothing else?" Paul asked.

Davonte looked at Paul. "I just told them I knew that little dude but that I didn't kill him."

"Did they take any blood samples, cut any of your hair, clip your nails, or test you for drugs or alcohol?" Sam asked.

"No, not last night."

"Davonte, I need to talk this over with Paul," Sam said. "We will be back in a couple of minutes."

Sam and Paul stepped into the hallway and spoke in low voices. "So, what do you think?" Sam asked.

"I don't know what to think, Sam," Paul said. "We never asked him about the crime."

"Yeah, well, I used to start with, 'What happened?' and got unicorns and rainbows from the client, so now I make the client tell me in his own words what the prosecution has," Sam explained. "It keeps them from blowing smoke up my ass."

"Okay," Paul said. "Makes sense. What are you thinking?"

"I'm not sure. If you don't have a strong feeling one way or the other, let's go back in and talk to him," Sam said. Paul nodded, and the two men started to re-enter the room.

"Sam, before we go back in." Paul put a hand on Sam's arm to stop him. "One more time: we've got bills to pay. You've got to cover. I can't keep this ship afloat much longer."

"I understand."

"Davonte," Sam began, when they were all in the room again, "before we make a final decision, I want your version of what happened."

"Nothing happened, man."

"Let me try this again: how long have you known the deceased?" Sam got the events of the past few weeks as best he could from Davonte before Tom told him it was time to cut it off.

Back at the office, the partners worked on other matters. Paul was clearly hesitant to take on Davonte's defense. Sam was interested and struggled to pay attention to the pile of real estate matters pending, but it had to be done. Finally, after drafting a set of covenants for a new subdivision to be located at the base of the mountains, he called it a day. On the way home, he decided to stop in the liquor store and buy a bottle. He'd made his purchase and was watching the clerk bag it when the headline on the *Bugle* caught his eye: ARREST MADE IN GAY SLAYING. Below the headline was a picture of an almost angelic-looking Miles juxtaposed against Davonte's defiant booking photo.

"And so it begins," Sam said.

"What's that?" The clerk handed him the brown paper bag. "You want a paper?"

"I might as well," Sam said.

"That's going to be a real mess," she said as she handed him the change.

Sam couldn't resist. "What do you mean?"

"Well, just that you got a fairy killed by that black boy. Now, what kind of mess is that going to be for us normal folk?" She tucked her blue hair behind her ear. Sam counted at least a dozen piercings in addition to the gauges visible. "I mean, nobody can help what he is, but I wish they'd leave all of that stuff where they come from and just leave us alone. What do you think?"

"I don't even know where to begin," Sam said, taking the bag and leaving the store.

"Right?" he heard the clerk say as the door closed behind him.

12

————

"Sam, I've been thinking. Even if the guy comes up with some money—which I doubt will happen—I think this case might be one we need to steer clear of." Paul was sitting in a chair in Sam's office. "I think he might be guilty and maybe this isn't such a good idea."

"It doesn't look good. But like everyone else, our guy has rights," Sam said. "That's really what we'd be defending."

"You and I understand that," Paul said. "But the average dude on the street, well, he doesn't get it. Besides, our client is a jerk."

"Most people don't get it," Sam agreed. "And as for Davonte, remember, he's a teenaged college jock. I'd like to see if he could come up with the money, at least."

"Sam, I think he is blowing smoke. Let the public defenders take the case. They've got some good people over there. They can try a case, and they've got state dollars to support them."

"He says he's got the coin," Sam said. "I say, 'Show me the money.'"

"Sam, this thing would become all-consuming." Paul was

up and pacing. "It would take our eye off the ball on virtually everything else we have going on for months."

"I know," Sam agreed. "That's why we bill his ass off. And I could maybe defer that school law thing?"

"Our financial situation sucks right now," Paul said, picking up and examining a hockey-puck-sized object on Sam's desk. It appeared to be made of clear plastic. Inside were dozens of sharp metal objects and a couple of ball bearings. "What the hell is this?"

"That's the stuff they took out of my leg," Sam said, smiling wryly at Paul's reaction. "Before they decided to take the leg. It's from the improvised explosive device that blew me up."

"You kept it?"

"Evidently. I was told later I insisted."

"Jesus, Sam!" Paul said. "I'm sorry. I thought it was a paperweight."

"It is now." Sam smiled as he watched Paul delicately place the memento back on the credenza. For a moment, he was back on the hospital ship under the bright lights and hearing the voice of the surgeon who had saved his life. Her name was Margaret. Major Margaret-something. Probably long retired and making a mint in private practice. He should find her and thank her, he thought, before returning to the subject at hand. "No sweat. But assuming for the sake of argument we got the money?"

Paul looked at Sam. "Up front, Sam. We've got to have the money in hand. I'm going to stomp my foot if you've got any other ideas," he said. "This isn't Tommy Olsen, right?"

"Oh, no. This is a business deal. Tommy was kind of a . . . project," Sam said. "Okay, let's do this: I'll go and tell him we won't consider making an entry of appearance until we have the cash."

In his old truck on the way to the jail Sam was listening to Wyoming Public Radio. They had the story and were playing up the racial and sexual orientation angles, just as the *Bugle* had. Just before he changed the channel, the radio personality cut to an interview with *Bugle* reporter Sarah Penrose.

"What's the picture on the ground in Custer?" Penrose was asked.

"Well, to be honest, the town is in a bit of an uproar," she responded. Sam was sitting at a red light, watching a mother and her children cross the street carrying paper cups from a national coffee chain. The interview continued, and as Sam drove by the college on the unseasonably warm Saturday afternoon, he noted a number of students on the vast property throwing footballs and Frisbees, while others lounged on the brown grass, looking at laptops. One even had a book.

"A number of college students have told me they are afraid to go outside in this environment," Penrose continued, as Sam stopped to allow three female joggers to proceed. "Vincent Beretta, Custer College president, has put out a statement urging calm and asking everyone to pull together, but it doesn't seem to be having much effect. On the one side," she continued, "are students seeking justice for the young man who died. Given Wyoming's history in these matters, they want to see justice for their gay friend."

"And on the other?" the host asked.

"On the other are civil rights activists and others wanting to ensure that the young African-American man accused of this heinous crime receives a fair trial," Penrose said. "As we all know, this country's history in that area is deplorable."

"Sounds as if things are tense in Custer," the host opined.

"Oh my, yes," Penrose said. "You can feel it in the air."

Sam arrived at the jail and sat in his truck, thinking about the coming discussion with Davonte. In the park across the street, two fathers were playing basketball with their sons while two women talked at a picnic table nearby. A dog, leashed to the picnic table, watched the basketball game, barking and wagging his tail. As he got out of the truck, Sam could smell dry leaves, charcoal fluid, and meat roasting in the crisp fall air.

———

After clearing security, Sam made it to the attorney/client room. A couple of minutes later, Tom brought Davonte in to see him. After chaining him to the table, Tom backed out of the room. "See you later, Mr. Johnstone. Let me know if you need something?"

"I will, Tom," Sam said. Because Sam had yet to make an appearance, he was deemed no more than a visitor, and he was still separated from Davonte by the plexiglass. "Davonte, how are you doing?" Sam began.

"I'm in jail for something I didn't do. The food sucks. I'm sleeping on a rock-hard bunk that was made for a midget. And the guards are all assholes. How the hell do you think I'm doing?"

"I think you're warm and dry and no one is shooting at your sad ass. That's what I think." Sam stood and was turning away when the pounding on the plexiglass got his attention. He saw Davonte motioning to him.

"Where are you going?" Davonte asked.

"I'm leaving. I really don't need this crap," Sam said.

"Wait!" Davonte said. Sam waved off Tom, who was looking through the window, questioning what was happening. "Look, man. I'm just pissed off. This place sucks."

"I get it, but I'm not your momma, I'm not your punching bag, and I'm not here to listen to your sniveling," Sam said as he sat back down. "I'll remind you that the charge is murder. You will talk to me like an adult, or you will find someone else. There is no other option involving me."

"You my lawyer yet?"

"Not until I see the money. All of it. I made that clear the other day."

"I'll get you the money, man."

"You've got an initial appearance Monday—that's two days from now. You won't have to say anything. They'll give you the paperwork for a public defender."

"I don't want no public defender, man!"

"Then you're not as smart as you think you are. Good public defenders try cases all the time. They're sharp, know the system, know the judges, and they've got the resources of the state behind them. They'll give you a good defense."

"I want my own guy. I want you."

"You don't even know me. You don't know anything about me."

"I know you are a hero. I figure you got big balls. From what these guys in here are telling me, there's people outside want me strung up 'cause Kaiden was gay and I'm black. I didn't kill that dude, and I need someone who isn't going to be afraid. I don't know about them other guys, but I know you won't be afraid."

Davonte looked tired, Sam thought. "Davonte, everyone is afraid," he said. "I'm not afraid of what those nitwits with their signs think or say, but I am afraid of representing another human being in a case like this. Everyone is. Can I control the fear? Yes. But that's all I'm doing. Now, I've spoken with Paul. We can't do this unless—"

"What is that dude's problem?"

"What do you mean?"

"I can tell that dude don't like me," Davonte said. "Is it because I'm black?"

"No. It's because he thinks you're a jerk," Sam said. "And to be frank, so do a lot of other people."

"Like Ronnie? That's his boy, right?"

"Yeah, but Ronnie seems to think you are a great guy. At least, that's what he is telling Paul."

Davonte sat quietly. "Ronnie is okay, man. Me and him, well . . . I didn't do this," Davonte said. "Can you do this by yourself?"

"No. Paul is my partner. We work together." Sam took a piece of paper out of his pocket, wrote a number on it, and pressed it against the glass so Davonte could see it. "That's the number. All of it. If you want me there, the money needs to be in my hand or on account by Monday." Turning to leave, he stopped himself. "One more thing, Davonte. A little free legal advice."

"Yeah?"

"Keep your mouth shut. Talk to no one about your case. Trust no one."

"That ain't gonna be a problem."

"Good," Sam said. "And eat something. You're already looking a little raggedy."

13

The afternoon on the Black Hills spring creek had done wonders for Sam's morale. The weather had changed overnight, and it was in the twenties when he left Custer at dawn. Several hours later, he was sitting on the bank thinking how the black pine and aspen contrasted nicely with the brown of the dead grasses, making the scene look like one of the photographs taken during Lieutenant Colonel General George Armstrong Custer's 1874 expedition into this very area. Best of all, when the temperature got to thirty-seven degrees, a small hatch of blue-winged olives went off. Having caught several small brown trout, he stopped in a small South Dakota town, got some gas, and prepared for the half day's drive back to Custer. While he was gassing the truck, he read several text messages and listened to a couple of voicemails. Apparently, members of Davonte's family wanted to meet with him. He finished fueling his truck, bought a couple packages of beef jerky and a cup of coffee, and drove west. Hours later he had parked his truck and was opening his office door when he heard a woman ask, "Are you Mr. Johnstone?"

Turning, he saw a tall, thin woman with her hand extended. Behind her were two large young men. "I am," Sam said, taking her hand. "Sam Johnstone. You are?"

"Davonte's mother. He's my baby. This is his brother Damon, and this is my sister's boy, Reggie," she said, introducing each.

"Nice to meet all of you." Sam nodded. "Come on in." He opened the door and extended a hand for Davonte's mom. The two men declined to follow. "After you," Damon said.

When they were all in the reception area, Sam looked at Davonte's mom. "Coffee?"

"Yes, please," she said.

Sam looked at the two men, who shook their heads. "Coffee for two coming right up, Mrs. . . . I'm sorry, ma'am, but I didn't get your name."

"Blair. I'm a widow, Mr. Johnstone. My husband died years ago in an industrial accident. Please call me Sharon."

"Sharon, please call me Sam," he said, and then indicated his office. "Why don't you all have a seat in my office while I make us a cup of coffee?"

Several minutes later Sam turned out the light in the kitchen and carried the two cups back to his office. Sharon was sitting in the chair directly in front of his desk with her purse on her lap. She was wearing heels and a plain blue dress and had a sweater across her shoulders. "It's cold here," she said.

"Sometimes we've got a foot of snow by now," Sam replied, putting the coffee on a coaster in front of her while watching the two men closely. Damon had taken a chair in the corner of the room and was watching Sam. He was not as tall as Davonte but had to be at least 6'6". He had on a light jacket, jeans, and an expensive pair of black basketball shoes.

Reggie, the shorter of the pair, had his back to Sam and was examining the law books and knick-knacks on the shelves. He wandered from shelf to shelf, picking things up, examining them, and replacing them with little regard for whence they came. "You a hero?" he asked, without turning to face the increasingly irritated Sam.

"I did my job," Sam said. Not thrilled with having this many people in his bubble, he was eager to get on to the business at hand. "How can I help you?" he asked Sharon.

"I want you to represent my son."

"I spoke with your son yesterday, ma'am—"

"Sharon."

"I spoke with Davonte yesterday, Sharon. I explained to him that defending against a murder charge is an expensive undertaking. As you can see, we're not a wealthy firm."

"I understand, Sam," she said. "He is my son. He has told us he wants you to represent him."

"I'm flattered, but I have a partner, and things haven't been great. See, I've had some trouble—"

"Tomorrow morning, I will go to the bank and have the full amount of your fee wired to your bank," she said. "I just need your bank routing and account numbers."

Sam took a sip of his coffee to mask his surprise.

"He thinks we're from the ghetto, Mom," Damon said. He and Reggie exchanged a knowing glance.

Sam looked steadily at Damon. "Your brother has spent the better part of both of our conversations trying to convince me he is a badass from Detroit," he said. "I've no reason—"

"To think he's anything other than some street thug?" Damon said, sitting up in his chair. Sam didn't know what Damon's problem was, but he was clearly spoiling for a fight.

"Damon, let the man finish," Sharon said.

"Thank you, Sharon," Sam said, then turned his eyes to Damon. "I was going to say, 'I've got no reason to believe he is anything other than what he says he is.'" He paused as if to think. When Damon had sat back, Sam finished. "Which, I guess, would be a street thug." He met the eyes of Damon and Reggie in turn, registering the fury in each set. "To use your term," he concluded. He looked at Sharon and could swear he saw a twinkle in her eye.

Except for the occasional indication that Sam had email arriving, the room was very quiet for what had to be a full minute. At last, Sharon reached for her cup, sipped from it, and wrapped her long, slender fingers around it, clearly enjoying the warmth. "You were a soldier, Sam?"

"I was."

"My Ronald was a soldier. We got married the weekend after he got out of basic training. I stayed in Detroit—we did live downtown, then—while he went to advanced something."

"Advanced individual training."

"That's right. Somewhere back east. He finished that, then came and got me, and the next thing I know I was living in a little apartment in Germany. Place called Schweinfurt," she said. "That's where my Damon was born."

"I've been there, believe it or not."

"Have you? Well, we had a good time. Still have some nice things from there. Anyway, we stayed there for a couple of years, he got deployed to Iraq or Afghanistan or one of those awful places—I can't recall which—and when he got back, I told him I didn't want him deploying anymore. No more being a hero. Told him I didn't want to be a war widow. So, we moved back, and he got a good job with the transit authority and we had Davonte and started raising the boys."

"Sounds like a made-for-TV movie," Sam observed.

"Doesn't it?" She looked around his office and smiled wistfully. "And then he got killed in an accident and I was a widow anyway. Raised Damon and Davonte by myself."

"I'm sorry," Sam said.

"I appreciate it," she said. "Sam, do you need anything from us? Besides the money, I mean?"

"Sharon, let me do this. Let me talk with my partner and make sure he is okay with this. If he is, I'll come back in tonight and draft an agreement. If you'd like to meet me here at nine a.m. tomorrow on the way to the bank, we can sign the agreement. There's just one thing, though."

"What is that, Sam?"

"Sharon, even though you are paying the money, my client is Davonte."

"And what does that mean?" she asked. In his peripheral vision, Sam could see the two young men listening closely.

"That means that I'm not going to be able to share a lot of information with you," he said, looking at each person in turn. "Whatever Davonte and I talk about is confidential. What happened, strategy, what he tells me—all of that will just be between me and Davonte and my partner, Paul. Anything said in front of you with Davonte present wouldn't be confidential and might have to be disclosed in court."

"I'm not worried about that."

"Okay, well, sometimes it can be a problem between lawyers and clients and the people paying the tab."

"Won't happen here. My Davonte doesn't have any secrets. He is a good boy. He didn't do this. It's not the way I raised him." She put down her coffee and stood, looking Sam in the eye as she extended her hand. "Sam, would you get me that bank information?"

After Davonte's mother had departed with the two young men and Sam's voided check, he wandered around the office for a time, unable to focus on real estate matters. He'd committed, but nothing would be final until the paperwork was signed. The first order of business, of course, was to discuss the matter with Paul, so he sent a quick text asking him to call Sam at the office. While he waited for Paul's call, he stood and worked his way around the office, repositioning items moved earlier by Reggie. When he got to the shadow box he stared for a long time at the contents. The rank insignia he had worn, medals and ribbons he had earned, the shoulder patches identifying each unit with which he had served were all arranged neatly and displayed underneath a tattered American flag that had flown over the forward operating base from which he'd deployed the day he got hurt. It all seemed so long ago. As he turned toward his desk, he bumped his prosthetic leg into the chair where Damon had been sitting. Smiling sheepishly, he repositioned the chair, sat behind the desk, and began looking for the form the partners used for a representation agreement. He was filling in blocks when his phone rang.

"Sam, what the hell are you doing?" Paul asked. "Single man, Sunday night, and you're in the office?"

"I've been meeting with Davonte's mom," Sam said.

"Aw, Sam," Paul said. "Really? I kinda thought we'd decided that maybe we didn't want to do this? I was going to see if you wanted to have dinner with me and Jeannie."

"They got ahold of me when I was coming back into town. I was fishing."

"There's a surprise. Do any good?"

"Yeah, I caught several nice browns," Sam bragged.

"Where?"

"Where I was. You want to know, you got to go."

Paul had always had a wonderful laugh. "You met with his mom?"

"Yeah, and his big brother and a cousin. The 'henchmen,' I think I'll call them."

"They all as big as he is?"

"Damned near. Hell, his mom—her name is Sharon—has to be six feet tall. They want us to take the case." Hearing nothing in response, Sam asked, "You hear me?"

"You quote 'em?" Paul asked.

"I did."

"And she's still interested?" Paul was incredulous.

"She's gonna have the money wired tomorrow morning," Sam said. He was typing and talking. "Sounds like her husband died in an accident, so maybe the proceeds from a personal injury case."

"So, you haven't signed anything?"

"Not without talking with you. I'm drafting the agreement right now," Sam said, correcting a mistake.

"I appreciate it," Paul said. Sam could hear a door slam. Paul must have walked outside. "Damn, Sam. I really don't want to do this, but—"

"It's a shit-ton of money. Tide us over."

"Yeah, it is that. How much trouble will momma be?" Every lawyer had stories to tell about conflicts with the mothers of their clients.

"Momma is a neat, neat lady. You'll like her."

"And the others? The 'henchmen,' I think you called them?"

"I don't know. I think on their own they might be trouble, but I think Sharon has a handle on them," Sam said. "She's beautiful, by the way."

"I can hear you typing," Paul said. "You are working on the agreement, you said?"

"I am," Sam acknowledged, leaning forward to see the screen.

"Make sure we've got an escape clause," Paul instructed. "Something like, 'In the event the parties deem themselves incompatible, blah, blah, blah.' Look at the file on my Thorson case. It was a civil matter, but I think there's some language in there we can poach."

"Will that stand?" Sam asked. The general rule was that once an attorney entered an appearance in a criminal case, he or she was on the case until a judge ruled otherwise.

"Doubt it," Paul said. "But I'd like them to think we have a little more leverage than maybe we do."

"So, we're in?" Sam asked.

"Yeah. God help us. Buckle up." Paul sighed. "I can't believe you got us into this."

Later that evening, Paul and Ronnie were in Paul's office. It was after nine, but Paul had called his son and asked to meet.

"Dad, what's up?" Ronnie asked when he came through the door. He was ten minutes late.

"You're late."

"What?"

"You're late. I asked you to meet me at nine. You will never get anywhere in life if you are late."

Ronnie said nothing. He was not up to arguing with the old man tonight. The two sat and looked at each other, saying nothing. Finally, Paul cut to the chase. "What are your mother and I going to find out about you in the next couple of months?"

"What do you mean?"

"I think you know what I mean. Sam is going to take on

Davonte's defense. That means everyone—cops, Sam, me—will be looking into Kaiden's background, as well as Davonte's . . . and yours."

"Nothing! There's nothing to find out, Dad. I told you that when we met before."

"Are you certain? I need the truth."

"Nothing."

"Drugs?" Paul asked.

"Well, maybe a little bit of weed, but nothing serious."

"Is that how you were raised?"

"No, but it's legal in Colorado. Better for you than beer—"

"Oh, stop. Save that shit for your dorm rat buddies," Paul said. "The fact is, the stuff's illegal. You are choosing to break the law. Society breaks down when people pick and choose what laws they will follow, son."

"Change isn't made by following the law!"

"Are you kidding me?" Paul asked. "What cause are you behind? Not having to make the bed in your dorm? Give me a break. I asked you what we're going to find out here. So we got drugs. What else?"

"I don't know." Ronnie was looking at the floor.

"Don't be petulant. I know that look."

"And I know you're a judgmental asshole," Ronnie said. "A racist, homophobic, white-privileged Generation Xer who doesn't understand what's going on in the world!"

"Wow," Paul said. "I guess I need to listen up, then. What's going on in the world? What's the bad stuff I'm missing? I look at the world and see full employment, every family with two cars, the big health issue being obesity, and schools and culture catering to people who are weirder than cat shit. Seems to me that for someone who is unhappy with tradition and culture, this is the greatest period in the history of mankind."

"All built on the backs of slaves, people of color, native Americans, LGBTQ+ people, and women. All by oppressing others!"

Paul watched his son for a moment. "Even assuming, arguendo, that everything you say is true—and it is more complicated than that—but even if we assume it is, all I asked is, 'Is there something you need to tell me?' So, let me ask again: is there anything you need to tell me?"

"No."

"Anything I need to tell Mom?"

"No. She wouldn't understand any more than you."

"Okay," Paul said, standing. "So, here is the deal, son: I'm going to help Sam defend Davonte. That means he will soon become my priority. I have given you the opportunity to tell me if there is anything going on with you, or you and Davonte, or involving you or Davonte or Kaiden. In return, you provided an insulting, frankly sophomoric rant. So, when and if you get caught in the crossfire between a prosecutor and Davonte, or between Sam and Davonte, understand that I was here, that I offered to listen, and that I offered to help. Good night, son." He opened his office door with one hand.

"Dad, I—" Ronnie began.

"Good night, son." Paul pointed to the hall with the other hand. "Good to see you," he said to his son's back.

* * *

"So, you got your money?" Davonte asked. It was Monday morning and outside visiting hours, but Sam had talked his way into the jail for what he'd promised would be a brief visit.

"Sharon says she will deposit the money later this morning. Assuming she does that, you've got yourself a law firm," Sam said.

"I got a lawyer, you mean."

"Davonte, I meant what I said. Paul and I are a package deal. If that doesn't work for you, let me know now." The young man looked at him for a long time. Sam met his stare. "This is a deal-breaker. Both of us, or none of us."

"Okay," Davonte said at last.

"Good. Now, we've got an initial appearance this afternoon. I'll be there with you. You don't have to say anything."

"Don't I gotta plead not guilty?"

"Not yet. The hearing is just to tell you what they are charging you with and to inform you of your rights—stuff like that. The judge we see today doesn't have the jurisdiction to take a plea on a charge like this."

"So, when do I get out?"

"Depends on how much money your family has. The judge will set a bond. I'll do my best to keep it down, but I'm expecting she'll set it at a million or so."

"A million bucks? You aren't serious, man! I didn't do it!"

"Keep your voice down!" Sam hissed. "The judge sets a bond based on her assessment of whether you are a flight risk and whether you pose a danger to the community. This is a murder charge and you're not from here."

"That's bullshit, man, I—"

"Davonte."

"I didn't do it, man. This is a bunch—"

"Davonte."

"White bread mother—"

"Davonte!" Sam barked.

"Yeah?"

"Think of this like a basketball game. There's two ways we can do this. One, you can piss and moan about the rules, the referees, and who we are playing. Or two, we can prepare the best we can to play the game, so to speak. How do you want to go? You want to help me, or not?"

Davonte nodded in understanding. "What do you need to know?" he asked.

"Let's start with everything good about you."

14

Later that morning Sam was loading his briefcase with the materials he would need for Davonte's initial appearance. When he was ready to go, he stopped in Paul's office. "You ready to go? Hearing's in twenty minutes."

"Why don't you handle this one?" Paul asked. "I just got a letter from an out-of-state attorney who is making noise about contesting a will I did twenty years ago. I better see what's going on here. Try to head this one off at the pass."

"Okay, got it."

"Good luck. And don't get run over by one of those protesters."

"What's that?" Sam asked.

"Didn't you see that gathering of idiots when you came in this morning?" Paul asked.

"No. It was still dark when I got here."

"Oh, yeah. Must've been thirty or forty clowns marching around, carrying signs and chanting."

"Whose side are they on?"

"Not yours."

"Nice."

Walking down the street from his office to the court-house, it occurred to Sam that he probably should have called court security to see if they would open the back door for him. He was pulling his phone from his pocket when a couple of the protesters saw him, pointed, and began moving toward him. Feeling his pulse quicken, he replaced his phone and then touched the pistol he'd put in a shoulder holster that morning. He hit the steps at a near-run, ignoring the insults and invectives hurled his way. "Good morning, Deputy," he said, and placed his briefcase on the belt to the metal detector. "You need me to empty my pockets?"

"No, Sam, I don't. Are you carrying?"

"I am."

"Okay, walk around the machine to the left here, okay? I don't want to start a riot by you lighting this place up."

"Thanks."

"No problem. Just remember, your carry permit for this building expires the day after the jury comes back."

"Got it."

Sam followed the deputy's instructions and was inside the courthouse a few seconds later. As always, he was struck by the grandeur of the place. Stone wainscoting complemented floors of gray marble. Ornate ceiling fans thirty feet above the gathering crowds circulated air. At opposite ends of the building, broad curving stairways led to the second-floor district court courtroom. He made his way down the hall to Judge Downs's courtroom while courthouse security, augmented by contracted off-duty law enforcement, struggled to keep onlookers in line. Sam nodded at head custodian Jack Fricke and his assistant as he made his way to the courtroom double doors. "Good morning Mr. Johnstone," the assistant—widely known as "Frac"—said shyly.

"Good morning," Sam replied, and flashed the young man a tight smile.

Judge Downs's first-floor courtroom was approximately half the size of Judge Daniels's second-floor courtroom. Perhaps fifty feet on a side, it was a windowless square dominated by the judge's raised bench, adjacent to which was a witness box. On the other side of that was the jury box. A lectern in almost the exact center of the courtroom was flanked by two library-type tables that would soon be occupied by the attorneys and parties from the prosecution and defense. Several chairs were arranged at each library table. Sam removed the items he'd need from his briefcase, then sat at the defense table, took a deep breath, and looked toward the ceiling and closed his eyes. Behind him, serving to separate the trial's active participants from the audience, was a waist-high divider known as "the bar." Since the mid-twentieth century, all courtrooms in Wyoming contained such a barrier. The rows of seats behind him were filled with observers. Cathy Schmidt arrived with Rebecca Nice and Chief Buck Lucas in tow. Sam stood and shook hands with Cathy. "Good morning," he said.

"Good morning, Sam," she replied, and he couldn't help but think of the stark professional contrast between Cathy and Ann Fulks, who had prosecuted the case against Tommy Olsen. So far, Cathy had impressed him as a smart, tough-but-fair prosecutor.

The parties waited for approximately five minutes before court security officers brought Davonte into the courtroom. Sam could hear the intake of air into the lungs of the observers as his client entered. Davonte's hands were restrained in front of him and each foot was connected to the other by a length of chain that allowed him to walk relatively normally but would impede his ability to run. Because the legs on the jumpsuit were designed for a normal-sized man, the white, jail-issued socks were visible all the way to their tops. Sam stood and pulled Davonte's chair back and seated him, then sat beside him and put his arm around the young man's shoulders. It was an old trick, designed to show anyone observing that Davonte was a human being. "All right, just as we discussed, okay?"

"I got it."

"Okay. Remember: just sit and listen and answer when she questions you," Sam reminded Davonte. "No commentary. Every question will require only a yes or no response. That's it."

"You told me all this yesterday, man."

"I did. I'm telling you again because it is important," Sam insisted. "You can't afford to dork this up."

"You want me to play the game."

"I don't really care," Sam said. "It might be worth one hundred thousand bucks for you to fake it—but you be you."

"My mom here?" Davonte asked, starting to turn around.

"Look straight ahead, just like I told you," Sam said. "Your mom, Reggie, and Damon are two rows back on our side on the aisle. You can nod to them as you are being led out after this hearing. That's it."

"Gotcha."

"All rise," the bailiff said as Downs entered. Sam and Davonte joined everyone in standing.

"Thank you, ladies and gentlemen. Please be seated," Downs ordered. "Court is in session. The first matter before the court is State of Wyoming versus Davonte Blair." Downs, as a circuit court judge, didn't have the jurisdiction to take a plea. Instead, the purpose of the hearing was to ensure Davonte understood his rights, the charges, and the possible penalty should he plead or be found guilty, and—since he had already retained Sam—to set the terms of his pre-trial release. "Mr. Blair, would you please step to the podium?"

Davonte rose and shuffled to the podium, followed by Sam. "Your Honor, Sam Johnstone, appearing for the defendant."

"Thank you, Mr. Johnstone. Have you been retained?" she asked. She was nervous, Sam thought. Her first big case; she had a slight quiver in her voice.

"I have, Judge."

"Well, if Mr. Blair has already retained you, we'll be able to dispense with a lot of what is usually covered and then we'll talk about the terms and conditions of pre-trial release."

"Yes, ma'am."

"Your client may be reached through you, Mr. Johnstone?"

"Yes, ma'am."

"Will Mr. Blair waive an advisal of rights?"

"He will, Your Honor."

"Thank you, counsel," Downs said. "Mr. Blair, you are here pursuant to an Information and Warrant alleging you are guilty of one count of first-degree murder, a violation of Wyoming Statute—"

"Your Honor, my client will waive a verbatim reading—" Sam began.

"Thank you, Mr. Johnstone," Downs said. "Not on my watch. Anything else?"

"No, Judge." Sam waited while Downs read the statute for first-degree murder and the warrant verbatim. "Mr. Blair, do you understand all that?"

"Yes, ma'am," Davonte said.

"Thank you, Mr. Blair." Downs moved the file aside. "Does the State have a recommendation for bond?"

Sam and Davonte sat at their table while Cathy rose and stepped to the podium. "Your Honor, as the court knows, Mr.

Blair has been charged with first-degree murder. While the State is still trying to determine whether to seek the death penalty, this is the most serious crime on the books. A young man has lost his life. Mr. Blair does have a prior record, albeit a minor one. For that reason, we would ask that the court allow no bond, and order him held until trial."

Downs had been taking notes. She thanked Cathy, then looked to Sam and asked, "Mr. Johnstone, does the defendant care to respond?"

"Your Honor," Sam replied, putting down his writing materials and walking to the podium. "As the court well knows, my client is presumed innocent until proven otherwise. Mr. Blair denies this charge and looks forward to the opportunity to defend himself. He is a college student athlete and a promising basketball player. His family is here today, and they provide him with the support and backing he needs. His mother has informed me she intends to rent an apartment to be on hand until this matter is over. His criminal record is such that it merits no discussion. My client would be amenable to curfew, and given his lack of a criminal history, we believe that curfew, combined with an electronic monitoring device he would gladly pay for, would be sufficient to ensure my client would appear for all further hearings on this cause and would present no threat to the community. We would ask that you set a reasonable bond, and we feel a bond in the amount of one hundred thousand dollars with the conditions I've outlined would be sufficient."

"Thank you, counsel," Downs said, while completing the bond form in front of her. "Having heard and considered the arguments of counsel, this court is going to hold the defendant in lieu of one million dollars, cash only." She looked up and waited while the audience quieted. "The primary considerations are the nature of the allegation and the defendant's limited contacts with Custer. Mr. Blair, you are remanded to the custody of the detention center pending trial."

Sam had prepared Davonte for the prospect of a high cash bond. To his credit, Davonte didn't flinch. "Davonte, I'll be over to see you tonight. Hang tight. We'll move for a modification when you get bound over. Could be a week or so."

"I'll be out tonight."

"Seriously?"

"Mom will have me out tonight." Davonte winked at Sam and was led away. When he was out of the courtroom, the spectators rose and left as well, eager to discuss the events they had just witnessed.

Sam remained behind, gathering his materials and thinking about what Davonte had said. "I should've charged more," he said aloud.

"I'm sure you got plenty," Cathy said. He hadn't noticed her walk up. She smiled. "I hated having to make the overhead every month when I was in private practice. What a pain in the ass."

"Yeah." Sam shook his head. "Just out of curiosity, what's the big downside to prosecuting?"

"Answering to the public," Cathy said. "I can deal with the long hours, relatively low pay, bureaucracy, and all of that. But . . . you know they've already figured out I'm prosecuting? I had people camped out in front of my house all night. Lights, noise—I could hardly get Kayla to sleep."

"That's unfair. How old is she?"

"Nine."

"Assholes—they couldn't care less."

"I mean, I'm not unsympathetic to the cause, right?" She poured water from a pitcher into a plastic glass and drank deeply from it. "I'm a woman, a member of a historically disenfranchised group and all that. But how does it help your cause to keep me awake all night? I have the gay supporters on one side of the street and the black supporters on the other. I'm in the middle, just trying to live my life, raise my kid, and do my job, you know?"

"That's not good enough for the zealots," Sam said. "But for the record, you do a great job, from what I can tell."

"Thanks." Cathy tossed the cup in a wastebasket and shouldered her bag. "I appreciate it. Doesn't mean I'm not going to kick your ass," she added. "But I appreciate it."

"I should have charged *way* more," Sam said to her back as she left.

"Why is that?" This time, it was Veronica. He hadn't seen her since he'd tried to talk with her weeks prior. She had apparently entered the courtroom while he was talking with Cathy.

"Uh, just talking smack," he said. "How . . . how are you?"

"I'm fine," she said. She was policing up the pitchers of water and cups on the two tables. "Hand me that pitcher?"

"Sure," he said, then added, "Are you okay?"

"I'm okay. How about you?"

"I'm fine. Better," he added.

"Really?"

"Yes, really," he said.

She looked at him for a moment. "Look, I've got to get this done and get back in chambers with the judge."

"I understand," he said. It was awkward. "Can I call you?"

She continued to stare at him, but she was not weighing her options. "Not yet. I'm not ready," she said, turning. "Take care of yourself, Sam."

"I promise," he said to her back as she left the courtroom.

Outside the courtroom, the press was ready with cameras and microphones. "Mr. Johnstone, how are you feeling about the bond set by the judge?"

"The charge is first-degree murder. The court has a balancing act to perform. Obviously, the amount is more than we would like, but we are not going to question the court's judgment."

"Are you confident your client, as an African-American, can get a fair trial in this community?" Penrose asked.

"I am," Sam said. "My client is not guilty of this charge. I believe any jury, anywhere, would acquit him."

"What do you say to the parents of the young gay man who was killed, allegedly by Mr. Blair?"

"That I'm sorry for their loss and hope that law enforcement can find out who did this," Sam replied.

"Cathy Schmidt says the State has arrested the right man, and that justice will be served." Another reporter stuck the microphone in Sam's face.

Sam stood quietly, looking at the reporter. "What's the question?" he asked.

"What is your response?" she asked impatiently.

"I believe the prosecutor is mistaken."

"Will justice be served?"

"I believe it will, and I believe that in this case, justice will be best served by the acquittal of Davonte Blair—if the State does not drop the charges before the trial. Now, if you will excuse me," he said, and side-stepped the reporters, quickly leaving the courthouse and ignoring the shouted questions.

"How did it go?" Paul asked Sam after he got back from the hearing. They were passing in the hallway between their offices.

"Fine," Sam said. "I think Judge Downs is starting to get in the swing of things. She set it at a million. I did a quick interview with the press."

"Cash?"

"Yeah. Davonte did well. Didn't move a muscle, kept his cool," Sam explained. "I was happy with how he handled himself."

"I'm glad you spoke to the press—they've been calling all morning," Paul said. "I guess you can move Daniels for a modification when he gets bound over, huh?"

"Davonte says his mom will make that bond."

"Seriously? We should've asked for a bigger fee!"

"That's what I said," Sam replied. "I don't know whether he is full of it or not. Sharon obviously has money, but I don't know if she's got that much lying around. I almost worry about him getting out. I don't think he realizes just how serious this is."

"Well, we'll see," Paul said, stepping around Sam. "I gotta go see Daniels. I've got an easement I'm trying to get done for the Scott family. They've got a land-locked parcel and the other party is being dick-ish."

"No surprise," Sam said under his breath. He walked down to his office, dropped his briefcase, and sat down. After checking his email, he looked desultorily through his in-box. Starting the day with an initial appearance on a first-degree murder charge was going to make everything else seem unimportant, but it all paid the bills and had to be done. He was going through his correspondence when he came across an unopened envelope with no return address—only the word "PERSONAL" and his misspelled name typed in all capital letters on the front. He slit open the envelope and blew into it, then extracted the folded piece of paper and read: MR. JOHN-STON, YOU ARE A THIRD-RATE LAWYER. YOU DEFEND KILLERS! WHAT THE HELL IS WRONG WITH YOU? WE WANT TO LIVE AS WE PLEASE! WE NO EVERYTHING YOU DO AND EVERYWHERE YOU GO. WE ARE WATCHING YOU.

"Well, that's pleasant," Sam said. He pushed the button on his office intercom, summoning Cassie. "The least you could do if you are going to threaten me is to spell my name right." When Cassie arrived, he asked her, "Where did this letter come from? There's no stamp or return address on it."

"Someone just dropped it through that old mail slot in the front door. Why? Is there a problem? I didn't open it because it said 'personal.'"

"You did the right thing. Nothing to worry about. Just some fan mail." He faked a smile. "Please take these with you," he said, handing her a stack of signed letters to mail. "And close the door, if you would."

Late that evening, Sam was finishing the installation of a home security system in his townhouse when his phone rang. It was an unfamiliar area code, but on a whim, he answered it.

"Yo, Sam, I just wanted to tell you I bounced," Davonte said.

"Wow. Not sure the last time anyone in this jurisdiction made a million cash bond," Sam said. "Can you meet me in my office? I think we probably need to talk."

"Sure. But right now, me and Damon and Reggie got some pizza ordered. Gonna catch up."

Sam was thinking there was no way the college would

allow Davonte in the dorms. "Where are you staying? You're going to need a place."

"Naw, man," Davonte said. "I've made myself eligible for the draft and hired an agent. He's gonna front me some cash to get my own crib. Me and my boys gonna live there."

"I'm not sure that's such a good idea," Sam said. "But let's talk tomorrow. And Davonte?"

"Yeah?"

"You should know I received a letter this morning," Sam said. He read the contents aloud and waited for a reaction. Hearing none, he continued. "Looks to be the result of my representing you."

"You gonna quit?" Davonte asked.

"Of course not, but keep your head down," Sam cautioned. "Be quiet and be aware of what's going on around you. Kaiden and his family have a lot of supporters here in town, and emotions are running high."

"I got it, Sam," Davonte said. "But I got my boys here now to take care of me. Now, we got some catching up to do."

"See you tomorrow—and Davonte?"

"Yeah?"

"A possession or use charge would result in your bond getting revoked," Sam reminded his client. "I doubt even your mom has enough money to get you out if that happens."

"Got it, boss."

15

The next morning, Sam, Paul, and Davonte were in Sam's office. "You got through the night okay?" Sam asked.

"I got my protection." Davonte nodded to the front of the building. Reggie and Damon—much to Paul's consternation—were cooling their heels in the waiting room.

"Yeah, about that," Paul said. "I want you to leave them home when you come to meet with us. They make my other clients uncomfortable."

"Because they're black?"

"No, because they sprawl over two or three chairs watching videos at full volume like a couple of assholes," Paul said. He and Davonte stared hard at each other until Sam spoke up.

"Okay," Sam said. "Davonte, leave them home or outside. I'm sure they've got something else to do. Frankly, we're probably not going to be meeting a lot here the next couple of months. It's the Christmas season, so the courts will slow down. Paul and his family will have things to do. We'll get back into the swing of things in January when Paul and I will start getting ready for trial. We'll need your input from time to time, but by and large this will be a lawyer deal for a while."

"So, no time for me, huh?"

"Jesus Christ, didn't you hear what he just said?" Paul exploded. "You spend your life trying to be offended! Just do what we tell you."

"I ain't your boy, dude. I'm your client."

"Right, and we don't need you," Paul said. "Remember that."

"Gentlemen, we need to focus here," Sam said. "Davonte, we need to start working up a defense. Now, there are essentially three strategies we can use. The first is that someone else did it. That's—"

"That's the one," Davonte said. "End of story."

"No, that's not the end of story," Paul said. "Let the man finish."

"I didn't do it," Davonte insisted. "Therefore, someone else had to. That's like, logical—right?"

"Perhaps," Sam said, looking at Paul and trying to reassure him. "The second defense is, 'I did it, but I was not in control at the time.'"

"What, like, I was crazy or something?" Davonte asked.

"Something like that, yeah," Sam said.

"But I wasn't. I didn't do it. I keep telling you that."

"The third way," Sam continued, "is that you did it, but you had justification."

"Like what?"

"Like self-defense," Sam said. "Like maybe he was assaulting you, and you—"

"That little faggot?" Davonte waved his hand dismissively.

"Seriously?" Sam asked. "You seriously are going to use terms like that when your life is literally on the line?"

"What?"

"Davonte, what you just said is homophobic as hell," Paul said. "Surely you know that?"

"I don't know what that word means, but I ain't queer," Davonte said.

"Jesus Christ!" Paul exploded. He turned to Sam. "It's going to be impossible with this guy."

"What are you talking about, man? 'This guy?'" Davonte said, standing. Paul stood as well, and the two men again squared off.

"Just a minute," Sam said, putting a hand on each man's chest. "At this point, it is safe to say neither of you is going to roll over and show his belly, so this is getting us nowhere. Sit down." He waited until they had complied. "Let's go back to our discussion from a few days ago in the jail. Davonte, you said you saw Miles leave after that little party, right?"

"That's right."

"You said you never saw him after that?" Paul asked.

"That's right."

"You ever touch him or any of his stuff?"

"No. Why would I?" Davonte asked.

"But you two got in a fight before he left?"

"No, man. We had a little argument, but that's all."

"Over what?" Paul asked.

Davonte looked at Paul and then Sam. "You know why. I'm sure your kid told you. Over money. I owed him a little money."

"How much?" Paul asked.

Again, Davonte looked at Sam before answering. "I don't know. That's what the argument was about."

"According to Ronnie, you owed him a lot."

"No sweat." Davonte shrugged. "He ain't gonna testify, man."

"Why not?"

"He knows better."

"Are you kidding me?" Paul burst out. "Sam, he's either

threatening a witness—who just happens to be my son—or he is suborning perjury!" He sat back, folded his arms, and crossed his legs.

"If he does testify, it won't hurt me." Davonte shrugged again, then looked at Paul and Sam in turn. "I'm just sayin'."

Sam looked at Davonte for a long time before he continued with his questions. "So, you never fought?"

"No."

"How'd you get the bruises and scratches on your hands Detective Polson mentioned in his affidavit of probable cause?"

"Playin' hoops, man," Davonte said. "I told Polson that."

"How do you explain that the college's surveillance video shows you following Miles across campus the night he disappeared?"

"Coincidence, man. It's a small campus." Davonte looked at Sam and then Paul. "Be cool. Those two won't testify against me."

Sam sat back and looked at Davonte for a long moment. "You've said that twice now. Davonte, we can't count on that. We have to believe they will testify. I'll come back to that in a minute. Now, Davonte, you said you didn't see Kaiden after he left the room."

"That's right."

"But that's not true, is it?" Seeing Davonte's look of surprise, he continued. "According to the affidavit of probable cause, Detective Polson pinged your phone and subpoenaed your phone records. They show your phone in the area where Miles's body was found on the night he disappeared. How do you explain that?"

"Someone took my phone, man," Davonte said.

"You have got to be shitting me!" Paul said.

"Hold on, Paul." Sam held his hand up toward Paul and

looked to Davonte. "Davonte, are you telling me that someone just happened to take your phone on the night that Miles disappeared, and they just happened to be in the vicinity of where the guy's body was found, with your phone?"

"Yeah, man."

"This is bullshit," Paul muttered.

"What's your problem, man?" Davonte's eyes narrowed.

"My problem is you are a damned liar."

"Whoa, mother—"

"Gentlemen, I'm going to remind you, we're all on the same team here," Sam said.

"Sam, you know this is crap!" Paul said. He waved his arms. "We're wasting our time."

"Let me finish," Sam replied, then turned to Davonte. "I'm having some trouble here. Remember when you told me you never touched any of Miles's stuff?"

"Yeah?"

"Then how do you explain your DNA on the watch cap found at the scene?"

"I don't. I never touched his hat," Davonte said. "I got my own. We all do."

"Did you hear me? I said *your* DNA is on *his* stuff."

"I can't explain that," Davonte said. "You're the lawyer. Maybe I saw it, picked it up, looked at it, and dropped it."

"It was next to his body. So it had been covered with snow for the two weeks he was missing." Sam watched Davonte closely. "Meaning you had to have touched it before he disappeared. But then, I think maybe you know that, and yet, you keep telling me you didn't know him."

"I didn't *know* him, man, but I *knew* him. Know what I'm saying?" Davonte said.

"For Christ's sake," Paul said.

"Let me ask you something else, Davonte," Sam began.

"Who is picking up the tab for your apartment and living expenses?"

"My agent."

"So, it's one thing to declare for the draft—you can always go back," Sam began. "Unless you sign with an agent. Then it's a one-way street."

"Right on, Sam."

"So, you've committed yourself. You don't get drafted as high as you want—or at all—and you're done in college," Sam mused.

"My boy says that isn't gonna happen."

"So it's a draw against expected future earnings."

"Right on. I can't lose," Davonte said. "Why do you wanna know?"

"Because I'm sure Detective Polson already knows, and I want to know everything he knows." Sam looked at his notepad and then back at Davonte. "So, he wasn't paying your expenses when Miles disappeared?"

"No. I just told you that."

"So, let me ask you this. You are a non-qualifier—I get that. But why are you here? Why not red shirt for a year?"

"No game action, know what I'm sayin'?"

"I hear you," Sam said. "What about overseas? Aren't there guys taking their game overseas right out of high school?"

"Yeah, but they don't have my mom." He shook his head.

"That makes sense," Sam said. Paul had gotten up and was looking out the window. Sam could almost see the tension in his shoulders. "Developmental league an option?"

"Chump change, man."

"So, your mother didn't think you were ready to be on your own overseas. I get it. So we here in Custer get a future NBA draft choice for a year. One and done, huh?"

"One and done, baby," Davonte repeated, and smiled,

showing his straight white teeth for one of the few times since Sam had known him. "Do my time and get the hell out of this shit-hole."

"Well, I personally cannot wait to see your ass heading east," Paul snapped. He turned from the window and pointed at Davonte.

"Man, I've about had all of you I'm willing to take," Davonte said, reaching for Paul's outstretched hand, which was quickly withdrawn. "Get him out of my face, Sam."

"I think we're done for today," Sam said. "Both of you need to cool off. Davonte, we're gonna need to talk again. Your story is not matching what I think the evidence shows."

"Sam, I—" Davonte started to say, but stopped when Sam put up his hand.

"I'll walk you out," Sam said, and opened the door. Davonte walked slowly down the hall, followed by Sam and Paul. When they got to the waiting room, Sam took one look at the three old women crowded together in one corner, and the two younger men sitting with their legs splayed wide, taking three chairs each, and knew there would be no stopping Paul.

"Get the hell out of my office!" Paul barked.

Reggie and Damon looked at Davonte, then at Sam, and then at Paul before moving. At last they stood, put their phones in their pockets, and followed Davonte out the door. "Tell your client," Paul said to Sam, "to leave those two wherever he found them before he comes back." Then, turning to the three ladies, he cooed, "It's the Morrison sisters. I am so sorry for my language. Please forgive me, ladies, and come on back to my conference room. Can I get anyone anything? Water? Coffee?"

Sam gradually opened his eyes, straining to see through a sort of fog. His mouth was dry, his head was pounding, and his stomach was doing flip-flops. He put on his leg and struggled to his feet, then made his way quickly to the bathroom and vomited. After washing up, he drank a glass of water, then brushed his teeth, showered, and ran a comb through his hair before dressing. He made a pot of coffee and then sat back down in the chair where he'd slept. While listening to the coffee brew he tried to recount the events of the evening. He grabbed his phone and examined it, beginning to remember some of the calls he'd made. He couldn't really remember what all he had said, but he could recall enough to know the call to Veronica had been a huge mistake. He thought about what to do while he poured and drank the first cup, then threw up again. It was going to be a long day. Might as well get it over with, he thought, and dialed her number.

"Hello?" Veronica said.

"Hi," he offered. "I'm calling to apologize."

Because there was no response, he continued. "Listen, I got a little wasted—"

"A little?" Veronica asked. "You were out of your mind."

"Yeah, vodka does that," he said. "Look, I'm sorry. I was just drunk and—"

"And trying to get me to hook up with you."

"Well, yeah, but there was more to it than that. I was hoping you might want to come over and talk, and maybe—"

"Well, you weren't talking about talking last night, Sam. That was a straight-up booty-call," she said.

"I might have said some dumb stuff—"

"You did."

"But I didn't mean anything by it," he said. She was quiet, so he went on. "Look, I miss you. I miss us. I've been working on some stuff."

"Well, how is it you were drunk last night if you are 'working on stuff?'"

"I just . . . I just had a couple of New Year's Eve drinks and I guess I lost count."

"Sam, I am uncomfortable around you when you drink. You get . . . I don't know. Sad. Weird. Scary."

"I'm sorry."

"I know, Sam," she said. "But that's not good enough. You said some hurtful, stupid things that indicate to me that what you want is not the same thing I want."

"I said I'm sorry. Can we get together and talk about this?" He sipped coffee and waited.

"No."

"Seriously?"

"Yes," she said.

"Veronica, I made a mistake. I need you to—"

"Sam, you're not the only one with needs. I can't do this. Don't call me."

Sam started to speak, but the line was dead. "Sonuvabitch!" he yelled.

———

"Davonte," Sam said. "Have a seat. How are things, considering?"

Paul and Davonte had joined Sam in his office. It had been a couple of weeks since their last meeting, and Sam wanted to touch base.

"Just ready to get this over with and get the hell out of here, man." Davonte was on Sam's couch with his legs extended, staring at the wall hangings. One in particular caught his attention. It was a picture of Sam rounding third after hitting a home run in college. "You play?"

"I did. *We* did." Sam gestured toward Paul and then himself. "That's where Paul and I met."

"What'd you play?"

"Outfield. Paul here was a pitcher. A good one."

"You look like an outfielder," Davonte said, ignoring Paul. "I always liked baseball. Probably more than basketball. But when you're 6'9", well, people be pushing you one way, you know what I mean?"

"Sounds like you got pushed in the right direction," Sam said, looking at an irritated and insulted Paul. "Now, we need to talk about the hearing next week. It's called a preliminary hearing. The purpose is for the judge to determine whether there is probable cause to believe a crime was committed and you committed it. Understand?"

"I think so."

"So, the State will just put an officer on, and he'll testify to what he and others saw, heard, and found out. If the judge decides that there is probable cause, then you'll get bound over to district court, which is where trial will be."

"What if she don't?"

"She will," Paul said.

Davonte ignored Paul and repeated, "What if she don't?"

"Well, I tend to agree with Paul—she will. All they have to show is that a reasonable person could believe Miles was murdered and you did it. It's a low bar."

"That's bullshit, man. Why not just skip it?"

"Well, we could," Sam said. "But I don't generally like to do that."

"Why not?"

"Well, I like to hear what the State's witnesses are going to say. Gives me a head start on preparation for trial, and we can lock down some testimony."

"So, my trial has to be held, like, speedy or whatever, right?" Davonte asked.

"Well, the 180 days start from your arraignment in district court. That will happen after you get bound over."

"What? My 180 days ain't started yet?" Davonte asked.

"Not yet," Sam said.

"Then bind me over, man!" Davonte said. "Let's skip it! If you already know what's going to happen, why do it?"

"I'd like to see if we could gain some information," Paul said.

"Does that happen?" Davonte asked.

"Not usually," Sam admitted. "The prosecution plays things pretty close to the vest."

"Sam, I need this shit behind me before the draft!" Davonte said. "Let's skip this and get to district court. What I gotta sign?"

"Just a waiver."

"Let's do it."

Sam looked at Paul. "What do you think?"

"We waive a right, things go bad, we're up to our ass in alligators with the malpractice insurer. It's not smart," Paul concluded.

"Ain't bright to waste time and energy on a foregone conclusion, is it?" Davonte asked.

Sam thought about it for a minute. "We waive this, you get bound over, we are on our way," he explained to Davonte. "That speeds up the clock with us a little bit in the dark. Your choice."

"What's the surest way to have this behind me the quickest?"

"Plead to manslaughter," Paul interjected.

"Man, be serious." Davonte waved a dismissive hand at Paul. "Besides pleading to something I did not do, I mean."

"That's a discussion we will need to have," Sam said. "Pleading to a lesser."

"Ain't happenin'."

Sam watched Davonte closely, then looked to Paul. "All right. That's good for today," Sam said, standing. "Hang out in the waiting area. I'll have Cassie draft a waiver of preliminary hearing, we'll sign it, and I'll get it filed today. We should be getting a call by early next week with a setting for the arraignment. That will start your 180-day clock ticking."

"The sooner the better, man. The draft is in June. I got workouts to attend."

Something—perhaps the chili or the several beers or both—was bothering Sam's stomach. He'd been rolling around in his bed for an hour when at 3:15 a.m. he finally sat up, attached his leg, and made his way to the small kitchen, where he took a spoonful of baking soda in a little water. Remembering to remain upright or face a potential volcanic upchuck, he wandered the house for some time before sitting down at his desk and checking the college basketball scores, and then the news. The Colorado Rockies had (again) made no move in free agency; the Middle East was (again/still) in an uproar; domestically, politicians were (as always) at odds; and locally funding was (forever) insufficient for various projects being considered.

His email wasn't any better. His inbox was filled with unsolicited ads from travel companies, fly-fishing product manufacturers, insurance reminders, and men's health companies promising both renewed youth and sexual prowess. He spent some time deleting the spam and thought briefly about sending Veronica a note before thinking better of it and closing the laptop. He stood and stretched, debating whether to try and go back to sleep or to give it up, shower, get dressed, and go into the office. He had a hearing at ten a.m. on a contract dispute, so he decided to try and get a little sleep. He turned out the light in the kitchen, and while walking to the window, took a quick look outside and thought he saw something moving in the junipers lining the driveway.

He dropped below the level of the window and moved to the entranceway of the townhouse, drew the pistol from the holster hanging on the door handle, and moved back to the kitchen, staying low. Leaning over the counter, he put his face as close as possible to the sill and peered out with one eye. He scanned the area where he had seen movement for a couple of minutes but saw nothing. He donned his shoes and walked through the house, out the back door, and into the small space serving as a backyard. Keeping as close as possible to the side of the house, he slowly worked his way around the back, scanning every inch of the perimeter for signs of an unseen enemy and vowing silently to buy the newest in night vision optics if given the chance. Having cleared the backyard, he performed the same drill up the side of the townhouse, until he was at the front corner and in position to the junipers if he moved his head enough to look around the corner. He was getting ready to risk a look when movement in the lilacs bordering the yard caught his attention. He swung the pistol to the target in time to see a large black housecat scramble over the fence and into his neighbor Bill's yard. The cat's movement was detected by Bill's security system, which illuminated, bathing Sam—who tried to minimize his exposure by pressing up against the wall —in blinding light. Hiding was futile, so he retreated to his home as quickly as possible, fearful every step would be his last. He was inside and still breathing heavily when his phone rang. Looking at the number, he saw it was Bill, and answered.

"This is Sam."

"Sam, what the hell are you doing?" Bill asked. "I saw you running around with a gun outside. What's going on?"

"I, uh, thought I saw someone."

"Well, did you call the cops?"

"No."

"Why the hell not?" Bill asked.

"I was, uh, gonna take care of it myself."

"Damn, Sam. This isn't Iraq or whatever. You see someone, you can call a cop," Bill said, adding, "You okay?"

"I'm fine. I'm fine. I'll talk to you tomorrow."

"Okay, Sam. Take care of yourself, now."

Sam hung up, then walked around the house and checked all the doors. He ate a bowl of cereal and took a couple of hydrocodone, then sat down on the toilet and took off his leg. He hopped in the shower, then got dressed and made his lunch, which—since Veronica had stopped seeing him—he had been eating in the office. While backing his truck out of the drive, he had a thought. He grabbed a flashlight, got out, and walked over to the juniper bushes lining the drive. In the small circle of light, he noted footprints in the dirt considerably larger than his own size 12s. He remembered the note.

16

It was early February and Sam was in his office pouring coffee and getting increasingly irritable. Davonte's tardiness had become habitual, and Sam was mentally rehearsing the ass-chewing he was going to deliver when Cassie called to let him know Davonte had arrived. In January, Davonte had been arraigned, bond had been continued, and the trial had been set—at Davonte's request—for May. The clock was ticking. Sam took a couple of deep breaths and vowed to practice the relaxation techniques Martinez had given him. In the meanwhile, when Davonte finally arrived, he decided to overlook his lateness one more time and focus instead on the positive. "So, Davonte, tell me what's going on."

"You know," Davonte began. "Hanging out, shooting some hoops, working out, playing some video. I'm pretty good at this one war game. Think I'da been a pretty good soldier. Maybe better than you."

Sam took a deep breath and let it out. "So, we need to talk a little bit. I want to run through some scenarios with you."

"Like what?"

"Like what happens if you get convicted."

"Didn't do it." Davonte shrugged. "Ain't gonna happen."

"What if it does?"

"Then you did a shitty job."

"Okay, so let's say I do a shitty job and you get convicted," Sam said. "Right now, the State isn't seeking the death penalty, so you understand you could get life in prison with no possibility of parole, right?"

"I understand it—but I don't see it happening, because I didn't do it, man."

"So," Sam said, ignoring Davonte for the moment. "Worst-case scenario is you go away for life without possibility of parole. Best case is you go away for life, with the possibility of getting out at some point on parole. Like, way down the road."

"Not happenin'," Davonte insisted.

"That's first degree. Mandatory life sentence," Sam said. Davonte was looking at his nails while Sam spoke. "Now, just so you know, I don't see that happening. I think the State over-charged this. I think the most that could be proved is second degree. You get second degree, and you're looking at anywhere from twenty years to life."

"Still not happenin'," Davonte said, biting at the nail on an index finger.

"So, second degree, worst case is life with parole," Sam explained. "Best case is twenty years in the can—get me?"

"Got it, boss."

"Now, the next step down is manslaughter. That's punishable by up to twenty years—are you listening to me? Because we're not having this discussion for *my* benefit," Sam said. Davonte was looking at his phone. "Put your damned phone away and listen or find yourself another boy!"

"Dude, relax. It's my agent."

"Really?" Sam said. "Then go ahead and take the call."

"Yeah?" Davonte said, and prepared to push "send."

"Yeah. Ask him what the market is for sixty-year-old ballplayers," Sam began. "Because if you don't start taking this shit seriously, you're gonna be the baddest dude on the basketball court in Rawlins."

"What's Rawlins?" Davonte asked.

"That's the location of the Wyoming State Penitentiary."

Reluctantly, Davonte put the phone in his pocket. "You a hard man, Sam."

"Harder than you know. Now, listen up for a minute. I think I could maybe get the State to agree to a ten-year sentence for manslaughter. You are young, you've got no serious record, and you'll be under thirty when you—"

"No, damnit!"

"—get out," Sam finished. He leaned forward and looked Davonte in the eye. "Davonte, I'm going to do the best I can. But twelve people—twelve regular, ordinary people—are going to decide what happened. I cannot guarantee results."

"I didn't do it!" Davonte was on his feet now. Sam was afraid Davonte's hair was going to get caught in the ceiling fan. "I am innocent!"

"Lower your voice and sit down," Sam commanded. Davonte sat down hard, like a scolded child might.

"Sam, I'm telling you, I didn't do this. I did not kill Kaiden."

"I understand what you are telling me, okay?" Sam softened his voice. "Look, it doesn't happen as often as television and movie types would like us to believe, but innocent people do get convicted. The choice is this: you can swallow hard and do maybe ten years, or you can roll the dice and possibly do life without parole."

Davonte looked down at his expensive sneakers for a

moment. He had tears in his eyes when he again looked at Sam. "You don't understand. I've worked my whole life for this. I'm almost there. I didn't do this," he said, shaking his head. "It's like a nightmare. I just want to get through this and get onto my dream of playing in the NBA."

He was either one hell of an actor, Sam thought, or he was showing real emotion for the first time. "Davonte, think it over. Talk to Sharon. I'm just saying it might be better to delay your dream and ensure a life worth living, versus taking a risk and having it all taken away—possibly forever."

"I can't do it, Sam." Davonte shook his head again. "I can't admit to something I didn't do. Not the way she raised me."

"We don't have to decide anything today. Hell, the State hasn't even made us an offer yet. I just wanted to get you to understand what's at stake here."

"I understand, Sam. Look, man, don't ever think I don't know what's at stake. It's my entire life, man!"

"I got it," Sam said, standing. Davonte extended his hand —a first. Sam took it and held it tightly. "Now get out of here," he said. "And make good choices."

"Thanks. I will," Davonte said. "You got somewhere I can clean up? I don't want. . . well, my boys. . ." He wiped his eyes with the back of his hand.

"Down the hall," Sam said. "Third door."

Moments later, Sam watched as Davonte crossed the street to where Reggie and Damon were waiting. Apparently, Paul had run them off for good. Davonte walked up to them, running his mouth and acting like he had the world by the tail. Damon looked at Sam, then looked at Davonte. Sam noted Damon was wearing workout clothes featuring the Custer College logo, complemented by black basketball shoes. The shoes were large—like twin black limousines large.

A few days later, Sam was in court with David Ebert, a client who was a terrible alcoholic. This was a guy, Sam thought, whose story could be in the back of the Blue Book. He'd been convicted nine times for driving under the influence, most recently less than a year prior. Because his most recent conviction was a felony, Ebert had been sentenced by Daniels, who'd given him three years. Daniels had suspended two years and ordered Ebert to serve one year in the Custer County jail, a sentence referred to as a "split." Ebert had spent the year behind bars and had gotten out just three weeks ago. He was appearing this morning on charges of violating his probation. According to the affidavit, he'd found a way to drink and drive again by defeating the Intoxilyzer in his car. Sam hadn't had much of a chance to talk with Ebert and was not terribly familiar with the details, but it wasn't going to matter, as Ebert was determined to plead, do his time, and be done with it. As Daniels called the case, Sam thought about his exchange with Ebert earlier that morning.

"I'm no good on probation, Sam."

"Dave, you plead guilty and you might very well do two years in Rawlins. I mean, given your history. . ."

"I know it, Sam, but I just can't *not* drink."

"Look," Sam had said. "Let me argue for treatment. We'll get you a bed date."

"I been there. Six times. I don't want to go back."

"Dave, you're going to die if you keep drinking."

"And I'll die if I don't," Ebert had said.

Now, after Sam waived an advisal of rights and a verbatim reading of the charges, Daniels asked Ebert for his plea.

"I admit it, Judge," Ebert said as Sam sat back, helpless.

"I'm guilty." While Daniels advised Ebert of the possible repercussions stemming from his persisting with an admission, Sam was looking at the scratches all over his client's arms and face, wondering if he'd gotten in a scrap in the holding cell.

"So, Mr. Ebert, what happened?" Daniels asked.

"Well, me and a couple of the boys were drinking some beers over at the Longhorn—"

"Which you were not supposed to be doing, right?"

"Right, Judge," Ebert said. "But I got a little thirsty. Anyway, them guys got too drunk to drive, so I figured I'd get everyone home safe."

"Ah," Daniels said, removing his readers and rubbing his eyes. "No good deed goes unpunished?"

"Well, kinda, Judge. So, anyway, I knew my car wouldn't start if I had alcohol in my system, and everyone else had been drinking, too. So we was wondering what to do when this cat walked by."

"A cat?" Daniels asked. "Like a housecat?"

"Well, yeah, but he was a little wild. And he was a big sonuvagun, too. Like that." Ebert held his hands a couple of feet apart. "So, I had an idea. I walked over to him and grabbed him and . . . uh . . . got him in the car. Then I wrapped my hands around his head and put his mouth around the Intoxilyzer, and then I squeezed him to try and get the air outta him and into that Intoxilyzer thing," Ebert said. Sam was afraid he was going to burst out laughing but pursed his lips instead to try and maintain a properly serious bearing. "See, I was trying to see if I could get enough air into the damned thing to start the car."

"So, what happened?" Daniels said, swiveling in his chair as if to check one of the bound volumes behind him. Sam could see his shoulders shaking from laughter. "Go on, Mr. Ebert."

"Well, the cat . . . he started to squirm, and he got his mouth off the thing and then he bit my hand and I dropped him, and he got loose in the car. The doors were closed, of course, and that bastard—I'm sorry—well, he decided he was gonna get even, I think, and he attacked us and bit the shit, er, bit the hell out of me, Ray, and especially Ed. I guess a cop was patrolling and saw the commotion and checked on us and ended up arresting me."

"That where you got the scratches?"

"Yeah." Ebert shook his head and looked at his outstretched arms. "That cat kinda ripped us a new one."

Daniels and Sam made eye contact. The old judge clearly couldn't resist. "So, what happened to the cat?"

"Well, last I seen he was stalking off, looking kinda pissed," Ebert said. "His tail was standing straight up with the hair on it standing straight out."

"Let's take a brief recess," Daniels said, wiping his eyes with a handkerchief. He stood and left the courtroom. Sam could hear the laughter from Daniels's chambers after the door closed.

"I don't know what you want me to do, Paul." Sam was getting exasperated with his old friend. They had been arguing over the client and strategy for twenty minutes. "He says he didn't do it, and he won't plead to a lesser. We've got to prepare for trial."

"The evidence is not overwhelming, Sam," Paul said. "But I think it is enough to gain a conviction. Hell, when I was prosecuting—and it's been a while, I admit—I took a few cases to juries where I had less than this."

"Murders?"

"Well, no. But we've got other disadvantages, too. Our client, for one."

Sam's hackles were raised. "Because he's black?"

"No, because he's an ass."

Sam sat back and looked at Paul for a long time. "I think he's young, Paul. I think the you and I of today would hate the you and I of twenty years ago."

"He's an arrogant prick."

"Uppity?"

"Give me a break," Paul said. "You and I both know he's not going to play well in front of a jury."

"That I agree with," Sam said. "But look, we'll use our guy's gifts the best we can. We'll get some character guys—like Ronnie," Sam suggested. "Ronnie seems to love the guy."

"I don't want Ronnie testifying," Paul said.

"But no one knows him better. How you treat the manager is a character check. As far as I can tell, they were—"

"I don't want him testifying," Paul insisted.

"And in an ideal situation I wouldn't, either," Sam said. "But it could come to that."

"Sam, look at us," Paul began. "We're doing a drill here to try and figure out what we can say that is positive about our own client. We've got a lot at stake here. The evidence is that he was there, and it tends to show something happened between him and that dead gay kid."

"I know."

"And the evidence is that Davonte doesn't like gay people."

"I think we can attribute a lot of that to youthful indiscretion."

"In this day and age? I think you're fooling yourself. I think when those jurors see and hear what he posted our stuff will be weak," Paul said. "Besides, how you gonna do that? You can't put him on the stand—you know that. Can't you work on him a little more about a plea?"

"I'll keep working on him," Sam said. "But I don't think it's gonna happen."

"Well, if he's not going to do a plea, at least get him to tell us the truth so we don't get ambushed. Because while I'm willing to admit I don't know what happened, I do know his story to date is bullshit. And I don't want Ronnie testifying," Paul repeated, then stood and left Sam's office.

***

According to the calendar, it was the first day of spring. Sam was looking out his office window at two feet of snow as he waited on Davonte, recalling his time in Washington, D.C. and thinking the cherry blossoms ought to be in bloom. He needed to run some things by Davonte, so he'd called him and asked him to come in. Surprisingly, he was on time this morning. "So, Davonte, I called you in here so we could talk about what happened."

"I don't know what happened."

"Well, I guess we are off to a poor start here. Let me begin again. The State can show that you and Kaiden were in a drug relationship. The State can show that you owed Kaiden money. The State can show the two of you knew each other well. The State can show that you had an argument with Kaiden the night he disappeared."

"So what?"

"Why are you interrupting me?"

Davonte looked at Sam for a long moment, then sat back.

"The State can show," Sam continued, "that you followed Kaiden out of the dorm." Davonte started to speak but Sam stopped him with a raised hand. "There is video and eyewitness evidence tending to indicate that. The State can show that your phone was in the area where Kaiden's body was found at the relevant time. The State can show you making demeaning comments about gay people, and the State can show you were the last person to talk with him. The State can show you had bruising and cuts on your hands a few days following his disappearance. The State—"

"That's all—whattaya call it?—circumstantial evidence!"

Sam nodded. "And the State can show your DNA on the cap found at the scene," he finished, adding, "Lots of guys doing life as the result of circumstantial evidence."

"Sam, I did not do this!" Davonte said, shaking his head. "This is all some small-town bullshit."

"I'm sure the State is developing other evidence as well. They are required to turn it over at some point, of course, but it will be icing on the cake. They've got enough right now," Sam said. "So, as a minimum, that's what the State has. Now, let's look at what we have."

"Okay, let's do it." Davonte leaned in eagerly toward Sam.

"I made a list," Sam said. He pushed a yellow legal pad over to Davonte. On the pad, he had written, "Davonte says he 1) didn't have a fight with Kaiden; 2) didn't follow him; 3) wasn't anywhere near the scene; and 4) didn't kill him." Sam waited while Davonte read what he had written. When Davonte looked up, Sam asked, "Do you see the problem?"

"No, I don't."

"Let me spell it out for you: they have admissible evidence tending to show all those things and more. We have you saying, 'uh-uh.' That, my friend, is the recipe for you to do the next forty years in an eight-by-ten room."

Davonte started to protest, but Sam stopped him. "My problem is I've got nothing backing your story. I'm not even really sure what your story is, because so far all you've told me is that you didn't do it. What you haven't told me is what you *did* do."

"What do you need?"

"I need the truth. All of it. Good or bad." Sam leaned forward. "I need to know exactly where you were the night Kaiden disappeared. Every second of the night. I need to know where you were, why you were there, who you were with, and what happened. Whatever it is," Sam continued, "if I know about it, I can deal with it. I don't give a shit if you are gay. I don't care if you use drugs. I don't care if whatever you tell me reveals your deepest, darkest secrets. But you cannot play 'stump the chump' with me any longer."

Davonte sat back and looked at his nails, then stretched his long legs to the side of the chair and looked at Sam. "So, I followed him—so what?"

"So, in the cops' eyes, that makes you one of the last people to see him alive. Try and follow me here: not infrequently, the last guy to see a victim is the one who made him a victim. Get me?"

"Yeah, I hear you. But when I left, he was alive."

"Left where?"

Davonte sat quietly, looking at nothing in particular. "Let me ask you a question," Sam began. "Do you have a desire to be locked in a small room with another man for a few decades?"

"Don't be a dumbass, man," Davonte said. "Of course not." He continued sitting quietly. Sam said nothing. At last, Davonte spoke. "So, if I did tell you, then what?"

"Then I would be better able to advise you and defend you," Sam explained. "If you don't come across, I'm going to talk with Paul. We might have to see the judge about withdrawing. So, telling me is a win for everyone."

Davonte stood and said, "I need to make a call."

"Seriously? There are guys your age leading rifle squads in Afghanistan right now, literally making life-or-death decisions for themselves and the men they lead, and you're gonna call your mom to see if you should tell your lawyer the whole truth? What am I missing here?"

Davonte ignored him and walked out of the office. Sam headed for the kitchen to get another cup of coffee and met Paul in the hallway. "Well?" Paul asked.

"He's going to come across, I think."

"It's not too late to call this off, Sam."

"I know. I've explained to him that I think we're done if I don't start hearing something that rings true."

"Sam, that ain't gonna happen. He doesn't trust us."

"I'm working on that."

"Not going to happen," Paul said. "Keep me posted."

"Of course," Sam said, and walked back to his office. He was sending an email to Cassie when Davonte returned, closed the door, and sat down. Sam turned to look at him. "Call your mom?"

"No, but I'm good," Davonte said. "Called the guy I needed to talk to. We good."

"What does that mean?" Sam asked.

"Don't worry about it. We're cool. So . . . the little bastard hit on me," Davonte said.

"What?" Sam asked.

"Kaiden. He hit on me, so I busted him one." Davonte shook his head as if to say he wasn't having it.

"Let's walk this back a little bit," Sam said. "You had an argument with Kaiden that night about money, right?"

"Yeah, and he embarrassed me in front of Ronnie and that

other dude," Davonte said. "That was disrespectful. I was gonna kick his ass."

"So, he left, you left, and you caught up with him where?"

"Outside his dorm."

"Then what?"

"We went to, like, the dayroom, or whatever. To talk it out."

"And then what?"

"Then he apologized," Davonte said. "I figured we were good, so I got up to leave, and he hugged me."

"So you thumped his melon because he hugged you?"

"It wasn't like a . . . hug, man. It was like a *hug*," Davonte explained. "Like he was hitting on me."

"Davonte . . . you had some stuff on your phone. Porn. Leads me to believe—"

"You are wrong, man."

Sam let it go. "What do you mean he 'hit on you?'"

"I mean, he was like crying and sad and everything, and then he wanted me to hold him."

"Hold him?"

"Yeah, no shit," Davonte said. "So, he put his arms around me and then tried to kiss me right there in the dayroom! I wasn't having it, didn't want no one to see, so I freaked out and punched him."

"Go on."

"Just what I said. Was trying to punch him in the nose, but he turned, and I think I caught him right here." Davonte indicated his jaw. "Don't know for sure, I was so mad. Then I hit him again, maybe in the eye. When I left, he was sitting on one of them couches, holding a rag to his face."

Sam looked at Davonte and then got up and walked around his desk to sit in the chair adjacent to the big man. "Okay, this is a start—but it is not a defense. Just so you know, what you've given me is a version of what they used to call the 'gay panic defense'—not a viable defense in the twenty-first century," Sam explained. "Plus, with that stuff on your phone, no one is gonna believe you panicked. The good news," he continued, "is that I now understand the cuts on your hands and the bruising on his face. I can explain that now."

"Shoulda busted him up more," Davonte said.

"Do yourself a favor," Sam said. "Don't ever say that again. Don't even think it. Now, let's go back for a second. What happened before he hit on you?"

"I got outside the dorm and he was being an asshole," Davonte said. "Dude was loud and demanding I come up with the money for the weed right away. I ain't got that kind of money. He was tellin' me he was going to rat me out to the coach and the college and the newspapers. Threatening to put 'his boys' from Fort Collins on me. I was scared, man. We were arguing and we went into the dayroom."

"So, did he touch you first?"

"Yeah, he came up on me and pushed me." Davonte demonstrated. "He was crazy pissed."

"And so you pushed him away and then what?"

"He hit the floor and tried to come after me. But he's just a little punk so I put two hands on his shoulders and shoved him to the floor."

"Then what?"

"He just sat there, crying and telling me his suppliers from Fort Collins were gonna kill him. That's when he apologized. Said he was scared. So, I tried to leave, and then what I told you. I popped his ass a couple of times and then just left. He was crying on that couch like a little bitch and I just left."

"So you hit him twice?"

"I think, yeah. I can't remember. I was kind of toasted, man."

"From the front?"

"Of course!" Davonte said. "I ain't no kind of chicken shit to hit someone from behind."

"Was he bleeding?" Sam asked.

"A little. Why?"

"Davonte, let me ask you another question," Sam said, ignoring Davonte's question. "Who else owed Kaiden money for weed?"

"You kidding? That boy had his hooks in everyone, including your partner's kid." Davonte nodded toward Paul's office.

"Are you serious?"

"Everyone knows Ronnie liked to vape. Dude was always cooking."

"Did he owe Kaiden any money?" Sam asked.

"Oh, yeah," Davonte said. "But me and Ronnie had a deal. I told Ronnie I'd cover him after I went pro if he'd do my papers and shit. You know, quid pro whatever."

Sam was silent for a moment. "How about Trent? He owe Kaiden money?"

"Dunno. Don't really know that dude," Davonte said. "He just showed up last month or so. Real quiet. Just kind of watches what's going on and doesn't say much."

"Is he a student?"

Davonte laughed. "How would I know, man?"

"Ever see him in class?"

"Class?" Davonte mocked.

"How were you going to pull grades to be eligible second semester?"

"I told you. I had people handle that shit for me, man," Davonte said, waving dismissively. "Like your partner's boy. Ronnie does stuff for me; I'll do stuff for him. That's the deal. Ronnie ain't all you thought he was, now is he?"

Sam was on the line holding for an expert. He was irritable to begin with, and as the time dragged on, he was getting tense. He was reading from a book on mindfulness suggested by Bob Martinez when he heard a voice he recognized.

"This is Russ Johnson, can I help you?"

Sam put the book down. "Russ, this is Sam Johnstone. We met—"

"Johnstone calling Johnson!" Johnson laughed. "That's hilarious!"

"It is," Sam managed to say. He waited for Johnson to stop chuckling before he continued. "You remember I'm in Wyoming, right?"

"Of course! Custer, as I recall. A beautiful place. You had that case with that soldier who was accused of killing his girl-friend—a lawyer, if I remember right."

"You do."

"What can I do for you?" Johnson asked.

"I've got another case."

"The black basketball player who killed the gay kid?"

"Well, that's the State's theory," Sam said. "How'd you know?"

"It's all over the news here in Denver. You got a gay guy killed by a black guy."

"Uh, yeah. Look, Russ, I've got some questions about DNA."

"I'm your guy."

"Touch DNA." Sam waited for a moment. "You still my guy?"

"I am . . . kind of complicated stuff. Lots and lots of variables."

"Give me a thirty-second primer," Sam urged.

"You going to retain us?"

"Depends on whether or not you can convince me you know what you are talking about without losing me."

"Okay, so most DNA is collected from fluids such as blood, saliva, or semen. But when people touch things, they can also leave behind fluid or a small number of epithelial cells—which is what I think you are asking about—under certain conditions. Thus, 'touch DNA.'"

"Bravo," Sam said. "Problems?"

"Plenty. First, the person usually has to have pretty good contact with the item. Second, depending on the surface structure of an item, there might not be any recoverable DNA even with a good touch. So, like a rock or something. Might be good, might not be."

"Okay," Sam said, thinking. "What else?"

"Bigger issue in my mind is the possibility of secondary transfer, tertiary transfer—there's a whole range of possibilities."

"Yeah?"

"Oh, yeah. And as a defense guy, most of them are good for you."

"How so?"

"Raise some doubt."

Sam thought about that for a moment. "Okay, send me a contract discussing your fee. What do you need for a retainer?"

"Twenty-five hundred for me to scope the problem," Johnson said. "I'll revise upward from there. So, we're in?"

"I think so."

"I'll check with my boss," Johnson said. "When's the trial?"

"Middle of May."

"Good. At least it'll be warm."

"Yeah. We oughta be up to forty or so."

"Are you freakin' kidding me?"

"I wish," Sam said. "Send me your contract. In the meantime, I'm going to send you some stuff to take a look at."

"Thanks, Sam. I'm looking forward to it."

"All right. Call you next week."

17

Weeks later, Sam was looking out his office window at a cold late April day when Davonte and the henchmen pulled up and parked on the street. It was snowing heavily, and Davonte put the hood up on his sweatshirt as he jogged across the street, once again leaving Damon and Reggie in the car. Sam met Davonte in the reception area. "Afternoon, Davonte," Sam said. "How you doing?"

"I'm all right. Just want to get this over with. This weather is killing me, Sam. Don't know how you deal with it."

"It's a bitch," Sam said. "Come on back. Got a question for you."

"Yo."

"Reggie and Damon. What's their deal?"

"What do you mean?"

"What do they do? I mean, what do they add to all this?"

"My friends, man."

"I get that, but it seems like they don't do anything. I mean, they don't play ball with you. They don't work. From where I'm at, it's like they're a cheerleading section or something."

"They don't gotta do nothin' except keep me safe, know what I'm sayin'?"

"Safe from what?"

"Trouble. Mom pays 'em a little to keep an eye on me, keep me company."

"Good work, if you can get it," Sam said, sitting and sipping from a cup with a pistol-butt-shaped handle. He gestured toward the chair across the desk. "Sit. Let's talk."

Davonte complied. "What's going on?"

"Wanted to have a little talk with you about the trial."

"Okay?"

"A couple of things you need to know. One, this is going to suck. And two, it's going to suck bad."

Davonte smiled wanly. "That the good news?"

"Just about," Sam said, smiling before turning serious. "Trials are intense. Think of a trial like it's a game. There are times when you've got the momentum and things are going well, and there are times when things are going against you and the other team's got the momentum. So, you've got to try not to get too high or too low. We aren't going to be doing any chest-bumps—get me?"

"I gotcha."

"And, remember this: part of their strategy will be to test you, to get you off your game. Nothing they'd like better than you getting pissed when they say something bad about you. So, just like when you're getting booed by the home team's crowd, you've got to keep your poise and show no reaction."

"I can do that."

"Good," Sam said. "Very important that you not react no matter how pissed you get. You've got to trust me to clean up the messes."

"I do, but . . ." Davonte's voice trailed off. He clearly had something to say.

"But what?"

"Well, I don't know how to say this."

"Just say it," Sam said, having a pretty good idea what was coming.

"It's gonna piss you off."

"You not wanting to communicate with me is pissing me off," Sam said. "We've got a couple of weeks before trial. I need to know what's in your head. We need to be on the same sheet of music."

"Paul," Davonte said at last. "That dude worries me."

"That's okay. We don't have to like each other to work together. It would be better if we all got along, but it's not necessary." Sam was watching Davonte closely. The young man was clearly unhappy with the answer. "What else?" Sam asked.

"I—I want him gone."

"Not your choice. We've already been down that road."

"I don't trust him, man," Davonte said. "I mean, if it comes down to it, will he allow Ronnie to testify on my behalf? I mean Ronnie—"

"What?"

"Nothing, man. I mean, he's gotta testify—know what I mean?"

"He doesn't have any choice," Sam said. "I subpoenaed him, so if I call him, Ronnie will have to testify or go to jail."

"Will Paul let you?"

"I'm lead counsel," Sam explained. "I will do what I believe needs to be done to represent you to the fullest."

"I still think it will be better—"

"No. Not a decision that is yours to make."

"Mom says I could fire you."

"You could. But you'd have to fire both of us. You do that and the judge may or may not allow you new counsel," Sam explained. "Not many lawyers—and no good ones—would take this case on short notice, so even if you could find someone, you'd likely be punching your own ticket to the pen at this point. Paul will do his job. He'll come around. Now, let's get to work."

For the next couple of hours Sam and Davonte went over the case together, with Sam explaining the evidence he expected the prosecution to present and watching Davonte's reaction to it. The young man was intelligent, insightful, and surprisingly witty when he wasn't in the company of the henchmen. The run-through complete, Sam walked Davonte back to the front door and the two shook hands. Back in his office, Sam watched as Davonte strolled across the street and joined Reggie and Damon in the big sedan. Reggie looked toward Sam's window, and their eyes met before Reggie put a foot to the throttle.

The snow had fallen all day, but Sam had intermittently shoveled the small deck behind his townhouse in order to attend to a rack of pork ribs. Because he'd had to work all morning, he'd gotten the ribs on the smoker a little later than he would have liked, and it was nine o'clock before he set his small table with the ribs and a potato he had baked. He'd made some barbeque sauce with a recipe he'd developed over the years featuring bourbon, horseradish, and apricot preserves. He slathered the sauce over the dry rub on the ribs, careful not to remove any of the top crust. He cut—separated, really—the ribs along every other bone and piled them on a platter. He'd had a little bourbon while he made the sauce and was enjoying its warmth in his stomach and the buzz in his head. He retrieved two long-neck beers from the refrigerator, sat down, said a brief prayer of thanks, and served himself a couple of ribs. He was buttering his potato when he heard a crash in the living room.

Because it was a weekend, he was carrying his pistol inside his waistband. He drew the weapon and moved quickly to the hallway that ran the length of the room. He turned out the lights in the kitchen and dining areas and moved quickly down the hallway. With his off-hand, he reached quickly around the corner and turned off the lights in the front room, enabling him to see through the broken window into the small yard and the street in front of his home. On the living room floor he could see a large rectangular object. Sam stood quietly, peering around the corner and through the window for a few moments.

When Sam was satisfied no attack would follow, he moved quickly to the window, drew the curtains, and turned on the light. In the middle of the floor he could see a common red brick with a piece of paper wrapped around it, held in place by baling twine. He carefully untied the knot in the twine and read: WE KNOW WHERE YOU LIVE. THE COPS ARE CROOKED. GET YOUR SHIT TOGETHER. YOU LOSE, YOU DIE!! He smiled wanly, dropped the note on the brick, and returned to his dining table. He sat and took a bite of his ribs before calling 911.

Minutes later, Corporal Jensen arrived. After letting him in and explaining the situation, Sam returned to his table—and his ribs. He could hear Jensen moving about the room and could see the occasional flash as the officer recorded the scene.

"Uhh, Mr. Johnstone?" Jensen called from the living room.

"Call me Sam."

"Sure, uh, Sam. Can I talk to you for a minute?"

"You bet. Come on in," Sam said. "Rib?" he asked when Jensen entered, indicating the platter.

"Uh, no. Better not. I'm working." Jensen smiled, looking at the ribs.

"How can I help you?"

"Well, it seems pretty obvious that whoever did this is trying to make sure you get Mr. Blair off," Jensen said.

"Yeah." Sam licked some sauce from an index finger. "But I got another one weeks ago. It was kind of anti-gay."

Jensen furrowed his brow. "Did you call us?"

"No."

"Why not?"

"Well, I figured it was a crank. This is different. This is my home. I'm a renter. I need the report for my insurer and my landlord."

"I see," Jensen said. "Did you keep that other note?"

"I did. How 'bout I bring it by tomorrow? I've had a little bit to drink tonight, and I'd like to finish my ribs," Sam said. "Have some?"

"Well." Jensen took off his hat and mopped his brow. "Maybe if you got a little foil, I'll take one to go. My lunch break is at midnight."

An hour after Jensen left, Sam helped his landlord cover the broken window with a sheet of plywood. "Sam," the man began, "neighbors are saying all kinds of weird things are going on around here."

"Yeah?"

"Yeah. Lights going on at night. You runnin' around with guns. I run a quiet place here, Sam. I can't have any trouble."

"You'll get no trouble from me. I pay my rent and mind my own business."

"I'm just saying—"

"I hear you. Now, if you'll get your stuff out of here, I can vacuum the glass off this carpet and maybe get some sleep."

Since he was in the courthouse, Sam figured he would take advantage of the opportunity and try to speak with Cathy. Her receptionist instructed him to wait until he was called. After five minutes, Cathy buzzed him through the locked door and shook his hand. She looked tired. "Mr. Johnstone, to what do we owe the honor? And I'll warn you in advance, I'm crispy and cranky. The yahoos outside drove me and Kayla out of the house. I'm bunking with a friend. The good news is it's quiet. The bad news is I'm sleeping on a couch that I'm pretty sure has been in their family since the Reagan administration."

Sam smiled. "Got a minute for opposing counsel?"

"Your guy ready to plead? It's gonna be cold or nothing at all." When he didn't respond, she shrugged. "What the hell," she said. "Come on back." Sam followed her to her office. She had a nice figure. He took the seat as indicated, and she moved and sat behind her desk. He was looking at the diplomas and family pictures around her office while she sat quietly, waiting for him to say something. Finally, she spoke. "I'm thirty-four, divorced, played basketball in college. Been prosecuting for eight years—ever since I passed the bar. Satisfied?"

"Sure," Sam said. "Point guard?"

"Bingo. Now, what do you want?"

"I'm hoping to get an offer," he said.

"On what?"

"Blair."

"None coming." She shook her head. "We took the death penalty off the table. That's as good as it gets."

"You can't show premeditation. The best interpretation of

the evidence shows Miles was in some kind of a mix-up and got whacked from behind after getting punched in the face—that's a fistfight gone bad. Second degree, best case."

"I'll let you make that argument to the jury, Sam."

"Besides—and you know this to be true—my client's not sophisticated enough to come up with a plan. He's nineteen years old, for Christ's sake."

"Every day, people with the IQ of a sheep develop and implement plans to do horrible things to each other," she said. "And if your guy is so dumb, put him on the stand to show the jury that." She smiled. "I'd like that."

"I'm sure you would," Sam said, returning her smile. "I think I could get my guy to plead to manslaughter in return for something like seven years."

"Are you kidding me? I'd have the gay mothers and friends of gays and everyone else lynching me."

"Lynching? Seriously bad turn of phrase for my client."

"You're not going to make this a race thing, are you, Sam?" she asked. "I've gotten calls from the civil rights leaders already. Told 'em I've got the evidence and I'm not backing down."

"No, Cathy, I'm not," he said. "I don't need to. You've got a weak circumstantial case. I'm thinking someone pressured Punch into arresting my client."

"It's not the best case I've had," she allowed. "I'll agree with that."

He nodded and looked around her office. According to a plaque on the wall, she'd been the defensive player of the year in the Mountain West Conference. "You're hard-nosed."

"I don't like to lose," she said. "You play?"

"Baseball. Small college. That's where Paul and I met."

"You look like an outfielder. You any good?"

"I was, and no, not really. I'm fast . . . well, I was at one point," he said, knocking on his prosthetic leg. "Good field, occasional power. If I could have stolen first, I mighta been something."

"Rebecca says no deals." Cathy shook her head sympathetically. Whether it was for the loss of his missing limb, his sorry batting average, or her assessment of his case, he didn't know.

"You can't prove first degree. I don't think the jury is going to be happy with second degree, either. If I put my client on the stand—"

"Oooh, really? I'm getting all warm and tingly just thinking about it."

"—he'll testify it was in self-defense. We go through this drill, you spend hundreds of thousands of taxpayer dollars, and if I get one juror to see it my way, my guy walks and you got no justice for Kaiden. You follow Ann out the door. Let's do a deal and everyone's unhappy, but everyone can claim a little bit of victory."

"I prefer to see it this way: you lose, and Davonte is locked up for life. This time next year, he's leading the prison league in scoring with fifty points per game. Absolutely dominating night after night, going back to his cell and dreaming of what might have been—if he hadn't killed Kaiden Miles."

"Ouch," Sam ventured. "Worst case?"

"I don't think that way." She shrugged. "Maybe you are getting a little nervous?"

"No," Sam said. "That's not it. No one's shooting at me." He stood with some difficulty. "Having a bad leg day," he lamented with a smile. "How is Kayla?"

"She's fine." Cathy smiled and looked at a picture of her little girl.

"What do you tell her?"

"I tell her there are people who are mad at Mommy."

"Oof," Sam said. "Tough stuff. See you soon, Cathy. Good luck, and let me know if you want to do a deal."

She watched him limp from her office and down the sidewalk, headed toward his own office, no doubt. She fiddled with a very expensive pen her father had given her following her passing the bar examination, then put it down and dialed Rebecca's number. "Can we talk?" she asked when Rebecca picked up.

———

Preston and Marci Daniels had lived in the same well-kept colonial revival on Main Street for forty years. It was a beautiful home, the source of great pride for both. The brick façade was accented with a small pediment and white columns on either side of a wide entrance and projecting bay windows trimmed in white. The roof was pitched steeply and side-gabled. A chimney was visible on one end of the home. Ancient cottonwoods—a favorite of the early settlers due to their ability to withstand the area's harsh winters and periods of drought—were evenly spaced on either side of the walkway leading from the street and sidewalk to the front steps. The attached double-car garage had a loft with two dormer windows, providing a good view of the driveway all the way to the street. Marci had planted and carefully tended the flower beds visible from the front and both sides of the home. Daniels still mowed the grass every Sunday afternoon, just as he had done before going to bed a little earlier than usual.

Just before midnight he was awakened by the motion-activated lights on his garage. Thinking it was probably a deer, he rolled over and closed his eyes, trying to get back to sleep. He was listening to Marci snore softly when he thought he heard voices. He sighed heavily and got out of bed to see what was going on. Walking to the window, he was surprised to see a number of people standing on the sidewalk in front of his home.

"What's going on?" she asked.

"There are people on the sidewalk in front of our house."

"What do they want?"

"I can't tell, but I'm going to find out." He walked to the closet and put on his bathrobe and slippers. "Maybe there was an accident or something."

"Be careful, dear."

"I will be. I'm going to give some sonuvabitch a piece of my mind, though," he said. He made his way down the stairs and into the living room. From the hall closet next to the front door he extracted a large black flashlight. He opened the front door and was immediately taken aback by the bright lights illuminating his home. He put a hand in front of his eyes and walked down his driveway to the edge of his property. He could hear chanting, but he'd forgotten to put in his hearing aids and couldn't make out what they were saying. "What's going on out here?" he asked.

"No justice, no peace! No justice, no peace!" several people chanted in unison.

"What the hell are you talking about?" Daniels said. "Get the hell out of here! It's the middle of the night, for Christ's sake!" Several of what he now recognized as perhaps two dozen protesters moved toward him from two different directions, chanting. Daniels gave ground. "I'm telling you to get off my property, and I'm not going to ask again!"

"Until there is justice for Davonte, there will be no rest!" screamed a young woman. "This racist community must change!"

"Get off my lawn, now!" Daniels yelled. "Or I will call law enforcement."

In response, the protesters changed their chant to one of, "All cops are bastards!"

"Who is in charge here?" Daniels asked. He turned out his flashlight and looked around him.

"We reject hierarchical systems," a young woman responded. "We are all in charge."

"Fine." Daniels turned and walked back down his driveway. "Tell your equals I'm going back in the house to call the cops." As he approached his home, he saw a camera flash. Turning, he watched two skinny young men wearing rainbow-colored wigs taking pictures of his home from behind the cottonwood to the east. "Get the hell off my property!" he yelled.

Back in the house, he discovered Marci awake and out of bed. "I called the cops," she said. "They should be here soon." Handing him the phone, she said, "It's Don." Donald Turner had been their next-door neighbor for almost forty years.

"Judge, what the hell is going on out there? Are you okay?"

"I'm fine, Don," Daniels said. "A bunch of rabble-rousers, is all."

"Marci okay?"

"She's fine." Daniels looked at his wife and smiled. She had started a pot of coffee and was putting some cinnamon rolls in the oven. "We've been through worse than this."

"What do they want?"

"They say they want justice," Daniels said.

"What does that have to do with raising Cain after midnight?"

"Good question."

"Did you call the cops?" Turner asked.

"Marci did." Daniels gratefully accepted a cup of coffee from her. Mouthing, "Thanks, dear," he took a sip. "What these people don't understand is that I'm almost seventy years old. Need my beauty sleep," he said to Turner while he winked at Marci, who rolled her eyes. "Keeping me up all night is not going to help see justice done."

"Judge, you be careful, okay?"

"I will be. Don't worry about us."

"I'm gonna go buy me a shotgun first thing tomorrow," Turner said.

"Now, Don. Don't do anything in response to this. I'm sure this will all be over soon enough."

"I know, Judge," Turner said. "But I've been thinking about it for a while. People are nuts."

"Just be careful," Daniels said, and hung up. He looked at Marci. "Go to bed, dear."

"Join me?"

"No, I'm up." He shook his head. "I'll wait for the cops and then probably take a shower and go on in. I'll work on my jury instructions. Been putting it off; might as well use the extra time."

"You'll be exhausted tonight." She smoothed his hair and gave him a peck on the cheek. "Okay, I'm going to bed. One of us will need to be functional this evening."

"Good night—or good morning, I guess." He smiled. He was thinking how he would be lost without her when the doorbell rang. Before answering, he first went to the china buffet and withdrew a small, single-stack automatic pistol he kept there. Marci had never approved, but it was the world in which they lived. Threats against judges were frequent and attacks rare but not unheard of. Taking a deep breath, he opened the door. "Good morning, Officer Goodrich," he said, exhaling. "Come in."

Daniels explained the situation and Goodrich took notes, occasionally asking questions. After taking the judge's report, Goodrich left to talk with the protesters outside. Daniels showered and ate a couple pieces of toast before packing his lunch and briefcase and walking into his garage. He opened the garage, backed out, and drove down the driveway, where he was surrounded by chanting protesters. A number of Custer Police Department officers then removed members of the surging crowd. "Go ahead, sir," Goodrich said to Daniels.

"Thank you," Daniels said, moving his car forward.

"You corrupt tool!" a young man yelled into his window.

Daniels couldn't help himself. "I'll follow the law!" he yelled.

"The law is corrupt!" was the response.

"Well, there you go," Daniels said as he rolled up the window. "A preference for judges to eschew the law to follow the will of the crowd. What could possibly go wrong?" He turned on the radio, took a deep breath, and sang along with Merle Haggard, who asked, "Are the Good Times Really Over?"

18

Several hours later, Daniels entered a packed courtroom. The dull buzz of conversation died immediately as everyone stood until he asked all to take their seats.

"Good morning, ladies and gentlemen," he began.

"Good morning," everyone responded at once.

"My name is Judge Preston C. Daniels, and I am the senior district court judge here in the 12th Judicial District of Wyoming," he said. "Welcome to the major leagues of trial courts here in Wyoming." Looking each juror in the eye in turn, he continued, "Most of you don't look happy to be here —and that's too bad, because we are thrilled to have you. What you are about to do is to fulfill one of the most important civic duties that you are asked to perform as a citizen, and that is to serve on a jury. You may recall from your high school civics courses that very few countries entrust their citizens with this kind of responsibility.

"I want to stress up front that what you are about to do is not for your entertainment. In the real world, trials are not like on television. They are not like the novels you have read or movies that you might have seen. As an initial matter, the judge is much better-looking." Daniels smiled while everyone in the courtroom laughed nervously. Because Daniels always used the line, Sam had Davonte prepared, and he, Davonte, and Paul laughed along as well. "Instead," Daniels said, turning sober again, "your job as jurors will be to search for truth. Truth that has consequences. Truth that will directly affect the liberty and perhaps the lives of those who are involved.

"If you are selected for this jury, don't expect to be entertained; expect to be asked to pay close attention to what's going on in this courtroom. Now, in just a few seconds, the clerk is going to call the names of twelve of you to be seated in the jury box. If your name is called, please come forward." Daniels indicated the jury box with a wave of his hand. "The bailiff will direct you to your seat. Madam Clerk, would you seat a jury, please?"

After the jurors were called and seated, Daniels continued. "The case that has been called for trial is entitled State of Wyoming versus Davonte Blair. The defendant in this case is present and seated at the counsel table to the court's left between his attorneys: Mr. Johnstone, who is closest to you, and Mr. Norquist, who is seated on the other side of Mr. Blair."

Davonte looked directly at each juror and smiled slightly, just as Sam had encouraged him to do. "Why I gotta do that?" Davonte had asked.

"Because that is what jurors expect. Remember, like I told you before: some percentage of jurors will make up their mind within minutes of seeing you. We don't want any of them deciding you're guilty because—"

"I'm black?"

"No, because they decide you're a petulant child or an asshole. How's that?"

"Okay, Sam," Davonte said. "I'll play your game."

"Good," Sam had said. Now, he and Paul flashed winning smiles as Daniels continued. "Seated at the other table is County Attorney Rebecca Nice, and Deputy County and Prosecuting Attorney Catherine Schmidt, who is lead counsel in this matter. They are the lawyers for the State of Wyoming; the burden of proof in this case rests with them."

To Sam's surprise, Rebecca actually waved to the crowd. Cathy merely sat up a little straighter. "Mr. Blair has been charged with one count of first-degree murder in the death of one Kaiden Miles, which is alleged to have occurred here in Custer County on or about last November 6," Daniels said. "Mr. Blair has entered a plea of not guilty, and as you look at him right now you should understand you are looking at an innocent man, and he'll remain not guilty until and unless you decide otherwise."

While Daniels spoke, Sam eyed each juror carefully. The clerk of court had provided both sides with questionnaires completed by each potential juror a couple of weeks prior. Sam and Paul had spent a lot of time reviewing and gathering what background they could on each, mostly through social media accounts. Here, too, Paul's familiarity with the community was invaluable. He'd ruled out some jurors who on paper appeared to be ideal candidates for Davonte; others, whom Sam might have struck, were graded positively after Paul's review. The initial slate wasn't bad from Sam's perspective, and he was pleased to see Davonte making eye contact with each.

"Ladies and gentlemen, we will now proceed to select a jury through a process called voir dire, which means 'to tell the truth.' The purpose is to select a fair jury. Ms. Schmidt will first ask questions of you as a group; she may follow up with questions to you individually. When she has completed her questioning, Mr. Johnstone may ask questions as well. Ms. Schmidt, please proceed."

Cathy stepped to the podium and for the next hour asked questions of the jurors relating to their knowledge of the case, the players, and the process, and their predisposition toward conviction and/or acquittal. She inquired of the jurors regarding their schedules, their state of mind, and their willingness to participate. Sam, Paul, and Davonte sat quietly, observing and taking notes. Davonte took notes in a surprisingly small and precise handwriting, Sam noticed. When she had completed her questioning, Daniels looked at Sam and Paul.

"Does the defense care to inquire of the panel?"

"Yes, Your Honor," Sam said, standing and buttoning his jacket. "Ladies and gentlemen, because Ms. Schmidt did a fine job of asking questions, I'm only going to ask you a few more. They will be simple and straightforward, I assure you. Again, all Davonte wants is a jury who will be fair. So, here we go. First, is there anyone here who believes my client is guilty because he is black?" Sam could almost feel the air leave the room; the jurors recoiled but quickly recovered and shook their heads—most did so vigorously. "So, we can all agree to judge my client not by the color of his skin or the fact that he is from Michigan, but by applying the evidence to the law Judge Daniels will instruct you on later?" Again, each juror shook his or her head.

"Okay," Sam said, looking at each juror in turn. "Let me ask you this: if you were Davonte, would you be comfortable having yourself as a juror?" Sam smiled and allowed his eyes to meet theirs. "In other words, do you see yourself as an open and fair-minded person?" Some of the jurors shifted in their chairs, some smiled slightly, but all met his stare and eventually nodded their assent.

"Well," Sam continued, moving to the side of the podium and gesturing with one hand. "How about this: is there anything you have seen or heard so far that would make it hard for you to judge my client and his witnesses just as fairly as you would the other side?" All jurors were still shaking their heads when Sam asked the next question. "Knowing what you know about this case, can any of you think of anything in your own life that would keep you from judging this case on its facts?" Seeing nothing but head shakes, he continued, "So no one here has a problem with gays or a problem with blacks that would keep you from judging this case on its merits?" Again, the air was still. "Can we agree that people who are gay are not automatically good? Can we agree that people who are black are not automatically bad?" Again, Sam met each pair of eyes with his own. He had his doubts about a female juror in the front row who was clearly afraid of Davonte.

For nearly an hour, Sam inquired of the prospective jurors. Some of them were excused for cause and new ones summoned to fill their place, whereupon Cathy and Sam asked questions of them as well. As voir dire wound down, Sam had two final questions. "Can we agree that people are people, and all people can be all things? Is there anything that any of you would prefer to discuss in private?" Sam asked, after seeing no juror react to the earlier question. "Raise your hand if you'd like to meet with us in private." No hands were raised, so Sam continued, "Is there anything we haven't asked you that you think we should know?" Seeing no hands, and nothing but blank stares or head shakes, he finished up. "Ladies and gentlemen, thank you for your patience." Turning to Daniels, he said, "Defense passes the panel for cause, sir."

"Thank you, counsel," Daniels said. "Ladies and gentlemen, we have a sufficient number of jurors from which to select the jury to hear this case. I am going to release you here momentarily so that we might select that jury in your absence.

We'll do this as quickly as possible, but it sometimes takes a while. Bailiff?"

Following the jury panel's departure, the parties selected the jury and the alternates. Sam and Paul were successful in getting the front-row female removed on a preemptive challenge.

"I think this is a good jury," Paul said. "Davonte, are you comfortable with it?"

"All look alike to me," Davonte said, causing Sam to laugh aloud.

Paul turned red. "I'm gonna get a drink of water before the judge comes back," he said.

When the jury had been reconvened and sworn, Daniels looked at the clock. "Well, ladies and gentlemen, you are the jury which will hear this matter. It's been a long day, so we will go ahead and take our evening recess, and we will hear opening arguments and get started in the morning. The bailiff will tell you where you need to be and when you need to be there. Are there any questions?" Seeing none, he stood, and everyone followed suit. "Thank you for your attention. Bailiff, you may escort the jury."

That evening, Sam was scrolling through the channels, looking for something to watch. He stopped on a national news cable channel covering Davonte's trial. "What I want to know is this," the young female host asked a man Sam recognized as Arick Jordan, a prominent African-American legal scholar, "why didn't the attorney for Mr. Blair seek a change of venue?"

"It's Wyoming, you bimbo!" Sam barked at the television. "Where the hell are we going to go?"

"Because he is a part of the same corrupt system of justice that has been keeping black people down for hundreds of years," Jordan responded. "How is a black man supposed to get a fair trial in front of a jury like that?"

"Because the jury will look at the facts and apply them to the law as instructed?" Sam said aloud. As the interview continued, Sam responded aloud to the questions posed to Jordan, fully aware he was wasting both time and energy. Turning off the television and the lights, he made his way around the little townhouse, checking doors, turning locks, and pushing windows shut. After brushing his teeth, he sat on his bed, removed his leg, and lay down to sleep.

What awakened him, he didn't know. But several hours later, Sam looked at the clock. It was 2:05 a.m. In the red glow from the clock he could see his pistol, still in the shoulder holster. He lay in bed, listening. It wasn't so much a sound as it was a feeling: someone was outside his townhouse. Reaching to the other side of the bed, he found his prosthetic leg and slowly, deliberately attached it. He stretched and moved to ensure it was properly affixed, then swung his legs down to the floor, donned a pair of slippers, and stood in the dark. He felt for the pistol, dropped the holster on his bed, and began to walk slowly through his bedroom, paying attention to the shadows and shapes he could see through his drawn shades.

He'd performed this drill a hundred times over the course of the past couple of years. Sometimes it was the wind, sometimes an animal, sometimes a dream, sometimes nothing at all. He would patrol the inner perimeter of his home, listening at the walls, scarcely breathing, anticipating an unseen enemy attacking in the pre-dawn darkness. Then, finding none, he would spend the remaining hours of darkness watching old movies and trying to get back to sleep. This time, having patrolled the entire house, he stepped out onto his ground-level back deck, forgetting that his neighbor had motion sensors in his backyard. Seconds later he heard Bill open the sliding glass door. Bill, too, was armed.

"Bill, it's me," Sam said.

"Sam?"

"Yeah."

"What the hell are you doing this time?"

"Thought I heard something out here," Sam said. In the beam of his flashlight he saw enormous prints leading from his dew-covered grass to his back door, and then back across his lawn.

"See anything?"

"No," Sam lied.

"Jesus, you scared the hell out of me!"

"Sorry, Bill," Sam said. "I forgot about your lights again. Go back to bed."

"Will do. Sam?"

"Yeah?"

"Damned glad to have you as my neighbor, but you are one weird dude."

"Back atcha." Sam laughed, then closed and locked his own door. He poured himself a bowl of cereal and ate it, thinking about the visitor.

The trial began in earnest on Tuesday morning. After everyone was seated, Daniels looked at Cathy. "Ms. Schmidt, does the State wish to make an opening statement?"

"We do, Your Honor," Catherine said. She stood and

walked to the podium. "May it please the court, counsel," she began. "Ladies and gentlemen of the jury, when Kaiden Miles awoke on the 5th of November, he had no idea it would be the last full day of his life. As a child, he wanted nothing more than to be a basketball player. His mother gave him a ball for his birthday when he was four, and he did not let that ball out of his sight for the next fourteen years. Day and night, summer or winter, fall or spring, young Kaiden was never far from a basketball court. But in the spring of his senior year he was injured in a terrible car accident that was not his fault. Doctors said he would never play basketball again, but that didn't stop Kaiden from being involved with the game. Instead of playing, he became a team manager for Custer College. In so doing, he met young men from all over this country—east and west, north and south, tall and short, black and white, rich and poor. Kaiden, you will hear, got along with them all. All except one of them," she said, pointing directly at Davonte. "All except Davonte Blair, who on November 6, with his fists and a murder weapon I'll tell you right now we have been unable to find, ended young Kaiden's life. Mr. Blair and his attorney might tell you it was an accident. Mr. Blair and his attorney may argue he didn't mean it, that it was self-defense. They might even try and convince you it wasn't Davonte who killed Kaiden. But ladies and gentlemen, the evidence will show that it was Davonte Blair who killed Kaiden Miles.

"The evidence will show they were partying, vaping marijuana, and drinking. Yes, ladies and gentlemen, you will hear some things about Kaiden that you might frown on. You may have heard that he was gay. You will hear that he used drugs. But Kaiden did not deserve to die. The evidence will show that on the evening of his disappearance, Kaiden demanded Mr. Blair pay him for marijuana he'd sold him. The evidence will show they had an argument and Kaiden left. The evidence will show Mr. Blair followed Kaiden. The evidence will show Mr. Blair caught up with Kaiden, and then assaulted him, first with his fists, and ultimately with a blunt object, killing him. The evidence will show—"

Cathy stopped short as the sound of raised voices could be heard outside the courthouse.

A deep male voice yelled, "What do we want?"

"Justice!" was the reply.

"When do we want it?"

"Today!"

"What are we?"

"Proud and gay!"

The chanting went on for several seconds before Daniels spoke up. "Ladies and gentlemen, whatever is going on out there is *not* evidence. The only thing that matters is what goes on in here." He turned to the jury. "Bailiff, I'm going to have you conduct the jury to the jury room while we deal with this." After the jury had been taken from the room, Daniels turned to court security. "Set up a perimeter. They are free to assemble and chant, but not so that it interferes with the defendant's right to a fair trial. Let's take a brief recess, shall we?"

Twenty minutes later the parties had reassembled, and the jury was back. "Ms. Schmidt, please continue," Daniels instructed.

Cathy stepped to the podium, cleared her throat, and began anew. "The evidence will show that after Mr. Blair killed Kaiden, he dragged his lifeless body to the bank of Custer Creek and dumped him like so much garbage. The evidence will show that Kaiden lay there, covered by falling snow, for the better part of two weeks, until an unfortunate couple walking their dog discovered the victim. The evidence will show the Custer Police Department conducted a careful and thorough investigation, and that, after ruling out all others, they arrested Mr. Blair, who—the evidence will show —is a homophobic, violent, and troubled young man.

"When all of the evidence is in, we will ask you to send a message to the people of Custer County, the people of Wyoming, and indeed people from across the country and the world. And that message is this: in Custer County, Wyoming, people should be free to live the life they choose. And when— as here—a person takes it upon himself to punish another because of his differences, he will face a jury of his peers. And when the evidence is in and you have been instructed on the law, the only acceptable message will be 'guilty.' Thank you."

"Mr. Johnstone," Daniels said. "Any opening at this time, or will the defendant reserve or waive?"

"Thank you, Your Honor," Sam said, stepping to the podium. "Counsel," he added, nodding to Cathy. "Ladies and gentlemen of the jury, the purpose of an opening statement has been explained somewhat by the judge and by Ms. Schmidt. Whatever I say here is not evidence. It is what I expect the evidence to be.

"The State's witnesses are, of course, under the control of the government. Most of them are employed by the government. She might call them; she might not. So as of now, all I can do is give you what we used to call a SWAG—a serious, wild-ass guess—as to what the evidence will show. This is my only opportunity to give you our theory of the case, and to tell you some of what we think took place. It's also my opportunity to call your attention to certain things so that you will be looking for them, and when you see and hear them, you'll realize they may have significance and you will be alerted to them."

Sam took a drink of water before turning again to the jury. "The one thing that is clear, the one thing that is certain, is that Kaiden's death was a tragedy by any standard of measure. The Miles family has already lost their son. The Blair family hopes not to lose theirs. Kaiden's life was important, and we mourn for his family's loss, just like you do. But Davonte's life is important as well, and it should not be forfeited or destroyed unless the State can meet its burden of proof—and it can't.

"I can state our theory of the defense in two succinct sentences." Sam held up two fingers. "First sentence," he began, holding up his index finger. "Davonte is innocent of murder as a matter of fact." Sam paused for effect and extended a second finger. "Second sentence: the State cannot prove beyond a reasonable doubt that Davonte murdered Kaiden Miles.

"Now, I want to directly address what might be described as a pair of eight-hundred-pound elephants in the room. First, Kaiden Miles was a young, white, apparently gay male. Now, I don't care, and I suspect you don't care. But to some people outside of this courtroom"—Sam pointed to one end of the courthouse—"the ones at *that* end of the building, that appears to be of great importance. Lord knows, for the past several months, we who live here have been bombarded with assertions in both mass and social media—mostly from those who neither live here nor have any knowledge of how life is lived here, I might add—that Mr. Miles was killed because he is gay; that because our legislature has eschewed passing certain laws we must be a people who are homophobic; that because Davonte may have expressed controversial opinions in one or more private communications he must hate gays and must therefore be guilty of murder; and that this trial is a test of us all vis a vis the gay rights movement. These people seek justice for Kaiden. They do not believe it can be attained in a rural Wyoming town.

"Arrayed in opposition," Sam continued, pointing in the opposite direction, "is another group—just as large and just as vocal—for whom Davonte's race is paramount. Here again, we've been inundated for months with punditry and commentary by folks who—again, it has to be pointed out—have never been to Custer County, and who will likely never grace us with their presence, yet who purport to know all about us. You. This group argues that because our population is largely Caucasian, there can be no fair trial for Davonte.

"Now, let me tell you up front that I do not stand with either side. Certainly, I believe one's race is generally important, just as I believe one's sexual orientation is generally important. But neither sexual orientation nor race is important in the matter before the court. I don't believe that your opinions regarding love or sex or skin color or religion will figure into your determination of my client's guilt or innocence. Because the only thing that is important—the *only* thing that is important—is whether the State can prove to you beyond a reasonable doubt that, on or about the 6th day of November, my client purposely and with premediated malice murdered Kaiden Miles. That's the question. That's the only question.

"Now, you will be happy to know that in this case we will probably stipulate to virtually all the evidence that Ms. Schmidt will seek to have introduced. We will do that because we agree with a lot of what she will say. The witnesses saw what they saw; the evidence is generally what they say it is. So, instead of quibbling about unimportant things, we want you paying attention to the areas where we disagree with the State. And let me tell you what we think is important: we think the timeline is important. Listen to the dates and times when events are said to have occurred. Listen to evidence regarding state of mind. I don't mean state of mind regarding somebody's feelings about the color of another's skin or their sexual orientation—the State will try and put you on that scent. I mean the state of mind of each of the State's witnesses. I mean the state of mind of Kaiden Miles, of Davonte Blair, and of any witnesses who take that stand there," Sam said, pointing.

"The government has indicated that they believe and expect to prove that Davonte beat Mr. Miles to death with his fists and/or a weapon they can't find. It will be important for you to be able to determine why my client would do such a thing. My client, a soon-to-be professional basketball player about to embark on the journey he has been preparing for his whole life. Why would he do such a thing? The State will likely float two motives. The first, of course, will be Davonte beat Mr. Miles because he was gay. They almost have to, don't they, given the pressure being exerted by outside groups? Listen to the State's witnesses and ask yourself, is this witness credible? We're nearing the one-quarter mark of the twenty-first century. Does anyone really care? Would my nineteen-year-old client really care? Or might he have merely said some things in a thoughtless moment? Teenagers have those. A second motive, you will be told, could be that he beat Mr. Miles to death over a minor drug deal. That Davonte—whose family members posted a *one-million-dollar cash bond* and who will soon be a millionaire in his own right if what my sources are telling me is true—threw it all away over two thousand dollars. Again, does that pass the smell test? Does it make sense?

"You'll hear they have no murder weapon. They don't even know what it was," Sam said, indicating Cathy. "They can't tell you. It might have been a log, a golf club, or a baseball bat—they have no idea. They'll probably tell you my client got rid of it. Think that through, now. Is it likely that my client—a nineteen-year-old, six-foot-nine black man with no car and no knowledge of this town—somehow found a way to hide a murder weapon with no one seeing him do it? Does that make sense?

"We will challenge the State's witnesses, of course, but I want to make one thing clear: whatever testimony is given, whatever evidence is introduced, we are not trying the police and we are not trying the prosecution. Instead, we think the evidence will show that the police and prosecutors are mistaken in their belief that my client killed Mr. Miles, and we believe that it will be so clear-cut that you will conclude Davonte Blair is not guilty.

"You have told the judge that you would try this case on the evidence, and that's all we ask. You have sworn to do what Davonte's supporters believe the US government has never done: be impartial and unbiased toward a man like him and give him a fair trial. And that is all Davonte Blair asks." Sam's last words were a near whisper, causing several jurors to lean forward in an attempt to hear. "Because when the testimony is heard, when the evidence is seen, and when argument has concluded, two things will be clear. First, that this situation is a tragedy. And second, that Davonte Blair didn't kill Kaiden Miles. And if the second is clear, then your verdict by law must be 'not guilty.' Thank you, ladies and gentlemen," Sam concluded, and sat down.

As the trial got underway, Sam struggled to maintain his focus. He was tired; no matter how many times he promised himself that he would get some rest during a trial, he found himself preparing until the last minute and sleeping poorly. Adding to that was the prior evening's visitor. He'd eaten his bowl of cereal and then—unable to sleep—he'd gone into the office and spent from three to five a.m. refining his opening. Racing home, he'd gotten in a quick shower and a couple cups of coffee before meeting with Paul at seven. He was jittery and his stomach was upset, and he'd been curt with both Paul and Davonte all morning.

The State began by calling Corporal Jensen, who was sworn by Daniels and took the stand. Cathy first had him explain his training, qualifications, and general duties.

"Corporal Jensen, were you employed by the department back on November 20?"

"Yes."

"Now, on that date, did you respond to an area on the south end of Custer College campus?"

"Yes."

"For what reason?"

"Dispatch got ahold of me. Told me a couple walking their dog had reported finding a body."

"So, the area you responded to, is that in Custer County?"

"Yes."

"Can you drive to the area where you were called?" Cathy asked.

"Not legally. There's a walking path, but I suppose it's maybe two or three hundred yards from College Drive. North of College Drive."

"So you drove up College Drive?"

"Yes. Then I walked—well, jogged, really," Jensen said.

"What did you observe?"

"As I got close to, well, I guess you'd call it 'the scene,' I saw a man, a woman, and a dog."

"What were they doing?"

"Watching me."

"Did you speak with them?" Cathy asked.

"Just him. He said, 'Over there,' and pointed toward the creek."

"Meaning Cavalry Creek?"

"Yes."

"And what did you do?"

"I walked in the direction of Cavalry Creek until I saw the body."

"And then what?" Sam noted Cathy was watching the jury closely. It was early and they were focused.

"Then I got on my radio and told dispatch about the body and that we would need the crime scene folks. Then I called Punch, er, Detective Polson, too."

"Then what?"

"Then I went back to the couple and asked them to stand by. I told them that I needed to ask them some questions, but that I had to protect the crime scene until I could get some other officers on scene to take over for me," Jensen explained.

"Did you check to make sure it was a body?"

"No. I knew it was."

"Did you check to see if that person was alive?" Cathy asked.

"No."

"Why not?"

"The guy who called 911 is a doctor at Custer General. I figured if the victim—"

Sam stood. "Objection. Assumes facts not in evidence."

"Sustained," Daniels said.

"The *person*," Cathy hinted. "What was your assumption regarding the person?"

"That the person was dead," Jensen replied.

"Why did you assume that?"

"Uh, because the reporting party was a doctor. I figured if the person was alive, the doctor would've been helping."

"Now, the person you saw. Can you describe what you saw initially?"

"Well, at first, like I said, I didn't get too close. But I got close enough to see a person's body. The body was on its front side, with its head toward the creek and its feet up the bank. The feet were splayed, and the body looked kind of . . . flat."

"When you looked at the body, did you know the body was that of a man?" Cathy asked.

The question was probably vague, but Sam let it go. "No. You couldn't tell at first," Jensen said.

"Did you see anything else?"

"Yes."

"What?"

"Like a watch cap. A beanie or a stocking cap. Not sure what to call it."

"You mean a hat like this?" She showed him a hat in a clear plastic bag that Sam expected would be introduced later.

"Yeah."

"Anything else?"

"Uh, not really?"

Jensen was thinking about something, Sam could tell. Cathy stood quietly, trying to decide whether to follow up.

"See any footprints?" she asked, staying on script.

"Some."

"So you were the first on the scene?"

"First officer, yeah."

"And what did you do when the other officers arrived?"

"I briefed each of them as they showed up, then Officer Goodrich and I taped off the surrounding area. I had him take pictures and I had other officers create a crime scene log."

"What's a crime scene log?"

"It's a list that tells who all walked around in the scene."

"Then what did you do?"

"Then I helped Detective Polson investigate," Jensen said. "Took notes, made calls. Whatever he needed me to do."

"Now, what other involvement did you have in the investigation?"

"Mainly helped do a neighborhood canvass," Jensen said. "I went into the dorms and the neighborhood that was nearest the crime scene and knocked on doors to ask people if they had seen anything. And I got the video from the college's cameras."

"So . . . at some point during the investigation you were kind of backtracking, trying to find out the whereabouts of Mr. Miles before his death?"

"Yes," Jensen said.

"Now prior to November 20, had you ever been to the spot where the body was found?"

"Maybe not that exact spot. But I've run by the general area when I've been jogging."

"Now, did you conduct the interview with the couple and their dog?"

"Not the dog," Jensen said. The audience laughed. Sam smiled with everyone else.

"And how did they seem?" Cathy asked.

"He was okay. He's a doctor. She was kind of freaked out."

"Did either or both eventually provide you with a statement?"

"Yes."

"And did you record your interview with either or both?"

"Well. . . yeah."

"Let me ask it this way: were you wearing a camera that day?"

"Objection," Sam said. "Vague."

"Sustained," Daniels said.

"Were you wearing a vest camera during the interview

with either the man, woman, or dog on the day you discovered the body?" Cathy asked with a glance at Sam.

Again, the audience tittered; again, Sam smiled along.

"Yes."

"Now," she continued, changing the subject. "Did you take any pictures that day?"

"Same objection," Sam said.

"Sustained," Daniels said.

"Did you take any pictures on the day the body was discovered?" Cathy asked.

"A few."

"Your Honor, may I approach?"

"You may."

Cathy walked up to Jensen and handed him several eight-by-ten photographs. "Corporal Jensen, take a look at those photos, and let me know when you are ready to answer some questions about them."

Jensen looked through them quickly and then nodded. "I'm ready."

"Have you seen those before?"

"Yeah, these are pictures I took of the crime scene before anyone else arrived."

"Do they accurately reflect what you saw and the condition of the crime scene at the time you took them?" she asked.

"Yes."

"Your Honor, move for the admission of State's Exhibits 1 through 8," Cathy said.

"Mr. Johnstone?" Daniels asked.

"No objection," Sam said.

"Exhibits 1 through 8 will be received," Daniels said.

"Your Honor, at this time I'd seek permission to publish these photos to the jury using the large screen."

"Very well."

Cathy then had Jensen leave the witness box and stand next to the screen to describe the contents of each picture. When she had finished leading Jensen through the pictures, she indicated that she wanted him to return to the witness box.

"No more questions, Your Honor," she said, and sat down. "Tender the witness."

"Thank you, Ms. Schmidt," Daniels said. "Mr. Johnstone?"

"Thank you, Judge," Sam said, and stepped to the podium. "Good afternoon, Corporal."

"Good afternoon," Jensen said warily.

"Do you have a photograph of the body we are talking about?"

"No."

"Why not?" Sam asked.

"I wasn't responsible for picture taking. I just . . . did. On those," Jensen said.

"Okay," Sam said. "What time did you get called?"

"I can't remember, sir. Could I look at my report?" Jensen asked.

"Would it refresh your memory?"

"I think so."

"Judge, may I approach the witness and hand him his report?"

"You may," Daniels said. Jensen looked at the report for a few seconds, then handed it back to Sam. "It took me about seven minutes from the time I was called until I reported arriving on scene," Jensen said.

"Was there anyone other than the man and wife on scene when you got there?"

"Well, not really."

"What do you mean, 'not really?'" Sam asked.

"People were walking by and riding by on the trail."

"Did you include them on the crime scene log?"

"No."

"Why not?"

"I hadn't started one," Jensen explained, shrugging. "I was waiting for Goodrich."

"So, we don't know exactly how many people were in the vicinity of the body even after you were there until Goodrich started keeping a log, do we?"

"No."

"And we obviously have absolutely no idea how many hundreds or thousands of people might have been on the scene before the body was discovered, right?" Sam asked.

"True."

"And you didn't really look at or photograph the body?"

"No."

"So, you don't know what it looked like before it was found, or if it was somehow moved or disturbed after it was found, do you?"

"Well, definitely not before," Jensen admitted. "After we got things taped off I can say no one moved the body."

"But you didn't take any pictures of the body, so we don't know that the crime scene photos of the body represent exactly how it was positioned before it was found, do we?"

"No. I guess not."

"You don't know when the footprints near the body were made?"

"No."

"So they could have been made after the couple called, but before you got there?"

"Well, I don't think so. They were kind of—"

"But you don't know, do you?"

"No."

"Same with the watch cap," Sam pressed. "You don't know how long it had been there or how or when it got there, right?"

"Well, I am assuming it, er..." Jensen stopped, realizing his mistake and looking at Sam expectantly.

"Are assumptions an acceptable part of the investigative process?"

"Not at my level," Jensen said.

Sam left it there. "Did you take the fingerprints of the couple who found the body?"

"No."

"Do you know if anyone else did?"

"I don't."

"Did you get samples of their DNA?" Sam asked, knowing there was absolutely no reason to do so but wanting to plant a seed.

"No."

"Do you know whether anyone else did?"

"No."

"No, meaning what? No, meaning you don't know, or no, meaning no one else did?" Might as well keep the seed watered.

"No, I don't know whether anyone else did."

"Thank you, Corporal Jenkins. No more questions, Your Honor," Sam said, and sat down.

"Ms. Schmidt? Redirect?"

"No, Judge."

"Thank you," Daniels said. "Is this witness subject to a subpoena?"

"He is," Cathy said. "We'd ask that he be released."

"No objection," Sam said.

After warning Jensen against talking about his testimony,

Daniels released him. "Ms. Schmidt, please call your next witness."

Cathy spent the remainder of that afternoon calling a series of effective and professional witnesses, experts in crime scene examination and analysis, who combined to paint a picture of a calculated killing of the deceased by none other than Davonte. Sam asked a few perfunctory questions, but Cathy had done a good job in preparing her witnesses. None colored outside the lines, and there was little Sam could do aside from sit there and attempt to portray what he was not: confident of his client's eventual acquittal.

⁂

Sam was in his office several hours later, polishing up his cross-examination of the State's DNA expert. His back was getting stiff, so he stood and stretched. He was rehearsing his first few questions to ensure he'd make good eye contact with the jurors when a story about the trial came across his favored national news website's feed. Sitting back in his chair, he un-muted the site and watched. This time, the host was a forty-something white male with a pencil neck and thick glasses. He too was talking with Arick Jordan, who was apparently following the trial on video for several television outlets. "What I saw, Bruce, well, frankly it disturbs me," Jordan said.

"And why is that, Mr. Jordan?"

"Just look around that courtroom. It looked like a Klan meeting. Judge is white, reporter was white, clerks all white, attorneys all white, jurors all white, court security all white. Only black thing in that courtroom was that prosecutor's heart," he said. "And all of them arrayed against Davonte. It was 1890s Mississippi all over again. It's emblematic of the problems with the justice system not only in Montana but in the United States as a whole."

"Wyoming," the host corrected.

"What?"

"They are in Wyoming, not Montana," the host said.

"Whatever. The point is the same," Jordan sniffed.

"Oh, Jesus," Sam said aloud. "Call the jurors racist trash. Always a winning strategy."

"Mr. Blair's attorney has said he believes the jury can reach a proper verdict," the host said.

"Did you see that guy?" Jordan asked, referencing Sam. "Talk about your deer in the headlights. That man lacks courage. And what did he do when that chanting started? Nothing. Not a damned thing. I would have been calling for a mistrial. I mean it. That lawyer is on his way to a lawsuit for malpractice!"

"You'da made that motion against the wishes of your client," Sam observed. "He wants this over so he can get drafted! And the motion would have been denied. If you granted a mistrial every time someone squawked, we'd never get a trial in."

Jordan looked at the camera as it pulled in for a tight shot. "We want Davonte to know that we stand with him. We think his choice of an attorney—an inexperienced white man—was unfortunate. Notwithstanding, we support Davonte and want to see justice for him," Jordan said. "The legal battlefield is slanted against defendants like him, and toward wealthy, connected individuals like Kaiden Miles."

Knowing that Miles's mother cooked lunch at one of the town's elementary schools while Davonte's mother had recently posted a one-million-dollar cash bond, Sam took a sip from a cup of tepid coffee and continued to watch, feeling his stomach tighten.

"I have personally called Davonte and told him that when and if he seeks our assistance, we will be there to assist him in appealing and in seeking redress through civil rights lawsuits," Jordan said. "Until then, we ask everyone to sound off, to let your feelings be known."

Sam stood, crumpled the paper cup, and fired it in the general direction of the face on the television. "You have got to be kidding me!"

19

The next morning, Paul marched into Sam's office. "Have you seen this?" Paul asked, tossing the morning's *Bugle* on Sam's desk. Sam looked at the headline: "TENSION IN BLAIR CAMP."

Sam scanned the article and put the newspaper back down. He looked at his red-faced partner. "Short version?" Sam asked.

"Davonte thinks we're a couple of red-neck, hick lawyers," Paul said. "He says he retained us not because we're worth a damn but because he felt like only a couple of mopes like us could communicate in mope-speak to the mouth-breathers who comprise the members of the jury. He's got some black lawyers group backing him, that essentially says we—you, really—have no business representing a black man charged with killing Miles. They're already lining up their appellate team!"

"No grounds to appeal." Sam shrugged. "No civil rights claim. It's bogus."

Paul closed the door to Sam's office and sat down. "I think we have cause to move Daniels to allow us to withdraw," he said. "What better cause than a client who has no confidence in us, a client with whom we are obviously not communicating, a client who is not helping in his own defense?"

Sam shook his head. "Daniels won't go for it. We're on the third day of trial. He's empaneled a jury. Huge costs to the taxpayer already. I can't see him buying off on it unless Davonte himself makes the motion."

"Will he?"

"I don't know, Paul. I'll call Davonte and have him meet us at the courthouse a little bit early." Sam picked up his phone. "I'll find out what the hell is going on here."

"I just think if there is any way we can abort this, we should do it," Paul urged. "Let's take our fee for what we've done to date and refund the rest to his mom. Short of an acquittal, we're going to be defending ourselves on an ineffective assistance of counsel claim. Our malpractice insurance is going to go through the freaking roof!"

"Paul, someone is whispering in his ear," Sam said. "He's nineteen years old. Not surprising that he's going to talk with them."

"Yeah, well, when the jury reads that—"

"The jury isn't supposed to read that."

"Sam, don't be naïve."

"Paul, that's the rule. The judge has instructed the jurors to not read anything."

"You're kidding me, right?" Paul was up and waving his arms now. "You can't possibly believe the jurors aren't reading the papers and social media and whatever else they can get their hands on, can you?"

"I know what they were told not to do," Sam said. He was on the phone and instructed Davonte to be early. "This is important," he concluded.

"Sam, this isn't the army," Paul said after Sam had hung

up. "In the real world, people don't always do what they are supposed to do. We've got a courthouse and a jail filled with people who don't do what they are supposed to do. Hell, half of the government's agencies exist because people don't do what they oughta be doing."

Sam was putting files in his briefcase. He looked at his watch. "We need to get going if we are going to meet with Davonte before court."

"Sam, let's call Daniels right now and tell him we need time," Paul argued. "Tell him we have an issue. We don't even need to tell him what it is about. He'll know."

"You coming?" Sam asked, ignoring the suggestion.

"Let me grab my briefcase," Paul said.

The partners had walked the two blocks to the courthouse in silence. As they mounted the steps, they were briefly surrounded by protesters shouting, "Justice for Kaiden!" Most held signs supporting Kaiden and his family and referring to gay rights. Sam noted that among the protesters was Custer County Commissioner Pat Morales. As they passed Morales, Sam could hear him shouting over the din to Penrose, "We are working every single day to build trust with the gay, lesbian, and trans community here in Custer. One of the things that would undermine the burgeoning relationship with that community would be a not-guilty verdict."

Penrose and other members of the press spotted Sam and Paul and rushed them, but neither commented and eventually they were through security and at the defense table. Enduring the stares from courthouse personnel, they quickly prepared for the day's session before Sam went to Daniels's chambers and retrieved a key from Mary to a room reserved for counsel to meet with clients. He waved Davonte in when he saw the young man sauntering down the hall with Sharon, Reggie, and Damon. Davonte took a seat as Paul closed the door in Damon's and Reggie's faces.

"What the hell?" Davonte began to protest.

"That's what I want to know," Sam said. "What the hell is your major malfunction?"

"What are you talking about?" Sharon asked. "Sam, what's wrong?"

"I'm talking about your son talking with that black lawyers association and saying Paul and I are essentially a couple of bums he's retained because he thinks we can relate to the dumb white folk on the jury."

Sharon looked at Davonte. "I didn't know they was gonna write a story," he told her.

"What the hell did you think they were going to do? Keep your secret? You got enough of those already," Paul snarled. Sharon looked at him steadily. Davonte tried to appear unfazed. "This isn't the time to give me your badass game here, son," Paul continued. "You need to speak up and you need to speak up now."

"*Son*? Who you callin' *son*? I oughta—" Davonte said, and began to stand.

"Sit down, Davonte," Sharon said quietly. She looked at Sam. He understood.

"Mrs. Blair . . . Sharon, my client and I need a minute," Sam said quietly. "You will recall I explained to you up front there were certain matters that were going to be between Davonte and us. This is that."

"I'll be outside." Sharon stood and looked down at her son. "Davonte, listen to the man," she said, and left the room.

Paul closed the door behind her. Davonte began to stand, but before he could do so Sam had moved across the room and put his forehead to Davonte's, forcing him back in his chair. "Sit down and shut up until I tell you to talk. And when I tell you to talk, you'd better stay on subject."

"Or what?" Davonte said, balling his fists.

"Paul, get out," Sam said, not taking his eyes off Davonte.

"What?"

"Get out," Sam said again. "I'm not asking."

"Sam, don't do this," Paul pleaded.

"Paul, it's time for me and Davonte to have a little 'Come to Jesus.'"

Paul left the tiny room. Sam had not moved. He was looming over Davonte. "Now, big man, I want you to know something: I'm sick of your screwed-up attitude, the games you play, and you and your henchmen spying on me, trying to intimidate me."

"What are you talking about, spying on you?" Davonte said. "No one talks to me like that."

"I am," Sam said, moving his face even closer to Davonte's. He could smell the young man's breath and was sure Davonte could smell the several cups of coffee on his own. "It's just you and me. You don't like the way I'm talking to you? Now's the time to do something about it. Let's go."

"You serious?"

"I am," Sam said, his voice lower. "Come on, Davonte. Put your money where your big mouth is."

"You only got one leg, man."

"I know, and I want nothing more than to stand on my bad leg and kick your ass with the good one. Let's do this. Make your move."

Davonte stiffened. "Do it, Davonte," Sam whispered. "Do it, or I'll know that you're a chicken-shit."

Davonte sat perfectly still for several seconds and then seemed to relax slightly. "Man, we got to do court."

"I don't know that I'm willing to 'do court' with you." Sam said. "I've busted my butt since day one, and I'm not going into court with a client who is undermining me. I don't need your shit, and I don't need your money. What I do need is to kick your ass. I need that bad. I just need you to make a move. Do it!" Sam yelled.

"Everything okay in there?" Paul asked from outside.

"Fine, Paul," Sam said. "Get away from the door." Sam turned his attention back to Davonte. "Time's almost up. I'm right here."

"That story in the magazine," Davonte said. "I was just talkin' shit, man."

"I know that, dumbass. And your shit-talking might get you convicted. But we're not here for that. We're here because I've got a score to settle."

"Sam, I . . . I don't want to fight you. How the hell's that gonna look to—"

"To who? What do you care?"

"Sam, I'm sorry. I didn't mean nothin'. I was just talking shit in front of Reggie and Damon. Just funnin' around a little. I screwed up. I admit it."

Paul was pounding on the door. "Sam! Mary says the judge is waiting!"

"Just a minute!" Sam said. He stepped back from Davonte and looked the young man in the eye. "Davonte, you should know that I'm going to walk into the courtroom with you, and I'm going to bust my ass to defend you. Not because of you—I think you are an arrogant, immature punk. And not because of the money—I couldn't care less. But because it's my job. Because somebody has to defend idiots like yourself. I signed up to do the job, and I'm going to do it. But there is another option, and it is yours and yours alone."

"What's that?"

"You grab yourself by the stack and swivel and tell Judge Daniels you need new lawyers. Sounds like you got some that are dying to come to Wyoming."

"How—?"

"Not my problem. I'm just giving you your options and I'm telling you this: you either get new lawyers or you do exactly what I say from here on out, knowing I'm perfectly willing to walk if you don't."

"This is bullshit," Davonte said. "I don't think you can do this."

"Tell your firm from back east," Sam said. "You already have their number. What's it gonna be?"

Two minutes later, Davonte and Sam exited the little room. Paul stepped in beside them, sweating heavily. "Mary says the judge is pissed."

"He'll either get over it, or he won't," Sam said.

"What are we doing?" Paul asked.

"I'm not sure. Davonte might want to speak with the judge."

"I'm glad to see that defense counsel is *finally* ready," Daniels said, shooting a scathing glance Sam's way after all but the jury were seated. It was an act; he'd read the paper and anticipated that Sam would need a little extra time with his client this morning. "Does the defense have a motion to present?"

Sam looked at Davonte. "Your move," he said.

Davonte shook his head, so Sam leaned behind Davonte and addressed Paul. "What do you want to do?"

"Your call," Paul said.

"Your Honor," Sam said, standing until he felt Davonte's hand on his sleeve.

"Sam, don't quit on me," Davonte said.

Sam looked at him. "It can't be the same."

"You got it."

"No, Your Honor," Sam said. He thought he could see both Daniels and Cathy exhale.

"Good," the judge said. "Bailiff, please call for the jury."

After the jury was seated, Daniels ordered Cathy to proceed. "Your Honor, the State calls Amanda Desmond," she said.

After Desmond was sworn and seated, Cathy began the direct examination. "Please state your name for the court."

"Amanda Desmond."

"How are you employed?"

"I am a forensic scientist with the Wyoming state crime lab," she said.

Cathy then asked a series of questions designed to show the jury that Desmond—as the result of her education, credentials, and experience—was an expert in the field of DNA.

"Ms. Desmond, can you tell us or give us sort of an overview of what DNA is?"

"DNA is a chemical found in various cells throughout the human body. It determines our unique individual characteristics," Desmond began. "The majority of human DNA is very similar from person to person, but there is a small percentage that varies a great deal from person to person and makes us unique. It is these regions or areas of the DNA that we use in forensic DNA analysis to generate a person's specific DNA profile."

"So, everyone has a specific profile?"

"Yes. Well, except for identical siblings."

"And I think you said the majority of our DNA is similar but there are areas that are unique—is that right?"

"Yes."

"And without getting into too much detail, when you are doing your analysis, do you look at the similar areas or the unique areas?"

"We look to the unique areas, the polymorphic areas. Those vary greatly from person to person."

"Now, Ms. Desmond, what can you get a DNA profile from? What sort of material?"

"DNA is taken from cells. We can obtain DNA from blood, saliva, semen, or skin cells."

"Skin cells?"

"Yes."

"What is touch DNA? If I hear that phrase, what is that?"

"Touch DNA refers to skin cells transferred to an item by having physical contact with it."

"And is it different from other DNA?"

"Well, the source is," Desmond said. "In touch DNA, we are obtaining nucleated cells in skin cells rather than in a fluid as in blood, semen, or saliva."

Sam was watching the jurors closely. They appeared to be paying attention.

"So, if I touch an item, my cells will be transferred to it?" Cathy continued.

"Possibly," Desmond allowed.

"But not in every case?"

"No. It depends on a number of things, such as the duration of the touch, the type of surface of the item—there are a number of variables."

"Could submersion in water or being covered in snow affect the deposit of skin cells?"

"It could."

"Could it affect the duration skin cells would remain on an item?"

"It could."

"Might it impact your ability to recover them?"

"It might."

"I am handing you State's Exhibit 10," Cathy said while she did so. "Will you take a look at that for me, please? Can you tell me what that is?"

"It is a sample of blood from Kaiden Miles."

"Have you handled that before?"

"Yes, I have."

"How do you know that?"

"It has my initials and I dated it right here," Desmond said, pointing to a pen entry.

"And what, if anything, were you asked to do with that?" Cathy asked.

"To develop a DNA profile of Kaiden Miles."

"Were you able to do that?"

"Yes."

"I am now handing you State's Exhibits 24, 25, and 26," Cathy said. "Take a look at those three items for me. Are you familiar with them?"

"Yes."

"How?"

"These are buccal swabs—cheek swabbings identified as coming from Ronnie Norquist, Trent Gustafson, and Davonte Blair," Desmond said.

"What were you asked to do with those items?"

"Develop a DNA profile."

"Were you able to do so?"

"Yes."

"I'm showing you State's Exhibit 32. Will you take a look at that for me, please?"

"I have."

"What did I just hand you?"

"This was a swab sample collected from a watch cap found near Kaiden Miles's body," Desmond said.

"How was the swab taken?" Cathy asked.

"I imagine a number of samples were taken from areas on the watch cap," she said. "I wasn't there, of course."

"What were you asked to do with this item?"

"To develop a DNA profile and compare it to known standards."

"So you would compare the DNA profile or profiles found on the cap to those of the three DNA profiles you obtained from the men using the mouth swabs?" Cathy asked.

"Yes."

"And when you did that comparison, what did you find?"

"Well, I generated a partial profile on that cap and found that it was consistent with a mixture of male DNA, meaning that there is more than one contributor, and the predominant profile matched to the DNA profile from Kaiden Miles."

"What does 'predominant profile' mean?"

"When you have more than one profile, one will have DNA on the item in a greater concentration."

"So, you had more than one profile? Were you able to determine who the, uh—"

"Minor contributors?"

"Yes, were you able to determine who the minor contributors were?"

"One of them, yes."

"And after you made that determination, did you perform a statistical analysis?"

"I did."

"What did you determine?"

"The sample came from a black male."

"Who?"

"The sample was 102 million times more likely to come

from Davonte Blair than another black member of Wyoming's population."

Cathy allowed the murmuring in the audience to die under the withering gaze of Daniels. "No more questions, Judge," she said, then turned to Sam. "Your witness, counsel."

"Thank you," Sam said. He stood, picked up a pile of papers, and carried them with him to the podium. "Ms. Desmond, I just have a few questions. Are you familiar with the term secondary transfer?"

"Of course."

"What does that term mean?"

"Basically, it is DNA transferred from one item that is also transferred to another item."

"Let me see if I understand. Let's say I'm sitting in a restaurant and I'm waiting for a friend—say, Davonte here. He arrives and opens the restaurant door, then walks over and shakes my hand with the same hand that opened the restaurant door. Is it possible that I could have Davonte's DNA—"

"Objection. Calls for speculation," Cathy said, standing and sitting quickly. The objection was not a good one, she knew, but she wanted to put the thought in the jurors' minds.

"Overruled." Daniels shot her a look. "She's an expert," he continued, looking to the jury. "She can respond to a hypothetical."

"Yes."

"So Davonte's DNA could be on my hand simply from him touching me?"

"Yes, that's called touch DNA. I thought we covered that," she said, looking bored.

"Continuing with my example." Sam paused for effect. "Is

it possible that in shaking my hand, Davonte could pass on to me DNA from *other* people who had touched that same door handle?"

Desmond shifted uneasily in her chair. "It is possible, but not probable. But it could happen."

"So, to continue with my hypothetical, if you were to swab my hand after my meeting with Davonte, you might find my DNA?"

"Almost certainly," Desmond said.

"Davonte's DNA?"

"It's not unlikely."

"And the DNA of a few other unknown people who touched the door handle of the restaurant but had never touched me?"

"Possibly."

"It could happen?"

"Yes," Desmond said. "But—"

"So, you cannot exclude as a possibility that the cells you found on that cap got there not from my client touching the cap, but from someone else—like Kaiden Miles—touching my client, or even something he had touched, and passing my client's cells to the cap?"

"No, I cannot exclude that as a possibility," she admitted. "I'd say it was remote."

"But possible if, for example, Kaiden had touched my client and then the cap?"

"Yes," she said tightly. "I already said that."

"When you are analyzing a sample, does your analysis tell you when the sample was placed on the surface that is being swabbed?"

"No."

"You have absolutely no way to tell how long a sample has been present on an item when it is swabbed for DNA?"

"Correct."

"You were asked to test numerous items in this case, correct?"

"Oh, yes."

"Do you have your reports there in front of you?"

"Yes, I do."

"I want to read some of the items that you were requested to test," Sam said. He picked up and read from a paper in his hand. "You were asked to test swabbings from the decedent's car, from his dorm room, from his pants, shoes, socks, and shirt—true?"

"You know it is."

Sam smiled broadly at Desmond. "Let's continue. You were asked to test swabbings from other items found near the body —sticks and rocks and those kinds of things?"

"Yes."

"And you were asked to test swabbings from the cap?"

"You know I was," she said.

Sam smiled at her again. "And you were asked to compare those matters in all cases to my client?"

"Yes, as well as the other standards that were submitted."

"Meaning other people's DNA?"

"Correct."

"Aside from the watch cap, you didn't find my client's DNA on any item you were asked to examine, did you?" Sam looked at the jury. They were still following.

"No."

"So, the cap only—and you don't begin to know when or how my client's DNA was passed to the cap?"

"No," Desmond admitted.

"And you can't exclude a secondary or tertiary transfer?"

"No."

"And in fact, regarding the hat, you found my client's DNA only in a mixed DNA sample, true?"

"True."

"And the major donor was Mr. Miles?"

"Yes."

"And you said one other minor contributor was, you believe, my client."

"Presumptively."

Sam had one more question, but he wasn't entirely sure of the answer he would get in response. He thought about it and then asked. "You said 'contributors' on direct—so were you able to determine the identity of the *other* minor donor or donors?" He assumed she had not, as there had been no disclosure. A name would certainly be exculpatory information his client had a right to know.

"Not to a degree of scientific certainty, no," she said. "That's why it's not in my report."

Sam was thinking. "So, there *is* another contributor," he mused aloud. "Any idea who it might be?"

"Objection," Cathy said. "She can't be certain; that's why it isn't in her report."

"Overruled," Daniels said. "You can answer, if there is an answer."

"I've got an idea," Desmond said.

Sam had been hoping for a simple no, which would have given him a phantom to point at in closing. He considered moving to have Desmond's answer struck because it wasn't responsive. He stalled by looking through the papers on the podium in front of him while he considered his options. He decided he needed to follow up. "Who else do you think might have contributed to the mixture?" Sam asked at last.

"I cannot recall," she said. "May I refer to my notes?"

"Would it help your recollection?" Sam asked.

"Yes," Desmond said. "That's why I asked."

Sam smiled tightly, then looked at Daniels, who looked at the witness. "You may," Daniels said. "Let Mr. Johnstone know when you are ready to answer."

Desmond looked at her notes, then looked to Sam and nodded. He indicated she could answer.

"I believe the other minor contributor was a male by the name of Ronald Norquist."

Sam tried not to let his surprise show. He now had a named alternate male contributor—albeit his partner's son and his star witness—giving him the ability to inject at least some doubt in the jurors' minds. He let the murmuring in the courtroom die down before he asked the follow-on question.

"Why didn't you disclose the identity of Ronald Norquist in your report?"

"Because I cannot say he is the minor contributor with the requisite degree of scientific certainty. I can only say that there is some arithmetic probability based on scientific assumption," she said. "But I have nowhere near the certainty I do with your client." She sat back and folded her arms, awaiting his next question.

"Can you explain what you mean when you say you cannot say 'with the requisite degree of scientific certainty?'" he asked.

"Certainly," Desmond said, and turned to the jury. She delivered a lengthy response explaining the biological and mathematical probabilities undergirding the method of analyzing mixed DNA samples, giving Sam time to think and get a drink of water.

"But you cannot say how, where, or when *that* sample was transferred to that mixture either, can you?" Sam asked.

"No."

"In fact, the old adage is, 'Your DNA goes places you do not'—isn't that right?"

"Correct."

"Mr. Norquist, like Mr. Blair, might well have never been near that hat, yet we find his DNA on the hat—true?"

"Well, the probability that Mr. Blair's DNA is on the hat is a lot higher than Mr. Norquist's."

"But only a degree of probability—true?"

Desmond sat quietly, thinking. "Right," she said at last.

Paul was trying to get Sam's attention. Davonte touched Sam's sleeve and nodded toward Paul. "Your Honor," Sam said. "May I have a moment?"

"You may," Daniels said. He watched as Sam and Paul entered into a discussion. As it got increasingly heated, Daniels looked at his watch. "Ladies and gentlemen, let's take ten. Bailiff?"

———

In chambers, Daniels was lighting a cigar and sneaking into his private bathroom for a couple of quick draws when Mary walked in. "Judge!"

"What is it, Mary?"

"You took your morning break early and didn't tell me," she scolded.

"I don't have to clear it with you," he said, puffing smoke and blowing it into the fan.

"Why did you break early?"

"To give Sam and Paul a chance to hash out a major issue," he said.

"What's going on?" Mary asked. She was straightening files on Daniels's desk while he smoked.

"Sam's questions just revealed the presence of DNA in a

mixture found on the dead guy's hat that belonged to a third party."

"Sounds like good news for the defense," she said.

"Ordinarily, it would be. You'd have an identified additional person of interest." Daniels watched a smoke ring get sucked into the fan. "But the DNA in question could well belong to Paul's son, Ronnie," he said, turning to Mary.

"Oh my gosh!"

"Yeah," Daniels said. "That's what Paul is thinking right now."

———

Paul and Sam were in a small conference room off the hallway to the side of the courtroom. "Paul, I had to chase that rabbit down the hole," Sam said. "This is our best chance to create reasonable doubt."

"No, Sam," Paul said. "I can't have Ronnie involved in this."

"It's too late. He knew Davonte and Miles; he worked with and was around both. His DNA is—"

"Might be!" Paul interrupted. "She didn't report it because the evidence is so weak. That's what she said."

"Exactly, and the presence of Ronnie's DNA—even the suspected presence of his DNA—is probably enough for us to raise reasonable doubt in the minds of the jurors."

"You can't use my son as a decoy." Paul was up and pacing the small room.

"Look, all I've got to do is make clear to the jurors that if Ronnie's DNA is there, then there's another . . . person who, uh, is . . . of interest."

"A *suspect*," Paul said. "You want to paint Ronnie as a suspect!"

"Paul, our client is Davonte. If we highlight the likely presence of Ronnie's DNA, we can create reasonable doubt. That is justice in this case."

"Only if he's innocent."

"Not our call. I'll ask her three or four questions to make clear that from the standpoint of DNA Ronnie is just as good a suspect as Davonte. Frankly, I think it is malpractice if I don't continue this line of questioning."

"You're going to want to call Ronnie," Paul said.

"We're not there yet," Sam said. "But I had him served with a subpoena."

"Without asking me. You are going to call him!"

"I might," Sam admitted. "The State's case is weak. DNA is important in the minds of jurors—sometimes too important. We have an opportunity to show the jury that in Davonte's case, the DNA is virtually worthless. We take away the DNA and they've got nothing."

"You can't put my son on the stand!"

"Paul, we put him on the stand, have him testify that he's been around the victim, just like Davonte. He testifies that he doesn't know how his DNA could have gotten on the hat. It's like having Davonte testify without having to call him. The jury will hear and see Ronnie and infer that, 'Hey, *he* was at the party, *his* DNA is on the hat, *he* didn't get charged. And *he* owed Kaiden money, too.' Ronnie—on paper—is just as viable a candidate as Davonte."

"No, he is not! He is my son!"

"Paul." Sam looked at his old friend closely. "What's going on?"

"What do you mean?"

"Is there something you are not telling me?"

"Of course not!"

"Paul, I know Ronnie's your son. But he is an adult and he

didn't have anything to do with the kid's murder, so what in the hell is the problem?"

Paul sat staring at the tabletop, saying nothing. Sam stood, looked at his watch, and said, "Time."

"Don't do this, Sam," Paul said. "For me."

"Paul, you are asking me to ignore my ethics, to forego a perfectly legitimate—frankly, probably required—line of questioning, and to put our client's life at risk. And I'm not sure why."

"Because he's my son," Paul said. He got up and walked out, leaving Sam alone.

Moments later, when all had reassembled, Daniels looked down the bench at Paul and Sam. "Counsel, please continue."

Sam stood and took a deep breath. He could feel all eyes upon him. "Thank you, Judge. Ms. Desmond, safe to say you don't know how or when Mr. Norquist's DNA was transferred to that hat?"

"That is true—I already said that. I don't even know for sure it *is* his."

"And similarly, you don't know how or when my client's DNA was transferred to that hat, either—do you?"

"I already said that, too."

Cathy was on her feet, about to object. With a quick look at the jurors, Sam saw two nod their heads. He sat down. "No more questions, Your Honor."

The next witness was the contracted medical examiner. Sam pulled a file from the banker's box he had prepared and quickly reviewed his notes. He didn't expect much to come of this testimony. Having gotten through Dr. Laws's bona fides, Cathy began asking the pertinent questions.

"What is the medical examiner?"

"The medical examiner is the physician assigned to the coroner's office. The coroner is an elected position and does not have to be a licensed physician," Laws said. "The medical examiner heads the office that is in charge of investigating the two major types of death investigations: non-natural deaths—the accidents, suicides, and homicides that take place in a community every day—and sudden unexpected deaths—deaths where there was not a doctor in attendance who might be in a position to sign a death certificate. We investigate those cases."

"Do you also perform autopsies?"

"I do."

"How many autopsies have you performed?"

"Well over one hundred, I would think."

"Let me take you back to November 21—were you employed as medical examiner on that date?"

"I was."

"Did you perform an autopsy on an individual named Kaiden Miles?"

"I did."

"Other than yourself, who was present during that autopsy?"

"I have an assistant who was present. I think Detective Polson was there as well for a time, but he may have left at some point. He wasn't feeling well watching. The coroner may have stopped in. I'd have to look at my notes."

"Now what did you first notice about the body of Kaiden Miles?" Cathy asked.

"Extensive bruising in the facial area. He had a black eye and a broken jaw. He had obviously been in some sort of physical altercation."

"A fight?"

"That's one possibility, yes."

"But there are others?"

"Well, of course. He could simply have been the victim of a battery," Laws said.

Cathy looked at the jurors and knew many were confused. "You are saying Kaiden might have been hit by someone, but not as part of a fight?"

"From a medical standpoint, it could have happened that way, yes."

"Now based on your training and experience and your findings from the autopsy, do you have an opinion as to the cause of death of Kaiden Miles?" Cathy asked.

"I do."

"And what is that opinion?"

"I believe the victim died as the result of hemorrhage following a depressed fracture of the back of the skull."

"So he suffered a blow to the back of the head and died of blood loss?"

"Yes. You could say that."

"Did you view any photographs from the crime scene?" she asked.

"Yes, and after reviewing the photographs, I feel like they supported my original opinion."

"Did you have the opportunity to observe how the victim's body was lying by the creek?"

"I did."

"And did that help confirm your opinion that this was a homicide?"

"I'm not sure my viewing the body added much. The deceased could not have inflicted the wound at the back of his head upon himself. Death would have resulted in a short time —minutes at the most—from the infliction of this blow.

Bleeding was sudden and massive. He would have lost consciousness within seconds."

"Your Honor, those are the State's questions," Cathy said, and sat down.

Daniels pointedly looked at the clock, then at Sam. "Mr. Johnstone, cross-examination?" he asked, and looked at the clock again.

"Yes, Your Honor," Sam said. "Just a few questions. Dr. Laws, as the result of the autopsy, were you able to determine a time of death?"

"No."

"Could you give an approximate date?"

"Not really. The body had been exposed to the elements. The time of year, snowfall . . . I wouldn't be comfortable beyond saying the man had been dead for ten days to two weeks," he said.

"You testified the blow that killed him would have done so in short order—is that fair?"

"Yes. It was a grievous injury," Laws said. "He would have lost consciousness almost instantly and would have died within minutes."

"And you said he had wounds consistent with having been struck in the facial area," Sam said.

"Yes."

"Can you tell from your examination whether the wounds to the face and the blow to the back of the head occurred at the same time?"

Dr. Laws sat back and thought for a moment. "Based on my observation of bruising to the facial area, I believe those injuries were incurred initially," Laws said. "The blow to the head came later."

"How much later, can you tell?" Sam asked.

"Not with exactitude."

"Weeks?"

"Oh, no. No signs of healing to the face."

"Days?"

"I would think more likely minutes—perhaps up to an hour. The bruising had not yet really begun to spread. The bleeding under the skin was really just starting."

"Was there a large loss of blood?" Sam asked. The question was vague, but Cathy didn't object.

"Not initially—not from the black eye or jaw."

"So, the victim was hit in the face at some point, and then whacked in the head at another?" Sam asked. He had a small opening here—one that accorded with what Davonte had been telling him and anyone else who would listen.

"I think that's fair to say, yes."

"By the same person or persons?"

Cathy was on her feet, but the doctor had it figured out. "I think that is Detective Polson's job." Cathy sat back down. Sam could feel Paul's eyes upon him.

"He'd have been able to walk after getting hit in the face?"

"Oh yes."

"So he could have been hit in the face at one location, and then whacked in the back of the head in another?"

"Objection," Cathy said.

"Overruled. You may answer, Doctor," Daniels said.

"Could have," Laws said.

"No more questions, Your Honor," Sam said. As he walked back to his chair, his eyes briefly met Jeannie's. He looked away.

"Any redirect?" Daniels asked Cathy.

"No, Judge."

"Okay, folks," Daniels said. He was anticipating the State would call Polson next. Thinking that examination would take a while, Daniels made a quick decision. "Let's take our lunch break before the State's next witness. As always, follow the bailiff's directions, and do not talk about the case. Bailiff, please conduct the jury to the jury room."

———

Ninety minutes later the parties had reconvened, and the jury was seated. Sam had spent the time reviewing the exhibits submitted by the State. Something was bothering him about the watch cap, but he couldn't put his finger on it. He was looking at a photograph of the room shared by Miles and Ronnie when it began to dawn on him.

When everyone had reassembled, Daniels looked to Cathy. "Okay. Let's proceed with the State's case-in-chief. Ms. Schmidt, please call the State's next witness."

"Your Honor, the State calls Kenneth Polson," she said. Sam and Paul exchanged a look, and Paul pushed a yellow legal pad toward Sam with the words "game time" scribbled on it. Sam shrugged and wrote back, "Not a lot we can do here." Paul's face clouded.

After swearing an oath, Punch took the stand. "Mr. Polson, please state your full legal name for the record," Cathy directed.

"Kenneth Polson—but everyone calls me Punch, ma'am."

Cathy ignored the temptation to ask why. She should have asked him earlier. "Never ask a question to which you do not already know the answer," the old adage went. "Mr. Polson, are you employed?"

"Yes, ma'am."

"What do you do?"

"I am a detective with the Custer Police Department, assigned to the major crimes unit," he said. He answered a number of questions from Cathy tending to show he was a qualified detective capable of conducting a thorough, professional investigation.

"Were you on duty as a member of the major crimes unit on or about November 20?"

"Yes."

"And on that date, were you called to a location near the Custer College campus?"

Sam knew Polson would be calm and collected, but he was still impressed by the detective's steady manner and his understated, professional accounting of the steps taken during the investigation. He would impress the jury, and cross-examination would have to be undertaken carefully.

"Detective Polson, you arrived on the scene when?"

"I got there about eight a.m. on the 20th."

"And what did you do?"

"I ensured that Jensen had a handle on securing the scene," he said. "Then I went with the crime scene guys to look at the body."

"Crime scene guys?"

"Well, photographers and DNA types first," Punch said, settling in to recall his actions. "The body had obviously been there for a while, and there was melting snow around it, so I wanted pictures taken before anything got disturbed. Then I sent the crime scene guys in, and when they were done, I started looking around."

"First impressions, as you recall?"

"Uh, the body had been there a while, so I figured he'd been killed shortly after he went missing."

"Killed? How did you determine that?"

"He," Punch began, then shifted his eyes to Ms. Miles before looking back to Cathy. "He, uh, had an obvious wound to the back of his head."

"Could he have sustained that in a fall?" She wanted

Punch to say no, but he was too experienced to do so. It was objectionable, but Sam let it go. If she wanted to open the door to the possibility of an accident, Sam was amenable.

"Um, not sure I'm qualified to respond," he replied, looking at Sam.

"Let's move on. So, you began your investigation?"

"We did," Punch said. "We began talking to people on the scene and from the surrounding neighborhood to see if anyone had seen anything."

"Results?"

"None."

"Then?"

"Well, we'd already looked at video from the campus and surrounding areas. Remember, he'd been missing almost two weeks. And we had already interviewed a number of persons in connection with the victim's, er, young man's disappearance," Punch said. "So, I felt a good place to start was with the guys our earlier investigation revealed had seen him right before he died."

"And who were they?"

"Ronnie Norquist, Trent Gustafson, and the defendant."

"So, what did you do next?"

"Well, I'd looked at the video, like I said, so I spoke with each of the young men about what they had seen, heard, and done that night. They each told me essentially the same story that they'd given me when I was inquiring into Kaiden's disappearance."

"What was that?"

"That Mr. Miles, Mr. Norquist, Mr. Gustafson, and Mr. Blair had been partying well into the evening, and that there was a dispute between Mr. Miles and Mr. Blair, and that Mr. Miles left, followed by Mr. Blair."

"What was the dispute over?"

"According to all parties, Mr. Miles said Mr. Blair owed him money."

"Why?"

"My investigation revealed Mr. Miles had been selling drugs to Mr. Blair," Punch said, looking first at Mrs. Miles and then at Sharon while the crowd murmured.

"What then?" Cathy said after the murmuring stopped.

"The party broke up following the argument."

"What time?"

"Well, the parties were a little . . . foggy . . . about times, but according to the video Mr. Miles left at around 1:20 a.m. and Mr. Blair a few minutes later."

"So, what did you do then?"

"Well, Mr. Gustafson and Mr. Norquist confirmed each other's story about being together the entire evening after the party ended," Punch said. "They had an alibi."

Sam watched as Punch looked toward Paul when he mentioned Ronnie's name, and out of the corner of his eye he could see Paul stiffen.

"Then what?"

"Well, at that point I knew Mr. Blair had been seen following Mr. Miles out the door of the dorm because I had the video as well as Trent and Ronnie telling me that. So, I'd already subpoenaed Mr. Miles's phone records and had seen a lot of communications with Mr. Blair, so I subpoenaed Mr. Blair's phone records as well as those of his internet provider. I had a forensic computer scientist go through all of that and produce for me the records."

"And what did you find?"

"I found some things that interested me," Punch said.

"Notably?"

"Mr. Blair was one of the last people to call Mr. Miles, and the last to send him a text message."

"Your Honor, may I approach?" Cathy asked while handing Sam a document. He nodded to her. After Daniels granted her permission, she walked to the witness box, handed Punch a document, and returned to the podium.

"I've handed you State's Exhibit 42. Seen it before?"

"I have."

"What is it?" Cathy asked.

"It's the printout of some of the text messages between the deceased and Mr. Blair gleaned from their phone records."

"Objection," Sam said. "May we approach?" Daniels nodded, and when Sam and Cathy were at the bench, Sam continued, "Judge, the probative value of the evidence is far outweighed by potential prejudice. The jury might convict my client based on some dumb things he said."

"Goes to motive, Judge," Cathy quickly responded.

"Overruled," Daniels said. "Return to your places."

Cathy looked to Punch. "You mentioned you had concerns as the result of your review of these records. Can you tell the jury why?"

"The defendant made several homophobic comments in here," Punch said. "Called the deceased a number of names indicating that he didn't like gay and . . . well, white people."

"Can you point out to the jury specific examples?" Cathy asked.

Punch then read into the record several homophobic and racial slurs that Davonte had sent to others, including Kaiden. Sam could sense the discomfort of everyone except his client.

"Anything else of concern in the phone records?" Cathy asked.

"Yes."

"What was that?"

"The defendant communicated a number of threats to the decedent."

"Same objection," Sam said. "Move to strike."

"Overruled," Daniels said.

"Any of special concern?" Cathy asked.

"Yes," Punch said. "On the morning of Kaiden's disappearance, at approximately 1:25 a.m., the defendant sent a text to the decedent that said, 'I've told your skinny white ass a hundred times, you'll get your money when I go pro. Keep pumping me and I'm going to beat your fag self.'"

Again, Cathy waited for the soft murmuring to die down before continuing. "What did that information indicate to you?"

"Well, two possible motives. One financial, one, well, homophobic, I guess."

"Anything else of value come back from the phone records?"

"Yes," he said.

"What was that?"

"Using the phone company's experts, we were able to place Mr. Blair in the vicinity of where Mr. Miles was eventually found on the morning in question, at approximately the time in question."

"Detective Polson, you heard Ms. Desmond's testimony regarding the DNA evidence in this case, didn't you?"

"I did."

"Did you play a role in the collection of the DNA?"

"I did. I collected it," he said.

"So, at some point, did you have contact with Ronnie Norquist, Trent Gustafson, and the defendant, Davonte Blair?"

"At various times, yes."

"So, not at the same time?"

"Never all three, no."

"And did you collect buccal swabs from each?"

"Objection," Sam said. "Vague."

"Sustained," Daniels said.

"Did you take buccal swabs from those three men?"

"I did."

"Can you tell the jurors the procedures you follow when you collect a buccal swab from an individual?"

"Well, I take a small Q-tip, have them open their mouth, and just rub it gently on the inside of the cheek. There are two in each package, one for the left side and one for the right side."

"So you are trying to obtain skin cells from inside their cheek?"

"I think so."

"You are not an expert on anything about DNA?" she asked.

"No, I'm just collecting the items to send to the state lab," he admitted. "I don't have any expertise in it; I just follow the instructions on the kit."

"Where were these samples taken?"

"I took Gustafson's at the station. I took the defendant's and Norquist's in the gym."

"And while you were speaking with Mr. Blair, did you tell him why you were there?"

"Oh, yeah."

"Was he a suspect?" she asked.

"Well, not really. More like a person of interest."

"So, no formal interview?"

"No, not really."

"Did you tell him you were going to take a sample of his DNA to use in your investigation?"

"Yes, ma'am."

"And he consented to this?"

"Yes, ma'am."

"What did you do then?"

"I placed the Q-tip thingy in a small white box that had a label with his name on it, then put that box into a white envelope. Then I sealed the envelope and had it secured at the police department."

Cathy walked back to the State's table and retrieved a package from her assistant. "Your Honor, may I approach?"

"You may."

"I'm handing the detective what is marked as State's Exhibit 26," she said. "Detective, please let me know when you are ready to respond to my questions."

"I'm ready."

"What is State's Exhibit 26?"

"This is the envelope I sent to the state laboratory containing the swab from the defendant," he said.

"The envelope is in substantially the same condition as when you placed the swab inside?" Cathy said.

"Looks exactly the same to me," Punch said.

"Your Honor, I offer Exhibit 26 into evidence," Cathy said.

Daniels looked at Sam. "No objection," Sam said.

"It will be received," Daniels said.

"Now, after you got the swabs from Mr. Norquist, Mr. Gustafson, and the defendant, you eventually sent them to the state crime lab for testing, right?"

"Yes, ma'am," Punch said.

"How did they get there?"

"An officer put them in his car and took them."

"Did you request testing?" she asked.

"I did. I requested that all of the swabs be tested for DNA evidence, and if any were found that they be compared to some DNA found at the crime scene."

"And you already had the sample at that point?"

"Yes."

"Have you received results back?"

"I have. According to the lab, the DNA from the defendant—"

"Objection," Sam said. It was hearsay. "Move to strike everything after 'I have.'"

"Sustained," Daniels said. "Granted. Ladies and gentlemen, you will disregard everything Detective Polson said after the words 'I have.'"

"Let's move in a different direction," Cathy said. "Now, at any point, did you try and backtrack to discover the location of the victim before he died?"

"Yes."

"Did you eventually retrieve some video from the college?"

"I didn't." Punch shook his head. "Corporal Jensen did and he showed them to me when he got back."

Cathy was watching the jury closely. They were watching Punch intently. "What other places did the Custer police look into to try and figure out the whereabouts of Mr. Miles before his death?" she asked.

"Oh, we looked at camera footage from shops and stores in every direction from the body. We of course got a warrant and looked at video footage from virtually every camera on the campus."

"So, like—"

"Fast food joints, gas stations," Punch explained.

"Did you find anything of value?"

"No."

"Have you ever had the opportunity to interview the defendant, Mr. Davonte Blair?"

"Yes."

"Do you see him in the courtroom today?"

"Yes, I do."

"Will you point him out to the jury?"

"He's sitting right there in a dark suit with a white shirt

and red tie," Punch said, pointing as requested. "The tall man between Mr. Johnstone and Mr. Norquist."

"How many interviews of the defendant did you undertake personally?" Cathy asked.

"Two or three, I guess."

"And who else was present during those interviews?"

"I think Corporal Jensen was there for a couple of them," Punch said.

"Now, in these interviews, was Mr. Blair informed of his Miranda rights?"

"No."

"Do you remember the first interview with Mr. Blair?"

"I do."

"What was your impression?" Cathy asked.

"I thought he was evasive. Not telling me the truth." Punch locked eyes with Davonte. "I had a general uneasiness about him. His story was not matching what others told me. He couldn't recall any details. He wasn't terribly cooperative. I feel like people who are telling the truth—"

"Objection," Sam said.

"Sustained," Daniels ruled.

"Did you notice anything about Mr. Blair's person?"

"I did."

"What was that?"

"Bruising and scratching on his hands," Punch said.

"As if he had been in a fight of some sort?"

"Objection; leading," Sam said.

"Sustained," Daniels said.

Cathy nodded. The jury had heard it. "So," she continued, "before you arrested him, you interviewed him a second time —true?"

"Yes."

"And after each interview Mr. Blair left wherever he was—he actually walked away a free man?"

"He did."

"What was his demeanor?" she asked.

"Surly."

"Objection," Sam said. "Move to strike."

"Overruled," Daniels said.

"Eventually, you arrested Mr. Blair?" Cathy said.

"I did." Punch nodded.

"When?"

"December 1."

"Why?"

"Well, the investigation revealed that he didn't like gay people, he owed the decedent a substantial amount of money, and he sent threatening texts to the decedent the morning of his disappearance. His phone records revealed he was in the area the decedent was found at about the time the decedent disappeared, he had injuries to his hands consistent with being in a fight, and his DNA was on an object near the body. He was the only person I could find who had motive, means, opportunity, no alibi, and who fit the evidence."

"Thank you, Detective," Cathy said. "No more questions. Your witness."

"Mr. Johnstone, cross-examination?" Daniels asked.

"Yes, Your Honor." Sam stood and moved to the podium. "Detective Polson, you never did find the murder weapon, did you?" Sam's plan was to hit the high points early.

"We did not," Punch admitted.

"That bother you?"

"Of course."

"The case would be stronger with that evidence—true?"

"True." Punch looked at Rebecca Nice and then Chief Lucas.

"Did you have any other suspects in this murder?"

"Not really."

"Why not?"

"Well, as I indicated, I don't have *suspects* as such. I begin with the premise that everyone could have done it. Then I eliminate folks by checking alibis, listening to their story, and looking at the evidence. Eventually I arrest the person the evidence fits."

"The evidence—such as it is—in this case is all pretty circumstantial, is it not?" Sam asked. He was looking at the jurors.

"That's not uncommon," Punch replied.

"Ever arrest the wrong man?" Sam had turned and was looking directly at Punch now. In his peripheral vision, he saw several jurors' heads move as they turned from Sam to Punch.

"Objection," Cathy said. "Relevance."

"Your Honor," Sam began.

Daniels held up his hand to stop Sam from speaking. He looked at his desktop as he thought it through. The reference to the Tommy Olsen case was obvious. It was certainly relevant—police do make mistakes, and this detective had in fact arrested the wrong man on at least one prior occasion. On the other hand, that didn't have anything to do with this case.

Daniels made a note, said, "Overruled," and looked at the witness. "You may answer."

"Turns out I have," Punch admitted.

"And again, you'll agree with me that the evidence against my client is entirely circumstantial."

"Yes, I'll agree that *all* of the evidence against your client is circumstantial," Punch said, heavily emphasizing the word "all."

Sam smiled. "Let's take a look, then, at *all* of the evidence, shall we?"

"Sure."

"Let's start with your assertion that Davonte doesn't like gay people."

"Okay."

"You learned this how?" Sam asked.

"He made a number of comments in his texts and on social media," Punch explained.

"And so you determined that he didn't like homosexuals?"

"Well, he wasn't exactly celebrating them, was he?" Punch said. Many in the audience smiled and nodded in agreement.

"Mr. Blair was a frequent companion of Mr. Miles, right?"

"Right."

"Anything secret about Mr. Miles's sexual orientation?"

"No."

"And Mr. Blair knew and associated with others who are homosexual—true?"

Sam saw Punch's eyes dart to Paul and then back to his own. "True."

"So, your presumption is that he doesn't like gay people, but it's fair to say he spent a considerable amount of time with them?" Sam asked.

"That's fair," Punch admitted. He looked at the jury and shrugged.

"In fact, Mr. Blair is fairly inclusive in the company he keeps—true?"

"And fairly homophobic in the language he uses," Punch said.

Sam ignored the nonresponsive answer, made a mental note to address the old adage regarding actions versus words in closing, and asked his next question. "You said he had a financial motive, in your opinion—is that right?"

"Yes."

"The information you had was that my client owed Mr. Miles for drugs—is that right?"

"Yes."

"And the texts between them you interpreted to mean that?"

"I did," Punch said. "There were dozens of texts between them where Davonte was ordering pizza and tires and kittens and sandwiches for himself and his friends."

"And you think those were euphemisms for drugs?"

"I do," Punch said.

"Why?" Sam asked.

"Your Honor, may we approach?" Cathy asked.

"You may," Daniels said, and hit the white noise button on his bench so the jurors and audience could not hear what was being said.

After Cathy, Rebecca, Sam, and Paul had assembled and the reporter donned her headset, Cathy began. "Your Honor, I object to this line of cross-examination. He is trying to put the deceased on trial. The fact that the deceased was involved in the drug trade is of no relevance. The issue is whether or not Mr. Blair killed Mr. Miles, not whether Mr. Miles was a good person."

Daniels looked to Sam. "Mr. Johnstone?"

"Judge, the State told the jury my client was arrested in part because he owed Mr. Miles money for drugs. The jury is entitled to know the extent of the deceased's drug dealing. It will show that a lot of people had the same motive."

"I agree," Daniels said. "You may proceed, Mr. Johnstone."

When everyone was back in place, Sam began again. "Why

did you think my client was not buying kittens, pizza, tires, and sandwiches from Mr. Miles?"

"Because those are common euphemisms for drugs in the trade."

"And why would Mr. Miles be familiar with drug euphemisms?" Punch sat quietly but did not immediately respond. Sam watched him closely, then prompted him. "Detective Polson?"

"Because Mr. Miles was a confidential informant for the Department of Criminal Investigation," Punch said at last.

"He was a drug dealer working for the State?" Sam asked, feigning surprise. He heard a commotion and turned to see Mrs. Miles being assisted from the courtroom by two others. She had her mouth covered and was shaking her head. After she had left, Sam resumed his questioning. "Have you seen Mr. Miles's books and ledgers?"

"We were unable to locate any," Punch admitted.

"So you don't know how many people might have owed Mr. Miles money—do you?"

"No."

"Could be hundreds?"

Punch sat quietly. His face was turning red. "Could be."

"So, no record of my client owing him money, either?" From the corner of his eye he could tell the jury was still following.

"Nothing tangible."

Sam thought he might be able to raise a little doubt on the financial motive. "Isn't it true that the managers of the basketball team do a lot of things for the players?"

"Like sell them drugs, you mean?" Punch snapped.

"Like run errands," Sam said quietly.

"Yes."

"Take exams?" Sam asked.

"So I heard," Punch said, looking again at Paul.

"Buy their beer?"

"Yes."

"Do laundry?" Sam asked.

"So I'm told." Punch shrugged.

"Help them with basketball drills?"

"Oh, yes."

"So," Sam pressed, "the request for a kitten or sandwich could have been the case?"

"I don't believe it was, no." Punch shook his head. "Unless someone really wanted half a kitten."

While the jurors and audience laughed, Sam felt his face redden. "But you weren't present when any of these requests were made, so you don't *know*, do you?" he asked, desperately hoping for a simple no so he could plow more fertile ground.

"I don't," Punch said.

Sam smiled as best he could. Not every tactic worked. He shuffled the papers in front of him. "You said he had some bruising and scratching on his hands?"

"He did."

"Did he allow you to photograph them?"

"He did."

"He told you he got them in a game?"

"He did."

"You doubt that?" Sam asked.

"Seemed convenient." Punch shrugged again and took a drink of water.

"Did you review the game footage to see if you could verify his story?"

"I figured he'd just tell me he got them in practice—"

"Move to strike," Sam said. "Unresponsive."

"Sustained," Daniels said. "Jury will disregard the response. Answer the question, please."

"No, I didn't," Punch muttered.

"The phone records," Sam said, changing subjects quickly. "What is the circular error probability of the location the phone company gets by pinging a phone?"

"As I understand it, anywhere from three to a hundred yards, depending."

"So, assuming for the sake of argument it was my client with the phone in that location at the relevant time, the error is enough that he could have been on the sidewalk where Mr. Miles was later found, right?"

"Yes."

"But he could also have been in this dorm, here—right?" Sam pointed to a spot on a demonstrative exhibit the State had introduced earlier, identifying the location of Kaiden and Ronnie's room. "And in fact, he could have been all the way over here—right?" Sam asked, pointing to the field house, half of which was within the circle on the map drawn by the State's expert.

"If that's within a hundred yards, well, yeah," Punch admitted.

"I'm going to represent *that* dorm is within fifty yards of the scene," Sam said, then indicated an adjoining building. "I'll represent that *this* dorm is within seventy-five yards of where the body was found, and that *this* half of the field house is within one hundred yards of the scene." Sam pointed at each in turn. "So, my client could have—could have—been in one of two dorms or the field house and had his phone show him possibly at the scene. Isn't that true?"

"It is," Punch admitted.

"Now, my question to you, Detective, is this: how many students reside in, or were in that area, during the relevant period of time?"

"I have no idea."

"So you can't tell the jury how many other potential suspects there were, can you?"

"No, but I can tell them how many other people's DNA was at the scene." Punch was fully flushed now.

"Let's look at that, shall we? I want to follow up a little on DNA," Sam said. "Would you agree with me that the producer of DNA—or whoever leaves it there—is not automatically the culprit?"

Punch thought about it for a moment. "I would," he said at last.

"Would you agree there is a good reason not to convict on the presence of DNA alone?" Sam asked.

"Objection," Cathy said. "The witness is not a DNA expert."

"I'm asking him the question in his capacity as a senior detective," Sam replied.

"Overruled," Daniels said.

"Yes, I'd agree with that," Punch said. "We always look for a fuller picture."

"A jury shouldn't convict on the basis of DNA alone?"

"Right," Punch said.

Time to change tactics. "Fair to say there has been a lot of interest in this case?"

"Certainly," Punch said.

"Fair to say you felt some pressure to make an arrest?"

"I always do."

"So, that's a yes?"

"Yes," Punch said.

"Fair to say you spoke with both the county attorney and the chief of police shortly before you arrested my client?"

"Yes, but I always—"

"Fair to say they wanted an immediate arrest?"

"Well, of course," Punch said. "But I made the choice to

arrest your client, counselor."

"Did you have the evidence you wanted?"

"Of course not. I never do," Punch said.

"In this case, though, you'd have preferred to wait, right?" Sam was guessing, but the worst he could get was a denial.

"I made the decision to arrest, counselor."

Close enough. "And you faced pressure from outside groups—true?"

"Me? No. Others may have."

Sam walked to the defendant's table and tried to squat between Paul and Davonte. He'd been on his feet for a while, and his good leg was killing him. "Anything else?"

"Good job," Davonte said.

Paul shook his head, indicating nothing else.

"No more questions, Judge," Sam said, and sat down.

"Ms. Schmidt, any re-direct?" Daniels asked.

"Yes, Judge," Cathy said, and proceeded to ask a number of questions designed to undo the damage caused by Sam's cross-examination. When she had finished, Daniels instructed her to call the State's next witness. Time was running out and he was starting to worry about the trial bleeding over into the next week.

Cathy stood. "Your Honor, the State rests."

The room began to buzz as spectators mumbled among themselves but quieted under Daniels's stare. At last, he swiveled in his chair toward the jury. "Ladies and gentlemen, we'll take our evening break at this time," he said. "There is a matter the court needs to discuss with counsel in the morning that does not require your consideration or your participation, so I'll have the bailiff allow you to get an extra thirty minutes' sleep tomorrow. I want to remind you: no discussing the case, no reading about the case online or in the papers, no watching television or listening to the radio or discussing the matter with anyone. Please let the bailiff know if anyone attempts to discuss the matter with you. Finally, do not make up your mind based on anything you have heard to this point. Wait until all the evidence is in, I have instructed you on the law, and you have been retired to the jury room to take the matter under consideration."

Following the jury's departure, Daniels looked to Sam. "Mr. Johnstone, I'll hear your motion—if you have one—promptly at nine a.m. Anything further we need to discuss?"

"No, Your Honor," Sam and Cathy said in unison. With that, Daniels was gone.

Sam nodded to Cathy. She beckoned him to her table. "Got a minute?"

"Sure," Sam said. "Let me get something set up. Mrs. Blair?" he said to Davonte's mother, who was sitting in the front row of seats.

"Sharon," she reminded him.

"Sharon, Paul and I would like to meet with you and Davonte in a few minutes. Could you meet us in my office in, say, thirty minutes?"

"Certainly, Sam," Sharon said. "Davonte, come on," she said, and led Davonte, followed by Damon and Reggie, out of the courtroom.

"Classy lady," Sam observed.

"I agree. How the hell she has a son like that," Paul muttered.

Sam ignored the comment. "Cathy wants to talk. Let's get to her office."

Cathy's office was in the basement of the old courthouse. She was sitting behind her desk when Sam and Paul were escorted in. Sam looked at the piles of paper that had accrued since the last time he'd been there and knew what he was seeing: work unaccomplished due to the murder trial. He had similar piles in his office.

"Have a seat, gentlemen," she said. When they were seated, she wasted no time. "Your guy pleads to murder two and we recommend he does the minimum twenty years."

Sam and Paul exchanged a look. "I think we—Sam, really—can get Davonte to agree to plead to manslaughter and do seven," Paul said.

"Are you kidding me? I make that offer and the gay coalition will have me drawn and quartered." She shook her head dismissively. "Besides, Daniels won't buy that."

"You've got nothing showing first degree," Paul pointed out. "The best you do is second degree."

"Which has a top number of *life*," she countered. "I'm offering the minimum."

"Daniels isn't going to give a nineteen-year-old life." Paul shook his head. "If you can get a verdict—which I doubt—we'll bring him in, have him apologize, and he'll get the minimum. This isn't an offer; it's a recognition of what's probably going to happen."

Sam had been quietly watching. "I think he's right, Cathy," he said. "I don't think Davonte will do the deal. I think I can get him to plead to manslaughter, though."

Cathy stood and walked to her window, then pulled the blinds. Through them she could see the upper half of protesters milling around the courthouse lawn. She watched them for a long time. "I can't do it," she said at last. She turned to face both men. "I can't do seven. I'll try and get Rebecca to agree to manslaughter, but that's it. I gotta live in this town, and I gotta live with the deal. Tell your client the deal is him pleading to manslaughter plus him doing twelve to fifteen and we're done."

"I don't know," Sam said.

"That's the offer. Get it to your client. And this is it," she said as they were leaving. "It makes me want to puke to make this one."

Moments later, Sam and Paul mounted the steps to their office en route to the meeting. Sam noticed a large black sedan with Michigan plates parked in the spot closest to the front door. The windows had been tinted, making it impossible to see who was inside, but Sam and Paul had the same idea. "The henchmen," Sam said.

"I cannot wait until this is over," Paul grumbled. He stopped Sam just inside the entryway. "Sam, we've got to get Davonte to do this deal."

"I know, Paul. I'll try—"

"This is a good deal. It won't get any better," Paul said. He opened the door for Sam, who walked through and saw Sharon and Davonte in the waiting room.

"Follow me, gang," he instructed.

When everyone was seated in Paul's office, Sam explained to Sharon the next steps. "Tomorrow, I'll start by arguing a motion saying that the State failed to make a reasonable case. I'll ask the judge to grant my motion and dismiss the charges. He'll deny it and—"

"Why?" Sharon asked softly.

"Because at this point in the trial, all the State has to have shown is that a reasonable person could find Davonte committed first-degree murder."

"But no juror could," she said. "He didn't do it."

Sam took a deep breath. This was always difficult to explain to clients. The differing levels of proof throughout the process were bewildering and maddening. When he'd finished the explanation, he continued. "Anyway, then we will present our side of the case. But before we get to tomorrow, we wanted to talk about a potential plea agreement." He turned to face Davonte. "The State has offered to cap their sentencing recommendation at twelve to fifteen years if you plead to manslaughter." Sam looked at Davonte, and then to Sharon.

Her dark eyes met Sam's for an instant before she turned to Davonte. "Davonte, how do you want to proceed?"

"Mom, this is a bunch of shit. These bitches—"

"Why are you talking like that?" Sharon asked Davonte. "Is that the way I raised you?"

"No, ma'am," Davonte said, looking down.

"There is no reason for you to swear or talk like an unedu-cated man," Sharon said. "How would you like to proceed?"

"Mom, I didn't kill him. I swear on Dad's grave!"

Sharon nodded, then looked in turn at Paul and Sam. "My son says he didn't do this. I do not want him accepting blame for someone else's actions. That is not what his father would have wanted; that is not what I want."

"Mrs. Blair," Paul began. She looked at him but did not correct him. "Sam has done a wonderful job so far. The evidence before the jury is such that they must be harboring doubts about Davonte's guilt. Worst case, they are thinking that—even if Davonte did kill Kaiden—it was likely in the heat of the moment. This is exactly what is contemplated by the statute. This deal—"

"Davonte says he didn't do it, Mr. Norquist. You were right here. You heard him."

"I did, ma'am, I'm just saying that it's our assessment that Davonte is at risk of being convicted of murder. Until now, the

State hasn't even put manslaughter on the table. Clearly, Sam has poked holes in the State's case. But one bad court session and all that goes away, and if Davonte is convicted, he will do a minimum of twenty and possibly up to life."

"Mom, he is selling me out! He—" Davonte stopped under Sharon's steady glare.

She looked at Sam. "Do you agree?"

Sam had been watching the jury closely and felt in his heart they would acquit. But it was risky. The safe play was to take the deal. "A plea agreement eliminates risk," Sam said. "If we do a deal, we have certainty."

"Certainty my son is going to prison." She locked eyes with Sam.

"Well, yes," Sam said. "But for an agreed-upon period of time."

"Mom—" Davonte began.

"Be quiet, son," Sharon said. Then, looking at both men, she asked, "Would you counsel your son to plead guilty to something he didn't do?"

"No," Sam said.

"Yes, if he could get life," Paul said simultaneously.

Sharon sat quietly, fingering a small gold cross she wore around her neck. She looked at her son, then Sam and Paul, and stood. "Well, I think I know what my Ronald would say, so I think we know where we are. Come on, Davonte. These men have more trial to prepare for."

Sam and Paul stood as Sharon and Davonte left. They remained in Sam's office until they heard the front door close, and then Sam walked to his office. Unknown to him, Paul had followed him down the hall.

"Damn it, Sam!" Paul exclaimed. "I thought we had a plan."

"We did, Paul—right up until I looked in that mother's

eyes."

———————

Hours later, Sam was in his office, awaiting Ronnie. It was after eight, and it had been dark for hours. He was getting tired and his eyes felt like sandpaper, but he had called Ronnie in late to go over his testimony in order to avoid having Paul around. He and Paul were still arguing whether to call Ronnie, but he needed to ensure Ronnie was ready. Sam's stomach hurt; whether it was nerves or the bad food he'd been eating of late he didn't know. He was quaffing antacids when Ronnie called.

"Mr. Johnstone? I'm at the front door."

"Be right there," Sam said. "I thought you had a key," he added after he'd let Ronnie in.

"My dad made me give it back."

"Okay," Sam replied. "Coffee? Soda? We might even have a beer in the fridge in the break area."

"No, I'm good," Ronnie said. "I just need to kind of get back to my room and study."

"All right, we'll make this quick," Sam promised. "I just wanted to go over your testimony so you've got a good feel for what I'm going to ask, okay?" Seeing Ronnie's nod, Sam continued. "Now, remember: our defense is that somebody else did it. So everything—"

"Someone else did do it," Ronnie interrupted. "You act like you don't believe him."

"Well, it really doesn't matter," Sam explained. "The fact is, I'm putting you on the stand to show that you were interviewed, that you were fingerprinted, that you gave DNA and all that and you weren't arrested, but Davonte was. Does that make sense?"

"Well, yeah . . . kinda."

"Okay," Sam continued. "So, my questions will be designed to make the jury see that really, you were just as good a suspect as Davonte, but you weren't arrested. I mean, I'll ask just enough questions to get them thinking that maybe Custer police had some preconceived notions—does that make sense?"

"It does," Ronnie said. He was tapping his foot nervously on the floor.

"So it will almost seem like I'm accusing you. I'll ask questions like, "Did you take a DNA test?' 'Did you give fingerprints?' and stuff like that," Sam explained. "You okay?" He looked at Ronnie's foot.

"Me? Oh, yeah," Ronnie said. "Nervous habit."

"Okay, well, you don't have anything to be nervous about, do you?" Sam chuckled.

Ronnie didn't respond.

"Something you need to tell me?" Sam pressed. He waited.

"No," Ronnie said at last. "What else?"

"I'll ask questions designed to make the jurors see that you were there that evening, that you owed Davonte money, that you had communication, that you were in the area—everything just like Davonte, see?"

"Yeah."

"And despite the fact that everything was the same, they arrested Davonte, not you—get it?"

"Because he's black, right?"

"Well, I don't know. It doesn't matter."

"It does matter!" Ronnie exclaimed. "Black people have been railroaded for centuries! We have to fix that!"

Sam watched Ronnie carefully. "Ronnie, I'm not going to put the Custer police on trial here," he said. "I just need to show enough to make at least one juror—and hopefully all of them—understand the police might have arrested the wrong guy. That's the task."

Ronnie sat quietly, tapping his foot.

"And we're going to have to talk about the drugs," Sam continued. "You know that."

"It's only weed. Weed's legal lots of places."

"I understand that," Sam said. "But it isn't here. And it isn't in Colorado or wherever for people under twenty-one, either. I'm just letting you know that is going to come out so you can talk with your folks or whatever. Let 'em know."

"My dad's not talking to me."

"Why not?"

"I think 'cause of the weed thing. He knows; he's pissed."

"I wouldn't worry about that, Ronnie. Fathers and sons. Ups and downs."

"You ever argue with your father?"

"No," Sam said. "My father wasn't worth arguing with."

Ronnie looked at Sam for a long time. It was one of the few times he had ever looked Sam in the eye. "So . . . what happens if they start asking me about . . . you know. . . what happened?"

"Well, I'll tell you the same thing I tell all my clients and witnesses," Sam explained. "The most important thing is that you tell the truth. You've got to do that, of course."

"Right." Ronnie was looking at his hands. "I told Davonte that."

"You've spoken with Davonte?" Sam asked.

"Of course," Ronnie said. "We're friends. When he gets to the NBA—"

"Ronnie, I don't have time for that right now. Tomorrow, it will work like this: if you can answer a question with a simple yes or no, do it, even if you think it is hurting Davonte's case. Trust me to clean up the mess. That's what I get paid to do —understand?"

"I guess," Ronnie said.

"So, no 'Yes, buts' or 'No, buts'—get me? Then, if you are asked something that requires more than a yes or a no, you need to answer in as few words as possible and then—and this is important—shut up. Don't ramble on or try to explain."

"What if it is complicated?"

"What do you mean?" Sam asked. He looked around his desk for the roll of antacids.

Ronnie was fiddling with a paperclip. "I mean, what if there are things that you don't know?"

Sam felt the blood drain from his face. "Ronnie, what exactly are you telling me?"

"Nothing. I mean . . . There's stuff that maybe you don't know." Ronnie had manipulated the paperclip into a small, straight piece of metal.

Sam assumed he knew what was coming. Might as well address it head-on. "Ronnie," he said, leaning forward in his chair. "I know you're gay, okay? It doesn't matter. There's no reason for that to come out in this trial. No one cares to begin with, and it isn't relevant." He watched the young man closely, hoping to see him relax. He did not. "Cathy doesn't know and doesn't care. You are not the accused; cross-examination—if she even bothers—will be perfunctory. I'm not going to bring it up, so don't sweat it."

"Well . . ." Ronnie began.

"Do your folks know?"

"What? Of course not! My dad would go nuts!"

"Maybe give him a little credit," Sam said. "He's a good man."

"Only when he deserves it." Ronnie tossed the paperclip into a nearby wastebasket. "What else?"

"Well, I think that's it," Sam said. "Ronnie, is there

anything I need to know? If I'm going to give Davonte the best defense possible, I have to know everything."

Ronnie started to stand and then sat back down. "Whatever I tell you is privileged, right?"

"Wrong. I'm not your attorney. I'm Davonte's attorney," Sam explained. Ronnie's face fell. "But you owe it to your friend to tell me what you know."

"What would you do with the information?"

"Depends on what it was."

"So, if it helped Davonte—"

"Then I will get it in front of the jury if it is admissible. If it's bad for you, well, it has to go to the jury anyway," Sam said. "That's my job." Ronnie was again looking at his shoes. In spite of himself, an irritable and exhausted Sam exploded. "Damn it, Ronnie! What is it?"

"It's nothing." Ronnie's eyes were wide with fear. "Nothing. I'll—I'll tell you later."

"There is no later! There's now, or there's never. There is no later!"

"Then it's never," Ronnie said. He stood and walked out of the room. Sam heard the office door shut behind him, then watched out the window as Ronnie made his way through the omnipresent protesters outside the office. Sam was about to intervene when Custer police arrived. Ronnie was able to make it to his car and drive away.

The next morning, after the parties and audience had assembled and before the jury had been called, Daniels looked at Sam expectantly. "Any motions from the defendant?"

Sam stood. "Yes, sir. On behalf of Mr. Blair we are moving for judgment of acquittal pursuant to Rule 29 of the Wyoming

Rules of Criminal Procedure. While we recognize the State's burden is low at this point, we do not believe the State has met even that low threshold of proof. May we be heard?"

"Yes."

"Your Honor, as you know, in order to meet its burden the State was required to present evidence to show that my client not only killed the decedent, but that he did it purposely and with premeditated malice or while committing or attempting to commit a felony."

Sam then cited case law in support of his motion. "Your Honor, we contend the State's evidence as presented in its case-in-chief is such that a juror must have a reasonable doubt as to the element of 'purposely or with premeditated malice.' The State has produced evidence which, if assumed to be true, a reasonable juror could use to determine my client killed the decedent. But there is *no* evidence from which that same juror could deduce malice. We know only that the decedent was a drug dealer and that my client owed him some money. Asking the jury to make the leap from owing someone money to killing them is simply too much under the law. We ask that you grant our motion to dismiss the charge of murder in the first degree. Further, with regard to the lesser-included offense of second-degree murder, we would ask—"

"Just a moment, Mr. Johnstone. Let's eat this elephant one bite at a time," Daniels said. "I'd like to hear from Ms. Schmidt regarding the first-degree charge. Ms. Schmidt, what says the State?"

"Your Honor," Cathy began, "the State's evidence is suffi-cient on every single element. First, we believe we have shown beyond a reasonable doubt the events in question occurred on or about the 6th day of November. There is no doubt as well that the relevant events occurred here in Custer County. Simi-larly, there is little doubt that Mr. Blair is the proper defendant. Finally, the State has shown the deceased was murdered. The only issue, then, is whether he was murdered by Mr. Blair purposely and with premeditated malice. The evidence on that point shows that the parties had a disagreement over money and that Mr. Blair hated homosexuals. The evidence shows that Mr. Blair followed the victim out of the party. The evidence shows Mr. Blair in the vicinity of the location where the defendant was found at the relevant time, and the evidence is that the victim was killed by a blow to the back of the head, virtually eliminating any argument of self-defense, accident, or the like. The State has met its burden, Judge, and we ask the court to deny Mr. Johnstone's motion."

"Mr. Johnstone. Your motion. You get the last word."

"Thank you, Your Honor. I think Ms. Schmidt's characterization of what was produced by the State in its case-in-chief is wishful thinking and we pray you grant the motion, Your Honor. With regard to the charge of second-degree murder—"

"Just a minute, Mr. Johnstone. Regarding the charge of first-degree murder, the court is going to find the State has met its burden and will deny the motion. It's a close call, and I'm not saying the jury *should* find premeditation; I'm saying they *could*." Daniels paused as two members of the press corps left the room to file their stories. After they had left, he continued. "So, that motion will be denied. Mr. Johnstone, I'm not going to hear you on the second-degree charge. In my opinion, giving the State every reasonable inference, a reasonable juror could find the defendant acted purposely and maliciously— assuming she believed the evidence, of course. In any event, let the record show you made the Rule 29 motion on second-degree murder and I denied it."

Sam felt adrenaline pulse through his body, and thought he heard Paul sigh heavily as well. Both first- and second-degree murder were still on the table, so Davonte would do between twenty years and life if convicted. "Now, has your client made a determination as to whether he will testify?"

"Not yet, Your Honor."

"Does the defense intend to offer evidence?" Daniels looked pointedly at the clock, clearly hoping for a negative response.

"Yes, Judge," Sam said. "Perhaps two witnesses, and perhaps Mr. Blair."

"All right," Daniels said. "It's still early. Here's what I'm thinking we do. Let's bring the jury back and the defense will put on its first witness. After the State does its cross, we'll let them go for a long lunch, then we'll meet and get the jury instructions straight so that we'll be ready to go when Mr. Johnstone's case has concluded. We'll start the afternoon with the defendant's second witness," Daniels said. "Now, not later than lunchtime today, Mr. Johnstone, I'll expect notification from you one way or the other. I don't like to move jurors in and out of the courtroom like cattle. Can we do that?"

"Yes, sir."

"Okay." Daniels nodded. "Bailiff, let's get the jury in here."

When the jury had reassembled and been accounted for, the trial continued.

"Your Honor, the defense calls Russ Johnson," Sam said. He was looking at the yellow legal pad on the defense table, upon which was written only the three points he wanted to make: that the producer of DNA was not necessarily the culprit, that no conviction should stand on DNA alone, and that there were a number of ways Davonte's DNA could have gotten on that hat.

Sam took Johnson through his background and qualifications quickly, then got to the substantive line of questioning. "Can you tell the jury a little bit about touch DNA?"

"Of course," Johnson said. "As I understand it, touch-transfer DNA was first discovered by an Australian scientist in 1997. The scientist discovered that tiny bits of DNA would transfer through touch, together with fingerprint markings, allowing for the collection and analysis of DNA from fingerprints left behind by culprits. So, it started as getting DNA from fingerprints. But scientists soon discovered the ability to search for touch-transfer DNA from other objects and surfaces. As you might imagine, this had law enforcement applications, and pretty soon we saw the prosecution of individuals based on DNA from these objects."

"Are there problems with the technique?" Sam asked.

"Oh, yes," Johnson said, warming to his subject. "While the sensitivity of the testing keeps increasing, making it possible to obtain DNA from smaller and smaller samples, it is kind of a double-edged sword."

"Why?"

"Because the technological ability to use smaller samples means it is not so clear-cut that the person whose DNA is found at the crime scene is actually involved in the crime, or that they were even anywhere near the crime scene to begin with."

"Why is that?"

"Well, think about it. If we're getting DNA results from just a few cells that somehow sloughed off someone, we have to ask ourselves how easy it is for just a few cells to arrive where they were found."

"Well, how easy is it?"

"Well, in study after study it has been shown that DNA transfers not only through primary contact with an item, but secondarily, and maybe even beyond that."

"Meaning?" Sam asked. The jury was following, he observed.

"It is possible that if you touch my hand, and I touch a

third person's hand, it is possible—I'm saying possible—that someone checking the third person's hand could find not only your DNA, but that of someone else you touched before touching me."

"So," Sam said, "is the science of any use at all?"

"Of course, but we have to be aware of the limitations. We cannot tell you when the DNA was deposited or how. We have to remember the DNA could have been deposited perfectly innocently, or even by someone else," Johnson explained. "And if that isn't complicated enough, the literature says that DNA can be transferred from one area of an item to another area."

"So, touch DNA is everywhere?"

"Yes," Johnson said. "Touch DNA is known to last for up to two weeks outside and six weeks or longer inside."

Sam walked over to the table where the admitted evidence was and retrieved the bag containing the watch cap. "So, Mr. Johnson, my question is this: if I were to tell you that this hat had lain outside in the weather for two weeks, that my client and the owner of the hat were friends, and that my client's DNA was found on the hat, would you automatically assume my client was the culprit?"

"Oh, no." Johnson shook his head sadly. "I wouldn't be surprised to find *your* DNA on that hat. I'd say that while DNA never lies, you have to evaluate all the evidence. DNA is just one part of it—especially touch DNA."

"Speaking of touch DNA, you mentioned that our cells slough off relatively easily—is that right?"

"Yes."

"So, can we expect that whatever we touch will have our cells on it?"

"No."

"Why not?" Sam asked.

"Well, we don't know for sure," Johnson admitted." "What we do know is that in controlled experiments, sometimes cells transfer, sometimes they don't."

Sam took a minute to walk to the table to feign getting a drink. What he really wanted was to be able to look at the jury and make certain he had their undivided attention. "So, let me ask you this. If you and I both touched an article—say, a hat like this," Sam said, holding the watch cap aloft, "what are the possibilities?"

"Well, there are many," Johnson mused. "First, we both could leave detectable amounts of DNA on the hat."

"Okay," Sam said. "What else?"

"Well, it's possible that neither your DNA nor my DNA would be discoverable."

"What else?"

"Well, it is possible that my DNA would be there but yours wouldn't."

"And?"

"It's possible that yours would be there and mine wouldn't."

"Okay," Sam said. "And that's if we know we both touched the item, right?"

"Right."

"Now, let me ask you this: those same possibilities exist for secondary or tertiary transfer, right?"

"What are you asking?"

"It is possible, isn't it, that I could, say, transfer your cells to an item without transferring my own?" Sam asked.

Johnson sat quietly, thinking.

"I am asking if it is possible," Sam prompted Johnson.

"It is possible, yes."

"May I have a minute, Judge?"

"Yes," Daniels said.

Sam walked to the defense table. "Two goals," he said to Paul and Davonte. "One, there could be a perfectly innocent explanation for Davonte's DNA on the hat. Two, someone's DNA might be missing or in a concentration less than maybe it should be."

"Done," Davonte said. Paul sat quietly and said nothing. Sam waited for him to speak, then returned to the podium when he saw that he would not.

"Thank you, Mr. Johnson," Sam said, gathering his materials. "Your witness," he said to Cathy.

"Thank you, Mr. Johnstone," she said, and moved quickly to the podium. "Your Honor, may I approach the witness?"

"Yes," Daniels said.

Cathy approached Johnson and handed him a pen. Johnson took the pen and looked at it curiously. "Mr. Johnson, would you set that pen down, please." Johnson complied and shot Sam a curious glance while Cathy walked back to the podium. Sam knew what was coming, but there was nothing he could do about it, so he ignored Johnson's look.

"Now, Mr. Johnson, you and I have both touched that pen. According to your testimony, there are a number of possible outcomes if we were to look at the transfer of DNA—is that right?"

"Correct," Johnson said. He was looking at her like a mouse eyeing a snake, Sam thought.

"Both of our DNA might be found?" Cathy asked.

"True."

"Or neither, you said?"

"Correct," Johnson said.

"Or yours or mine alone?"

"Correct."

"Now, it is also possible that mine alone could have been transferred to the pen by you, even if I had never touched that pen—isn't that what you said?" she asked.

"True," Johnson said.

"Which of the outcomes is most likely?"

Johnson looked to Sam for help, but he sat quietly. "Well, that's hard to say . . ."

Cathy asked him about a couple of what Sam presumed were the most recent, major studies in the field of touch DNA. Johnson acknowledged he was familiar with the studies. "Well, do you have any strident objections to the results of those studies?" she asked.

"Of course not."

"You are satisfied with the methodology?"

"I am."

"Then I am going to ask you again. Given the passing of the pen touched by both of us, and given your knowledge of the relevant literature, what is the most likely outcome, DNA-wise?"

"That my DNA would be present," Johnson admitted.

"Next most likely?"

"That both our DNA was present, I would think."

"Okay." Cathy looked at the jury before asking her next question. They were paying attention. "How likely, according to the literature, is it that my DNA could be where I've never been?"

"Well, that's hard to say," Johnson began.

"I'm not asking for specific odds," Cathy said.

"Well, it would depend on myriad factors."

"Is it almost always?" she asked.

"Oh, no."

"Possible?" she pressed. Sam was watching the jurors.

They were picking up on it.

"Oh yes."

"Probable?"

"No, I wouldn't say that." Johnson shook his head.

"Unusual?"

"I think that's probably fair," he admitted. She had him boxed in, Sam knew.

"Far-fetched?"

"No, more possible than that." Johnson again shook his head.

"So, somewhere between 'unusual' and 'far-fetched?'" she confirmed.

"Well," Johnson said. "Certainly closer to 'unusual.'"

"So, the science tells us in the grand scheme of things that —best case—it would be 'unusual' for you to have passed my DNA to that pen if I had not touched it?"

"I think so, yes," Johnson admitted.

"No more questions, Judge," Cathy said, and sat down.

"Redirect, Mr. Johnstone?"

Cathy's cross-examination—as expected—had been effective. Sam thought about attempting to rehabilitate Johnson with a few questions but decided that he could live with "unusual" as the characterization of the theory that was rapidly becoming central to his defense. "No, Judge."

"Thank you, Mr. Johnstone," Daniels said. "Ladies and gentlemen, let's take our lunch break. Bailiff, please conduct the jury to the jury room." After the jury's departure, Daniels looked to Sam. "Mr. Johnstone?"

"Judge, I'll have an answer after lunch, just as you directed."

"Good. We'll take our noon recess and come back and get the jury instructions in order before we bring the jurors back. I'm going to give them a ninety-minute lunch. So, everyone be back in an hour. We'll get your client's decision on the record when we get back, then we'll do the instructions conference, and then we'll call the jury and start winding up."

Sam, Paul, and Davonte were in the counsel room located adjacent to the courtroom. The door was closed, and courtroom security was posted outside. "So, what do you think?" Sam asked.

"I think we've got enough reasonable doubt," Paul said, taking a sandwich Sam offered. "Let's rest and call it good."

Sam passed a packaged turkey sandwich to Davonte. "I'm thinking we need to put Ronnie on."

"No."

"Paul, we already had this discussion. All I want to do is put him on the stand and have him testify that he's been around the victim, just like Davonte. He will testify that he doesn't know how his DNA could have gotten on the hat."

"No, Sam."

"It's as good as having Davonte testify," Sam said. He was struggling with the wrapper on a ham sandwich and gave up, dropping it on the table. "The evidence is almost identical. It's like having Davonte testify without having to call him."

"Call *him*," Paul said, pointing at Davonte. "He is the one on trial, not my son."

Davonte shook his head. He unwrapped Sam's sandwich and passed it to him. "You gonna throw my ass under the bus to save your boy."

"I am," Paul said. "And you'd do the same thing. He's my son!"

"Paul, we have to do this," Sam said, taking a bite of the ham and cheese. He chewed for a long time while looking steadily at his partner. "I'll limit his testimony with a few short questions, thereby framing the State's cross. I spoke with Ronnie last night. He's ready."

"You spoke with my son without me being there?" Paul asked, standing to leave.

Sam pointed at Paul's chair. "He's an adult, Paul. Sit down; let's talk about this."

"No. I'm done talking."

"Well, then, let's stay and discuss Davonte testifying."

"Doesn't matter," Paul said, opening the door. "I really don't give a shit."

After he was gone, Sam and Davonte sat for a moment, finishing their sandwiches and processing what had happened. "I told you, that dude don't dig me," Davonte said, taking a long pull from a bottle of flavored water.

"No, he doesn't," Sam agreed. "But he's not himself. Now, let's talk this over." He tossed the wrapper from his sandwich into the trash can across the room. "We've got to let the judge know whether you are going to testify after lunch. What do you want to do?"

"I'll go with whatever you think, Sam. I trust you."

Sam tried to conceal his surprise. "Well, it is your decision. The jury always wants to hear from the defendant. In a lot of cases, I'd go ahead and put you on. But in this case, the evidence is slim. Really slim. I think we've got to have planted some doubt in the mind of at least one juror—that's all it takes," he said. "And if I put Ronnie on the stand, he can help me plant doubt about the DNA."

"You gonna do that?"

"Put Ronnie on the stand?" Sam asked. Davonte nodded. "I have to."

"Might cost you a friendship."

"Oh, I don't think so," Sam said. "I think Paul is just being protective. He's a father."

"Maybe he knows something you don't." Davonte dropped the plastic bottle into the trash and then returned to his chair.

"What do you mean?"

"I mean I didn't kill Miles, man. Meaning someone else did. What reason you got for thinking it ain't Ronnie?"

Sam thought again about the dorm room photograph and Ronnie's comments from the prior evening. "Well, I'm not seeing any evidence he did," Sam said.

"That's because you ain't lookin'. Same evidence against Ronnie as me, right? How'd you put it? He's just as variable—"

"Viable."

"—just as viable a candidate for murder as me," Davonte said. "Yet we got the brother charged, right?"

"Right." Sam stood and walked around the room.

Davonte watched him pace. Finally, he asked, "What are we gonna do?"

"I think we'll have you stay silent," Sam said. "Unless you insist. I don't think they've got enough to get a jury to convict you."

"Even a brother like me?" Davonte asked.

Sam smiled. "Yeah. Even a brother like you." Then he turned serious. "Davonte, I gotta think the jury will do the right thing."

"Man, you are one red, white, and blue thinker," Davonte said, shaking his head.

"I have to be. If I didn't believe in the system, all of this would be a waste," Sam explained. "My men, those medics, that surgeon . . . they gave me a second chance at life. I can't waste it."

"Okay, but you gonna call Ronnie, right?" Davonte asked. "I think that's important to my case."

"I am." Sam sighed. It had to be done.

20

After lunch, the parties returned to their seats in the courtroom. Sam was looking at the crown molding twenty feet above him on the roofline and doing deep-breathing exercises to relax when Daniels entered.

"All right," he said. "We're back on the record. As an initial matter, Mr. Johnstone, will the defendant testify?"

"He will not, Your Honor," Sam said, and sat back down.

Daniels looked around the courtroom to quiet the crowd, who now understood the trial would soon end. "Mr. Blair, I need to ask you a few questions to ensure you understand the importance of your decision." He then proceeded to ask Davonte questions in order to satisfy himself that Davonte's decision not to testify had come after due consideration, a discussion with Sam, and that it had not been forced or coerced.

Having finished his inquiry, Daniels made his decision. "I'm going to find that Mr. Blair has made his decision to not testify knowingly, intelligently, and voluntarily after consultation with competent counsel with whom he is satisfied. I'll find that he understands his right to testify, that this is a one-time decision, and that he has waived his right to testify to the jury," he said. "Now, ladies and gentlemen, let's take a look at these jury instructions."

The parties had discussed the instructions in the morning conference with the judge, so Cathy and Sam proceeded to formally lodge their objections or support for certain instructions given. Davonte doodled on the yellow legal pad and answered occasional questions from Sam. Paul left the courtroom and played no part in the instructions conference. At last, after Cathy and Sam had agreed on the majority of instructions to be given, and after Daniels had ruled on the ones at issue, they were ready to proceed. Daniels summoned the jurors. After they were seated, he looked to Sam. "Mr. Johnstone, call the next witness for the defense," he said.

Sam stood, looked at Judge Daniels, and then down at Paul, who was staring straight ahead. "Your Honor, the defense calls Ronald Norquist."

Earlier that morning, Sam had spoken with Ronnie and reminded him there were three points to be made on the stand. First, that while Davonte had left after Kaiden, he wasn't particularly angry. Second, that Polson, in his conversations with Ronnie, had let it be known early on that Davonte was the main suspect; and third—and now that it had been revealed—while Ronnie's DNA was on the watch cap, he had no idea how it got there.

Sam turned to watch the court security officer retrieve Ronnie from the hallway. Hearing rustling behind him, he looked over his shoulder and saw Paul collecting materials from his part of the defense table. Sam walked over to him. "What are you doing?" he whispered.

"I'm leaving. I'm done," Paul said. "I cannot believe you are doing this to my son."

"Paul—" Sam started to say, but quietly gave up. The

judge, court staff, audience, and the parties watched as an angry Paul began walking toward the double doors at the end of the courtroom. All eyes shifted to the doors as Ronnie was admitted.

Ronnie stopped short as Paul walked by him. "Dad?" Ronnie said, but Paul did not answer and left the courtroom. Ronnie looked at Jeannie and P.J., who were seated in the last row of the audience. He then looked to Sam uncertainly.

"Mr. Norquist," Daniels said. "Please come forward, raise your right hand, and be sworn to an oath."

Sam looked at Ronnie while he swore the oath. He could see—and he was sure the jurors could see—the young man's knees shaking and hear his voice quiver as he said, "I do."

"Mr. Norquist, please have a seat in the witness box," Daniels directed. When Ronnie had complied, Daniels nodded at Sam and said, "Mr. Johnstone."

"Please state your full legal name," Sam began.

"Ronald Paul Norquist."

Sam then led Ronnie through a series of benign biographical questions designed to tell the jury who Ronnie was, and to calm him. Having established that Ronnie was a nineteen-year-old student at Custer College, Sam continued. "Do you—did you have a roommate?"

"I did."

"Who was that?"

"Kaiden Miles." Ronnie stole a quick look at Kaiden's mom.

"How long were you roommates?"

"Since August," Ronnie said. "When school started."

"Did you live together last year?"

"No."

"How did you come to live together? Were you assigned, or did you choose?"

"We chose. We were managers on the basketball team together last year. Well, this year, too," he added. "We met last year and hung out a lot, so we decided we'd go ahead and choose each other since we spent so much time together."

"So you were friends?"

"Yes."

"Knew him well?" Sam asked.

"I think so."

"In fact, you called the police to report him missing, didn't you?" Sam asked.

"Yes."

"Why?"

"Well, he was gone for more than a day. I was worried about him." Ronnie pulled a handkerchief from his pocket, wiped a tear from the corner of his eye, and then blew his nose. Sam watched him closely.

"So, let's walk backwards a little bit," Sam said. "When did you last see him?"

"I'd say it was about 1:30 in the morning on November 6."

"The day he disappeared?"

"Well, I don't know. I just know I saw him last at about 1:30, and I called the next day—no, the day after that—at around ten in the morning."

"Did you do anything before you called the cops?"

"Sure; I tried to call him. I called Davonte. I called his mom. Trent, I called him," Ronnie said. "Then, I called . . . my dad."

Sam struggled to keep his poise. This was news to him. "So, at approximately ten a.m. on the 8th you called the police?"

"Yes."

"And what did you say?"

"I told them my roommate was missing, and they said—"

"Objection," Cathy said.

"Sustained," Daniels said.

"Just stick to what you said and did, please," Sam instructed.

"Okay, I called the cops and told them Kaiden was missing. The next day they came over."

"Do you remember what time?"

"No. I do remember it was after class and after practice and it had been snowing for almost two days, because when I got to my—er—our place there was quite a bit of snow on the doorstep," Ronnie said. "And Corporal Jensen was outside my place."

"Then what?"

"Then he took a report of everything I said and told me he would get back with me," Ronnie said.

"Then what?"

"Um, a day or two later, I think, Corporal Jensen and Detective Polson came by our place and started looking around."

"Then what?"

"At some point—I can't remember when, exactly—I sat down with Detective Polson. We talked." Ronnie looked to the seats behind the prosecutors, where Kaiden's mom was crying softly. "Or, maybe it was the other way around. Maybe they found Kaiden and then came to talk with me. I can't remember."

"In any event," Sam said. "You interviewed with Detective Polson and Corporal Jensen a couple of times?"

"Right."

"Were you ever placed under oath?" Sam asked. He looked and the jury was following him.

"No."

"Read your rights?"

"No."

"Fingerprinted?" Sam asked.

"Yes."

"Did they take DNA?"

"Yeah. At the gym. Detective Polson did. Said he wanted to rule me out as a suspect."

"He said he wanted to rule you out?" Sam feigned surprise. Point number one was in the books.

"Yeah."

"Why?" Sam asked.

"What?" Ronnie asked.

"Why did he want to rule you out?"

"Objection." Cathy was on her feet. "Judge, the witness cannot possibly—"

"I'll withdraw," Sam said. If the jurors were listening closely, they could conclude Punch was trying to rule out certain persons. That was enough. "Did Detective Polson ever tell you who he did suspect?"

"No."

"So," Sam began, "you didn't know he suspected my client until when?"

Ronnie shrugged. "Well, after he got arrested."

"Were you surprised?"

"Well, yeah. Of course. Someone you know, ya know?" Ronnie looked at Davonte out of the corner of his eye.

"Let's talk about when Kaiden disappeared. Had he ever disappeared before?"

"No. Well, I mean he missed class sometimes—we've all done that." Ronnie smiled. "But then he missed practice. He wouldn't miss practice. I knew something was up then."

"What did you do then?"

"Well, I'd already called his mom, so I started calling other people. No one had seen him, so eventually I called the cops."

"Okay, so when was the last time you saw Kaiden?"

"After the game on the night of November 5. We were at Davonte's place. Playing games. Then Davonte and Kaiden got in an argument. Kaiden left."

"And that was the last time you saw him?"

"Yeah."

"What was he wearing?"

"Sneakers, a hoodie. Jeans."

"Hat?" Sam asked. He was watching Ronnie very closely now.

"I don't think so." Ronnie was looking past Sam toward Jeannie and P.J.

"Well, did he have his watch cap on or not?" Sam pressed. He could see Cathy and Rebecca consulting out of the corner of his eye.

"Uhhh, no. I don't think so. I don't remember."

"So, Kaiden left—then what?"

"Well, Davonte left a little later," Ronnie said.

Ronnie was looking beyond Sam and at Jeannie, so Sam moved enough to block Ronnie's view of his mother. "Was Davonte particularly angry?"

"Not that I recall," Ronnie said, and Sam had the second point made. "Not as mad as Kaiden was, for sure," he added.

"Move to strike," Cathy said.

"The jury will disregard that last bit," Daniels instructed. Sam knew that Daniels, not wanting to emphasize what was to be disregarded, had deliberately left the instruction vague. He considered objecting to ensure the jury understood what to disregard, but decided against it. He could clean it up in closing. It was now time to sow a little doubt regarding the DNA.

"Then what?" Sam asked.

"Well, me and Trent left."

"And did what?"

"Uh, we . . . went to my place," Ronnie said. He looked at his feet and shifted uncomfortably in his chair.

"Were you smoking weed earlier that night?"

"We all were," Ronnie said, looking away from the jury. "Vaping, actually."

"So, everyone being you and Kaiden?"

"And Davonte and Trent."

"Who brought the weed?" Sam asked.

"Can't remember. It might have been some of Kaiden's stuff, or it might have been what Davonte had." Ronnie tried to peer around Sam to see Jeannie.

"Where did Davonte get his stuff?"

"Your Honor," Cathy said. "Objection. Relevance."

"Please approach," Daniels said. When Cathy and Sam were at the bench, Daniels addressed Sam. "Mr. Johnstone?"

"I'll tie it up in a minute, Judge. Just going to show there were lots of folks with a motive."

"Overruled," Daniels said. "But Mr. Johnstone, this trial is not about Mr. Miles."

"Understood, sir."

Sam and Cathy returned to their places. Sam took a drink of water from a plastic cup on the defense table, then put both hands on the podium and addressed Ronnie. "Now, are you aware that your DNA is on the hat found near Kaiden?"

"Objection. Misstates the evidence," Cathy said.

"Sustained," Daniels said.

"I'll rephrase, Judge," Sam said. "Mr. Norquist, are you aware that the State's expert has located what she says *could be* your DNA on the cap found at the scene?"

"I am."

"Can you explain that?" Sam asked.

"No. I never touched it."

Sam had wanted Ronnie's testimony to help him raise

three points. All three were now on the record, and he was free to discuss them during closing to raise a reasonable doubt. It was enough. He could sit down. Instead, he walked to the defense table and poured himself half a cup of water. His stomach was boiling. He drank, put the cup down, and returned to the podium to face Ronnie.

"Are you certain?" he asked. In his peripheral vision he observed Cathy stir in her chair. Daniels, an inveterate note-taker, had his head up and was looking alternately at Sam and then Ronnie. Sam again moved slightly so that he was between Ronnie and his mother's line of sight.

"I—I mean, I can't," Ronnie said.

Sam returned to the table and retrieved the bag with the hat in it. He thumbed through admitted photos until he found the ones he was looking for. "Your Honor, may I approach the witness?"

Daniels looked at Cathy, who shrugged. "You may," he said.

Sam walked up to Ronnie and handed him the bag containing the watch cap, along with two photos of his dorm room. "Take a look at that watch cap. Ever seen it before?"

"Well, I'm sure I have," Ronnie said. "It's Kaiden's. The team issued one to all the players and managers."

"Where's yours?" Sam asked. He had positioned himself directly between Ronnie and Jeannie.

"What do you mean?"

"I mean, where is your watch cap?"

"It's back in my room," Ronnie said.

"Are you sure?"

"Of course I'm sure," Ronnie said, looking around the room. He shifted in his seat, trying to make eye contact with his mother. Sam was watching the jurors, many of whom were getting uncomfortable.

"I'm handing you what was marked earlier as Exhibits 12 and 13. These are pictures of your dorm room already introduced into evidence by the prosecution. Take a look at these pictures and let me know when you are ready to answer some questions, please," Sam instructed. He walked back to the podium, avoiding the temptation to look at Jeannie.

Sam noted Ronnie's hands were shaking as he looked at the photos. After a cursory look, he nodded and said, "Okay."

"Do you see a watch cap in those photos?"

"I do," Ronnie said.

"Why is it on Kaiden's bed?" Sam could hear the audience stirring behind him.

"That doesn't mean anything!" Ronnie cried. He shifted in his chair, again trying to see Jeannie.

"Move to strike," Sam said. "Non-responsive."

"Mr. Norquist, just answer the question, please," Daniels said.

"Your Honor, I object. He's cross-examining his own witness," Cathy said.

"Overruled, Ms. Schmidt. You know the rules. You may answer," he said to Ronnie.

"I—I can't remember the question," Ronnie said.

"Whose cap is in that photo?" Sam asked.

"I must have taken it off and thrown it—"

"Move to strike," Sam said.

"Mr. Norquist, I'm going to ask you once again to answer the question," Daniels said.

"Your Honor, I object," Cathy said. "That wasn't the question asked; I don't know where this is going—"

"Overruled," Daniels said.

"The watch cap on Kaiden's bed in these photos," Sam began, retrieving the photo from Ronnie. "It's Kaiden's watch cap—isn't it?"

"No." Ronnie folded his arms in front of himself.

"Your watch cap was the one at the scene, right?"

"No!"

"I think you wore the watch cap to a meeting with Kaiden. You argued. You struggled. Somehow, he got his hands on your watch cap." Sam lowered his voice. "Ronnie, isn't that true?"

Ronnie sat very still for a moment, then began to shake. His lip quivered and his eyes welled with tears as he looked to the back of the courtroom, where Jeannie sat. Sam turned and looked at Jeannie, who put her head in her hands. He wanted to vomit, but he had to follow up. "Ronnie, isn't it true that you had a struggle with Kaiden—"

"It was an accident!" Ronnie shouted, then put his hands to his face. "I didn't mean to!" Sam watched for a long time and said nothing. He looked at each juror in turn while Ronnie looked up and wailed. "Kaiden was going to call the police! That would ruin everything!"

Sam waited for Ronnie to continue. When he didn't, Sam was forced to follow up. "What are you talking about?"

"Kaiden said—"

"Objection!" Cathy was on her feet. "Hearsay."

"Sustained," Daniels said.

"So, Ronnie," Sam said softly. "What happened?"

"I couldn't let that happen. Davonte's been saying all year that when he gets drafted and goes to the NBA we are going with him. So if Kaiden called the cops it would ruin everything!"

"So—"

"So, me and Trent were in my room. Kaiden called me and told me—"

"Objection," Cathy said.

"Sustained," Daniels said.

"Tell me what happened without telling me anything Kaiden said," Sam instructed. He turned and looked at Jeannie. She was in tears.

"Sam, no," she mouthed.

"He needed a ride to the hospital and to the police station," Ronnie said. "We were walking from the sidewalk to my car. He was bleeding a little from his mouth, so I told him I would take him to the hospital first."

"Did you?" Sam asked.

"No. Well, I was gonna. We were walking from the dorm to my car and we started arguing because he wanted to go to the police station first. He slugged me here," Ronnie said, indicating the middle of his chest. "Then he grabbed my hat and threw it. I went and picked it up and told him to stop, and he told me he was going to tell the cops all about Davonte. He was going to ruin everything! He turned around on me and I grabbed a snow shovel that was on the sidewalk and . . . uh . . . hit him."

Sam sat down at the chair at the defense table. "Then what?" he asked, no longer intent on blocking Ronnie's view of Jeannie.

"He wouldn't wake up!" Ronnie sobbed. "I got scared and dragged and carried him to the creek. He wouldn't wake up! He was going to ruin everything!"

Again, Sam looked at the jurors. Two of them were wiping tears from their eyes. "No more questions, Judge," Sam said at last. He could sense, more than hear, Jeannie and P.J. leaving the courtroom, followed closely by a couple of the reporters.

Daniels observed Cathy and Rebecca consulting and gave them a moment. When Cathy looked up at him, he asked, "Cross-examination?"

"No, Your Honor," she said.

"Mr. Norquist, you may step down," Daniels said.

Ronnie left the witness box and walked slowly past the defense table, mouthing, "I'm sorry," to Davonte as he walked by. Davonte looked away. Every eye in the courtroom, Sam knew, was on Ronnie until he left. As courtroom security opened the doors, Sam could hear the questions being hurled at Ronnie. The doors closed and it was quiet again, except for the low buzz of spectators discussing what they had just observed.

Daniels stared down the crowd until the discussion abated. "Mr. Johnstone, call your next witness."

Sam stood. "The defense rests, Judge."

Late the next morning, Sam and Davonte sat alone at the defense table; Paul was nowhere to be found. That bridge had been burned, Sam knew, and rightfully so. He thought briefly about renewing his motion for judgment of acquittal prior to the jury delivering its verdict, but under the rules an uncorroborated confession by a witness—especially one from a witness called by the defense—was an insufficient basis for a dismissal. It was more than enough to raise reasonable doubt, though—assuming the jury believed it.

"We good?" Davonte had asked moments before, when they were alone in the counsel room, awaiting the verdict. After Sam had concluded his case, Cathy had eschewed presenting any rebuttal evidence, and Daniels had instructed the jury. Cathy and Sam made their closing arguments and Daniels had given the case to the jury late in the afternoon. The jury had spent a couple of hours deliberating before being given the night off. Sam never slept well while a jury was out; instead, he'd lie there and replay the trial—always with an eye toward what he might have said or done better.

He'd finally given up and had gotten to the courthouse before seven a.m., where he drank coffee and looked at his phone until they brought Davonte over. He and Davonte had talked quietly about basketball, the army, and the future—everything and anything except the trial—until the bailiff informed them that the jury had reached a verdict.

"I think so," Sam said. He looked steadily at Davonte. "But like I told you all along, there are no guarantees."

"The time they were out—that good or bad?"

"I wouldn't begin to guess," Sam said.

"I'll say one thing," Davonte said, shaking his head slowly. "You got balls, man."

"What do you mean?"

"You burned your partner's son." Davonte smiled. "But I gotta tell you: I knew you would."

"My job is to get the jury to find reasonable doubt on behalf of my client," Sam explained. "To do that, I needed to have Ronnie on the stand. Honestly, I didn't know what I was going to be able to get from him. I thought maybe Paul got to him."

"You let Paul stay on the team," Davonte said. "He could have screwed me if he talked you out of callin' Ronnie. You risked my ass." Davonte stretched his long legs in front of him. "How'd you figure it out?"

"Well, I can't say I did—at least not all the way through," Sam admitted. "Like I've said before, when it looks like the State has enough evidence to convict, you've got to look for ways to create reasonable doubt. So I worked to try and poke holes in the State's evidence, one piece at a time."

"That's it?" Davonte was incredulous. "That was my defense?"

"That's it." Sam shrugged. "You didn't give me a lot else to work with, now did you? What else did we have? I can't make chicken salad out of chicken shit." He smiled briefly, and then turned serious. "But I started thinking about something you said."

"What was that?" Davonte asked.

"You said—and it made sense—that the State had generally the same evidence against Ronnie as you. So, I decided to try and eliminate the drugs as a motive. Then the phone stuff —I could mess with that a little. But when their expert testified that Ronnie's DNA was on the hat, I got to wondering why. Kaiden's DNA on the hat made sense. After you finally explained what happened, your DNA on the cap made sense. But Ronnie's didn't make sense, unless he was somehow involved or except as a secondary or tertiary transfer or whatever—which was unlikely.

"So a couple of nights ago I remembered the photos and I noticed there was a hat on Kaiden's bed that was exactly like the one found at the scene," Sam explained. "None of you said he had a hat on when he left, and I got to thinking, 'What if the cap at the scene wasn't Kaiden's?' Again, I just needed one juror to buy the theory, right? So I put Ronnie on and figured he'd deny any knowledge. If he would have denied everything, then I'd have been done and we would have submitted to the jury based on the doubt I'd got to that point. But he admitted everything—I didn't see that coming. He's just not that kind of kid," Sam concluded.

Davonte laughed out loud, then remembered where he was and quietly asked, "When did you come up with that?"

"After you refused to cop to manslaughter."

Sam and Davonte stood as Daniels entered and approached the bench. When he had been seated and the jury returned, Daniels turned to the jury and asked, "Has the jury reached a verdict?"

"We have, Your Honor," said a short woman in the front

row. Sam could hear the crowd outside the courthouse. They'd been on site for days, and now that the verdict was in, there was an anticipatory roar from each direction.

"Please give the verdict form to the bailiff," Daniels instructed. When the bailiff had the form, he took it to Daniels, who read it to ensure it was properly completed. Satisfied, he handed it to the clerk. "Ladies and gentlemen, upon the reading of the verdict, there will be no demonstrations, remonstrations, celebrations, disapproval, or sound of any sort. Violators will be removed summarily," he concluded, nodding to the security officers arrayed around the courtroom.

"Mr. Blair, please stand," Daniels instructed. Sam and Davonte stood, Davonte taking Sam's elbow as Sam's leg was feeling a little tight that morning. "Ms. Marshall, please read the verdict."

Violet Marshall, the county's elected clerk of district court, stood, and with shaking hands and a quiver in her voice, read: "As to the charge of murder in the first degree, we the jury find the defendant, Davonte Blair, not guilty." She took a deep breath. "As to the charge of murder in the second degree, we the jury find the defendant, Davonte Blair, not guilty."

Sam felt relief swell through him. Over the roar emanating from outside at one end of the courthouse, he accepted a handshake from Davonte. "Hang tight," he said. "We've got one more thing to do."

They listened while Daniels thanked the jury, formally acquitted Davonte, released the million-dollar bond, and sent everyone on their way. It was over. While Davonte accepted congratulations from his family and supporters, Sam sat alone, thinking about Paul and Jeannie.

21

Late that afternoon, Sam was packing up the books and personal items in his office and happened to look out the window. The television trucks were no longer in front of the courthouse, and the activists who had been staked out for weeks had left as well. He'd tried to contact Paul, to no avail.

"Who has the time to do that?" Cassie asked, startling Sam. He hadn't heard her come up behind him. "I mean, I've got things I feel strongly about, but I don't have the time or interest to travel around complaining about stuff. I've got my own stuff."

Sam smiled and took the box she was offering him. "A lot of those folks get paid to do exactly that. Of course, others are truly committed to the cause."

Cassie shook her head. "I don't understand it. You come into someone else's town and tell them how to do business. That takes gall."

"Indeed," Sam said. "Did you get those copies made?"

"I did . . . So, Paul said to send you an invoice—" Cassie began.

"Invoice it."

"But I don't feel right about doing that," she said.

"Do it."

"With you getting started somewhere else, I just . . . well, it's just not right. You and Paul have been friends for a long time."

"We have. Things are a little raw right now. I can't blame him. Ronnie is his son. Nothing can overcome that."

"It's all so sad," she said. "Ronnie. You and Paul. All of it."

Sam had turned back to the window. "It is," he said. The meteorologists were predicting hail in the afternoon. With the wind picking up and the temperature dropping, Sam wasn't so sure it would take that long. He sipped coffee and watched the trash and detritus left behind by the protesters dance in the wind.

"It sucks, Cassie," Sam said. "But we know one thing: the jury did its job. Despite the unrest brought to town by the outsiders, twelve Custer jurors did what they had to do. They listened to the testimony, they saw the evidence, and they applied the law Daniels gave them to what they had seen and heard. They made a decision. We don't always have to agree with jurors; they have the right and responsibility to make up their minds. But we should respect the process." He watched as two signs, somehow separated from the cheap wooden handles that had held their messages high for all to see, floated down the street like a pair of ghosts.

"I'm going to miss you, Sam," Cassie said to his back.

Penrose was pacing back and forth in Bill Gordon's office. "I think there is still a story here!" she said. "I think the next trial will be just as controversial as this one."

Gordon looked away from his computer screen and drank his soda. "Really? And why would that be?"

"Well," she said. "My sources tell me that young man— Ronnie—might be gay."

"Meaning?"

"That we might have a killing of a gay man by a gay man. That's a storyline. Don't you see?"

"No, Sarah. I don't. I don't see anything but an American tragedy. You see gay, you see black, you see whatever color or gender preference or sexual identity you want to assign. I see people. You see a gay-on-gay killing. I see a situation where two young men got in a dispute—apparently over nothing important. One killed the other in a fit of pique. It's incredibly sad. It's incredibly tragic. One family has lost a son, one almost lost a son, and one more might lose a son. Mothers and fathers and sisters and brothers must now go through the remainder of their lives with a hole in their hearts. I think *that* —and not their race or gender or sexual identity—is your story. Write that. This is the twenty-first century. The gay thing is passé. But young men killing each other is, unfortunately, a tragedy apparently without end. Write that."

22

Sam took the next week off to rest and recuperate. Like all trials, Davonte's had been a draining one, and like all trial attorneys, he needed some time to catch up in other areas of his life. He'd found a location to open his own office, and the night before he was to do so he was drinking beer and tying flies at his kitchen table when he heard the knock on his front door.

It was ten p.m., and because he didn't get many visitors that late, he assumed it was a drunk neighbor at the wrong door. He was completing a size 16 Royal Wulff with a whip finish when the knocking resumed. He sighed heavily, put down his tying tools, slipped the small revolver into his waistband, and went to the front door. Peering through the peephole, he saw the top button of a dress shirt.

Smiling, he opened the door to Davonte. "Come in," he said, and Davonte—followed as always by Damon and Reggie —entered. Davonte sat down and watched curiously while Sam applied a small drop of clear finish to the fly.

"You catch fish with those?" Davonte asked. He pointed a huge finger at the tiny fly.

"I do."

"Where at?"

"I've caught fish all over the country with these," Sam said.

"What kind of fish?"

"Trout."

"So, little ones." Davonte smiled. So did Damon and Reggie.

"Usually. But I like where the little ones live," Sam replied. "Water is clean and pure. No people."

"I hear that."

"What can I do for you?" he asked, turning in his chair to face Davonte.

"Just wanted to say thank you."

"Well, it's my job."

"I know, but my momma said to come and say it. She'll stop by your office tomorrow. She really liked you. She told me all along to trust you."

"She's a classy lady," Sam said. "What's next?"

"Got to get to Raleigh," Davonte said. "My agent has got some guys lined up to help me get ready for the draft."

"Very cool. NBA still an option, then?"

"Of course. Why wouldn't it be?"

"The drugs? The gay thing?"

"Weed ain't no issue," Davonte said, dropping the smile. Damon and Reggie quit smiling, too. "Lots of guys do that."

"And the other?"

"Hey, man." Davonte spread his arms wide and looked at Damon and Reggie. "All anyone knows is I was hanging out with a couple of gay dudes. As far as they know, I'm just an equal opportunity kind of brother. Inclusive and accepting, you know?" He looked at Reggie and Damon again. They nodded their approval.

"That's you," Sam said, looking at each man in turn. "Inclusive and accepting."

"Right on. So, I just kind of wanted to thank you, and to remind you that I'd prefer no one know about that other thing."

"What thing?" Sam asked.

Davonte smiled. "War hero and smart, too."

"I get by."

"Yeah." Davonte stood. "Well, me and the boys need to get back to civilization."

"Right." Sam stood as well. "It's been . . . interesting."

"Thanks again, man," Davonte said, extending his huge hand. Sam took it, shook it, and was ready to release, but Davonte was hanging on. "Keep that stuff under your hat, you understand?" He tried to release his grip, but it was Sam's turn.

"You had your chance," he said, feeling the henchmen stiffen and staring at Davonte for some time before releasing his grip. He stepped back and gave the three men a wide smile. "I hear you. Now get the hell out of my house so I can finish my flies."

Sam escorted Davonte, Damon, and Reggie to the door and closed it behind them. He got a fresh beer before returning to his chair, then sat and threaded his bobbin, put a tiny hook in the jaws of the vice, and drank from the bottle in preparation to begin tying the next fly. The goal was to get a dozen tied tonight that he could use tomorrow. The weather was supposed to turn for the better, and he was hoping to get in a little early spring fishing before the run-off started. Tonight, he would enjoy the buzz and anticipate the fresh air on his face.

He picked up a fly that he'd finished three beers ago and

frowned. It looked like something a cat coughed up. "Okay, let's get re-focused here," he said aloud.

Five minutes later the front door to his home opened, and Sam realized he'd failed to lock it after the three men had left. Assuming it was Davonte and the henchmen, he looked around his immediate area to see if they'd forgotten anything. Seeing nothing out of place, he said, "Davonte, what'd you forget?" Hearing nothing, Sam felt goosebumps rise on his forearms. He reached back and touched the pistol, just to be sure. "Davonte? Don't be dicking around."

When he felt the presence of someone on the other side of the kitchen door, he drew the small double-action revolver, dropped his hand to his side, turned toward the door, and waited. After what seemed like a full minute, Albert Smith stepped through the door and pointed a pistol at Sam's chest. His eyes were red, his cheeks were wet with tears, and Sam could smell the booze from ten feet away. "You ruined our lives, you sonuvabitch!" Albert said.

"Mr. Smith, put the gun down," Sam said quietly. "Let's talk."

"Ain't nothing to talk about!" Albert said. "I warned you. You are a third-rate lawyer screwing with people's lives! We just wanted to live as we please."

Sam felt the hair on the back of his neck standing on end. "It was you," he said quietly. "It was you making the threats. It was you following me."

"You finally figured that out, mister smart lawyer? Who else would it be? How many other lives did you ruin, you bastard?" Albert wiped the tears from his face with a big paw. "I tried to warn you! You turned her against me. You ruined us with your protective order and your tellin' her I'm bad for her! She said she was going to leave me!"

"Mr. Smith, you've been beating her up for years. You won't get help. She's leaving because of you."

"No!" Albert said. "She loves me, but she told me this morning she was leaving and not coming back! It's your fault!" Albert raised the pistol's aim point from center of mass to Sam's forehead. "You put the idea of leaving in her head!"

"Albert, put the gun down," Sam said. "Shooting me gets you nothing."

"It gets me even! You took Raylene away from me!" Albert shouted.

"No," Sam said. "No, it doesn't. Look around—you see anything I'm going to miss here?" Albert looked around the little apartment, then back at Sam when he started to speak again. "I've been blown up, shot, freaked out, and lost my girl. I've got nothing except an old truck and a couple of fly rods." Sam shrugged. "Shoot me and I lose nothing. But you'll do life. Then you'll never see Raylene again. Let's talk."

"I'm done talking, and I'm done listening!" Albert said. He was waving the pistol around as he ranted. "But you bastard, you should know you are going to suffer, just like you made me suffer!"

"What do you mean?" Sam asked.

"That little lady you been seeing?"

"You mean Veronica?" Sam's stomach was in knots.

"I dunno," Albert said. He lowered the weapon and then smiled, showing an uneven row of yellow teeth. "I asked around. That little brunette who works at the courthouse? Well, if I can't see my woman, you ain't gonna see yours, neither. I seen to that."

Sam felt his blood run cold, and he stood. "Albert, I swear to God, if you did anything to hurt her—"

"What? You gonna threaten me? I'm beyond that, counselor," Albert said. "You might be a war hero and all, but it's too late. It's over. It's all over."

Sam raised his weapon and pointed it at Albert. "If you hurt her—"

"Too late, counselor," Albert said, raising his own weapon.

"No!" Sam shouted, as Albert put the weapon in his mouth and pulled the trigger.

23

"I need to speak with Detective Polson," Sam said, trying not to look at Albert. There was nothing to be done.

"Just a minute, please," the dispatcher said.

"Please hurry," Sam said. "I've got a dead man in my kitchen and there's somewhere I need to be."

Moments later he heard Punch pick up the line. "Polson."

"Detective Polson, this is Sam Johnstone."

"What's going on, counselor?" Punch asked warily.

"Albert Smith—you know who he is?" Sam asked.

"Yeah. A world-class jackass and wife-beater."

"Yeah," Sam said. "He was that. Long story, but he just put a gun in his mouth and shot himself. In my kitchen. Before he shot himself, he told me he killed Veronica Simmons. I'm on my way over there now."

"No!" Punch said. "Stay where you are. If it is a crime scene—"

"I'm on my way now," Sam repeated, grabbing his wallet and keys. "I'll leave the door to my apartment unlocked so your boys don't need to break it down."

"I see we're getting calls about a shot at your place already," Punch observed. "Everyone else is okay?"

"Fine."

"I'm sending an officer to Veronica's place. If she doesn't answer the door, wait for my guys. Do not—I say again—do *not* screw up my crime scene, counselor."

Sam could travel anywhere in Custer in a matter of minutes, but even with the short duration he was able to make five increasingly plaintive calls to Veronica en route. Despite the cold night air, sweat was pouring from him, and he could hear his own breathing and the blood pounding in his ears.

Arriving at her home, he sprinted to Veronica's door and pounded on it, yelling, "Veronica, open up! It's me, Sam!" He repeated the pounding and yelling to no avail. He heard the sirens emanating from approaching cop cars, turned his shoulder to the door, and was about to break it in when Veronica opened it. Her feet were bare, her hair was wet, and she had a towel wrapped around her.

"Sam Johnstone, are you drunk again? What are you doing here? I told you I need time to—"

Sam stepped through the doorway and gave her an enormous hug.

"What is the matter with you?" she protested, trying to push him away. "What's happening? What's with all the cop cars?"

Daniels rolled over and answered the phone. It was just after eleven o'clock. "Your Honor, are you awake?" Punch asked.

"I am now, Detective."

"I need a warrant signed, Judge," Punch said. "I tried to get

Judge Downs to sign it, but she isn't answering. It's about Albert Smith."

"What about him?"

"He . . . well, he just killed his wife, we think. Then he broke into Sam Johnstone's house and killed himself in front of Sam."

"Aw, shit!" Daniels said. "What are you looking for?"

"Just the evidence from the crime scene where Albert killed her and where he shot himself," Punch said. "I'm . . . Well, I'm sorry, Judge. If I didn't need this signed right now, I wouldn't worry about it. I know that this has to be tough."

"Just bring it over and let me take a look at it," Daniels said, getting out of bed.

"What's going on?" Marci asked.

"Cops coming over," Daniels said. "Guy I let out of jail just killed his wife and then himself."

"Oh, honey!"

Half an hour later, Daniels handed Punch the affidavit and warrant and took off his reading glasses. "Here you go, Detective. Be safe."

The next morning, Mary took a deep breath. The door to Daniels's chambers was ajar. For years, she'd had free rein to enter as she felt necessary, but this morning was different. Finally, she exhaled and knocked before she entered.

"Your Honor?"

"What is it, Mary?"

"Judge," Mary stammered. "I—I guess I don't know how to say this."

"Then just go ahead and say it."

"I'm sorry."

"I appreciate that. Nothing you can do. Brought this on myself." Daniels stood and walked over to the cabinet where he kept his bottle. "That will be all for today. I've got some paperwork to sign and we'll be done here."

"What? But it's only ten o'clock!"

"That's fine," Daniels said. "I am done for the day. Lock the door to the outer office when you leave."

"Judge—"

"Mary, we're done here," he said. "No cases, no calls, no nothing. Tomorrow, I will write my letter of resignation and have you mail it to the Supreme Court."

"But you can't quit! You can't blame yourself!"

"Well, Mary, then just who the hell is to blame?" Daniels asked.

"Obviously, he is!" she said. "Albert is the one who killed his wife and then killed himself. There is nothing you could've done about that."

"I could've kept him in jail. I could have denied the motion to amend bond. For twenty years that is exactly what I would have done, but for some reason I thought I saw something in him." Daniels drank two fingers of whiskey in a single gulp and poured another two fingers. "I don't know what the hell I was thinking. But I made the decision to amend his bond and the sonuvabitch killed her. He should have been in jail!"

"It is never the judge's fault when someone gets out and kills another person," Mary insisted.

"Tell that to the people of the Twelfth Judicial District," he said. He walked slowly to the chair behind his desk and sat down. "They are going to want my head on a platter, and I deserve it."

"What can I do?"

"Nothing, really," he said. He stood again, walked to the window with his glass, and looked out over the courthouse square. "Mary, to be honest, I'm not so sure I want to do this anymore. I've done the best I could do. I can't say I've always been comfortable and confident that I made the right decisions, but I haven't been reversed much—if that means anything. But now, two people are dead because of my decision to amend Albert Smith's bond. I just don't know that I could ever feel confident in what I'm doing again. Hell, I only had a couple of years left, anyway."

"Judge, you have been a wonderful help for this community," Mary said, her eyes welling up with tears. "You've saved hundreds of lives and made thousands of other lives better."

Daniels turned and looked at Mary, smiling wanly. "Thank you, Mary. You are so very kind. But as you know, the district courts are the big leagues—big cases, high stakes. I made a major miscalculation. The world has changed; people are much less forgiving. I think we both know that from now on, no matter what I do or how hard I try, my entire tenure will be gauged against my decision to let Albert Smith out on bond."

"It's not fair!" she said, moving his drink to a coaster. "I refuse to believe that people will forget all the good you have done."

"No one said it would be fair," he said. "When I took this job, I promised to do my best. Do you see those people forming up on the sidewalk outside?"

Mary went to the window, stood on her tiptoes, and opened the blinds ever so slightly. She was quiet for a moment before turning to face him. "Oh my God."

"Right," Daniel said, sitting back in his chair and opening a small humidor on his desk. "Mary, results count. It doesn't appear my best was good enough for that bunch—now does it? So, if you would be so kind, please close the door and lock up on your way out. And leave some sort of message on that phone answering thing."

After Mary left, Daniels sat smoking and reflecting on days and cases gone by until the afternoon sun began to make the office uncomfortably warm. He then stood and straightened things around the office. He closed and locked the door on his way out. He and Marci would come and get his belongings after dinner and pie.

"Davonte! Man, I am glad to see you," Ronnie said through the phone on his cell block. "I've been waiting for days!" He looked around and saw a couple of the black inmates watching him closely. "Thanks for coming to see me. What's going on? How is getting me a lawyer going?"

"Just wanted to stop in and tell you I'm leavin' town, little man," Davonte said. He was in the detention center's area reserved for visitors, talking on a handheld phone. Behind Davonte, Ronnie could see Damon and Reggie standing with their arms crossed in front of their chests. "Wanted to remind you that the way to succeed in jail is to keep your mouth shut."

Ronnie looked at Davonte, confused. "What do you mean?"

"I mean I got to go. Just reminding you there are certain subjects that, you know, are off limits. Shit no one needs to know about."

"Davonte," Ronnie began, swallowing hard. "You know you can count on me. I mean, we're friends, right? I got rid of . . . the thing . . . and testified just like you said."

"You done good. That acting stuff—you're good at it, I'll say that. But you just remember to keep quiet," Davonte said, ignoring the question. "Because, if you was to forget, well, then my other friends—the ones probably watching you right now—they might take offense. You know what I'm sayin'?"

Ronnie stole a quick glance at the two black inmates standing behind him. One of them faked a big smile, the other drew a line across his throat in a slashing motion. "I understand," Ronnie said, his mouth suddenly dry. "I helped you—"

"And I'm gonna help you, man. Just as soon as I get drafted and get my boys here taken care of." Davonte smiled. "Right now, those are my priorities—you know what I'm sayin'?"

"But we're friends!" Ronnie said. "You said if we did this, then when you got off, you'd square me away at my trial! You said you'd testify for me and be in the clear because of double jeopardy or whatever you learned in that class! You said if we did it this way, no one could prove anything against either of us!"

"Well, I'm gonna be busy here for a while. You know, the draft—things like that. Don't know I'll be back this way," Davonte said. He stood. "Now, you just go on back to your cell and think about what I said. I gotta get ready to fly out east to meet with my agent."

"Davonte!" Ronnie exclaimed as Davonte rose to leave. "Davonte! After you get drafted, you'll hire me a lawyer— that's what you said, right? I'll need you to testify or I'll get convicted! You got my back, right? Then I'll get through school and be your agent, just like we agreed, right? Davonte!" Ronnie watched, his eyes filling with tears, as Davonte and the henchmen left the phone room. After they were out of sight, Ronnie hung up and slowly turned around. The two inmates were gone.

The June sun was low on the mountainous western horizon. Sam had gotten the keys to a friend's cabin, and Veronica had agreed to spend the weekend. They had spent the day exploring local streams—Sam fishing, Veronica handling the net.

"They are so small!" she had laughed at one point.

"They are," Sam agreed. "But I like where little fish live."

"I understand."

Now, he and Veronica were sitting on the deck, reveling in the sun setting over the pine- and spruce-covered mountains. The sound of birds settling in and the creek just yards away added to the beauty. He'd been up and down the steps, checking on the fire. She remained in her chair, without shoes, luxuriating in the late afternoon's warmth. She was drinking a white wine of some sort, and he was having sparkling water with lemon.

"We're about ready," Sam said, looking at his watch and checking the coals. "You want a steak, a burger, or what?"

"Whatever you are having," she said. "I don't really care. I'm only here for the after-dinner s'mores."

"I should have known," he said. "Well, then, if you've no preference, I'm going to toss on a T-bone. I'll eat the strip; you can have the filet. How's that sound?"

"Sounds good. As does another glass of wine."

"I've got you covered."

While he grilled the steaks, they caught up. He felt relaxed and comfortable for the first time in a while, and must have been staring at her wine glass as he listened to her talk about family and friends and work problems, because she suddenly stopped and brought him out of his brief reverie.

She pointed at her glass. "Does this bother you?"

"Not at all," he said. "Wine isn't worth the trouble."

"What do you mean?"

"I mean, I drink with a purpose: to get loaded. I can get drunk on wine, but it gives me a roaring headache, and liquor is quicker. If you were drinking whiskey or vodka it might trigger me a little, but wine? No."

"Do you miss it?"

"Not tonight. I've been talking with a sponsor and attending some groups online and meeting with my counselor," he said. "You know, except for when I was deployed, I've spent the better part of my adult life about half in the bag. It was a good run, but it's time for me to find another way to deal with things. I'm getting comfortable with the idea. How do you take it?"

"Medium."

"We're ready, then. Let's eat."

After dinner, she made s'mores outside while he tended the fire. She had more wine, the elevation soon took its toll, and back inside the cabin she fell asleep on his shoulder on the leather couch. Without disturbing her, he managed to grab the remote and turn on the television. "Thank goodness for satellite," he said quietly.

"Hmm?" she asked.

"Nothing," he said. "Rest."

He found the channel he was looking for and watched as dozens of young men from around the world were selected to play for teams in the National Basketball Association. Sam drank soda and watched the video of families from around the world as they waited for or received the once-in-a-lifetime call and listened as the commentators discussed the possible choices for the next few teams. At one point, Davonte was mentioned, video highlights were shown, and the announcers commented on his physique, athletic ability, and potential. Later, the feed was switched to show him surrounded by family and friends, phone to his ear. As the camera panned over his mother, she smiled shyly; Reggie and Damon then folded their arms and stared intimidatingly at the camera as if on cue.

Still later, after the last name was called, Sam shook the melting ice from his glass into his mouth and crunched it. Veronica stirred on his shoulder. "What's going on?" she asked.

"Davonte didn't get drafted," he said. The live feed showed Davonte with his head in his hands. This time, as the camera panned, Reggie and Damon rose and stalked off. Sharon put her arm over her son's huge shoulders. Sam chewed more ice.

"Well, that's disappointing," she said, yawning. "What do you call it again? When they play one year and then leave?"

"One and done."

"Well, there you go," she said, and repositioned her head on his shoulder. In a moment, she was again fast asleep.

FALSE EVIDENCE

After a fall-out with his business partner and a breakup with his girlfriend, lawyer Sam Johnstone thinks a long vacation might be just what the doctor ordered.

Before he can quit town Sam gets a call from Lucy Beretta, the wife of the missing local college president. With a shocking accusation against an acquaintance and a plea for protection, Lucy derails Sam's plans for a quiet escape.

But when her alleged attacker turns up dead, Lucy is charged with his murder—and Sam is appointed to represent her. As he struggles to prepare his defense, Sam discovers that Lucy is lying—about a lot of things. The facts are not in her favor, and to make matters worse, Lucy is also a suspect in her husband's disappearance.

If Sam is successful, a guilty woman may go free—and if he's not, he will have failed at his job. Facing a client who can't seem to tell the truth, an aggressive prosecutor eager for a conviction, and an ethical dilemma of epic proportions, Sam faces his most challenging case yet.

Get your copy today at www.James-Chandler.com

JOIN THE READER LIST

Never miss a new release! Sign up to receive exclusive updates from author James Chandler.

**Join today at
www.James-Chandler.com**

YOU MIGHT ALSO ENJOY...

Sam Johnstone Legal Thrillers

Misjudged

One and Done

False Evidence

Never miss a new release! Sign up to receive exclusive updates from author James Chandler.

www.James-Chandler.com

ABOUT THE AUTHOR

James Chandler spent his formative years in the western United States. When he wasn't catching fish or footballs, he was roaming centerfield and trying to hit the breaking pitch. After a mediocre college baseball career, he exchanged jersey No. 7 for camouflage issued by the United States Army, which he wore around the globe and with great pride for twenty years. He holds a Bachelor's degree from Eastern Oregon University and a Master's degree from Marshall University. James earned his Juris Doctor after attending night school at the George Mason University School of Law. When he isn't working or writing, he'll likely have a fly rod, shotgun or rifle in hand. James and his wife are blessed with two wonderful adult daughters and one grandson. He loves to hear from readers and can be reached at james@james-chandler.com.

f

Made in the USA
Monee, IL
27 April 2022